Nameless

MW01235114

Published by Lulu.com.

Copyright © 2015 by Teddy G.R. Morgan

All rights reserved.

This is a work of fiction. Names, characters, businesses, places, events and incidents are either the products of the author's imagination or used in a fictitious manner. Any resemblance to actual persons, living or dead, or actual events is purely coincidental.

Cover design by David Buehler and Teddy G.R. Morgan.

ISBN 978-1-329-34123-4

Prologue

The year is 2087.

Every day there is news of more people dying and more people disappearing. No one talks about it either because they are scared or because they don't care. The people responsible are called Preachers and my family used to be a part of them. The Preachers say they are "cleansing" Earth, but in reality, they have been killing and persecuting anyone they think is different, useless or unclean. Or anyone who gets in their way.

When my family figured out the errors of the Preachers' ways and wanted to leave, the people that we thought were our friends and supporters all turned against us. We fought our way out and managed to escape. Since my father knew their plans and secrets from many years of working for them, the Preachers couldn't just let us go. So my family was hunted. We ran, going from town to town until they finally lost track of us. Then they claimed that we were dead. I guess they were just trying to scare the other Preacher followers, but it made it easier for us to start a new life with new identities.

Even when I was young, I made it clear to my family that I will have my revenge, destroy the Preachers, and help all those who they have persecuted. My father had been making some sort of weapon for the Preachers before we escaped; something that could change everything. He has continued his work in hopes that it will help me in my crusade against the Preachers. I have been training and waiting for my chance. I have waited eight years and I know that I am ready to start my work.

Chapter One

Beep! Beep!

My alarm clock goes off meaning it is time for my morning run. I get up quickly knowing that if I don't, the alarm clock will spray water on my face. I quickly change into my running pants and a sweatshirt, pull my hair up into a ponytail rush out of the room. Walking down the hallway and down to the main floor, I try to make as much noise as possible. It's my eighteenth birthday today, and I want everyone to be up. I get down to the living room, and surprisingly there is no one there. Usually my father is up by now.

Despite being a little concerned, I unlock the front door and step outside. The sun still hasn't risen yet and there is a slight breeze. This is the perfect running weather in my opinion. I turn on my headphones before heading out. The headphones can read my brainwaves, so all I have to do is think of a song and it will play. A thought barely has time to form in my head when a steady drum beat starts pounding in my ears. It is soon joined by bass guitar riffs and synth. I easily recognize the song even though it is wordless: Revolutionary Pawns by The Chalk Outlines, my favorite band.

With the music blasting in my ears, I start my trek that circles the entire city. I have been running for a long time, so runs like this are easy for me. My family and I live in one of the biggest cities in North America. It is in the northern part of where Lake Michigan used to be and is called Tieced. It is pretty easy to hide here amongst all the people, I guess that is why Dad decided that this would be a good place to settle. Our house is on a lonely street between the Circumference, the rougher section of town, and Halfway, the busier part. I have not been to the richer, central part of the city called the Inner Ring since I finished school. There is a park near the house and a small restaurant down the block.

I have multiple routes mapped out for my runs to make sure I stay away from the more dangerous parts of the Circumference. I switch them up every couple days to make sure no one can track me. Running is just one part of the training I do to keep my body and mind in shape. My daily activities include the jog in the morning, then breakfast, and training in the small and secluded backyard for a few hours. I also do a lot of research and read articles from the only reliable news-site I have found, The Hearing. I search for clues of the Preachers' whereabouts and activities and recently have been looking for small apartments in the surrounding cities. Now that I am eighteen I can leave whenever I see fit.

The burning in my legs as I sprint quickly wakes me up. I find that the city is most beautiful when the sun is rising; before everyone has woken up and gone to work and just as the drunken party-goers begin to stumble home. The cold light burns through the barrier, casting an odd blue light over everything and reflects off of the tall buildings. I often wonder what the sun is like outside of the barrier, without the gas distorting its color.

Circling the city only takes me about two and a half, and by the time I get home the sun has climbed halfway up the tallest building. I stop on the porch and watch the city come to life. Then I notice some strange noises coming from inside my house. At first I am nervous and the worst case scenario pops into my head — *Preachers are here.* But after that I recognize my brother's voice commenting, "I don't know, she's usually back by now."

I decide to knock on the door and announce my arrival so my family members won't be surprised. They are probably waiting for me with some kind of birthday surprise. I roll my eyes before my mom answers. "Come in, Helena!"

I hate the name Helena. She doesn't usually call me that. It might be the name on my original birth certificate, but I like to be called by my new name: Wren. Besides, that document was burned and replaced by forgeries years ago.

I open the door and look around the room. Nothing unusual so far. "Why so formal?" I ask.

"No reason." My mom leaves the living-room and rushes into the adjoining kitchen stifling her laughter. I wish they could be a little better at hiding secrets.

Beck, my older brother lounges on the couch next to my dad's big comfy chair.

My father looks up from his book, "What is going on?" he asks sheepishly.

"Come on, guys, stop being so childish. I know you're pretending to not know it's my birthday."

"Fine, you saw through our lame attempt at tricking you, you are so much smarter than the rest of us." Beck rolls his eyes and then quickly gets up from his sitting position and calls upstairs, "Piper!"

My older sister runs down the stairs holding a thin cylinder in her hands. My mom comes in from the kitchen and Dad finally puts down his book. Piper crushes the cylinder with her hands and throws the remains high into the air.

"Happy birthday!!!!" Fireworks pop and go flying around, their confetti falling on my head. I shake the pieces out of my hair.

My sister hugs me, "Happy birthday, Wren." she says and then whispers in my ear, "We have some good news."

I don't have time to think as they rush me into the dining room and sit around the table. Mother sets a blue birthday cake in front of me. "Isn't it a little early for cake?" I ask, but I am not complaining.

"It isn't just your birthday; I also have an announcement." My father starts cutting the cake. There is a huge smile on his face. He doesn't smile every day, this must be something really important. "I apologize for acting so silly but…"

"What is it?" I urge him on. The exhilaration is getting to me too even though I do not know what is going on.

"I have good news for you, Wren." *Yes, yes, we have already established that.* "Piper and I—" *Dad's excitement and Piper's involvement... That can only mean one thing. The weapon has been completed.* I wait for him to finish his sentence despite already knowing what he is going to say. "The invention that I started researching with the Preachers is finally complete. We should be able to start testing in the next few days."

Dad and Piper have been working on his invention since we settled down five years ago. I have been trying to wait patiently, but I cannot control my excitement now. Excitement and surprise aren't things I am familiar with so I have trouble getting out the next sentence, "That's great. So now we can continue with our plans." I am surprised, and happy.

The way my dad sighs next makes me stop. I can tell that there is something he is not telling me. And that I am not going to like it. "Yes, Wren, it is true. But you are going to have to put your plans on hold." *Come on, Dad. Don't say that.* "Piper and I are not completely sure the weapon is safe for use."

"Hey, do not bring me into this." Piper holds her hands up.

"So we are giving it to more capable hands to test it and make sure everything works properly and safely." Dad ignores Piper. "I will still be working on it, but they have better technology and more workers that I can use. A representative is coming over today. He will ultimately be the first subject." *Not me. This wasn't the plan.* "He will be staying for a few more days while Piper and I put on the finishing touches. I need someone to volunteer to pick him up at the park, Be—"

"I will do it." I want to be the first to meet this guy and size him up. The only way I am going to let anyone else use the weapon before me is if I know they are more qualified than I.

"Okay…" My dad does not trust me with this mission. He probably shouldn't. "He said to give him some sort of signal so he will know it is safe to approach."

"Sure, sure." I already know what I am going to do to him. I want to know more about the new invention, "So what does the weapon do, exactly?" I ask. Piper and Dad have been insanely secretive about the whole thing. I don't really blame them, the stakes are pretty high.

My father reluctantly goes back to the subject, "This device can give an ordinary person super-human abilities, but I think we should wait to discuss it with Hawk."

"Hawk?" I ask. *What a ridiculous name.* "How did you meet this guy and decide he should take my place?"

"Your time will come." he sighs, not wanting to get into an argument with me. "Hawk can explain everything when he gets arrives… That should be in an hour or so."

It could take longer than a year for my dad to replicate the weapon, and he told me that I would be the first to wield it. I know I should be furious, and deep down inside I probably am, but anger won't change my father's mind or speed up the process of making another.

Still, a little voice inside my head keeps telling me that I should be the first one to use the device, I have trained for years to get here, and now…

"I am going for a walk." I inform my family somewhat angrily and leave the table before I do something I'll regret. I march out of the kitchen and through the living room before slamming the front door behind me.

I run, fast, to that playground near my house and climb to the top of the rusty monkey bars.

I sit there for what seems like hours thinking and watching the few children that walk by gazing longingly at this abandoned park.

No one has played here in many years. It doesn't take me too long to fully calm down.

A figure appears down the road and I immediately know who it is. I wait patiently for him to approach the park all the while taking note of his movements and behavior as I squint in the sunlight.

Hawk is probably in his mid-thirties. He is of average height and has broad shoulders. *This is it? Eh. He isn't anything special.* I could instantly recognize him because he isn't dressed like most of the people around here or behave like them. He walks with confidence and strength ripples through his limbs.

Hawk knows I am here, but does not acknowledge my presence as he sits down on a bench. *Time for me to give him the signal.*

Hopping down from seven-foot high bars, I go and sit next to Hawk. I decide to take the straightforward approach. "So... You're Hawk." I state.

"Yes I am." Hawk answers clearly. Now that I am closer I can see little grey hairs mixed in with his regular light brown hair.

Unfortunately, I haven't confused him like I wanted to. "Cool," I say casually, "I'm Helena." I don't want him to know my real name.

"I have heard a lot about you, Helena." I wrinkle my nose at that stupid name. The way he says it makes me hate it even more. *Funnily, I haven't heard anything about you until an hour ago.* "I am very glad to meet you, but I thought you were supposed to give me a signal or something so I will know who you were sent by."

"Oh, yeah. I almost forgot." Of course, I really didn't.

He turns his head just as I throw a punch that connects with his jaw. Hawk tumbles over the side of the bench and pours onto the gravel. I'm already on my feet by now, and he gets up too, dusting his shirt off. I am fully aware of my actions and don't let the adrenaline and anger take over. This is merely a test.

He doesn't ask questions and he doesn't retaliate. "Not bad." he mutters, and holds out his hand in greeting. I grab hold of his long sleeve and place the rest of my arm in his armpit while twisting my body around. He is bigger, stronger and heavier than me, but I use that to my advantage when I lift him onto my shoulder and flip his dead weight over my back. He accepts the pain and stays in the dirt, rubbing his bruised elbow. "You know this is pointless, right?" He puts his weight on his arms and gets to his feet slowly. "We shouldn't be fighting each other; we should be fighting the Preachers." I don't pay attention to him; he shouldn't even be here, meddling in my life.

I try to kick him with my left leg, but he grabs it, and twists it so I have to turn around. I try punching him, but he grabs my right arm and twists it behind my back. He then kicks the back of my right knee and I fall to the ground. He is kneeling behind me, still gripping my leg and arm; I am almost in a full split. I cry out in pain and he lets go, shoving me forward. *Damn it, he's good.*

I roll over on my back; he is standing, looking down at me, "You are a pretty good fighter. I'm sure NEST could train you to be even better."

"A nest? What's that?" I wheeze and stare at him above me, the sun almost directly behind him.

"You haven't heard of NEST yet? Your father has a lot more to explain than I thought." Hawk pauses and sighs before explaining, "NEST is an underground organization. They help refugees whose families have been killed by the Preachers, and people who were once Preachers but have escaped. They train them, give them a home and give them a purpose."

For years I thought my family was alone, and that I would have to take down the Preachers by myself... A part of my identity is washed away with the revelation that we aren't. "Wait, so there are more like us? More like me?" These are the more capable hands my father was talking about.

He looks me in the eyes, "Yes, there are a lot more like you, people who want to take down the Preachers; give them what they deserve."

"And why should I trust you? How can I know that you will do a better job with my dad's life's work than me?" I ask.

"I can tell that you're very capable of fulfilling this task and have reasons to, just like many of us." Hawk holds out his dirty hand again. I grudgingly grab it and he helps me up with ease. It is clear to me that he wants to tell me more so I follow him.

We make our way silently to the lonely swing set and rest there. As I wait for Hawk to explain I notice the empty swing beside me gently moving with the breeze. "I have as much of a right to test it as you do." Hawk finally speaks up, "The Preachers... Preachers killed my family. My in-laws, my wife, my two young children, they killed them all. They all had a hereditary disease, passed down from the parents." He is looking down at the mulch, with his elbows on his knees. Hawk doesn't look like the strong man I first met and fought just seconds ago. I suppose everyone has a side that they hide. I can't help but feel sorry for him. "They came in the night, knocked down our door and killed every one but me. We were eating dinner in the living room. We had no time to react. In minutes my whole family was dead, lying on the living room floor in front of me."

He pauses, "Then-then they said 'You're welcome.' like they did a good deed, like they were curing the world of pests. They just left me there, alone in the living room, looking at my dead family members' corpses. I felt so helpless. That was five years ago. Then I made contact with NEST, they helped me, gave me a place to live. They gave me a way to get my revenge."

I spin on the swing and the chains coil around each other above my head.

"The Preachers work above the law," he continues, "the government can't do anything. So we have to take matters into our own hands."

"I know, and that is why I need to take them down."

"Your father doesn't know for sure that the weapon is safe to use, and he doesn't want to risk you getting hurt." Hawk watches me twirl.

I stop the spinning by digging my heels into the ground and look him right in the eyes, "I do not care what happens to me."

"He is just doing his job and protecting you."

Hawk gets up and starts walking to the house; or at least in the direction he thinks the house is in. "What I suggest is that you come with me to the NEST headquarters and get situated there; I'm sure you'll have an easier time on your mission with us than you would by yourself." He pauses when he sees that I am not fully convinced and then continues, "We have a whole building to ourselves with training facilities and instructors; and more importantly, you can meet people on the same path that you are on."

He waits for me to get up and show him the way to my house. I feel like running ahead and leaving him to get lost, but this means too much to my family. I turn Hawk's words over and over in my mind. I don't like it, but they make sense. *I should join NEST. I mean, they probably have more resources than I would have living in an empty apartment alone. And they'll have first access to my father's weapon, so if I ever want to use it, I guess I'll have to do it the long way.*

***

As soon as I make up my mind, I tell my family that I am going to join NEST. None of them seem too surprised, so I guess it is a smart move.

Hawk stays with us and sleeps on our couch for the next couple days while we wait for another NEST correspondent to arrive.

***

"Wren!" Beck knocks on my bedroom door.

"What do you want?"

"Everyone's ready and in the lab." The lab is downstairs in the basement. My dad and sister create a lot of things down there.

I wait for Beck's footsteps to fade before jumping out of bed.

I rush downstairs. This is it. They're finally going to experiment on Hawk. Is it bad for me to want him to get injured? The door to the basement is in the kitchen, it has a lock and code. My dad usually changes the code every month. This month's code is 'Hummingbird'. I type it in quickly and open the door. I slow down when I get to the last couple steps; I don't want anyone seeing me acting unprofessional. Everyone is already waiting for me; my dad, Piper, Hawk and two other men that I have never seen before.

I suppose the first man could be called middle-aged. He is probably around sixty years old, has silver-grey hair and walks with a cane. The second man might not even be referred to as a man. He is in his early twenties at the most, has dark brown hair that is almost black and light brown eyes that are almost orange. His hair is cut short on the sides, a little longer on the top. The military haircut does not suit his round face, but it doesn't make him look bad either.

"Oh, Wren, you are just in time." My father says.

"So you already have a codename; good. I was happy to hear that you will be joining us." The mysterious man says to me.

Hawk answers him, "No, Wren is her real name. Wren, this is Albatross. He is on the board of NEST leaders and the main supporter of your father's work. And this is Swift." Hawk gestures to the young man. "As soon as I heard you would be joining NEST, I sent for him. He will be your guide when you get to the NEST headquarters." Albatross holds out his hand and I shake it. Swift reaches for my hand almost identically and nods his head. He looks friendly enough; I will have to get used to this Swift for the next few weeks while I settle into my new life and then be able to forget about him.

"So you are all probably wondering what the weapon does." My father interrupts the introductions and brings the attention back to himself and his work. He ushers us over to a work table, and on it is something that looks like a hybrid of a taser and a needle. A few buttons reside on the side of the device. Next the table is a plain metal chair. "It alone is not a weapon, but when it is connected with a human, the human becomes the weapon. It enhances your abilities, like speed and strength. It also makes your strengths even stronger, which ultimately depends on the person. The Preachers are not very far behind in manufacturing it, and I am certain they will have the technology soon." My father gestures toward the chair, and Hawk sits in it. "It also gives you another ability, but I think it would be easier to show you." When Hawk places his right arm on the table, Dad picks up the strange thing, "This might hurt a little." I am surprised that Hawk trusts my father enough to let Dad experiment on him without knowing exactly what this thing does.

My father pushes the tip of the needle into Hawk's arm, just above his wrist. Dad then presses one of the buttons and something is injected into Hawk's arm. Dad then pulls the needle out of Hawk's flesh.

"What I just injected into you is my invention, it is a microchip that releases special chemicals which enhance almost every aspect of your bodily functions." My father unlatches Hawk's straps and holds up a remote with a single button. "Once it is turned on it can never be turned off. Well unless you die, but that is beside the point. Are you ready?" He asks Hawk. Hawk nods his head with conviction and my dad presses a different button.

The chip lights up and digits and letters ripple across Hawk's skin. Beginning at his right arm they spread all over his body, appearing and then quickly disappearing.

Hawk waits a moment before asking, "So what will I be able to do?" He is trying to act cool, like he gets a computer chip that gives him superpowers stuck in his arm every day, but I can tell he is excited. And nervous.

"I will show you, or I guess you will show the rest of us. Maybe everyone should step back a little." Dad picks up a marker from the table, walks over to the wall furthest from our small group and draws a large X in the center of the wall with the marker. "I mentioned before that all of your regular abilities will be enhanced, you will be able to run faster and carry more weight, as well as receive another power based on your strengths. Those things can be used for many things, but the last ability the microchip will give you can only be used as a weapon. All of this is only in theory of course, and I must admit that not all of the elements of the invention were my idea, so we really need to be careful when figuring out and testing this device." My father notices the marker in his hand and remembers what he was initially talking about. "But anyway, the last thing." He walks back to us and motions for Hawk to step towards the wall. "I imagine that the weapon will be triggered in times of danger, but for now you will want to focus on your gut."

Hawk doesn't know exactly what my dad wants him to do but he closes his eyes, and holds his hands at his sides in fists. I can tell he is straining, trying to get something to happen. All I can see is the back of him and a weird slight shivering. He starts glowing, or I guess, some field around him is glowing. Something about my dad's simple and seemingly strange words have caused a change in Hawk.

He roars, and the glow increases until I can barely look at him it's so bright. I cover my eyes with my hands, and then uncover them just in time to see a blast of light shoot from Hawk's body. A strange sizzling noise fills the room until impact, when what seems like a small nuclear bomb erupts. The light fades and we can all see the missing chunk of wall. Hawk staggers back towards us, winded.

"Very good!" My dad exclaims, I guess he was worried it would not work. "You better sit down, those things will wipe you out." Swift quickly grabs the chair from the desk and takes it over to Hawk. Hawk practically collapses into the chair, but smiles, relieved that it actually worked.

"Nice job." Swift pats Hawk on the back and mutters. He turns to look at my father, "What was that anyway?" I stare at Swift, somewhat surprised that he said something. The back of his neck gets red, but he still has the courage to smile at me. The corners of his eyes crinkle. Everyone else in the room is smiling too, relieved that it worked.

"An energy-blast. Hormones from the microchip use ATP—"

Piper hugs my dad and exhales deeply, "Dad, I don't think they're interested in that stuff right now, let's just celebrate."

I go over to congratulate Hawk, even though I'm still feeling a little resentful, passing by Swift. I quickly leave them to pat my dad on the shoulder. "Do not forget Piper, she helped a lot." he tells me. I had almost forgotten about her even though she stands at my elbow.

I look down at Piper and then put my arms around her shoulders. "Do not worry, you will be next." she whispers in my ear.

The whole group eventually makes it back upstairs for dinner and celebratory cake. We usually only have cake for important birthdays, because the ingredients are so expensive and it's rare to find someone who knows how to bake one properly, so having two cakes in the span of a few days is extremely special.

After a nice and joy-filled dinner, I grab a piece of cake and go outside on the porch. The sun is just about to set and the sky is a nice blue color, not the usual green. I lean against the railing and stare at the red sun that is sinking behind the roof tops.

I suppose tomorrow I will head to NEST headquarters with Swift. My chance to actually do something is finally here. I've been waiting for my chance to fight back ever since we got away and yet I feel a little sad. The cake is really good and I start stuffing it in my mouth; the way that I usually eat.

I hear the front door open, and expect Piper to step out, but instead Swift appears, "Is it okay if I join you?"

"Um, sure." I try to say but my mouth is still full and all that comes out are inaudible mumbles. I nod my head and swallow the cake that's in my mouth.

"I will take that as a yes." He mutters and starts walking towards me. He stands next to me and stares at the starless sky.

"Happy belated birthday." He says, still not looking directly at me. Swift is only a couple of inches taller than I am. He notices the way I look at him suspiciously and quickly adds, "I was talking to your mom and she mentioned it."

"Thanks." I say quietly and stuff the last of my cake in my mouth. He hasn't touched his piece.

"Are you going to eat that?" I ask, the last bit of cake still in my mouth. I am not sure if he understood me or not.

"No, you can have it." I take his plate with a smile and hand him my empty one. I probably look like a pig, but I don't really care. Swift stays silent while I eat.

"So how long have you been a part of NEST?" I ask when I am done eating his piece.

"A few years." Swift answers. He looks me straight in the eyes and says, "It's okay to be sad to leave. I would be if I were you."

"So you are going to be my guide when we get to the headquarters?" I ask, avoiding his remark.

"It looks like it." He says cheerfully, "Tomorrow"

The door bursts open and Albatross, Hawk and my father walk out.

"I am glad you two are getting along," Albatross says, "You will be seeing a lot of each other for the next few weeks."

"And what about Hawk?" I ask. There is no way I am taking my eyes off of that weapon.

"Hawk and I are leaving now. You will leave tomorrow and your father will be joining the NEST team soon to finish the testing on Hawk."

"What?" I ask and send a glare at my father. He never told me he would be going anywhere.

"I will need their technology and workers if I am to mass produce the Enhancer. That is what I have decided to call it, and Hawk is the first Enhancement." he answers as if he hasn't done anything wrong, and I guess that technically, he hasn't.

"You better get your stuff ready; you two need to set off early in the morning. Come see Hawk and I when you arrive." Albatross tells us.

"See you guys soon." Hawk says, and he and Albatross begin to walk off the porch. I watch them as they continue to walk down the road until the reach a black car. They get in it and the car literally disappears before my eyes.

***

Swift sits in the corner of my room on a chair as I begin to pack.

I shove three or four casual outfits into a small suitcase. The outfits mostly consist of long-sleeved shirts and jeans, so I pack a pair of sneakers, a sweatshirt; and my favorite black leather jacket. Swift said that I will have my own room so I add a poster of my favorite band, The Chalk Outlines; and two of my favorite stuffed animals. I know they are childish, but they were my only friends as a child, moving from city to city. And even now, I don't have any friends.

Swift interrupts my thoughts, "You don't have many friends, huh?"

"What?" *Can he read my mind??*

"When your mom was talking about your birthday party she only mentioned your family members..."

"Oh." *Mom;* I glare. "Yeah."

Swift looks at the clock on my bedside dresser and says with a straight face, "It's getting late. We better get some sleep; we need to leave by ten o'clock tomorrow morning."

"Ten? That is okay with me." I usually wake up before dawn.

He gets up and opens my door, "See you tomorrow, bright and early." He winks and slips out my door. I jump in bed and manage to fall asleep quickly.

Chapter Two

I have had a dream—or nightmare—every night for the past eight years, so when I wake up this morning, without having dreamt anything, it feels very strange, as if I am taking a step in the right direction.

I wake up before dawn and after failed attempts at going back to sleep, I quietly get out of bed and sneak out of my room. My family and I have lived in this house for almost five years, after spending three years on the run. This is the only house that has felt like a home. I don't remember anything about my house when we were Preachers. I don't remember most of my childhood. Sometimes I see that as a blessing. Not knowing what horrors my family went through, or what horrors they caused, might be a good thing. There are some things that I do remember, of course; mostly tragedies branded into my mind forever. It is not just the people that the Preachers persecute who are hurt, but also the members of the Preachers. We were restricted, lied to, used. We weren't allowed to ask questions, question our leaders' actions, or question their authority.

I walk through the swinging doors and enter the kitchen. I hear the doors open again behind me, and I automatically switch into combat mode. I do some quick calculations; *The person just came through the door, from the sound of his footsteps and creak of the wooden planks he weighs around one-hundred and seventy pounds and is a little shorter than average height, so his head should be... right... there* — I grab a knife from the kitchen counter then spin around while throwing the knife towards the entrance. Swift dodges just in time as the knife goes soaring into one of the doors, which after impact, swings slightly.

Swift gets to his feet, "What the hell? Are you trying to kill me?!" He has an alarmed look on his face and I see a bead of sweat trickle down the side of his face.

"Do not sneak up on me! I didn't know who it was, so yeah; I was trying to kill you." Everyone in my family knows not to sneak up on me. My brother is missing a toe from a similar incident.

"Holy crap, you are paranoid." Swift rips the knife out of the door, which was imbedded a few inches in, "And deadly." He says with a small grin and hands the knife back to me.

***

Swift's and my luggage sit by the front door and my family is gathered in the living-room, ready to say goodbye. As I wait at the top of the stairs, I can already hear my mother sniffling; she must be crying. Saying goodbye never gets easier.

"You should probably get down there." I jump. Swift is now standing behind me and just whispered in my ear.

"What did I tell you?" I shout at Swift and shove him away. I realize now, when the moment is finally here and my family is waiting to say goodbye, that I'm going to miss them, and that I don't want to face them. "Let's get this over with." I mutter and begin to make my way down the staircase that seems longer than usual.

I stop on the bottom step and look at my family huddled in the living-room. I was right; I can tell my mom has been crying even though she is trying to cover it up. Piper is on the verge of tears as well. My dad looks the same as always. I stand in the same spot for a couple minutes, while everyone stares at each other, saying nothing.

"Um, we need to leave soon." Swift says while adjusting the sunglasses on his head. As soon as he says this, my mom rushes at me. She hugs and kisses me as the others come over slowly and then say goodbye.

"Don't forget to call or message us as much as possible." My mother says, already missing me. Swift picks up our bags and we start heading for the door.

"Make sure to tell Albatross that you want to be filled in on anything Enhancer related. I have heard rumors that he will be starting an elite team of future Enhancements." my father says quickly as Swift and I open the door and step outside.

"Bye!" I yell as Swift and I step off the porch. My family looks out the screen door as we leave. I walk quickly down the dusty road, trying to put as much distance between me and my family. The sooner I get used to being away from them the better it will be for all of us.

"Where are NEST headquarters? And more importantly, how are we going to get there?" The question had not dawned on me before.

"We'll be taking the light-train."

"Oh." I was hoping that we were going to ride in an invisible car.

The light-train is the only transportation from city to city. It isn't like we are trapped and not allowed to leave; it just isn't very safe traveling between cities. All that's out there is chemical waste, desert, the occasional forest and endless piles of garbage.

Tieced's train station is on the other side of the city. Swift and I walk along the Circumference for about two hours, keeping our heads down and avoiding any other humans. We don't talk very often, but when we do it only lasts for a couple seconds.

We finally get to the train station around twelve o'clock. The train station is practically deserted except for a very young couple; a mysterious, dark man; and a sophisticated, professional woman wearing a suit-jacket with shoulder pads. I am sort of glad we missed the busy hours.

"When does the train get here?" I ask Swift, hoping we won't have to wait very long.

"In about ten minutes." he says as he points to the mechanical sign that says when the different trains to the different locations come.

The only train that is coming in ten minutes is heading to Nevada. I sit down on a bench in the shade and adjust my suitcase beside me.

The last time I was on a train was almost five years. My family used to take the light-train almost every day while we were on the run, hopping from city to city. Just seeing the train station gives me a bad feeling, the same feeling of anxiety, of looking behind my shoulder, the same feeling that I had all the time back then.

After ten minutes of staring and thinking, Swift says, "It's here." The train flashes past us and comes to a halt. "Come on." He starts walking towards the train and I follow.

We get to the door and he hands me some money, "I'll go in first and find us some seats."

He puts money in a slot on the side of the train and the doors open. *That's new;* I think. The doors close after him and I step forward, put all the money Swift gave me in the slot, step through the door when it opens, I drag my suitcase to where Swift is sitting. He stands up and lets me sit near the window. When we finally get situated, I take in my surroundings. We are sitting seven rows behind where the driver should be, except there's no driver. Five rows in front of us, the young couple—they look like they are thirteen years old—sits facing us. They start making-out and I am totally disgusted. I have never even kissed a boy; I do not have time to waste on pointless relationships.

Swift must see the disgusted look on my face because he says, "You must not get out a lot." in a tone that suggests that I'm the weird one here.

I decide to keep my mouth shut and just shake my head as a response. I haven't been out of the house much since I finished school two years ago, except to go to the park near my house or to run. Even then I don't pay much attention to what others are doing and keep my head low. I used to love school. History was my favorite subject even though I did not get very good grades in it. I loved to

23

hear the real history, instead of listening to the lies that Preachers taught me. At first, when the teacher would ask a question, I would be the first to raise my hand, say the answer that the Preachers taught me, and get laughed at by the other students. I soon learned that almost everything I was taught is wrong, so I stopped answering and just listened.

The train starts up and as soon as we pass through the city barrier the sun's rays are so bright I am blinded.

"What's wrong with you?" Swift tries to keep his voice low, but I can tell that he is frantic.

"What?" *What's going on? Are we under attack, I can't see anything.*

"Your eyes." Something is put over my eyes and settles on my nose. After a few seconds I can see again. "Are you crazy? Why didn't you bring sunglasses?" Swift once again has a worried look on his face.

"Oh, crap." I forgot. Outside the barrier, we are unprotected from radiation and Ultra Violet rays from the sun that could permanently damage my eyes.

"The train windows protect your skin against radiation, but if you do not wear Glares..." He points to the glasses on his head.

I hadn't noticed before, but the lenses of Swift's glasses are completely black, and I can't see his eyes. All of the other passengers also have Glares covering their eyes.

"Sorry, it has been a while. I forgot." *I must look like an idiot.* The sun suddenly disappears behind dark grey-green clouds and rain and sleet begin to hit the train like bullets.

"Whatever, I'm tired." Swift says abruptly, slides down the seat until his head can rest on top of the back and then closes his eyes. *This kid is supposed to help me? I don't think he could even take care of himself.* He lifts his head a little and says, "You can sleep too, if you want." I just shrug and he closes his eyes again. *What an idiot.*

24

If I sleep too, then we will be completely unprotected. Everyone calls me paranoid, but I have reason to, after all of those years looking over my back.

I stare out the window and watch the sky change from stormy to sunny every couple minutes. After a long while the sun begins to set and the overhead light flicker on.

***

"Wake up." A hushed voice mumbles in my ear. *Dang it; I fell asleep.*

"What's up?" I say out loud and I am quickly shushed. I open my eyes. Everything is dark, but I can feel the sway of the train. *I am blind.*

"The lights went out." Once again it seems that Swift can read my mind. *Thank the gods I'm not blind.* I hear a rustle and something brushes past our seats.

"They are here," a rough voice I have never heard before says, "I followed them from Tieced. I am honored to be in your presence, but why have you come in person? Who are they?"

"We can't let the filth roam around free anymore." A man with a strange accent simply states.

"Preachers." Swift murmurs beside me. Hearing that name brings back the memories, and puts a knot in my stomach… I slide down my seat.

"Are they here for us?" I breathe.

"There is no way they know who we are."

"Do you think they realize we are here?" I whisper to him.

"I don't think they care."

Outside, a lamp-post flies past the train, which illuminates our cabin for a few, brief seconds, showing two dark figures. One of them is short, plump and balding; the other is tall and wearing a black

25

overcoat and hood. They stand over the teenagers, who are huddled together. Their backs are pressed against their seats, as they try to get away from the Preachers. I catch all of this in the one and half seconds before the lamp-post disappears.

I hear the girl whimper.

"How are we going to do it?" The scruffy voice utters. I assume he is the short one.

"The usual way, there is no need for special treatment here." Declares the taller of the two. I hear the familiar clink of metal on metal. Before I realize what I am doing, I am up on my feet, climbing over Swift.

"Stop!" His hushed voice calls after me as he grabs my hand.

My training has taught me to only interfere if I'm sure I'm going to get out uninjured, but I'm not a kid anymore. "No. I'm not running anymore." *I am not going to stand by while two kids are murdered. That would make me as bad as the Preachers.* I yank my hand away from him. He gets up and stands next to me.

"Don't try to stop me." I threaten.

"I'm not going to." My stomach is filled with a peculiar feeling. I quickly dismiss it as gratitude.

Together, we walk the few steps between us and the Preachers. I hear a rustle of cloth. "Do not touch them." I say with authority. The train is again lit up; another lamp-post soars by.

The two men turn around. The squatter one holds a machine pistol and points it at us. I kick it out of his hand before he can do anything. The lamp-post flies by and leaves the train cloaked in darkness again.

The lights above us flicker and turn on. After spotting the weapon, Swift dives and scoops up the pistol.

"You idiot!" The larger man says, "Our time is up, I will take care of this myself." Using his left hand, he wrenches out a machine pistol similar to a Beretta 93R from the depths of his cloak, points it at the girl, and pulls the trigger.

No noise is heard except for the girl's scream. I see her fall back and crumple over. *Was she shot?* The man is still facing the girl. I see now that a mask hides his face, but I can guess the expression on his face: joy.

I rush at him; ready to grab his gun. He turns around, swinging his arm, barely missing my nose, and makes me come up short. Fortunately for me, his arm keeps swinging. He aims at the window next to me, and once again pulls the trigger, shattering the glass. I cover my head with my hands, dive and flatten myself to the floor as the broken glass falls around me.

I stay laying on the floor for longer than I would in a normal fight, thinking that we should be dead. The radiation should have killed us by now.

I decide to look up. The hooded figure stands above me, his gun barrel pointed at my forehead. His long jacket flaps in the wind, the hood threatening to fall. His mask is pearly-white and seems to shine.

Out of the corner of my eye, I see Swift raise the stolen gun. The gun shot rings out and my assailant's gun goes flying out the broken window, into the night. He realizes that he has lost. He dives out of the window and disappears. *Where is the other man?* I lost track of him in the struggle. His figure waddles past me and he too jumps through the window just as another gunshot rings out. His body falls, hovering in the air for a second and then goes falling fast, out of sight.

I turn my head. Swift stands a few feet from me, arm still raised, gun still pointed towards the broken window. Swift drops his hand, tucks the gun in his waistband and helps me up. The first thing I do is look out the window. I notice the buildings zooming past us and realize that we are already in city-limits. Soon the train will stop and Swift and I will have to escape the scene before the police arrive.

"Wren, get over here!" Swift shouts to me. He is over by the two teenagers.

I brush the glass shards off my clothes and hurry over to the couple.

The girl is sprawled across two seats, blood covering her torso. Her companion is standing over her, wide-eyed and trying to rip off her shirt, which is plastered to her skin. I push him aside and crouch down beside her. I tear her shirt over her abdomen, where it looks like the most blood is coming from. The wound I uncover is like nothing I have ever seen before: the wound is about four and a half inches wide, I am not sure about depth, but is probably a few inches deep, because I can see part of her intestines. I can also see the bullet, which is lodged in her large intestine and is oozing some kind of green liquid. *There is nothing I can do.* Slowly, the flesh surrounding the wound foams and disappears. The green liquid is eating her alive.

I realize that I am not the only one staring: Swift stands behind me; the boy is on his knees, hands over his nose and mouth; and the girl stares into my steady eyes. She holds her hand out towards the boy and he stands up, kneels beside us, and grabs it. She extends her other arm and I grip her hand in both of mine. Now all we can do is wait until she dies.

I can feel her pulse in her wrist. As soon as her heart stops beating, the chemical sizzles and smokes, evaporating into the air. The girl's dead eyes stare into her partner's. He knows she is gone.

"Nooooo!" He gets on his feet and shakes her limp body. Blood trickles out of the corner of her mouth, and her body slumps over. Once again, he falls to his knees. The train suddenly comes to a stop and I almost fall. The doors burst open, and the suit-jacketed woman dashes through one.

I let go of the girl's hand. She only has four fingers on her right hand.

"This is why." I say and I stretch out her hand so Swift can see. "This is probably why she was murdered." He does not counter my statement, but as soon as I utter the words I know that they are only half true. The tall man was wearing a mask, telling me that he is some sort of leader. *But why would a high-ranking Preacher kill someone themselves? Even that lower-ranking Preacher was somewhat surprised to see him.*

I notice the movement of people outside at the train-station.

"What should we do with the body?"

"Leave it." Swifts says, and motions to the boy to follow him, "Come on."

But the boy is glued to the floor. Swift grabs him by the waist, gets him on his feet and directs him towards the door. I seize our bags and hurry after them. From behind me, I hear the train doors open and close and then they are followed by gasps of horror. I hasten my strides, catching up with Swift and the boy in a few steps. I lift my hood over my head.

As we walk, Swift asks, "What's your name?"

But the kid isn't listening and doesn't answer.

"What is your name?" Swift repeats. The harshness in his voice somewhat surprises me and it brings the boy back to reality.

"Orion." He mumbles.

"Where were you heading?" Swift continues his interrogation.

Orion doesn't answer at first. "I don't know. We were just looking for somewhere safe… heard about some organization…"

"NEST. That is where I work." Swift states.

Unspoken words agree that we will go together.

I follow Swift and Orion through the alleyways and back roads of the city. All of the cities I have visited are the same: circular with the Center Building in the middle. First comes the Circumference, the poorest and dirtiest part of the city. The crime rate is understandably higher in this area. Next comes Halfway, I guess you could call it the neutral zone. Shops, businesses and apartment buildings, all architectural giants, form the Inner Ring.

My mind is blank and my body tired. I notice the strange looks we receive. After all, we are three kids walking through the streets covered in blood, wearing ripped clothes and grim faces. It's dark out already; the sun replaced by a grimacing moon. The night sky is speckled with a few stars.

Tiny cuts litter my arms, and my hands are coated in her blood. I might have to throw out these clothes altogether.

"We better take the back entrance. We don't want to draw too much attention." Swifts says and we turn into another alley.

I walk in the shadows created by the dark concrete jungle and the lampposts, when Swift stops. We are not that far from the Center Building. I can see it from here, but that doesn't mean much since it is the tallest building in every city.

What I assume is the NEST building is about twenty floors tall, but only because it has a narrow and tall structure with a bulbous point at the top. Swift stands facing the wall a few feet away from it. The only thing between him and the wall is the top of a dumpster chute. Dumpster chutes are designed to look like old trash cans. Garbage is thrown through the chute and it falls down, below the city, landing in a current of trash. It eventually flows out of the city boundaries to join the endless piles of filth and waste. *Great, we are going to have to go through sewage.*

"This is the back entrance. For Proxies." Swift places his hand on the garbage can lid and a light appears. It seems to be scanning his hand. Swift eyes Orion for a moment before turning back to the wall. A chunk of the wall flickers and fades, forming a door. An empty corridor leads from the entrance.

"My lady…" Swift says, gesturing to the doorway and stepping aside so I can go in.

But I don't know where to go; "Maybe you should lead the way."

He walks in and Orion and I follow.

The walls, ceiling and floor are made of white, square tiles, about three feet wide. We make our way down the hall and halfway through, orange tiles are mixed in with the white ones. Walking along, I soon realize that there is a pattern: two white, one orange, two white, one orange… all in one line, straight down the middle.

"There shouldn't be a problem getting in. We can drop off Orion at the lobby and then get the key to your room—"

Five armed men hurry down the corridor from both ends. I am ready to fight them off but Swift sighs and says, "Do not move, and do not say a word. Everything will be fine, let me do the talking."

"Freeze! Put your hands above your head!" I quickly obey and so does Orion.

 Swift keeps his arms at his sides though and asks casually, "What is going on, guys?"

The one closest to us lowers his MTAR-21 and the others follow his lead. "News of an attack. Upped security measures. Who is this?" The guard nods to Orion.

"Refugee. Could you escort him to the living facilities, Ruff?" The guard's eyes drift to me. "New recruit." Swift explains. "We are late for a meeting with Albatross."

Ruff motion to Orion to follow and the group of guards hustle down the hallway.   They walk down the passageway turning right where the hall splits.

Swift waits until they are out of earshot to speak, "Nice welcome party." He mumbles, trying to not lose his cool. "We need to hurry up, Albatross and Hawk are probably waiting."

We walk faster. As I get closer to the split, I notice a metal door directly in front of us.

When Swift and I reach it, he punches a bunch of numbers on a pad on the wall next to it. A retinal-scanner pops out of the wall,

31

above the key-pad. There is a short hallway to the left. Another door keeps me from seeing where it leads.

He moves closer; opening his left eye wide, squinting his right. A blue light appears, scanning his amber eye.

"Agent Swift." He says and then whispers to me, "Getting places isn't this hard when you're inside." It is nice to know that I won't have my fingerprints scanned every time I have to go to the bathroom.

"Welcome, Agent Swift." A robotic voice comes from above. The door unlocks with a click and then Swift pulls it open, revealing a large and open room. I don't get to look around a lot because Swift immediately whisks me off towards an elevator. The elevator door slides open revealing a shiny, clean compartment. We enter. I set my bag on the elevator floor, tired of carrying it. The doors close. There are no buttons on the wall, but the elevator rises fast. We only ride for what seems to be a hundred floors and by the time we come to a stop, my head is spinning.

I grip Swift's arm. "You'll get used to it." He assures me. "This one goes directly to the main headquarters, the Viewing Deck."

Once we finally arrive at our destination the doors slowly open, displaying a huge round room. The walls are made of tinted glass; desks are curved and pressed up against them. I pick up my bag and slowly step out onto a platform that looks down on the whole room. One desk with two computer screens is the only thing on the platform other than Swift and I. Straight ahead of us, the desks are cleared. The room is empty except for two men that are standing next to the window, they seem to be arguing. A large round table stands in the middle of the room; it can probably seat eighteen people. We descend one of the two staircases leading down from the platform, with me holding on to the railing carefully. As we approach the men, I recognize them.

"We need to act fast!" Hawk yells and touches the window with his finger. Images appear, covering the exposed glass; news stories and their photographs. Corpses in all different positions and locations fill my view.

"And these are only the bodies The Hearing has found and was able to report." Hawk adds. The Hearing. That is the name on the top of every news story. They all seem to be from the same source.

Ding ding! A short alarm beeps. A new picture pops up on the screen, flashing red twice in time with the beeps. The girl. My body freezes and I look at Swift. He clears his throat to get their attention. Albatross and Hawk turn around.

"Swift!" Albatross exclaims. "How long have you two been standing there?"

"We met that girl and her friend on the way here." He nods towards her dead body on the screen, "They were attacked by two Preachers. We tried to protect them, but she was shot by some chemical weapon. The higher ranking Preacher got away. I shot the other while he was escaping. His location and condition are unknown." He stands legs apart, back straight, hands behind his back. He looks at me; telling me to do the same. I emulate his stance.

"And the friend?" Hawk asks.

"Escorted by some Security Proxies to the civilian living quarters."

"Did you get any samples of the chemical?"

"No. It evaporated when it was done with its job."

"Thank you for coming up here like I asked. I expect a full report on everything that happened." Albatross states. I yawn loudly and try to cover it up, "After you get settled in." he adds. We have been traveling for about eight hours and I am already tired.

Albatross dismisses us and then Swift and I head back to the elevator. The elevator begins to descend, and I lean against the curved back wall, closing my eyes.

"We will go down to the lobby and get your room key and everything."

I nod slowly.

Even though we have to travel the same hundred floors it feels like we have been standing here for a while, "Um, Swift?" I ask, eyes still closed.

"Yes?" He answers.

"When will we arrive at the lobby?"

"Oh, we got here like thirty seconds ago." My eyes burst open. It's true; the doors hang open waiting for someone to pass between them. Crowded voices and footsteps echo outside.

"Why didn't you tell me?" I punch his arm and stomp out of the elevator.

He smiles innocently and follows me, "You looked too peaceful to be disturbed."

I sigh and take a glance around the lobby. To the left of the elevator bank white couches line the walls and corner, small windows illuminating that sitting area. An opening to a hallway breaks the wall next to the couches. The room is pretty large. It could fit quite a lot of people. Right in front of us is a secretary's desk. A round clock hangs high on the wall.

The secretary notices us and stands up. She is stunning. Her blonde hair is in a bun, her bright turquoise eyes pop out against her milky-white skin. She looks too young to be a secretary. She smiles kindly to Swift. My intestines feel as if they are knotting in my stomach. *Why do I keep getting these strange feelings? I must be sick.*

Swift smiles as she grows closer, "Good evening, Blue-jay." *She must be one of Swift's friends.*

"Swift." She says, nodding her head.

Another wave of sickness rushes over me, "Um, Swift. I'm not feeling too good." I clutch my stomach. The attention is drawn back to me.

Swift takes my bag from me and puts his hand on my shoulder to keep me steady, "I better take you to your room." Blue-jay slips something metallic into his hand. He pulls my arm over his shoulders to support my weight. **Whoosh**. Another rush so powerful I almost fall over. "Careful, now." We hurry away from Blue-jay and back to the elevators. *Not again.* I close my eyes, only opening them for a couple seconds and then shutting them again. As soon as we begin our ascent I am instantly knocked back into the vertigo. When the elevator comes to a stop we exit and walk through another door and an echoing hallway into a larger room. From a door on the right I can hear the clank of silverware and dishes.

"Is she ok?" I hear a young male voice ask from behind us.

"She will be fine, but can you two help me get her into her room?"

"Sure." A new female voice says.

My curiosity gets the best of me and I open my eyes for a quick moment. A flash of orange. I keep my eyes open, but hang my head. They follow us; I can hear their footsteps. More footsteps join theirs; people walk past us from both directions, they are all wearing combat boots.

"I got your key from Blue-jay. Number one hundred and forty-five." Swift mutters. We had come to a turn-off and he appears to be considering which way to go.

"That is this way," the girl says, "I am in one-fifty-one." We head right as the girl and boy lead us. As we go along I stand up straight, taking my weight off Swift and I rub my eyes with my left hand.

I try to pull my arm off his shoulders, but he grips my hand with his right hand, "You don't want to fall again, do you?"

"I didn't fall in the first place." I groan.

35

There are doors on both sides of the wide hallway. Every door is white with black numbers. One-forty-one on the left, one-forty-two on the right, one-forty-three, one-forty-four. As we approach door one hundred and forty five, Swift digs in his back pocket for my key and throws it over his shoulder, I hear someone catch it. A boy steps forward and puts the key in the lock and unlocks the door, letting and Swift and I walk in.

"Thanks for helping us." I say and turn around to face the two. They could be twins, except for the age difference, so they must be siblings. They both have flaming ginger hair and green eyes. The boy has curly hair and freckles; the older girl has bangs and large eyes.

"No problem. I am Robin, and this is my brother, Owl." The older sister says. She looks to be about my age. Her brother is a few years younger, maybe fifteen. I shake their hands.

"Well we have to get going," she says, and smiles kindly at me, "And you have to unpack. Good luck." She steers her brother out of the room, he waves before Robin closes the door behind them. I quickly notice the queen sized bed in the center of my room. I look around, to the left there is a couch facing a huge screen and a bathroom is past the bed. A desk and a chair stand to the right of the door. Walking to the bathroom I notice the closet between it and the bed. I consider attempting to stay up, but the white fluffy blanket and pillows are too inviting. I collapse, face first, onto the bed.

Swift chuckles, "Good night." he says with a smile in his voice.

"Good night." I mumble into a pillow.

Chapter Three

The sound of something heavy falling wakes me up. I roll off my bed, trying to take cover and reach my gun, which is lodged somewhere between my mattress and the bed. But it isn't there. *Where is my gun?* I peer over the mattress, looking for my attacker.

Swift stands near the door. He chuckles once before explaining, "Sorry. I knocked over your suitcase." He bends over and sets my suitcase upright. "You really need to relax. You're safe here, this building is almost impregnable. I have your key and a brand new T-Screen." he says and then places them on the desk.

For a brief moment I had thought that yesterday was a dream and that I had woken up in my bed. I remain quiet for a moment and wake up. "Well, I need a gun." I say clearly. Nothing makes me feel safer and more comfortable than having a gun on my person. I should have brought one with me from home.

"After we fill out a report on yesterday's adventures," he says in a way that annoys me. "And after basic training."

"Ugh." I moan and get up.

I get dressed in the bathroom and Swift tells me that we're going to eat breakfast. I follow him out of my room, head right and then turn left around a corner. We walk along a long hallway which eventually leads into a wide room; almost like a courtyard, but indoors. We walk across the 'courtyard', and enter a cafeteria through two large swinging doors.

"This is the cafeteria for Proxies." Swift informs me. "We take in refugees, but they eat in their private apartments."

He and I stand in line, pick up a tray and get our food from one of the many workers on duty at the moment. There is a small selection of dry cereal and different flavors of yogurt. Then Swift walks me over to one of the many circular tables and we sit down. As soon as we settle down, Swift pulls out a folded sheet of paper. The report for Albatross, I assume. While he flattens out the paper, I start eating.

The food isn't bad, but is pretty much flavorless. I guess that's better than disgusting food, though.

The two of us sit in silence while Swift fills out the report, sometimes asking me questions about certain details that he forgot. Mid-meal Robin and Owl walk in. As soon as they see us Robin waves and Owl smiles. They quickly pick up their meals and join us at our table without hesitation. Swift doesn't talk much, but Robin tries to make conversation. I wonder if Robin, Owl and Swift were acquaintances before I arrived, or if these people are accidently my new friends. I don't need any friends at the moment.

"You guys—" I am suddenly interrupted when a loud girl with a purple mohawk a few tables away bursts out laughing hysterically about something that I am unaware of. I take a moment to glare at the woman and collect my thoughts before trying again. "If this is the Proxy cafeteria, than that means you are both Proxies, right?" I ask the pair. Owl seems a little young to be an agent.

"Yes, we are both Proxies," Robin explains, "Owl works in building security and I—"

"Sorry to interrupt you guys, but I need to get this to Albatross." Swift holds up the filled-out report, "You coming, Wren?" Swift asks abruptly.

The question takes me by surprise, "Um, I guess so." I was trying to learn some more about being a Proxy, but I guess Swift doesn't think it is important at the moment.

I say goodbye to Owl and Robin while Swift grabs our trays and disposes of them.

Swift and I head back to the round room at the top of the building. I mostly just follow his lead, still not familiar with the large building. Every hallway, corridor and room have the same white walls, white tiled floor and fluorescent lights.

After taking two different elevators, we arrive. Like Swift said would happen, the ride doesn't affect me as much this time. Unlike last night, there are people working at every desk and there is a low buzz of talking. We find Albatross at the front of the room again. He is talking to the secretary from downstairs, Blue-jay. Hawk is nowhere in sight.

"Albatross, sir?" Swift interrupts them formally, "I have the report you asked for. Morning Blue-jay."

She smiles at him kindly and I can't help but scowl.

"Oh, thank you, Swift. I was just discussing the Enhancement program with Blue-jay. So far the plan is to form a team of about ten people who will eventually become Enhancements." He explains and continues, "But first we need to make sure Hawk's implant is safe. So it could take a couple of months before it is officially organized."

It annoys me that she was informed before I was, but I leave it be. "Count me in, sir." I say firmly.

"And me." Swift says beside me. I wasn't expecting that. Now I know that Swift and I will still be together in the future. For a moment I wonder what Swift's reasons are for getting Enhanced. I guess I'll find out when we are on the 'Enhancement' task-team.

"I already knew you two would be interested." He says with a grin. "Well you better get going, Wren still needs to get used to how things work around here."

***

"In four days." Blue-jay tells us after a few seconds of her touching her fingers on a computer screen.

I groan.

Swift and I had gone down with Blue-jay to the main information desk to ask when the next training course would begin so I could become a Proxy. She had politely looked up the information on the secretary's computer.

Now Swift and I sit on one of the couches in the lobby. "It could have been worse. I guess we'll just have to hang out till then." Swift resolves.

I have not 'hung out' in years. "Maybe we should do something actually productive." I hint to Swift.

"You're not one for relaxing, are you?" Swift chuckles and leans back against the couch. "I suppose I could show you around the facilities..."

"I think that would be best."

Swift hops to his feet and walks over to the elevator bank, "Fifteen stories above ground, seven below. And not to mention the civilian lobby. Where do you want to go first?" He gestures to the four elevators.

The civilian lobby sounds interesting, but so do the underground levels. "Um, the training facilities." I decide, unsure of my decision. "Or someplace with guns."

Swift smiles again. "Fine, first I will show you the weapons cache, and then the Proxy training rooms. After that, we can go grab a bite to eat in the civilian lobby."

"Great." I say and then get up myself.

Swift takes us down a hallway that turns off from the lobby and into a low-lighted room. A shorter man stands behind a tall desk that reaches to about my lowest rib. Behind him are two shelves. The space between them forms an entrance to the long room behind him filled with more shelves and rows of table with all sorts of weapons. I wish I could get a closer look.

"Jardah, Buzzard." Swift greets the man. *Does he know everyone?* "I am just showing this new recruit around the building." Swift tells Buzzard and then turns to me, leaning against the desk. "You will get your rifles from here whenever you are on duty. Do not get any ideas right now; you can only retrieve a weapon if you are a Proxy. Just wait a few weeks." I roll my eyes in response.

40

I want to stay and look at the guns for a little longer, but Swift leaves soon after he is done explaining, so I go after him. Entering the lobby again, I see Swift standing in front of the closest elevator to me. I hurry over to him.

"These two elevators," Swift points to the two elevators on the left. "Take you upstairs to the Proxy floors and the science floors. We're going to check out the Proxy training rooms." The door opens for our elevator and a few people exit, making Swift and I take a couple steps back. When the area clears, Swift and I enter the pod and he presses the button for the fifth floor. "Proxy dorms are on the second, third and fourth floors. Five and six are Proxy training floors."

Swift and I get off on the fifth floor and he shows me the many different training rooms. They have rooms filled with exercise machines, mats for yoga, gun ranges, punching bags and they even have a fighting ring. As we pass through each of the rooms, my confidence in the choice I made to come here grows stronger. *I would never have any of these things if I were on my own or at home.*

I linger in the rooms for longer than Swift had expected. "It's getting late; we better get to the cafeteria before the food runs out. We won't have time to explore the civilian lobby today."

The two of us rush to the second floor, where we both have apartments, and into the dining hall. A heap of feithid is plopped onto my plate by a lady who looks less than happy. By the time Swift and I find a place to sit, the bugs have already started moving around on the plate. Some of them have even left the plate and are roaming slowly on the tray. That's why I like feithid, because I sort of have to fight for my food.

"So what do I have to do to become a Proxy?" I ask Swift. I have been wanting to know all day and have expected him to explain it to me, but I have grown impatient.

"It is pretty simple." He tells me and then takes a bite of his own dinner. "You just have to pass a training course. I am sure it will be easy for you."

I simply nod my head and go back to eating.

After dinner Swift walks with me back to my dorm and helps me unpack. He assists me in hanging the Chalk Outlines poster above my bed and watches me arrange my clothes in the small closet. I catch him nodding off on the couch just as I put the last jacket on a clothes hanger. "You can leave." I inform him and grab the last things from the bottom of my suitcase. The two stuffed animals, which I was taught are a tiger and a dog. I toss them onto the bed, "I'm done now."

"Oh, okay." He slowly gets up and stretches. Swift walks towards the door, "Tomorrow we'll explore the bottom floors, okay?"

"Sounds great." I answer so he'll just leave already; I am tired too.

"Cool, see you tomorrow."

Chapter Four

Tap, tap, tap. I hear someone knocking on my door; I'm guessing it's Swift.

"Coming!" I yell, then roll out of bed and quickly get dressed.

I yank the door open to see Swift's happy face, "Ready for another fun day?" He asks.

"Yeah, yesterday was loads of fun." I say sarcastically while rolling my eyes. After seeing Swift's offended expression I quickly add, "Don't you have anything better to do? Like a real job."

Swift waves his hand toward the hallway and we start walking. "Right now, my job is to help you get used to this place." I stop in front of the doors to the cafeteria, but Swift keeps going. When he sees me stay behind, he says, "Oh, you slept in and missed breakfast, but don't worry, we can pick something up outside." *I never sleep in so late that I miss breakfast. I love breakfast. This place must be getting to me already.*

Swift takes me down to the lobby, past the main desk and through a pair of doors. I don't know what was expecting, but it certainly isn't what I see now. I went from walking in a clean, white, closed-off lobby to an open and very public place that looks like a mall. *Why is there be a mall here? What about security?*

Swift steps forward into the madness and then turns back to face me, "Welcome to what Proxies call the 'civilian lobby' and to what the outside world knows as the Phoenix Shopping Center. Yeah, I know." Swift grins and then pulls me closer to him, so no one will overhear our conversation. Despite Swift's infectious mood, even now I can't be anything but serious. "We have all sorts of shops here, and even offices up there." He points upward toward a balcony that rings the ground floor. Now I notice the high, arched ceiling covered in dark lines and apparently made of yellowish glass. He drags me over to a bench and we sit down together, "The five floors here are filled with small businesses, all run by refugees. This way, the building is not as suspicious." *But what about Preachers just walking in?* "We have security all over the place; cameras, Proxies, and a lockdown in case something does happen." Swift pauses to look at me, "Now let's go get you something to eat."

A small café is where we end up. I wait outside at a small round table while Swift goes in and orders me some pastries. I see him reach into his own pocket and give the waitress the money for the food. I don't like owing people anything, but I currently don't have any money. "Why are you being so nice to me?" I ask him when he returns with a square plate filled with muffins and small cakes.

Swift does not seem taken aback by this question at all, which surprises me. "Three reasons—one: I am your guide and my job is to help you; two: we should get to know each other because it seems we'll be with each other for a while; and three: you look like you could use a friend." He snatches up a muffin and starts to take off its wrappings. "Go on and eat."

His words answer my question sufficiently so I grab a small cake that's oozing some sort of red jelly and begin to devour it. *He is right;* I decide; *if he's going to be in the Enhancement program, we're going to be together for a while and may be in tough situations together.* Throughout our meal I ask Swift to explain some more about this place, but he tells me that it is not safe to talk out loud up here, so I save my questions for later.

After I finish the last pastry, Swift clears the table and we start our trip to the underground levels of the NEST building. Swift presses the button for floor minus six and I send him a curious look. "The bottommost floor is pretty much empty, but we sometimes use it for special training. We will now go check out the refugee quarters." I follow Swift's lead as he walks me through the six floors of refugee homes and I even get to see some of the people living down here. Whole families walk past us and go about their own business. I wonder why I never ended up here.

As Swift and I explore, he explains the life here, "The refugees are split into three categories: regular people who disagree with the Preachers, targets of the Preachers, and ex-Preachers. Every group usually helps out in some way, but most of the Proxies come out of the first group.

"In each apartment there are two bedrooms, a kitchen, one bathroom and a living room. The only problem is that a lot of them cannot leave these floors in case they are seen by Preachers."

We take an elevator to the Proxy lobby; neither of us speaking the whole way up.

Swift walks straight to the secretary's desk when we arrive on the main floor, "Anything important going on right now, Crow?" he asks a Proxy I have never seen before, who looks up from a computer screen. Blue-jay must be on a break.

Crow goes back to typing on the computer's keyboard. "Actually yes; an Agent Hummingbird has just arrived at the building. He is important for some reason, but I have never heard of him. What about you, Swift?" Only his dark eyes rise to look at Swift.

"Nope." he answers quickly. *Liar*. Next thing I know Swift is grabbing my arm and pulling me back to the elevator bank. "Dinner time." Swift tells Crow and waves goodbye.

As soon as I get into the elevator, I pull my arm away from Swift's grasp, "Why did you lie to him?" I ask him; he was obviously lying.

"I wasn't lying, it actually is dinner time." Swift says this while stepping onto our Proxy floor. I rush after him.

I walk right next to Swift now and talk at him, "Don't patronize me, Swift. Who is Agent Hummingbird?"

"It's your father, Wren." He pauses and then ducks into the cafeteria. When I catch up to him in the line to get food he finishes explaining, "I was going to wait for us to get somewhere safer, because I don't know how much of a secret the Enhancers are, but you were being a pain so..." *So Dad has finally arrived.* I should want to go see him, but for some reason I don't. I should keep my distance and he should just focus on the Enhancers.

Swift swallows a large forkful of food and then says, "We should go see him tomorrow."

"Actually, what I—"

"Great, it's a plan. I need to show you the research laboratories anyway."

My first instinct is to tell him what I really mean, but I keep my mouth shut. Right now and in this place, I am the new kid and I need to learn how things actually work around here. And I can't always let my anger take ahold of me.

***

"Good morning, Agent Hummingbird."

My father stands a few feet away from me in a bright room filled with all sorts of clean instruments. Right now he is looking through the lens of a microscope. I wait just inside the door for him to acknowledge my presence and respond. Swift stands beside me.

I wait a few seconds, but Dad still continues with his work as if he didn't hear me. Even at home my dad could get a little distracted and ignore the rest of the family for a couple days, so I am used to this behavior. But Swift is not. Swift steps away from me and moves closer to my father's work desk. "Agent Hummingbird." he says louder than I did.

"Oh, Swift!" Dad exclaims and then almost knocks over the microscope. As I join the two, I notice the bags under his eyes and the way his greying hair sticks up in strange places.

"Dad, have you been sleeping?" I ask him, trying to make sure concern can be heard in my voice.

He rubs his eyes before looking at me, "I just got here and there is a lot of work to be done... I must have lost track of... What time is it?"

I look at Swift. "We just ate breakfast." I answer. Swift and I had sat with Robin and Owl again. "When was the last time you ate?"

"Sometime yesterday."

"Dad..." I want to tell him how irresponsible that is and how he should worry about himself before the Enhancer and work for NEST, but Swift does not give me the chance.

"I'll go get you some food. Wren, you stay here and catch up." Swift rushes out of the room and down the hall. *We've only been apart for two days...*

Because Swift is taking care of the situation I decide to drop it. "So what are you working on now?" And anyway, Dad won't want to talk about anything else.

"I am glad you asked." He pulls a stool up next to him and beckons for me to sit on it. "Well I have already started the tests on Hawk—nothing out of the ordinary except for the super human factor—and this is a tissue sample. Would you like to take a look?" Dad moves the microscope closer to me. I shake my head no; despite what my father might think, I'm not that into science or biology or chemistry or whatever. "Everything is going according to plan, so you will be Enhanced soon."

Don't get your hopes up just yet, Wren; "How soon is soon?"

Before Dad can answer Swift comes back, his right hand holding a plastic bag, "I got some leftovers from the cafeteria... I have no idea what it is." He places it on my father's work desk.

"Thank you, Swift." is all my dad says and then he goes back to writing in a notebook.

"Why don't we leave your dad to his work and we can go explore the rest of the floor."

I sigh and get up, "Sounds like a great idea." *Swift is full of them.*

47

Dad doesn't even say goodbye.

Swift shows me the different laboratories on this floor and then takes me to check out the hospital. "Two stories of hospital rooms for the residents of the building. The Medical Proxies work here of course, but we have a few civilians too." We pass the circular main desk right in the middle of the floor. Each of the rooms for patients is equipped with a classic hospital bed, a couple cushioned chairs for company, all the necessary medical machinery that I don't understand, a window looking out on the city with floral curtains, and an adjoining bathroom. And everything is super clean. *Piper would like it here.*

Swift and I are just about done with the hospital when I feel like being cocky and say, "I think you might be visiting here pretty soon."

"Oh, really?" Swift grins and looks my way, "And why do you think that?"

"Well tomorrow is my last day before training and I was thinking that maybe we should have a little fun. My kind of fun." I press the button for the elevators. It should be around dinner time. Even if it's not, I am still hungry.

"And let me guess… Your idea of fun is beating up a poor guy like me."

"Pretty much."

"Challenge accepted." Swift steps into the elevator first and then I quickly follow. *Tomorrow should be interesting.*

Chapter Five

After quietly entering the cafeteria for breakfast, I spot Swift sitting at a table near the left wall with Blue-jay. I hurry over to them while shouting, "Are you ready to get your butt kicked?"

Swift takes a sip of juice before answering, "If I beat you you'll be really sorry you said that."

I pull out a chair next to him and sit down. "So you think I might win."

"It's a possibility."

For once Blue-jay decides to speak up, "Everything is a possibility, but I have not seen Swift lose a fight." I would rather she hadn't.

"It's because I make her look away." Swift chuckles humbly. "Now go get some breakfast." He pushes me softly off my chair. I think he's just trying to butter me up so I won't be so hard on him.

While waiting in line, I look back at Swift and Blue-jay who look like they're deep in conversation. Or maybe an argument. I'm sure they're talking about me until Swift notices my staring and then grins at me. I turn my attention back to picking out which kind of yogurt I want and the upcoming match with Swift. From what I've seen he's just a kid pretending to be a man; I can easily take him.

Blue-jay and Swift stop talking when I return, but Swift tries to keep our conversation going, "So I was thinking we should take this fight upstairs, duke it out in the fighting ring."

"Perfect."

I consume my breakfast quickly, getting pretty excited about my match with Swift. Other than the argument with Hawk, I haven't fought an actual person in months; I hope I'm not out of practice. Swift clears the table when I'm done eating and then we head up the couple floors to the fighting ring. Unfortunately, Blue-jay comes up with us.

Swift glances at the empty ring and asks, "Ready, Wren?"

I don't hesitate with my answer, "Of course." and then I quickly step onto the elevated mat. I place myself in a corner. "What are the rules?" I ask as Swift enters the ring too.

Swift thinks for a moment before responding, "Um, first one to tap out or fall off the mat loses. Blue-jay is the judge." He nods his head towards Blue-jay and then moves to the opposite corner from me.

I lift my fists and place my feet, getting into a fighting stance, "That's it? Okay."

Swift gets into a fighting stance too and then Blue-jay calls for the match to begin.

Swift comes at me much quicker than I had expected, especially from someone as big as him, and swings his fist at my head. *A lame move on his part;* I step back with my right foot and move out of the way easily if not a little out of balance. Next thing I know Swift thrusts out both of his hands; they land flat on my chest. The combination of his force and my unbalance causes me to be simply pushed backward. I can't do anything as I stumble off the mat in what seems like slow motion. Both of my feet land firmly on the floor.

Blue-jay seems way too smug when she announces, "Wren stepped off the mat, Swift wins."

Shit, shit, shit; I think, furious with myself, and stand up straight. With the shame of failure on my back, I finally notice the other Proxies in the room who, only a few seconds ago, were doing their own thing, but now seem to be looking at me.

Swift hops off the mat next to me and places a hand on my back. "Sorry, looks like—"

"Let's go again." I say while shrugging his hand off of me. I climb back into the ring and silently wait for him to either deny my request or agree.

For an answer Swift steps back into the ring. He brushes past me on his way back to his corner. "I hope you're not being too hard on yourself, Wren."

Of course I'm being hard on myself, I'm supposed to be this big, tough girl and I got knocked out in the first five seconds. I underestimated Swift's abilities and overestimated mine. "Can we just start?" I ask and immediately hear the harshness in my voice. I don't want Swift to feel sorry; I am the one who should be sorry about losing in the first place.

"Right…" Blue-jay looks at Swift nervously. "Let the match begin."

The first thing I do is breathe. And then I do my best to ignore the other Proxies in the room as they move closer to the ring to get a better look. Ready to really begin, I lock eyes with Swift and take my first step forward on the balls of my feet. Swift moves towards the center too and we meet in the middle. A foot apart now, Swift is the first to strike, swinging wildly at my head. I duck and crouch, then move closer to his body, shoving my right shoulder against his chest. Swift staggers back, but is nowhere close to the edge of the mat. He regains his balance quickly and kicks his right leg at me. I block it easily with a knock from my hands and then send three quick jabs at his chest. Each one makes contact. But instead of looking worried or hurt, Swift smiles. Even though I know he isn't doing so in malice, it irks me.

I am preparing to attack again when a voice booms throughout the room, "Is she a Proxy?" I turn my head to see a muscular, tall man standing near the entrance with his arms cross his chest. A rifle is slung across his back and he has tattoos all over his body. He wears a dirty tank-top and cargo pants. I can tell that this is someone I don't want to mess with.

Swift gets off the mat and walks to the man with a kind smile on his face, "No, but—"

"I do not care what your excuses are, if she is not a Proxy then she does not have permission to be in this room or any of the other floors." The Proxy then turns around and leaves before Swift or I could explain my situation.

Blue-jay goes over to Swift and places a hand on his upper-arm, "We had better go."

"Yeah." He says quietly and then turns to me and waves to the door, "Come on, Wren, let's get out of here."

I jump down and go after Swift and Blue-jay as they exit. *Damn, that guy is a spoilsport.* "Who was that guy?" I ask at the elevator bank as we wait.

"Vulture, he's one of the trainers here." Swift answers and right after the elevator arrives and the three of us enter. He drops the topic quickly, "Where are we headed to now?"

"I have to work now..." Blue-jay presses on the button for the main floor.

Swift looks at me with excitement in his eyes. I wonder what he has planned, but I'm also not in the mood to do anything anymore. "And I was actually thinking about taking some time to relax by myself." I hit the button for the second floor.

"Oh, okay." Swift says. "But we'll hang out later, right?"

The elevator arrives on my floor and the doors open to show the empty hallway. I step out and look back at Swift over my shoulder, "Sure."

When I get back to my apartment I decide to take a nap for a few hours. After that I just sit on the couch and catch up on the news via T-screen.

During a particularly interesting article about The Chalk Outlines' most recent concert, Swift knocks on the door, "I got you something." can be heard from the other side.

I quickly hop off the couch and unlock the door for him. Swift smiles and holds up a paper bag. "I picked up some snacks and thought we could go check out one of the only spots we haven't completely explored yet." Immediately I think — *he's just really bored.* "You'll need a jacket."

"Okay." I hurry over to my closet and grab the first jacket I find and get into it quickly. Swift takes me down to the main floor and at first I don't know what exactly he's going to show me.

Swift turns to the furthest elevator to the right, "This one, as you might have noticed, goes to the Viewing Deck. It's twenty five floors above ground level, but it is on top of a structure that's width is relatively small. You can see practically the whole city from up there."

"Seems cool, but I've already been there a couple times."

"But did you actually take the time to look around, I mean really look around?"

"I guess not."

As soon as I answer Swift types in a security code to the Viewing Deck elevator. I try to pay more attention to the elevator as we zip up the twenty five floors, but nothing seems different than the rest of the building. The white walls, the shining metal, the bright fluorescent lights—they can all be seen over and over again throughout the Proxy section of the complex. When the doors suddenly pop open, I expect Swift to take me down the stairs to the main area of the Viewing Deck with the desks and computers and the large table and the people, but instead he grabs my arm and leads me to the left. "My little secret." he says quietly and then pushes open a steel door leading somewhere outside.

I feel the cool evening breeze hit me even before I step through the doorway, and once I do everything is magnified by a billion. The wind, the temperature, the noise, the view.

Something that could only be described as a deck made out of old scraps of wood and steel runs along the outside of the Viewing Deck structure with only a flimsy metal fence between the edge and the open air. So this must be the real Viewing Deck.

I slowly walk to the railing, taking my time with each step, and once I reach it, I hold onto it firmly. From here, about three hundred feet above the ground, I can see everything, hear everything and feel everything. I can see past the barrier, out onto the dead world and mountains beyond. I can see the sun about to set. I can hear the air, the cars, the buses, the people and the whole bustle of the city. I can feel the wind pushing me this way and that, threatening to throw me off the edge or push me back inside.

Swift comes up beside me; I try my best to listen over the wind. "I like to come out here when I need a break from it all. From the busy Proxy life, from the danger, and from the stress. Or when I lose sight of what's really important."

Any normal person would ask him what he means, but I don't really have any desire to get too personal with him. "It's like your secret hideaway, huh?" I try to speak without shouting, but it is practically impossible.

Swift nods his head yes and then motions for us to move away from the edge. I walk with him around to the other side of the Viewing Deck where three chairs rest with their back to the structure. Swift sits down first and pulls one of the other chairs closer to his spot.

I sit down somewhat reluctantly for a reason unknown to me. "So do you come up here often?" On this side of the building, with the Viewing Deck acting as interference, the wind doesn't impact us as much and Swift and I don't have to yell to be heard. Almost as soon as the words exit my mouth I realize that I am making small talk; I hate small talk. I never really talk to people unless I can get something out of them. I must expect to get something out of him.

Swift opens up his bag of goodies and produces plastic containers full of flower-shaped corn chips and sugar candies that are architectural beauties. "I actually haven't been up here in a while. Not since my last, well…" Swift hands me a container of each of my own. "I got these at the three-D printer shop downstairs."

Not since his last new recruit… He must have had a lot of people up here. I ignore any feelings of jealousy, lean back in the chair and pop a few sugar candies in my mouth. When they land on my tongue, they sizzle and crackle, making me smile uncontrollably. I take a couple silent minutes to just eat.

Swifts swallows down a big handful of chips, "Where'd you get that scar from?"

"Hmm?"

"This scar." Swift lifts his arm and touches the spot above my right eyebrow.

I subtly pull away from him, "Oh… yeah." I actually haven't thought about that scar for a while. When I was younger, though, it used to bother me a lot. Most days I can barely see it. "I don't remember exactly, but it was during one of the Preacher attacks after we escaped."

"Oh…" Swift looks away from me and turns back to the glowing city below us. "Excited about your first day tomorrow?" he asks after a couple minutes.

"I guess so, I'm kind of indifferent."

"Well it's basically collecting your information and meeting a few of the instructors, it'll be over quickly." Swift looks at me and smiles a genuine smile, one that makes the sides of his eye crinkle. "You'll be an official Proxy before you know it." He adds.

And then I'm that much closer to the Enhancer.

Chapter Six

I hear a knock on the door and quickly open it. Swift stands in front of me. I smile.

"Let's get going."

I follow him out, locking the door behind me.

"Like I said yesterday, today is just the introduction, you'll officially start tomorrow."

Swift escorts me to the inside 'courtyard' where a group of people stand around. A low buzz of nervous talk is heard. There is a portable stage of sorts in the front and a rectangular table off to the side; two people sit behind it with computers.

I breathe in; suddenly becoming aware of just how nervous I am. But I shouldn't be.

Swift waits with me until someone yells over the crowd telling everyone to be quiet. "Good luck and play nice." Swift whispers to me and then leaves.

Slowly, everyone stops talking and I can see and hear the only person who could possibly be our instructor. Vulture, the guy from yesterday stands on the stage making it easier for everyone to see him. He wears the same dirty clothes as yesterday. I notice a jagged scar on his cheek that I must have missed yesterday.

"Jardah!" He welcomes us with a common greeting. "For those of you who do not already know, we are in the Agent sector of the NEST HQ building. This is where you will live when you finish the training course. Right now we are standing in what has been named the 'Courtyard'. My name is Vulture," *Of course, I had to piss off the guy that is going to be my instructor.* "If you are here it means that you want to become an agent or 'Proxy' of NEST," His voice is rough. "It will not be easy and if you don't have any experience with guns or combat of any kind, I would not suggest going through this course." I see a couple people look around nervously and someone even walks away. Probably a smart decision on their part. "This is your last chance to leave; we will not accept any quitting once the course has begun." Three or so people sigh and decide it's better to not continue. He waits until they exit and then continues speaking, "Because of the increase of applicants, we are forming two groups instead of the usual one. My colleague, Tui, and I will be your instructors." He motions to a woman standing to his right, my left.

She is small and has sandy hair cut into a short bob. She is not pretty, but not ugly either; just... plain. She smiles kindly and nods. I instantly decide that I want to be in her group.

"We have already split all of you into the separate groups." he informs us. For some reason this feels like a competition, even though it isn't one. We all just need to try our best and eventually fight against Preachers. "We will be announcing who will be in each group later, but first you will be 'logged'. This means taking your measurements, weight, fingerprints and ten milliliters of your blood." Vulture gestures toward the table and people start walking over to it.

I wait for the line to thin out and then join the others. As I get closer, I can see that each of the new recruits, one by one, stand on a round metal platform maybe four inches tall. There are two of these platforms set up and they are connected to computers on the table. A light bursts from the platform and extends until it reaches the top of the person's head. It then swirls, wrapping itself around the person's body, and then spirals downward and disappears into the metal contraption.

There are only four people in front of me; then three, two and it is my turn. I step forward and take a deep breath.

I'm not usually this nervous, but I don't want my personal information locked up somewhere for someone to access at any time. It's just an easier way to control me. I wonder who among these people will try to control me.

I take another deep breath and step onto the disc anyway. I will do anything to become an agent, which will take me one more step closer to getting what I want: Revenge.

The light comes from below me and encircles me, looping around my head, torso and then my legs. It raises the hair on my arms and on the back of my neck and sends shivers down my spine. And then it vanishes.

"Come this way." a man helping the new recruits instructs me and then backs away from the computer, "Type your name here and then place your hand here."

Which name? Wren or Helena? My face goes blank, like it usually does when I am having an internal war; a hard decision between two options. After a few moments I type in 'Wren MacGregor'. I am Wren now; Helena is a stranger to me.

I put my hand on the screen and the computer scans it.

He lifts a small cool-box from underneath the desk and takes a syringe out of it. I hold out my arm and he takes my blood. He then places the syringe back into the cooler.

"Is that it?" I ask.

"Yes. For now." That makes me somewhat uneasy.

By this time, almost everyone has been logged.

Vulture steps back onto the stage, tells the crowd, "I will see you all again tomorrow; same place, same time. You will know which group you are in then." and then gets down and begins packing up with the other agents.

Everyone else walks into the hallway leading to the elevator. It is only about one in the afternoon so I turn around about to head to the cafeteria for lunch. Swift stands in the entrance to the cafeteria a few feet away, "How did it go?"

"Pretty well, I couldn't screw anything up this time." He smirks when I say this. "Were you watching me the whole time?"

"No, only for the last minute or so. Looks like a good group." Swift hands me one of the grey trays.

After picking up our meals, we head to an empty table.

Those agents taking all of my personal data has made me on edge. I should have all the information before officially joining NEST. "We should go over the details again, so everything is clear."

Swift nods, "Okay, that's fine with me."

Swift clears his throat with a sip of water before beginning, "After a two and a half week course, participants are made agents of NEST, also known as Proxies. At the concluding ceremony each of you will receive a bird's name for your code-name." Swift clarifies and stabs a piece of pasta with his fork, then pops it into his mouth and chews quickly. "I already talked to Albatross and he said it would be okay if you keep the name 'Wren'." *Good. I don't need another new name to get used to.* "Proxies protect this compound, help the refugees already in the NEST facilities and retrieve any persons trying to make it to the NEST facilities or anyone we know that Preachers are targeting. At graduation you will be notified which jobs you qualify for."

And I add with a sigh, "And I have to be an agent before I can be Enhanced."

"Of course." He finishes and we throw our garbage in a trashcan. *Great.*

Chapter Seven

"Are you ready?" Swift asks upon arriving at my room the next morning.

I stand up straight and salute, "Sir, yes sir."

He smirks and looks me over, "No."

"What?"

"Your clothes."

"What's wrong with my clothes?"

"Good thing I brought these." he says and pulls out a package from seemingly nowhere, "NEST approved Proxy training uniforms."

I take them from him and change in the bathroom. I take a moment to look at my reflection in the mirror. It doesn't look too bad. Tight but comfortable grey sweatpants and a black tank top. I haven't worn a tank-top in a while. It makes me glad we're indoors; we can't show too much skin outside mostly for medical reasons but also for 'religious' reasons. Mainly because the Preachers don't like it, while most of the other religions have accepted that others do not think the same way as they do and have stopped trying to change them. Some speak up, some don't, and then there are Preachers who take things to the extreme. Well I guess the Preachers aren't really a religion; they are more like an ideology.

I shake my head, coming out of my trance and then tie my hair in a bun.

Once again we walk to the courtyard and then he leaves me to do whatever he does when I am not around.

"It is great to see you all again today." Vulture's harsh voice calls over the crowd. I notice that there are fewer people than there were yesterday. I am the only new-recruit wearing the 'NEST approved Proxy training' clothes.

"I will split you into groups now."

Tui hands Vulture a T-Screen, which lights up when he taps it with his fingers. "First I will tell you who is in my group." He reads off the names of ten people in turn and then says, "Everyone else is in Tui's group."

That means I'll be taught by Tui.

"My group, follow me. The rest, go with Tui. Good luck."

Tui beckons for us to follow her. She leads us through the hallway and away from the dorms and the cafeteria, back to the elevator. The group rides it up one floor and then exit. We pass a couple rooms filled with mats and punching bags or shooting-ranges, but keep walking to the end of the hallway where we turn into our training room. It looks just like the rest of them; punching bags hang on the left side, mats stacked against the opposite wall, and I can see more equipment through an open closet door. Windows line the far wall.

"Sit down." she orders us. I sit down on the hard floor along with the others. "I hope you memorized the route, because this is where we are going to meet every day for the next three weeks.

"Now, let's get down to business!" Her voice is nothing like I expected. From the outside you would think that she has a soft, kind voice, but in reality it is loud and... tough. "So you all want to become 'Proxies', do you? Well I don't think most of you have what it takes." She specifically eyes a chubby, balding man sitting near the front. "Unfortunately, my opinion doesn't mean much at this stage and practically everyone who takes this course passes and continues on to becoming a Proxy... for better or for worse."

She starts walking back and forth at the front of the room, "I will be teaching you fighting techniques, hand to hand combat, basic medical-aide and training you all in firearms. The methods that I will teach you are simple yet effective and have been proven in real life situations. There will be no fancy moves like in those old movies, because they are not as effective when your life is at risk. We will practice the techniques over and over again until they become second nature." Tui stops and puts her hands on her hips, eyeing a girl with a long braid who has been talking non-stop to a young boy next to her. She purses her lips and continues, "You cannot give out any personal information about yourselves at any time, not even your names. Who you were before this does not matter."

The girl's hand shoots up right away, "How will we address each other, then?"

"After the first few days you all should have been assigned nicknames based on your behavior and physical appearance. Until then I may just point and call 'you'."

This answer doesn't seem to appeal to the girl.

"There are several different departments agents can work in: Security, Field, Civilian Liaison, and Medical. But first, I want to make sure everyone is here, let me check my list." She pulls a T-Screen from her back pocket and looks over it. She looks up every once in a while, matching everyone to their description.

"Well it seems that we already have a Proxy among us." She says mockingly.

Everyone looks around at each other.

"You have a name, uniform and everything. I even think I saw you training in a Proxy room yesterday."

When I realize that she is talking about me, I am about to answer her, but I keep my mouth shut and lower my red face; I don't want to get in trouble on my first day.

She eventually moves on, "A few people are missing, but that is to be expected." She concludes.

"Let's get started." She pauses and we all stand up, "First, I want you all to do as many sit-ups as you can in sixty seconds, or up to fifty sit-ups. I will take your scores afterwards."

I get on my back and finish the fifty sit-ups in half the time. While everyone else continues to work, I can get a good look at my classmates. I will only be around them for a few weeks, so I should not get close to anyone.

I sit back up on my knees and notice that a man is finished as well. He has a dark complexion and wears cargo-pants. He is probably the oldest one here and already has graying hair. He looks like a soldier, perfect for this course, perfect for a Proxy. He notices me watching him and stares back with electric-blue eyes that raise the hair on the back of my neck. I avert my gaze.

The talkative girl is doing the sit-ups fast, but gets tired out and rests for a few seconds before continuing. She does this a few times. She also finishes before the time is up and when she sits up her bronze hair is coming out of her braid.

The chubby, balding guy is barely keeping up and is breathing heavily.

"Time is up." Tui's annoying voice informs us. "You, score." She points to the talkative girl.

"Fifty, but does the time I did it in count or just the amount?" She asks really fast while rocking on her knees.

"Spaz," Tui mutters under her breath and types in her mark, "Only the amount... You." She points to a female with large, muscular legs. She has short hair.

"Fifty." She says in a flat and bored voice.

"You." She says to a young man who lies on the ground, eyes closed. His dirty-blonde hair is tousled and he doesn't seem to be paying attention.

The dark, lean girl next to him lightly hits him and he jolts awake, "Oh, um, forty eight."

Most of the rest got fifty except for the plump man and the gangly kid who got thirty two and thirty seven respectively.

Tui tells us to do pushups and other exercises afterwards. Everything is easy for me and I end up finishing before everyone else.

63

"You guys did pretty well for the first day. Now, you must run a mile and then I will dismiss you." Tui orders us.

We all slowly get up, dusting ourselves off. I look around the room. *Does she expect us to run in here or is she going to take us somewhere else?* Everyone else is just as confused as I am.

"Get going! It should be about two hundred and sixty-four laps from wall to wall."

The sleeping man scoffs and the soldier-like one walks to the right wall and begins jogging to the wall across from him. The rest join him.

It takes me eight minutes and twenty nine seconds to run the mile.

Starting at eight thirty, the 'lessons' with Tui are only about six hours long.

***

On the third day, we start training in hand to hand combat.

"While learning the basic straight punch you will need to have a partner, so choose now."

I look around the room searching for a good partner, someone who looks somewhat experienced and is taking this seriously. This causes me to over think things and before I realize it, everyone else has partnered up and the only person left is the guy who fell asleep yesterday.

"It looks like we'll be partners." The young man says with a boyish grin and tries to fix his messy hair.

"Yep." *Oh, joy.*

"Every pair, grab a pad." Tui instructs us and takes out a sack full of medium-sized, rectangular cushions from the closet.

I expect the guy to go get one but he just stares blankly at the wall. I guess I didn't get that serious partner I wanted.

"Hey, sleeping beauty, think fast!" Tui calls out and throws a pad in his direction.

I want to warn him that a pillow is soaring through the air aimed at his head, but I don't know what to call him. I can only watch as the cushion hits him square in the face. The impact makes his hair whip around his face. I let out a small laugh and pick it up from the floor.

Tui stands in front of our group and instructs us, "Always have your hands up to protect your face. The point of impact for this punch should be with your two big knuckles: on the index and middle fingers. Your arm moves out straight from your body. Close your fist on the way out while rotating your elbow, and then you make contact. The elbow is never fully locked. Your striking hand's shoulder should be facing the opponent, while the opposite leg should be back. The strike is done when your hand is back up protecting your face." She demonstrates while talking, "Get to work!"

"I think we should try it a couple times in the air."

"Whatever you say." agrees my partner.

I drop the pad and we shadowbox.

"Well, well, well. It looks like I was right, you are a Proxy. Are you sure you do not want to teach the class?" a sarcastic Tui says.

I know I'm right so I don't keep quiet, "No. I just have some personal experience learning these techniques and thought it would be better to know the punch before trying out on a punching bag or pad. To avoid injury, of course."

Her face goes blank as she realizes that I could be right; which I usually am, but for some reason, people don't seem to listen to me.

"Do whatever you want." she eventually says and turns toward another pair.

My partner laughs and gives me a high-five. Victory!

After a few more tries in the air I say, "I think you should try first."

I pick up the pad and hold it at the perfect height for him to punch. His first few tries are sloppy, but he eventually gets the hang of it.

"Your turn." He yawns and takes the pad from me.

He doesn't hold it tightly enough, so when I punch it, it flies out of his hands and hits the muscular, dark-skinned guy in the shin. It probably didn't hurt, but he looks annoyed.

My companion jogs over and picks it up, muttering his apologies, "I am s-sorry s-sir. We didn't mean to, I promise."

I roll my eyes and he comes back, wiping his forehead.

***

"Today I re-learned the basic straight strike, palm heel strike and the hammer fist." I talk to my mom, Beck and Piper on a computer in The Viewing Deck. Somehow Swift convinced the usual worker to let me use it for the hour. Swift stands to my right.

"Well I'm happy to hear that your first couple of days are going well. How long do we have to talk?" My mother asks.

"Uh, ten minutes." I lie. She probably knows I am lying, but I don't really want to talk and I need to let go of my family.

"Have you made any friends?"

"Not really."

"Well I'm sure you will." My mother smiles kindly at me.

My goal right now isn't to make friends.

"We do stretches, push-ups, sit-ups and run every day. At the end of the course we'll have combat, medical and fire-arms tests. I'm sure I could pass them all now." I tell them about my father's work and how I don't get to see him very often. They know more than I do, apparently he calls them once a day. Nothing new has happened in their lives recently. That makes me remember the boring days I had at home. I feel sorry for them now.

***

I burst out of the dining hall doors and jog in place, lifting my knees high. Swift walks beside me to the elevator, "Looks like you are having fun in the course."

"I'm just glad that I'm actually doing something now." I say with a smile, turning to face him.

He frowns; I didn't mean to hurt his feelings. I stop bouncing and scowl.

I turn into the elevator doors just as they're opening and bump into an older man, "Oh, sorry."

"Hello, Wren."

It's Dad. He wears a lab coat and glasses. I've only seen him with his glasses when he comes up from his laboratory.

He hugs me awkwardly, "I wish I could talk with you, but I am really busy right now."

"Oh, yeah. So am I."

"How about we meet later for dinner?" he asks me, his mind is clearly somewhere else.

"Sure, down here?"

"Yeah." He says and brushes past me, "It was nice seeing you. Uh, talk to you later."

"Yeah, you too." I say to his back that is currently walking away.

My dad is too busy for me and I'm being pushed away. I sigh. This was to be expected and what I wanted in the first place. I had better get used to it.

Swift pats me on the back when we are inside the elevator. I ride it up one floor and then get out.

"Bye." I grumble to Swift.

My good mood is ruined. I walk down the hallway to the last training room, my training room. I stand at the edge of the room near the entrance and watch the others as they wait for the lesson to start.

"Hey, there." The guy who was my partner a few days ago comes up behind me. He yawns and rubs his left eye, "You okay?" he asks, apparently noticing my bad mood.

"Yeah, I am fine." I lie and put on a smile. It's nothing.

Tui walks in behind us and all of the recruits hurry to the center of the room.

"Kicks." Tui starts, "We will not use them very often because it's easy for our attackers to redirect the attack or grab our leg. But they are good to know. I will teach you the 'groin kick'."

She stands directly in front of us facing towards us so we can all see. "The stance is very important: The heels of your feet are off the ground, legs are slightly bent. The kicking leg is farther behind than the non-kicking leg. Chin down; you are obviously aiming for the groin."

She then moves to the punching bags hanging on the left side of the room. I move forward so I can see better.

"Swing your foreleg up and out. As the knee goes past the target, you snap your shin out making contact. The point of impact should be with the bridge of your foot and the bottom portion of the shin. The knee is slightly bent on impact. You lean back while kicking." She kicks the bag and it swings after impact.

She faces us again, "A 'front kick' is very similar to this. You just lift your knee higher if you are aiming for the chest or that area."

We do not need partners for this one; I'm much happier working alone. Each trainee picks a different punching bag and soon the sound of legs hitting padding and chains swinging fill the room.

***

68

Later that evening I wait at a table by myself for my dad. I told Swift that I wanted to talk to my dad alone so he sits at a table across the room with Blue-jay and a cluster of other Proxies. They laugh every once in a while and it annoys me. I have been waiting for Dad for half an hour now.

Swift strides towards me, his group following. "Do you want me to wait with you or—"

"No, it's okay. You go have fun with your friends. You're stuck with me most of the day anyway." I tell him.

"Thanks, Wren." he says and smiles wide.

I try my best to smile back. His friends also grin and laugh. Then they head out the door.

"The old ball and chain letting you lose for a little while, huh?" one of the guys asks.

Everyone else laughs and I am unable to hear Swift's reaction.

The group parts in the middle as my father comes through the double-doors. He looks like he's been busy; his hair is tousled and there is a pencil behind his ear.

"Sorry I am late. Did you have to wait long?" He kisses the top of my head and sits down next to me.

"No, I just got here." I lie. There is no point in telling him that I waited for forty-five minutes and still have not eaten. He can't change it or bring back the lost time.

"I will go get us some food." he says and stands in line in front of the counter.

I fiddle with my hands until he gets back.

"So what did you want to talk about?" I ask him as he sits down again and places a tray on the table in front of me.

"I just wanted to catch up… And to talk about the great progress my team is making on the Enhancers."

"That is good to hear." I give him a small smile and start to eat.

"So how are your Proxy training classes?"

69

"Going well. After tomorrow I only have two more weeks. In those two weeks, there will be some pretty intense combat scenarios, where I will be fighting another person in my group with a bunch of different things going on in the background. Oh, and I will finally get to shoot a gun. It's been too long." I sigh, "Tomorrow we're going to have a lesson in medical-aide. How is your research doing? And the testing on Hawk?"

"Hawk's chip is working really well; the hormones are flowing exactly as they should be." He gets excited, "You see, the chip releases hormones that enter the blood stream and eventually get to the brain. The hormones send signals to the brain to speed up the metabolism and produce more energy at a faster rate. That is how he creates the energy-blasts. But that means that Hawk has to consume more sustenance." He has stopped trying to eat and just talks really fast.

"And what does that have to do with me? Other than that I am going to have it implanted into me soon, right?" I hint.

"Of course, but I wanted to talk about something else. I said when I first implanted the chip into Hawk that it will enhance his abilities, making his strengths even stronger, which really happened. Hawk used to be really strong, physically able to carry great amounts, but now he can lift a car with no problems. Super-strength!" He gets this crazed look in his eyes.

I laugh. *That is amazing!* And it dawns on me how awesome my dad is. And how smart he is.

"But because his strengths are improved, his weaknesses also seem to have been enhanced. He is weaker in certain areas than he was before; his weaknesses have been increased. More pronounced. So I was thinking that maybe the new batch of Enhancements would completely get rid of the weaknesses, cure them."

I did not quite get the biology aspect of it before and this also confuses me, "What do you mean?"

70

"Say someone's greatest weakness was that they cannot run fast and they get Enhanced. Then they would gain the ability of—?"

"Super-speed?" I ask.

"Yes, or something like that."

I keep it rolling from there, "And if someone one who is deaf got Enhanced? They would probably get their hearing back. So the Enhancer could be used as both a weapon and a cure, a treatment that could heal someone of any disease." Of course my dad would invent something that could be used for good as well. I realize that I have also stopped eating, despite my hunger.

"I had never thought of it like that. It could be used as a cure, but only as long as the illness or handicap is truly their greatest weakness."

I think about it for a couple of minutes, "What do you think my greatest weakness is?"

He exhales deeply, "I do not know, that is for you to discover and for you to know."

"I guess we'll find out when I get Enhanced."

"Yes, I will continue my work while you finish your Proxy course and then an Enhancement course that Hawk will instruct."

Another course? I almost scream out loud in frustration. *Why can't I just get Enhanced already and kick some Preacher butt already?*

"It can be dangerous if you do not know how to use it." he answers my unasked question.

And with that we stop talking about the Enhancer.

After dinner I lay in my bed, finding it hard to actually fall asleep. *What is my biggest weakness?*

How much will my life change after that problem is solved? It couldn't get much different than what I've mentally prepared for. I just have to work on the complete separation from my family, but I guess that will have to wait until I am Enhanced and doing what I know I am meant to do: stopping the Preachers and then helping to pick up the pieces afterwards.

Chapter Eight

A dummy rests on the floor. Tui stands above it and the group is gathered around her.

"Medical-aide." Tui begins, "What I will be showing you right now is very basic, but if you are interested in learning in depth medical-aide then you have the option of taking the Medical Proxy course afterward." Spaz perks up when hearing that; that is the bronze-haired hyper girl's nickname.

There are seven others in the group with me. We have been at it for a week and most of us have nicknames by now. My partner from the third day has been dubbed 'Sleepy'. "As in one of the seven dwarfs." Tui said when she called him that for the first time. The muscular soldier with dark skin is 'Sir', and the fat guy is 'Baldy'. One of the other girls, who is slightly more masculine, is called 'Dude'. The young boy who is probably fifteen years old and is the youngest of the group is 'Junior'.

Other than the dark haired girl, I am the only one without a nickname. I can't *wait* for mine. Tui doesn't like me very much so I bet it's going to be a good one.

"I am going to teach you CPR and how to bandage wounds." Tui kneels beside the dummy, "First, CPR. If you find someone who looks unconscious, the first thing to do is get him to safety. Reviving him will not do any good if he gets hit by a bus a second later. And you should always call for help." She drags the dummy a few feet back, away from the 'danger'. All this talk of Medical-aide reminds me of my sister. She's a nurse at the main hospital in Tieced and a really good one. She has taught me all sorts of things including CPR, so I kind of zone out during Tui's instruction. I remember one time on her birthday a few years ago, we were taking the bus to the Inner Ring to have dinner at a fancy restaurant when an old man seemingly passed out and spilled out of his seat onto the floor of the bus. No one knew what to do except Piper. She jumped into action, checking his pulse and quickly gave the diagnosis of a heart attack and cardio arrest. Then she went right into performing CPR on the man while everyone else just stood around in awe. Piper was still in medical school when this happened, but she knew exactly what to do and gave the correct diagnosis. My parents couldn't have been more proud.

Tui raises her voice and it brings me out of my memories. "If the victim is breathing you should lift their legs a foot or so into the air. Does anyone know why?"

Sleepy stands to my right and elbows me in the ribs. I know the answer, but I decide to let someone else respond. Waiting for one of the others to speak up, I glance at the others in the room. Junior looks like he wants to say something, but is too nervous. He looks more pallid than usual today. He is also sweaty; his sandy hair clings to the sides of his face.

"It helps the blood-flow, which carries more oxygen to the brain." The darker-complexioned girl says. She's usually quiet, so I don't usually pay much attention to her, but I do now. She is slender and has dark brown hair and nut-brown colored eyes. She currently stands across from me, next to Sir.

"That is correct." Tui says, also surprised at the woman's knowledge. "You are quite sneaky; quiet and barely visible, but also smart and strong." Tui ponders; I can feel a nickname coming. But in the end, Tui can't seem to figure one out and gives up, continuing with her instruction, "So if the victim is not breathing you will have to start with the resuscitation. You put one hand over the other, locking your fingers. The stronger hand, which is usually the one you write with, should be on top. You need to find the place in-between their nipples." Sleepy chuckles at this. He is so immature. I block out the rest of the Tui's long and boring speech until she stands up and says, "Now it is your turn. Everyone has to practice at least once on the dummy."

"I would rather practice on you." Sleepy says and winks at me.

Dude punches him in the arm for me.

"Thanks." I say to her.

Spaz has been quiet this whole time, which is a miracle, "Can I go first?" she pipes up.

I assume she wants to work in the hospital after this.

"You haven't been talking, so sure. We'll take turns around the circle. So Cat will go after Spaz, and then Junior."

Cat smirks at her new nickname; it suits her perfectly. Junior looks nervous and sweats even more.

"What is 'cat'?" Sleepy asks, whispering in my ear.

I answer quickly and quietly thinking that he probably embarrassed that he doesn't know, "It was a type of fast and stealthy animal." After that, I turn my attention to the task.

Spaz executes the whole CPR process perfectly, even removing the dummy from mock danger. Cat also does well, but forgets to pinch him to see if he reacts to pain.

Junior steps up and kneels beside the body, his hands shaking. He fumbles around, making weird noises and missing some key points. When he is done, you can see sweat stains on his shirt. Junior gets up hastily and hides behind Sleepy, but it's his turn next, so Junior only gets a few seconds of cover.

"You okay?" Dude asks and places her hand on his back. She quickly takes it off and wipes it on her pants.

"Yeh-yeah, it is just that my—" Tui gives Junior a death look and he stops speaking. "Never mind, I am fine."

When I perform the procedure, I do it perfectly. Of, course.

Sir almost crushes the dummy; his big hands would obviously crack some ribs.

Almost everyone succeeds and then Tui brings out scraps of cloth. She explains that we'll learn how to dress wounds and that we won't always have bandages with us. She tells us to split into pairs. I can see

75

Sleepy walk towards me in the corner of my eye, but I make a beeline for Cat, knowing I'll be able to think and concentrate with her.

I lay on my back and lift myself up on my elbows as she begins wrapping and tying the cloth around where my wound is supposed to be. It takes me back to when I was a kid and got hurt when I was training; which was a lot. Piper or my mom would take care of me, using the same technique that Cat is using now. Whenever I was out of school I would train; shadowboxing in my backyard, or sitting on the edge of my bed thinking of different battle situations; 'What would I do when...' 'How would I react if....' In his spare time my dad would help by making little trinkets for me to fight with. He even made me a working replica of a Desert Eagle.

A grin grows on my face as I remember the day he gave it to me and the way it fit perfectly in my hand... and then how mad I was when it broke.

"Um, ow." Cat says. I have been twisting the tourniquet too tightly around her thigh.

"Oops, sorry." I apologize and give it some slack.

"We do not want to have to actually amputate her leg do we, Scar-face?" Tui was standing right behind me.

My hand automatically goes up to the scar above my left eyebrow; a great nickname.

"Okay, we are finished for today. As I have told you, we are coming up to the last few days of the program and the remaining days will be made up of the final tests that help determine which areas you will qualify for: combat, medical and fire-arm evaluations. The combat and medical tests are combined in one exercise where two people will fight each other in the midst of all sorts of distractions going on in the background. Two other people will be chosen to be their Medical Proxies. If one of the fighters gets hurt, their Medical Proxy will have to mend the wounds as best they can. The whole process will be the final contributor for your results;

determining whether you qualify for Security, Field, Liaison or Medical. Then we will go to the firing-range for your fire-arm evaluations. Be prepared." She claps her hands together and we are dismissed. All of the trainees head for the exit, when Tui calls out, "Wait a minute, Junior, I want to talk to you. And Scar-face, it's your turn to pack up the equipment." She pulls Junior over to the side of the room.

I begin collecting the fabric scraps and drag the dummy to the closet.

"I wanted to talk to you about your results." Tui begins, her voice is softer and lower than usual. "So far you've only qualified for Liaison, and only just barely."

"But I really need to make it to Security." he whines and sounds like the little kid he is.

"I know. We will just have to see what happens after the combat-scenario. You will have to do really well."

"I'll try my best." He promises and the conversation is over.

I lock the closet door and leave.

***

Swift is waiting for me outside the door to my dorm room when I get back from the lesson.

"Are you excited for graduation?" he asks as I unlock the door.

He follows me into the room and then crashes on my couch.

"Yeah, I guess so. Which areas do you think I'll qualify in?" I sit on the edge of my bed.

"Well you have to at least get Security to be Enhanced, but I am sure you'll qualify for everything."

I throw a pillow at him; I'm not used to compliments.

"Except maybe Liaison; you are *not* a people person." He laughs to himself and catches the projectile.

We wait for an hour or so before it's time for dinner, and then head to the cafeteria. Robin and Owl are already sitting at a table engaged in some sort of argument when Owl sees us and waves us over.

"You will not sign up for that program!" Robin says sternly, but trying not to raise her voice.

"So you get to, but I don't? Please, just let me tell them I'm interested, I might not even be accepted." Owl begs from his sister. He pouts and tries to make his eyes as big as possible.

"You're too young; I am not going to let you endanger yourself—"

"What are you guys up to?" Swift asks as we sit down.

"Nothing, Robin is just being a big sister." he sighs, leaning back in his chair and looking away.

I am about to push the question further but Swift speaks before I can, "Wren is going to graduate in a week, do you guys want to come to the ceremony?"

"Sure." Robin breathes strongly through her nose, "We would be glad to." She looks uneasily at Owl.

I sigh, "There's a ceremony? Swift, you keep forgetting to tell me stuff."

"I 'forget' because I know you won't want to participate. I tell you too late so you can't get out of it." He gets up, "Now are we getting food or what?"

Although I'd never admit it out loud, he is right at least somewhat; if someone forces me to do something I automatically want to do the opposite.

Chapter Nine

Swift and I walk down an unfamiliar hallway. Earlier, he had just mentioned that the Combat Scenarios are held in a different room than the training ones, but now we are seven floors underground. The lighting is darker and spookier, but for the most part, things here are the same as on the other floors.

"I thought you said the bottom floor was empty." I eye him.

"It usually is, but they like to have the last part of training down here to scare the newbies. There are a few storage rooms as well, but I actually heard that it is going to be renovated soon."

He turns into a lit room and I follow him. Tui is currently looking through a list of names on her T-screen, while the trainees that are already here, mingle. I hope that I don't have to fight Sir, Dude or Cat. I might be able to take them on, but those three will probably be the hardest to beat.

Most of the floor is slightly rubbery, softer than a normal floor. It would still hurt to get smacked down on it, though. In the middle of the room, a square patch of the floor is dark blue instead of black. I guess that that is the fighting area. Different things hang from the ceiling: lights, smokers, some random ropes.

Tui then moves behind a desk and computer located in the corner of the room. She touches the screen in a couple places, causing the lights to dim and the temperature to drop. Smoke pours out from the ceiling. *That's pretty cool.*

Swift wishes me luck and then leaves. Sleepy walks in after him and the session begins.

"I hope all of you are prepared." Tui welcomes us and consults her T-screen, "Scenario-combat. As you know, two people will fight, two people will be their medics; the first person to give up or not be able to fight any longer will be the loser. The medics have to take care of their patient after the match. The first pair fighting is…."

Sleepy slaps his thighs, making a drumroll sound.

"Cat and Sir." *This should be interesting.* "Do I have any volunteers for Medical?"

Spaz's hand shoots straight up and when Tui looks around the room in the other direction, she makes straining noises.

"Yes, Spaz?" Tui asks patronizingly, "Would you like to volunteer?"

Spaz bounces up and down and nods her head multiple times.

"Did you forget to take your medication today?" Tui asks jokingly.

"Maybe." Spaz answers under her breath, pouting her thin lips and crossing her arms.

"Okay, Spaz will be Cat's Medic and Baldy will be Sir's."

Cat and Sir walk into different corners of the blue area and their Medics stand a couple feet behind them. Tui yells for the two to begin.

"My money's on Sir." Sleepy whispers into my ear.

I push him away and tell him, "I would not overlook Cat's intelligence and agility."

He stays quiet and I focus on the match.

With lights flashing and loud music blaring from unseen speakers, I can barely see what is going on and I wonder what is going through Cat's and Sir's minds. I won't have to wonder for very long as I will be in the ring soon enough.

Cat sways and dodges as Sir throws punch after punch and kicks the empty air. He quickly tires and Cat eventually wins, her strategy beating Sir's brute force. But she did take a few hits so they both visit their Medics. Tui walks over to the pairs in turn and looks over the Medics' techniques.

When they're both patched up, Tui pauses the lights and sounds and calls out the next names.

"Spaz and Baldy, your turn to fight! Your Medics are Dude and Scar-face." It looks like the Medics are next in line to duel.

Tui doesn't say who is whose medic so I give Dude an apologetic look and then run to Spaz's corner. When she understands what I did, Dude frowns at me and slowly walks towards Baldy. I can deal with a pissed-off opponent.

"You ready?" I ask Spaz.

"As ready as I'll ever be."

I give Tui the thumbs up and she motions for the match to begin.

Both opponents reluctant to attack first, Spaz and Baldy circle each other for some time. The loud music threatens to blow out my ears and the flashing lights make it hard for me to focus on any certain thing.

Tui yawns, "This better get interesting fast."

Spaz looks at Tui with resentment and rushes Baldy, punching him in the gut. In this moment, his fat is useful because he doesn't feel a thing. Not so with Spaz, who grimaces and tries to shake the stinging pain out of her hand. He tries to strike back, but she's too fast, dodging and blocking all of his attacks. But then she gets over confident and when she looks over at me and gives me a big smile, Baldy takes his shot. He runs up behind her and before I can say anything, Spaz's arms are pinned to her side in what looks like a giant hug. Baldy squeezes tightly until Spaz can't breathe. Desperately, she tries to squirm and wriggle out of his grasp, but she just can't break free. Baldy kicks Spaz's feet out from under her and one of her legs lands at an odd angle. She gasps in pain and Tui quickly calls it. Surprisingly, Baldy has won. And now I have to mend Spaz's wounds...

I drag Spaz out of the fighting area and easily bandage her hand, but can't manage to set her leg properly.

After fumbling around for a minute or two Spaz snaps, "Just give it to me." and snatches the dressings away from me.

"Fine." I walk away and run my fingers through my hair.

I notice Tui standing directly behind us. She must have seen the whole thing; *Great.*

"You better do a better job fighting, Scar-face. You are up next; get in positions! Junior and Sleepy are your medics!"

"Oh, I call the pretty lady!" Sleepy runs up behind me and begins to rub my shoulders.

I shrug off his hands. "Back off." I growl in a hushed tone.

He retreats like a wounded puppy, "Sorry."

I may not be good with people, but at least I know I can fight.

As Dude prepares, I grin at her from across the room. She cracks her knuckles and steps forward. I shake my arms and legs, stretch my muscles and then meet her in the middle.

"Have fun kids." Tui leaves us to rip each other apart, turning on the distractions.

The music I am used to and it doesn't have much of an effect of on me, but then it changes to traffic noises and explosions and I begin to worry. The lights are thin like lasers, burning neon green.

I pretend to watch Dude's every move while I actually plan out my offense. We're both pretty stubborn, so I doubt that either of us will surrender willingly. My best strategy is to take her out fast. *Jaw, temple or wind-pipe?* I shouldn't go for the wind-pipe except as a last resort; so I will save that for later.

I have learned a thing or two from the previous fights: don't waste all of your energy and don't lose sight of your opponent. Those are rookie mistakes and I am not a rookie, but for some reason I don't think Dude is either.

"Okay, ladies, you can start." Tui announces.

I put up my hands and then block an immediate punch to the jaw with my forearm. I send two blows to Dude's stomach while she's unprotected. She stumbles backwards, obviously not thinking that I would be this good. After faking a swing with my left, causing her to lean back, I kick her in the stomach, not very hard, but strong enough to make her lose her balance. She lands flat on her butt.

"Come on, Dude, you should just give up." I try to bluff confidence so that she might leave quickly without hurting me.

She grunts, stands and dusts off her pants. Dude shifts into a fighting stance quickly and comes at me with a few spinning kicks. They are mostly just for show, to scare me and to get closer to me faster. I step backwards and avoid each of them. Dude lands right in front of me and throws one lucky punch. It connects with my nose. *Damn it, that hurts.* I feel the warm crimson liquid drip down my face as she tries to hit me again. I stop her fist with my left arm, absorbing the power and energy of her punch. With the same movement I grab and twist her arm with my free right hand. And while it doesn't look too painful, she gasps in pain and stops what she is doing. We stand there staring each other down. The loud sounds blast in my ears and the lights illuminate our faces. I had not noticed them while fighting.

I threaten to twist her arm even more, "Surrender." I say nonchalantly.

"You wish." She says through gritted teeth and then tries to kick me, but I punch her in the jaw with an uppercut, causing her brain to slam against the inside of her skull. And Dude passes out. She falls quickly to the floor and I walk back to Sleepy.

"That was pretty ruthless, Wren." Sleepy says and hands me a towel.

"Thanks." I mutter, not really paying attention.

I put the cloth under my nose and sit against the wall. Junior tries his best to drag Dude out of the fighting area and revive her. He doesn't do a very good job and just leaves her laying half in, half out of the ring.

Sleepy needs to fight Junior next. I don't know how this will end, and I don't really care.

83

I watch from the side lines as the two most lethargic people I know duke it out.

In the end, Junior gives up easily and goes back to his Medic, Cat. When Sleepy returns from the mat he expects to be congratulated. I don't say anything.

And that's everyone. I stick one of the corners of the towel up my nose and get off the floor.

"That looks very attractive." Sleepy jokes. At least I didn't ruin his mood.

"Good, that is what I'm going for." I really couldn't care less what I look like.

"Next up, we will head to the firing-range and I will evaluate your results. After that you are let out early because of today's tests and tomorrow's graduation. We will still meet tomorrow morning at the regular hour to go over some last minute information." Tui says all of this with a bored tone. I wonder how many courses she's held and how many people have been under her command. *Is this her only job?*

The group crowds into the tiny elevator and travels seven floors up, to the lobby, and then to our main floor. The firing-range is not far from our usual training-room, the one we have trained in several times since we started training with firearms in the second week. We have all gotten pretty good. Well, I've always been good.

Now, we each stand in our separate booth thingies with ear plugs in. I don't see the point of the ear plugs, we should get used to the sound because we won't have them in real combat.

I run my fingers across the cool surface of the Gibbs B14 and then stand up straight, facing the target like I've done a hundred times. Breathe in, breathe out, **Boom** and recoil. Straight through the heart. I let loose another four rounds that pierce the head, the chest, the neck and then the heart again, exactly where I want them to go. Tui marks something down in the T-screen and I assume that I am free to go. I leave the plugs and the gun on the table and exit the room.

Something feels different about today. It's like I'm in my own little bubble where nothing on the outside really matters. I just travel from one station to another, accepting whatever I discover. I'm probably just excited to be moving on, even though these symptoms don't really match that idea.

"You okay?" Owl bumps in to me.

"Oh, sorry, I was not paying attention. Yeah, I am fine. You?"

"Feeling a little bummed. Robin is still upset with me because I've decided to apply for the Enhancement chip program, whatever it is, when the time comes." I have noticed that he has not been his usual bubbly self recently. Neither has she.

I don't really care and am already distracted, so I simply respond with "Yeah, I have noticed." and continue on my way back to my room.

"It's not like this hasn't happened before. Robin and I get into arguments every once in a while; but never for this long. Anyway, I have a shift now. Don't cause any trouble or I will have to detain you." Owl smiles and hops into an elevator. I can't imagine him detaining anyone.

***

"Field trip, ladies!" Tui shouts as soon as I enter our regular room. "We are heading upstairs for a special, new recruiting video that all of the up and coming Proxies will have to watch." She says this as if she is reciting a long speech. "It should not take very long and then we have the stupid ceremony this evening; which really is a waste of time."

She and I finally agree on something. We file out of the room and down the hallway to the elevator.

85

"Which button should I press?" Cat asks after we all squish in.

I barely have room to move my arms and Sleepy, who stands next to me, wiggles his eyebrows. I roll my eyes and look in a different direction.

"Ten. We are going to the computer laboratory." Tui is flattened against the back wall by Sir.

I suppress a laugh when I notice her failed attempts to get past him.

The group pours out of the elevator as soon as the doors pop open. Before I can look around, Tui walks into a lab and I have to follow. Two rows of long tables with touch screen tops fill the laboratory. I sit at the far end away from the entrance and everyone else.

"Just tap your chosen screen and the introduction video will start. It explains the Proxies' roles and what options you have."

I stare at the loading screen, wait for everyone else to begin and then touch the cool surface in front of me.

"Jardah." A friendly female voice welcomes me. "NEST is an organization that works above the law to protect the citizens of UCNA from Preachers. We welcome refugees from all different backgrounds and train humans to do what the government is not willing to do." Images of burning buildings and bloody bodies stay on screen for a few seconds before fading into the next photograph. "After receiving your Proxy training, you can qualify for four areas: Field, Security, Liaison, and Medical. Let us start with Field." The program displays photographs of supposed Proxies walking the streets of different cities. "Becoming a Field Proxy is the hardest of the four. Field Proxies help in the outside world, protecting innocent civilians and helping them to NEST's safety if needed. Field Proxies are also the first line of defense in the event of a high-scale attack.

Many of you may have had 'guides' that brought you to the NEST headquarters and then helped you adjust to your new way of life."

Swift, of course, pops into my head. I had not realized that guides were so common and that a lot of other people have them. "Guides are a branch between Field and Liaison, the next area we will discuss." More photos flash on the screen, but this time with friendly looking people interacting with others. *This definitely is not for me.* "Liaison Proxies assist in the communication between the refugees and Proxies and even between our organization and others, such as the UCNA government or outside factors. Most of our intel comes from the Liaisons' research and communication.

Protecting this building and the residents who live here is very important. These are the Security Proxies' duties. Patrolling the corridors, breaking up any fights that might occur and arresting persons who try to break into the building are just some of the things a Security Proxy has to deal with." *They're just trying to make it sound more interesting than it really is.*

"Last, but not least, is Medical. Medical Proxies work in the hospital on the higher floors. After finishing the basic Proxy training program, those who seek to become Medical Proxies must go through an additional and more detailed training course.

As you may know, we also have scientific laboratories in the upper levels, led by Agent Hummingbird. You do not have to be a Proxy to work in these labs and do important research to help our cause, but not everyone can. If you have any interest in working there, I would suggest talking to the nearest Liaison Proxy about the subject.

The last course to discuss is the new Enhancement program." *What? They're announcing it now?*

"The Enhancement program is an experiment run by Agents Hummingbird and Hawk, supported by Albatross and a board of high-ranking Proxies. It is only for Proxies who are at least qualified for Security. This program is an experimental procedure and could be potentially dangerous. Only ten applicants will be selected to continue and the training program will begin on the third of January.

Testing will begin in the next few weeks; apply with great caution. If you have any further questions, talk to a nearby Liaison." *Liaisons, shmilaisons, they seem to know everything.* "Thank you for your service. Good luck, stay safe, think fast, run, and don't get too attached."

The last statement worries me.

I can't believe they announced the Enhancement program already, and to everyone.

Even though I began after everyone else, they still seem to be watching something on the computers. Mine dings in front of me and more photographs appear on the screen.

Apparently, 'The Hearing' just posted another article on its webpage. It could only mean something bad happened. "Congress Members, Myers and Smith, missing" reads the headline. Those names sound familiar. A few photos from the crime scenes are under that. Blown out windows in an apartment; and another of a partially caved in roof. "Two congress members have gone missing. Abruptly taken from their homes, little doubt what happened to them as they were known anti-Preacher activists.

"If you have any information on these cases, please contact—"

"That is enough; that does not concern you at the moment." Tui declares when she realizes the video is over and sees what's on all of our screens.

I reluctantly get up from my chair and leave with everyone else.

Preachers are getting bolder and bolder. Kidnapping, or murdering, two relatively famous people is a bit much. Unfortunately, this doesn't mean anything is going to change. The police aren't going to do anything about it and neither is the rest of the government. I suspect that Preachers are going to do something even bigger next time.

Tui leads us to the courtyard. "I have nothing else planned for today." Tui actually seems to be a little sad that our time together is coming to a close. I, for one, am not. If I could, I would run up to my dad's laboratory right now and inject myself with that amazing chip, then find the closest Preacher lair and tear it apart. But no, my father wants me to do this the proper way: safely, wisely and boringly. I know he is right, of course, but I still feel resentful. Who knows if the Preachers are not planning a devastating hit that will keep us from being Enhanced; we should act as soon as possible.

"I hope to see you all later, for your official passing of the class… even though literally anyone can." I catch her glancing at Junior.

Taking that as a goodbye, each trainee disperses to their separate areas.

***

This is so cheesy; I thought I had gotten past this when I finished high school.

I wait in the cafeteria, just behind the double doors, with everyone else that took the course. The 'graduates' from Vulture's group are here too, but mine is first; a small victory. I hope I can leave after my turn. I am fourth from the front; after Spaz, Junior and Dude.

Sleepy stands behind and pokes me in the ribs, "Ready?"

"Mmhmm."

"Jardah," Vulture starts off the ceremony, "Thank you for coming and supporting our new recruits. Now let us welcome our two graduating classes." Vulture announces.

The two groups march into the Courtyard in line formation. A loud roar of clapping erupts from a relatively small collection of supporters.

Swift stands with Robin, Owl and Blue-jay in the back. He and Owl clap enthusiastically; Owl whistles.

My parents sit in the first row. I think I have the most people here to support me; most of the other soon-to-be Proxies don't have and family or friends here.

I feel blessed, but not really. I have that much more to lose.

"Spaz." Tui calls. She stands next to Vulture. "Congratulations to Agent Sugarbird! You have qualified for Medical and Liaison."

The biggest smile I have ever seen breaks across Spaz's freckled face as she shakes Tui's hand. She got into Medical as she hoped.

Spaz walks away and sits by herself in the crowd.

"Junior." Tui says; a proud smile on her face. She must not have thought he would make it. "Agent Goldcrest, congratulations; you qualified for Security." Junior eagerly grabs Tui's hand. That is what he was aiming for at least.

"Dude." Tui nods, "Welcome to NEST, Agent Dipper. You qualified for Security and Field."

I am next. I've done a lot of standing in line and waiting my turn in my life, and I am sure I will have to do some more before I can get Enhanced, but right now I am coming to the end of a period and am that much closer to my goals.

I feel nothing, no nerves at all, when Tui calls my nickname and tells me that my code-name is Wren. Big shocker. "You have qualified for Security and Field. Welcome to NEST." I shake her hand firmly and head straight for Swift and Robin, Owl and Blue-jay, but mostly Swift.

They, of course, greet me with high-fives and pats on the back. Swift gives me a hug that lasts a couple seconds longer than it should have. Thankfully though, before it could get awkward, my parents ambush me.

"You weren't planning on leaving without talking to us?" My mother asks, joking.

"Of course not, Mom." I give her a hug.

"Jardah, Wren. Your father—" She looks over her shoulder at the talking people. "Let's find a quieter place." She smiles.

Everyone that came to support me, except for Blue-jay, heads away from the small crowd. Blue-jay seems to just disappear.

"Where are Beck and Piper?" I ask while we walk to my dorm. I hope there will be room for everyone.

"Beck has work that he couldn't miss and your sister has an extra shift."

Like I have mentioned before, Piper works as a nurse. I guess that's her way to change the world. I like to think bigger; more exaggerated and theatrical. Beck just works in an old museum, I find it boring.

I unlock the door and somehow we all squeeze into my room. Three on the couch, one on the extra chair and I sit on the floor. Swift sits on the edge of the small desk that I don't use.

His amber eyes scan the area and then focus on me. I was looking at him for too long.

He mouths, "What are you staring at?"

I avert my gaze quickly as Swift chuckles.

My dad speaks, "First of all, Wren, congratulations. I know it was hard for you to wait this long to finally be done with the course, but I am afraid that you will have to wait even longer. The Enhancement program will start in about a month, towards the beginning of the year." *Yeah, I already know. And so does everyone else.*

"I can probably get you a shift working in Security." Swift jumps in before I can say anything.

"Thanks, Swift." I say through gritted teeth, trying to keep my cool.

"I am sorry, Wren." My father says and he seems genuinely apologetic.

"It is okay, dad." I try to smile.

Seeing my parents here, it does not seem like I am doing a very good job staying away from them.

"Awesome, so I have time to get ready." Owl, who has been quiet so far, smirks and then scowls at his sister when he notices her giving him the evil eye. "Robin *and* I will be applying for the Enhancement program."

"It's nice to hear that other people are taking interest and are willing to go through the procedure." My mother smiles at both of them kindly. She then adds quietly, "So far the program hasn't gotten a great response. I don't think many people will be applying."

"The entrance tests will begin in a couple weeks, but only ten people will ultimately be chosen. I hope to get people from different backgrounds and from different age groups to see how the Enhancer affects them. That is all I can tell you for now, though." My father stands up slowly, "That is all I wanted to tell you. Congratulations, again."

I give my parents hugs and we all say goodbye. My father herds my mother out the door.

"Who else do you think is going to participate? Hopefully there won't be too much competition." Owl states and runs his hand through his curly hair.

"Blue-jay mentioned something about it... I don't think a lot of people will apply for an experimental chip thingy. Even I don't understand what it is. But you're a shoe-in no matter what." Swift pats Owl's back and sits next to him on the couch.

I don't know if Owl is a good fighter or not; Swift is probably trying to make him feel better.

Owl rubs his arms and smiles at Swift, "Thanks."

"Do *not* encourage him." Robin mutters.

She has really been annoying me lately. It's his choice to make, she isn't his mother. "Let the kid do what he wants, he is old enough to decide for himself. Obviously he has a strong conviction to join." I leave it at that and look away from Robin's shocked face.

Swift also seems to be surprised to see me express myself like that.

"I think we should go." Robin says, hopping out of her chair.

"Maybe I want to stay."

I didn't want to rekindle the fight between them, just put Robin in her place. "Actually, I think I am going to leave." I slowly stand and move towards the door. I wait for the others to leave before shutting the door behind me. Robin goes storming off, to her room, I presume, and Owl marches in the other direction.

Swift waits for me while I lock the door. "Where did that come from?"

"What? We were all thinking it."

"I think I like the more expressive Wren." He smiles radiantly at me and my heart skips a beat. "But maybe tone it down a little bit."

He ignores me as I clasp my hand to my chest. *What is this all about?*

"Where are you going now?" I ask after I recover.

"Back to my place." Swift answers casually.

This is the first time he has mentioned his dorm. Secretly, I wish for him to invite me.

"Oh, cool." But it might appear that I have plans, which I do not.

"See you around." Swift heads further down the corridor to where his allusive room must be.

A weird lonely feeling sets on me and I don't know where to go or what to do. I decide to just move. My feet step without me thinking too much and I end up in the courtyard. Some empty chairs still remain, but other than that there's not a sign of the ceremony that just took place.

Sleepy bursts out of the dining-hall, trying to run away from some Proxies who are spraying him with foam.

93

"Ah, Wren, protect me!" He runs behind me and uses my body as a human shield.

My hair gets soaked as the foam lands on it. I scoop some into my hand and rub it on Sleepy's face.

"Welcome to the real world, Nightjar." One of his friends calls.

"Yeah, I'm sure Preachers spray foam at people." he calls back. Sleepy laughs and explains, "Just a little after-graduation partying."

"Oh, yeah, sorry I didn't stick around, Sleepy. What did you qualify for?"

He puts on a straight face, "Please, call me Nightjar. I have been accepted into two fields: Security and Liaison. By the way, what do think about my serious voice?" He giggles at the end so it ruins his attempts at being a cold-hearted Proxy.

"It does not suit you." I answer honestly.

He smiles anyway, "We were about to hang out; do you want to join us?"

"Sure, why not?"

Nightjar introduces me to his friends. Most of them have multiple tattoos and piercings. And swear a lot.

"So what do you want to do?" A woman named Nightingale asks me. Her purple hair is spiked in different directions. She has ink all over her shoulders, chain links are tattooed on her collar bones. She looks a little familiar.

I have no idea what these people do for fun, thankfully Nightjar interrupts before I can make a fool of myself.

He motions to the can of foam that Nightingale is holding as he sneaks behind the group without attracting too much attention. I get the hint and follow his lead. Counter-attack.

"So?" Another male asks.

"Now!" Nightjar shouts while smiling.

I sweep Nightingale's legs before grabbing the can from her falling hands. Nightjar has a can too and we spray the unsuspecting group between us.

They still have foam cans, so it turns into an all-out foam war. It's the most fun that I've had in a while. I smile the whole time. There are no victors in a battle like this, just empty metal cylinders and goofy-looking participants.

After that we go to the front desk and get Sleepy's dorm number and key, because he had been staying in the civilian living quarters until now. I am sure he will spend a lot of time in his new room taking naps in between jobs. His friends and I pile in his room and eat cookies that he and his friends had snatched from the cafeteria.

"Wren, you and I need to spend more time together after we get settled in." Nightjar states and hands me a cookie.

"Yeah, sure." I say absentmindedly. I know that in reality I probably won't see him at all after this.

"You're really cool."

"Oh, thanks." I respond.

But Sleepy is out. His head hangs back over the edge of the couch and his mouth is wide open. At least he lives up to his name.

All of his friends laugh when they realize that he is asleep and after several failed attempts at waking him up, draw on his face. One of the big guys drops him in his bed, before we leave. Nightjar doesn't react at all. *Wow, he is a deep sleeper.*

I turn out the lights and close the door. *Sweet dreams, Nightjar. Good luck, stay safe, think fast, run and don't get too attached.*

Chapter Ten

Swift, thinking he is doing me a huge favor, gets me a Security job.

I can't decide if I would rather travel the country or be stuck in the NEST building for the next month, but hopefully I will be able to do a little of both. I need to see first-hand what is going on in other people's lives; people who are not lucky enough to have the power and protection that I do. I will be immensely powerful when I am Enhanced. I will no longer be a ghost in the background, I will be the face fighting on the front line. I can hardly wait.

My job takes me to the lower, underground levels of the NEST building, where the refugees and civilians live. I have seen Orion walk by a few times, but I keep my distance. Work here is mostly boring, walking back and forth through a hall where not many important people live, but I do get to see children and adults live their simple but grateful lives. They are happy just to be alive, which makes me think about my role in life. I know that I'm meant to do something amazing.

Seeing these people live down here in peace, it makes me wonder if we could build a hidden, safe society and ignore the Preachers completely. I know it couldn't work, once the Preachers take care of the bigger threats, they would branch out until they realize where we are. And then they won't stop until we are eradicated. It wouldn't be right to hide anyway, as humans we shouldn't leave our brothers behind to be murdered. We need to stop it, stop the killing, even if it takes... more killing.

A tiny voice in my head asks if that is really the answer. For now that's the only answer I can come up with and until there is another solution, I'll follow this one.

***

I turn up the volume on my T-Screen as loud as I can.

"What do you think?" I ask Swift after he has had a chance to take in the brilliance that is The Chalk Outlines.

He looks me in the eyes and says, "Not bad."

"Not bad???" I move closer to him on the couch, making sure he can actually hear what I'm hearing.

Swift chuckles, "I was kidding." He takes the computer from me. "I can see why you like them so much." he says but doesn't elaborate. Swift sets the T-Screen on the couch between us.

We sit in silence for a few minutes, just relaxing on the couch together and listening to music. *Is this what having a friend is like?* I ask myself after a moment. "I'm gonna do something useful." I jump to my feet and walk over to my closet which has now turned into a giant pile of laundry on the floor. I start picking through the pile, throwing all of the dirty clothes into a separate pile to be taken to the laundry room on the eighth floor and washed, and hanging up all of the clean ones. I look over at Swift when I'm done, watching him move his head to the music. "I see that." I tease and walk back over to the couch.

Beep beep beep! A message appears on the T-Screen. "What does it say?" I ask and lean over the back of the couch and Swift's head.

"Something about the Enhancement program..." Swift mumbles and then shifts his weight to see the screen better.

Before he can get a better look, I jump over the back of the couch, my butt landing on the cushions hard, and snatch up the T-Screen. I read out the message quickly, "First entrance test tomorrow. Psychological assessment. Only eighty applicants will continue." I pause, taking in the news. A flood of emotions washes over me. Excitement, happiness, worry, anxiety. I try to ignore them all, but apparently Swift doesn't.

"That's amazing!" he practically shouts. Next thing I know, he is wrapping his arms around me and pulling me into a tight hug. I sit still until he lets me go. "Aren't you excited?"

Quick knocks on the door keep me from answering him. "Hurry up!" Someone shouts from the other side.

I rush to answer the door, jerking it open once I get my hand on the handle. "Eighty? Your mom said no one would apply!" Owl strides into the room half excited, half nervous.

I respond quickly, "Apparently a lot more Proxies are interested than we thought, which isn't really that surprising."

Owl takes my place on the couch, "But what if I don't get in?"

"There's no need to worry, Owl." Swift places a hand on Owl's shoulder and comforts him. "If you want to, I'll be willing to help you prepare for the psych test." *You can't really prepare for a psych test, though.*

Owl turns to Swift, "Oh, thank you. That sounds great." he says genuinely.

"Wren?" Swift asks.

"Oh, no thanks. I think getting a good night's sleep would be the best preparation for me."

Owl leaves just as quickly as he came, taking Swift with him.

At first I think Swift is going to leave without saying goodbye, but just as I'm about to close the door behind them, he pops back into the entrance and says, "Sorry about all this. Goodnight."

"Goodnight, Swift."

***

"Nervous?" Swift asks as I place my tray of food on the table and then take the seat next to him.

"Not at all." I answer with a small grin. It's true, I'm not nervous; I don't really need to be. Whether I pass this test is not in my control.

I couldn't have prepared or studied for this, so I just leave it be; no matter how much I want to be in control of the situation.

In between spoonfuls of yogurt I ask, "Did you find out where the test is?"

"The same floor as the computer labs." he answers briefly before taking a bite of his chocolate muffin. Swift checks his watch, "And starts in four minutes." and then shoves the rest of the muffin into his mouth and grabs his empty tray.

I try to spoon up the rest of the yogurt while walking to the trash can. I don't finish it all, but I should be set for the next couple hours.

Swift and I walk swiftly to the elevator and have to wait a minute or two for it to arrive and empty itself of the few passengers. We ride the elevator to the tenth floor and then step out of the elevator and immediately into the line for the test. *Oh, crap* is the first thing that comes to mind.

"Looks like we might be here awhile." Swift mutters into my ear.

There are three separate rooms meant for testing, but the line moves slowly, each assessment taking about nine minutes for each person. It seems to be first come, first serve. There are no chairs, so we have to stand the whole time. My feet grow tired quickly.

Swift tries to entertain and distract me while we wait and anytime he sees someone he knows, he is sure to call them over to talk. We converse with Owl and Robin separately since they're still not getting along. Fortunately for me, neither of us spots Blue-jay during the wait.

Many people file in behind us and I wonder just how many people signed up and how the testers are going to decide who passes. I just wish there was some order to the process. My dad must not have had much control over this part of the entrance exams because he would never let it get this way.

As Swift and I grow closer to the doors of the testing rooms, butterflies begin to form in my stomach. I try to stop them, because being nervous now is silly, but they don't seem to go away no matter what I try. I decide to just ignore them instead.

Swift places his hand on my arm and lightly pushes me, "We're up next."

I pop out of the haze I was in and wait for the current Proxy to open the door.

Swift's door and mine open at the same time, their Proxies hurrying out of the rooms and down the hallway. They must be just as eager as I am to be done with this.

"Good luck." Swift wishes me before stepping forward. He strides confidently to the open door and closes it lightly behind him.

I try to do the same when I enter my assessment room, but overthinking things, I slam the door shut loudly.

"Please sit down." A man says.

I walk to the table in the middle of the room and sit in the chair behind it. The room is constructed in a perfect square, with just enough space to hold the tester, his assistant and I, and all of their equipment. A large blinking machine stands near the table.

"I work with Agent Hummingbird, and I will be conducting your psychological assessment with the help of my assistant." He motions to the woman at his side. She nods her head silently. "First, I will take your basic personal information and then we will begin." He only pauses a moment before he starts with the questions. I wonder if this is already part of the test. "Your name?"

"Agent Wren." I respond quickly.

"Age?"

"Eighteen."

"Okay..." he draws out while typing my information into a T-Screen. "Now we can start."

As soon as he finishes his sentence, his assistant begins her work attaching me in as many ways as possible to the machine to the left of the table. She attaches some stickers to my chest, wraps stuff around my left forearm and places something on my head that I don't catch. All of these things are attached to the machine by wires.

"Ready?" The man asks the woman and she nods again. "Okay, let's begin."

The woman steps closer to me and speaks for the first time, "What is your favorite color?"

I'm so surprised at first that she is actually speaking, that I almost forget the question. And then I just say the first color that come to my mind, "Um, blue."

It takes me time to think about the questions and their answers at the beginning, but after a minute, I get into the flow and rhythm of the test.

"Who is the family member you most connect with?"

"My sister."

"And why is that?"

"Because she knows what she wants to do with her life; so do I."

The man and woman take turns asking the questions, probably attempting to mess me up somehow, but I focus easily and ignore any outside distractions.

"And the last question for the day: what would you say is your greatest weakness?"

"Oh, um—" I stumble over the question. This is probably the most important question they have asked so far and the one I've been supposed to be thinking about. I blurt out the first thing that comes to mind, "I have a really bad sense of time and am usually late for appointments." I want to bang my head on the table the second the words come out of my mouth.

"Well okay then..." The man types the final answer into the computer and says, "Congratulations on making it through the first step, if you have passed this level you will be contacted later today and informed when the next level of testing is. You can go now."

Like the people before me, I get up and leave the room as fast as possible. I think they only asked me about twenty-five questions, but for some reason my brain seems to be fried. When I'm out of the room and back in the hallway, I take a few seconds to look for Swift, but with the other Proxies in line watching me and the relief of the test being over, I easily give up the search and head back to my dorm.

After checking the clock on my T-Screen, I realize that the testing didn't make me miss my shift, so I decide to throw on my Proxy clothes, pick up my gun and head down to the refugee floors. I do my job late into the afternoon; walking the same boring hallways and corridors ready to protect the refugees here against something that hasn't penetrated these walls yet. And I hope it never does.

"Jardah, ma'am?" I hear a small voice call to me and someone pulls the hem of my shirt.

I turn around and try to smile at the little girl I find.

"Is there a problem, miss?" I ask and kneel next to her so we are at the same height. I twist my rifle around to hang on my back.

In general, I try to be nice to children, but sometimes it doesn't come off like I am. I guess I just don't connect with them as much. I never really was a child; I was very mature for my age when I was younger and already exposed to so many things.

"No, I just wanted to thank you for protecting us. It is nice seeing you here every day." She looks at her feet when she speaks.

"It is no problem; my duty, in fact. Hopefully I will help you even more in the future, but you will not see me as much."

I hear shuffling down the hallway and then finally I make out the footsteps of quick paced running coming this way. I turn to face the noise and the person who's coming, moving the child behind me slowly. "Wren?" someone calls just beyond the corner.

I recognize the voice and stand up, "Yes, Swift?" I call out to him. He turns the corner just as I finish my sentence.

Swift looks right at me as he approaches, with a huge smile on his face. His eyes seem to glow with his joy.

"I came as soon as I saw it." Swift holds his T-Screen in his hands and when he's close enough he passes it to me.

'Congratulations, Agent Swift.' I read. 'You have successfully passed the first entry test to the Enhancement program.' He did it. Now I have to find out if I made it too. Without finishing the message, I hand the T-Screen back to Swift and start the trip to my dorm, where my T-Screen awaits. Swift follows me at a fast pace.

"Good luck." the young girl hollers after me.

"Thank you!" I shout back before rounding the corner.

I maneuver through the hallways back to the elevators with ease, Swift right behind me.

"Enhancement is so close, I can almost taste it." Swift says while we ride an elevator to the main floor. "I—"

I interrupt Swift before he can go on, "Don't get too ahead of yourself, Swift. You will only set yourself up for disappointment."

Swift gives up on what he was saying and keeps his mouth shut until we're on our Proxy floor and outside my dorm. "I know you're nervous about the whole test and Enhancement thing, but you shouldn't take it out on me."

This would be the optimal time to apologize, but I just slip the key in the lock and turn it to the left, ignoring what he said. I remember the reason I'm here, and swing the door open wildly, dashing to the computer I left at the foot of my bed.

As soon as I touch the screen, a flashing message pops up, and I can almost taste the Enhancement too. I tap the notification and the message appears in large, written is the same thing that Swift was sent, except with my name on it. I read to the bottom of the page this time, 'The next test will take place in two days. Good luck, stay safe, think fast, run and don't get too attached."

Chapter Eleven

I'm on the computer lab floor again, ten stories above ground. The second test is about to begin and I sit in my own private cubicle, behind a desk fitted with a large T-Screen in the center.

I sit up straighter and stretch my neck above the cubicle's left wall and spot Swift at the cubicle right next to mine. I don't know what this test is about and am a tiny bit nervous, but seeing Swift next to me is comforting. I take a brief look around the room and eye the other nineteen participants. I will have to be better than everyone in here and in the other rooms if I want to make it into the Enhancement program. I wish I could just rely on my dad to get me in, but I know that I have to do this the right way.

Something flashes in the corner of my eye and I turn my head back to the T-Screen which was blank a second ago. 'The examination will begin in ten seconds and will be testing your intelligence. There will be a total of one hundred and fifty questions and you will have fifty minutes to answer as many as possible. Good luck.'

In the remaining two seconds I take a deep breath. Here we go...

A series of seven numbers appears on the screen, five more numbers are below it. 'Which number should come next in the series?' Reads the question. I quickly identify the pattern and press the option that I think should come next.

'Which shape completes the pattern?' is the next question. I examine the original shapes in the sequence and then select the shape that is correct.

I continue with ease along more similar questions about patterns and shapes and numbers and then come different types of questions.

'If you rearrange the letters Ruaroa, you will get the name of a: lake, city, ocean, desert or country?' The letters form the word Aurora, which is the easternmost city in the country. I tap the screen where the correct answer is.

'Which word is least like the others?' I read the five different options and choose the one I suspect could be right.

At the end of the fifty minutes I manage to answer most of the questions, even if I did just guess for a few of them. Over all, I'm pretty positive I passed this section.

I join Swift at the exit and we wait for Owl in the hallway. He also passed the psychology test and came up with us earlier, before this one. He was put in a different room, though.

Swift spots him coming out of the room to our left, "How was it?" he shouts as Owl comes closer.

"I failed." Owl exclaims when he reaches us and rests his head on Swift's chest. "Halfway through I gave up and started pressing random answers."

"Come on," Swift pushes Owl away from him kindly and looks him in the eyes, "What happened to the confident and happy Owl we used to know?" Swift's right, Owl hasn't been the same since the Enhancers came into the picture.

I am not exactly sure how Swift's words could make Owl feel better, but Owl stands up a little straighter and nods his head, "You're right, I guess this whole thing with the Enhancement program and Robin has gotten me a little upset."

"I'm sure you did your best," Swift lowers his voice a little, "but even your worst is better than some of these Proxy's best." Swift grabs Owl's head and ruffles his orange hair like an older brother would. Sometimes I envy Swift's skills with people. "You just need to have more confidence in yourself."

Later that day I receive the news that I passed, which doesn't surprise me.

***

105

The next phase is a physical test, which I take five days later along with fifty-nine others. It is quite simple and basic, running and weightlifting and then a medical check-up. Swift and Owl pass these stages with me and I start to imagine the three of us being in the final team. Owl's been keeping his distance from Robin, but is keeping an eye on her, so he informs Swift and I that she has made it thus far as well. So has Blue-jay, which excites Swift, but annoys me.

***

The lines keep getting shorter and shorter and the crowds thinner and thinner; I think they said only fifty people have made the cut until now. I can sense the end of the entrance process and hope that I'll make it through to the end. Right now I'm waiting to take a turn in the Combat Scenario room. I heard that it will be different from the ones at the end of Proxy training; that there will be guns and a team to help me. I am ready to get in there and show the instructors just how good I am. I was nervous taking the previous tests, but after getting through the first couple stages, I realized that I am meant for the Enhancement program; I know that I can make it and flourish in the program.

There is a lot more order to the way this test is being done today. Instead of first come, first serve, when it's your turn they'll call your name and the list seems to be in alphabetical order, which sucks for me. Swift has already gone in, probably kicked butt, and was escorted off the Proxy floor by one of the instructors. I didn't get to talk to him at all.

"Agent Wren?" A young woman stands next to me and bends down to get my attention, "Will you come with me, please?" I stand up slowly and follow her a little ways down the corridor, "The goal of this exercise is to test your leadership skills and see how good you are with a weapon. You will be in charge of a team of five Proxies and your goal is to enter the building, take out any threats and rescue the hostages. Is everything clear?" She stops outside a door and I know that as soon as I say yes she'll open it and I'll be thrown into action. I take a moment to collect myself and focus. *You're almost there. You're going to do fine.*

I nod my head in confirmation and she turns the handle and throws the door open.

I step into the dark room carefully and a rifle is immediately shoved into my arms. "Team leader, we have a situation." I move forward through the room, noticing how it must be split into different sections by walls. Right now I'm in a small sliver near the entrance, a wide window with tinted glass shows off the actual testing area—the first floor of a house. A large man moves towards me through the darkness, "Three of our Proxies have been taken hostage by a group of Preachers. We think they are being kept in the basement of this building, but we are not sure how many Preachers are guarding them."

Five Proxies come through the door behind me, all holding similar rifles. All of the Proxies in here look the same to me because of the lack of light. I might have trouble differentiating between the good guys and the bad guys, which is most likely part of the test too.

The main instructor breaks character for a moment to say, "You have eight minutes to complete the mission, good luck." and then he leaves the room through the door behind me.

The five Proxies wait for me to make a move and I am reminded that the test has already started and I'm being timed. The first thing to do is find an entrance. I squint my eyes slightly and feel along the wall to the left of the window for a hole in the wall or a doorknob or something. I find what must be the front door of the house shortly after I begin my search.

Holding onto the doorknob with my left hand, I instruct my teammates in whispers, "On the count of three, I will open the door.

107

You five go in first and I will follow. Two to the right, two to the left and me and another will head to the center. Our intel says that the Proxies are most likely being held underground, but even if they're not, they will most likely be restrained, so shoot anything that moves." I make sure we are all on the same page before holding up my hand. I lift three fingers slowly, one by one. When the third finger is raised, I twist the knob and pull the door open wide. The five rush in and I quickly follow, my rifle up and ready to shoot. We enter what appears to be a poorly furnished living room. There's a tall lamp in the right corner ahead of us, giving off a little light, and a small table and two chairs close to it. The room has two doors, one in the right wall and another in the left. I motion for the left pair to move into the left room and the right pair to move into the right room and I soon hear that the right room is empty.

"It is clear over here too," one of the Proxies from the left room calls, "but there is a back door."

In a brisk walk, I guide my partner and the Proxies from the right room through the left doorway and into the room. The Proxy that spoke points to a door in the wall right ahead of them. I join them by the door, lower my weapon and listen intently to what's happening on the other side.

"There is definitely someone on the other side of this door." I whisper, "I will go in first; be prepared for a fight." I bring the butt of my rifle up to my shoulder and ready myself. Then I nod my head for the Proxy to open the door and when he does, I charge into the next room followed by my team.

I am ready and so are the others, so when we enter the room and seven Preachers are just sitting around, we take them out in about ten seconds. I shoot one Preacher in his left shoulder and another in her chest. I head straight to the next doorway and room, taking out a waiting Preacher before he can get off a round from the automatic he holds in his hands. I find a hatch in this room, tell two Proxies to come with me down the hole and instruct the others to stay and guard. I strap my rifle on my back before dropping to the floor next to the opening, swinging my legs into the open air and plummeting down into the darkness until my feet hit the ground about seven feet below. I land in a dimly-lighted room; three motionless forms are tied up in a corner. The Proxies. Just as I'm about to run over and untie them, I hear voices coming from an adjacent room. I move to the wall behind me and crouch next to it.

I swing my gun back into its correct place, my arms, and wait for either my teammates to come down or for the Preachers to walk in. Just as the others land, three Preachers walk through the opening.

Knowing that my teammates won't have their guns ready and will be unprotected, I stand up and shout, "Get down!" right before shooting off a few rounds right at the approaching Preachers, taking them all down. I don't let the Proxies rest and immediately shout, "Stand guard at that entrance, I'll take care of the others." and rush over to the captive Proxies, untying them as quickly as I can.

As soon as the last one is free, the lights come on full power and the simulation shuts down.

The instructor from before comes out of the other room and says, "Great job, kid." He makes me hand over the rifle and then shows me the way out and onto the main floor. "You will be contacted soon if you have made it."

After he leaves, I take a breath of relief; I actually did really well.

"Wren!" I hear Swift's voice call out to me and I turn around, looking for him. I spot him on one of the couches in the corner and hurry to him. "How did you do?" Swift pats the empty couch next to him.

I answer honestly, "It was great. How about you?" I sit.

"It was good for me too, but I'm still a little anxious because the number of applicants keeps getting sliced majorly."

"Yeah, I bet the last test is coming up." I pause and then ask, "What time is it?"

Swift takes a moment to check the digital watch on his left wrist, "Just about supper time."

I am surprised that it's so late. "I missed my shift then."

"You know what we need?" Swift asks and then gets to his feet. "A treat. We have been working too hard."

"You are right." I respond and stand next to him. We then head through the big doors and into the Phoenix Center and grab some real food while we wait for answers. I need to know if I passed or not. I actually have no idea what I'm going to do if I don't get into the program... I should start making a backup plan just in case.

"Hey, Swift." I say, breaking the silence that was between us, he was probably deep in thought too. "What are you going to do if you did not pass?"

Swift takes a moment to ponder my question and I go back to looking at all of the people walking through the Phoenix Center, who are completely oblivious to what is actually going on behind the scenes.

"Just continue with the way things are now I guess."

I don't know exactly what I wanted his response to be; for him to leave with me? Like that would happen. I just nod my head in response and finish my meal.

"Have you gotten a message yet?" I ask Swift when he is done with his food. He reaches into his pocket and pulls out the T-Screen. "Nope." He answers.

That is not the answer I was looking for. Swift's eyes move from me to something behind me. I turn in my seat and spot Blue-jay making her way to the Proxy part of the building. Swift quickly catches her attention and she changes her course. "Where are you rushing to?" Swift asks her when she reaches our table.

"Agent Hummingbird is having a meeting with Hawk and Albatross about the Enhancers in the Viewing Deck." she says in a hushed tone. *How come she knows about it and I don't?* "I guess you could come too." She says this while looking at Swift, not me.

I stand quickly, "So let's go." I say, not caring whether or not she wants me to come.

Swift and I hurry to clear our table and then follow Blue-jay to the Viewing Deck.

The walk to the elevator isn't far at all, but the ride seems to takes forever.

The elevator door whooshes open revealing the almost empty Viewing Deck and it occurs to me that maybe we aren't wanted. But now it's too late, Albatross has spotted us and I step out of the elevator uneasily.

Swift smiles nervously and then we walk down the stairs to where Albatross, Hawk, my father and a few others are sitting at that huge, round table.

"Good evening, Blue-jay, Swift, Wren." Albatross says somewhat sarcastically as we stand awkwardly beside the table. "Since you are already here, I suppose it is okay if you sit down. Please begin, Hummingbird."

My father smirks at me before going through a list on his T-screen and then stands. "All of the tests done on Agent Hawk have had positive results and we have received permission to start manufacturing ten more chips. I have made some changes to the design and these chips should be able to work in two or three months." He's already told me about those changes. "Right now, narrowing down the final ten participants is coming to a close. After that, Hawk will be training those ten chosen subjects in the Enhancement program. The special training facilities being built for the Enhancement program are nearly complete. The course will go on for three months and then Enhancement will take place. They will receive another month or two of training after that. After Enhancement, the task force will lead the fight against the Preachers." Dad sits down, bringing the meeting to an end. My dad always did know how to be thorough. I remember the one minute family meetings in my living room.

Albatross starts a private conversation with some other Proxy and then everyone is talking in small groups except for Swift, Blue-jay and I.

Blue-jay stands up and leaves without saying goodbye.

I get up to leave too, "Why did she even join?" I murmur to Swift in case she is still lurking around.

"I'm sure she has her reasons." Swift says vaguely, but I can tell that he knows more. He stands too.

"You guys better go get some sleep." Hawk says and walks toward Swift and I, stopping us in our tracks.

"That's exactly where we were headed." Swift responds to him.

"Well then, I will not keep you," Hawk smiles and it makes me uneasy. "Good luck." *With what?* Hawk just walks away after that.

Swift ignores Hawk and pulls me to the elevator.

"When do you think the next stage is going to take place?" I ask after the door closes and we begin our descent.

Swift smiles, "Soon, definitely soon."

I go to bed soon after I get back to my dorm, or at least I try to. Still not having received word about the Enhancement program, I keep my T-Screen under my pillow and check it about every five minutes. Eventually I do fall asleep, but while feeling very anxious and nervous even though I'm sure I did well.

Chapter Twelve

"Agent Wren?" The voice pauses and so does the knocking. "Agent Wren, please open the door."

Why is someone at my door in the middle of the night? I wrap a blanket around my shoulders and crawl out of bed to the door. I slowly open it, "What do you want?"

"Um, hello." A young woman stands in the hallway; she tucks a strand of loose hair behind her ear. "I work with Agent Hummingbird and the Enhancers and I was told to wake you up and take you downstairs." At least she looks a little sorry for waking me.

I yawn before saying, "Downstairs?" *Wait, did she say Enhancers?* I wake up a bit. "Does this have something to do with program?"

"I can't tell you a whole lot now, but yes."

"Okay, wait a minute." I shut the door lightly.

Tossing the blanket onto the bed, I rush over to my closet and pull out some clothes. It only takes me about a minute to get dressed, wash my face and get back to the woman. "I'm ready, let's go." I say, close the door behind me and lock it. I fit the keys into my right jacket pocket.

The woman doesn't speak as I follow her to the elevator bank, reach the main floor, and enter the elevator that leads to the refugee floors. She seems nervous, so I stay alert. I wonder where we're going.

She hits the button for the very lowest floor.

"That's where the training is going to be held, right?" And that's where my Proxy combat-scenario was.

The woman seems a little hesitant in answering but she says, "Yes, the renovations are almost done." Right before the elevator door opens, she checks the time on her watch, "We should hurry." and then she rushes through the opening and into the corridor. I follow her lead.

113

Jogging down the hallway, I don't see many changes, but I'm sure the insides of the rooms are completely different.

"It's right up here." She points to a door on the right and slows down. We come to a stop in front of the door, "Good luck."

I take a deep breath before entering; I do not know what is going on, but it is definitely something big.

When I enter the room, I am greeted by about ten others just standing around, looking just as confused and curious as I am. The room is fairly large, but has a low ceiling. An elevated square mat sits in the center and punching bags hang from the ceiling in the far corner.

"Wren!" Owl spots me and calls out my name.

I am about to go over to Owl when Hawk comes into view. "Oh, good, Wren's here. We can begin." He has a T-Screen in his hands. "Please, everyone form a line in front of me."

The other nine people and I move through the room, trying to make a straight line as quickly as possible. I want answers and so do they. I grab Owl and we stand next to each other.

Hawk looks us over once before shouting, "Congratulations, everyone! If you are here, that means you have passed the stages of testing and are the final ten in the Enhancement program!" He pauses a moment and it gives everyone a chance to celebrate. Half of me is excited and relieved, the other half is worried and confused. *Where are Swift and the others?* "First of all, I think we should all get to know each other. My name is Agent Hawk and I will be your instructor.

Each one should introduce themselves and then I will tell you a little more about the program. Let's start with you then." Hawk motions for me to step forward.

I do, "Um, I am Agent Wren."

I stand back in line, aware of how awkward that must have looked.

Then it is Owl's turn; his red hair is curlier than usual and is sticking up in places. He tries to have a brave face on when he greets the group, but I can tell that he is as worried as I am. When he steps back next to me he whispers, "Where's Swift? He should be here with us."

"I guess he didn't make it." Even as I say the words, I know they can't be true.

I wait patiently as everyone says their names, waiting for them to be done and then ask Hawk what exactly is going on. Raven, Yellowhammer, Grosbeak, Pheasant, Kestrel, Osprey, Warbler, and finally Nightingale, one of Sleepy's friends. The one with the spiky hair and the tattoos and piercings.

The second Nightingale says her name, Hawk is already pushing us to our next activity, "Okay, everyone. I should give you the tour of our facilities." so I don't get a chance to speak with him.

Hawk leads us into a classroom with desks and a giant touch screen on one wall. I get caught up with the tour and forget about my other questions and worries. "Here we will learn history and strategy, and ask some very important questions." That makes me wonder what kind of questions.

Hawk leaves his statement in the air and guides us into another seemingly empty, but huge room. The ceiling is so high; the entire room must span over two floors. But for some reason I sense that we aren't shown the entire room.

"There will be some very interesting training in here," He grins while walking to a panel on the wall. It slides up, revealing a screen. Hawk presses some buttons and knobby things and different parts of the room rise while others drop making alleyways and side streets to a small city. If this room can change on command, there are an endless number of training scenarios; parts of cities, different compounds, and all sorts of other things. All of the walls move and reform a couple times except for one; the back wall just stands there

115

as if it doesn't belong. "This is where you will train the most; a special room programmed with a console called the 'holographic adaptation breadth intended for training and teaching' also known as 'HABITAT'." *Wow, someone really wanted the name to be bird related.* "It was designed and created by the inventor of the Enhancers, Agent Hummingbird."

The other Proxies are about to leave the room when Hawk calls us back to him, "Oh, and guys, I forgot to mention—in about sixty seconds, this room is going to turn into a maze." *Wait, what?* Owl grabs onto the sleeve of my jacket and sends me a questioning look. "On the other side of this wall, another group of ten, that was also told that they are the final ten, is now realizing the truth just as you are—there are actually twenty of you and this is your final test. The ten spots are still up for grabs and to get one, you have to make your way to the center of the maze." Hawk backs away and returns to the console before the others or I have a chance to react. I knew something was up, but couldn't have predicted this. "Good luck."

I place my hand on Owl's shoulder so we won't get split up. As dividers and barriers begin to rise around us, we form a plan. "I think we should stick together." I tell him.

"I couldn't agree with you more." His voice shakes and I can tell that he is really nervous. "We should find Swift; he should be in here too."

"Right." I agree. A wall brushes past me, growing up and up until it stops, reaching about fifteen feet high. "Robin could be out there too; do you want to look for her?"

"Um…" Owl thinks about it for a few seconds. He must be conflicted.

"It is your decision." I tell him in hopes that it will make his choice easier. The room has almost stopped moving and changing now.

"No." he says firmly. "Let's just find Swift and get to the center before the others." Owl begins to run when he finishes talking. I catch up to him almost immediately and then take the lead.

As we run, I obviously take a look around. The room seems to have expanded, making it look as if the maze goes on forever and ever. For the most part the ground stays level, but occasionally Owl and I will reach an incline or decline. The walls of the maze are plain and white. With no way of knowing the direction of the center, I take random turns.

"Left or right?" I pause at an intersection to catch my breath and consult with Owl.

"Right." he answers and plows past me and into the right corridor. I admire his spirit; we were woken in the middle of the night and yet he hasn't stopped running this whole time.

I jog behind him as we continue down the new corridor until we reach what appears to be a dead end. Something is different about this wall though.

"Darn it." Owl says in disappointment. "Come on; let's head back the other way." Owl turns around and begins to walk back the way we came.

I step closer to the back wall, "Wait, something's off." I eye it suspiciously.

"It's just a dead end, Wren!" he shouts to me.

I press my hand against the wall and a screen appears under my fingertips. I grin; I knew it. Words form on the screen: 'In what year did World War Three start?' That's easy, everyone knows that. I move my face closer to the screen and speak clearly, "Two thousand twenty-four."

I hear a soft popping noise and the wall shudders a little. I put all of my weight against the wall and push. It slowly swings open. I pass through the entrance and further down the new passageway while chuckling. "The reason the wall seemed off is because it's not a wall at all; it's a door!" I call to Owl. I turn around to see Owl round the corner back at the intersection and then the door closes behind me, cutting Owl off from me. *Oh, shit, no!* "Owl!" I run back to the closed door that has merged back with the wall. "Owl!" I shout again, but know that it is futile and he can't hear me. I'll just have to keep going without him. I spin around and keep pushing forward.

After running a few steps, I feel a sharp pain erupt in my right leg. I look down to find a dart with a red flight sticking out of my thigh. Just as I reach down to pull it out, my vision blurs and I stumble forward. A tranquilizing dart.

I lean up against a wall and yank it out as quickly as possible. I rest for a moment and then continue my trek at a relatively slow pace, trying to shake off the effects of the tranquilizer. I have to keep going. I have to get there in time. I have to get into the program.

Once my sight and balance fully return, I quicken my pace through the identical white halls and corridors, avoiding any other Proxies. From a hall up ahead and to my right, I hear a woman's scream. I slow down and turn to see the yellowish-blue glow of electricity and the woman's body convulsing atop one of the tall barriers. She must have climbed up there somehow and apparently we're not supposed to. *It would have been a smart move if only the walls weren't booby trapped. The whole area must be booby trapped too.* The idea that the maze actually is booby trapped and that Hawk and my father are okay with it makes me want to vomit. It makes sense in an analytical way, but it just doesn't sit right within me. To shake the feelings, I go back to running, this time faster than ever before.

Bounding down the corridor, just as I realize that I could be running right into one of the traps, my left foot finds open air instead of the tiled floor. In what feels like slow-motion, I plummet into the square-shaped hole. Bent at the elbow, I stick out my arms. Miraculously, they actually help and I am caught in the opening. The sudden stop sends shots of pain through my arms and my face flies forward, smashing into the edge of the trap door. The right and left side edges sit firmly in my armpits, everything below my shoulders in a dark pit and everything above out in the open maze.

The first thing I do is cry out in pain. And then I swear. And then I call for help. Of course no one comes to help, so I try lifting myself up and kicking to find something to push off of, but there is nothing below me. As I start my second attempt at lifting with my arms, someone runs up behind me.

"Scar-face!" Even before they are in view, I know who it is. "Fancy seeing you here." Sleepy says with a smile in his voice. He moves from behind me to my left and then to right in front of me. He bends over to get a better look at me. "Surprised I made it this far? Well so am I." I didn't even know he was trying out to be an Enhancement.

Like everyone else, he was woken from his sleep and dragged here, so he's still wearing his pajamas. This just makes his nickname so much more appropriate. I strain to keep myself up.

Sleepy is about to say something more, but I interrupt, "I would love to chat with you, but I kind of have a problem."

"Oh, I can help you with that." Sleepy shoves his hand into my face, waiting for me to grab it.

If I let go of the edge to take his hand, then I'll fall.

His lips curl into a half-grin and then he speaks in his most calming voice, "Come on, trust me." I shake my head no.

I make the situation very clear, "If I move, I will fall."

"Fine." He mutters and then in one smooth movement he bends down even further, sticks his hands under my armpits, holds on tight and pulls me up. It feels like I pour out of the opening and onto the floor. He takes a few steps back.

I rest and catch my breath there for a moment before saying, "Thanks." Not many people in his position would stop and help me.

"Don't worry about it." Sleepy then helps me stand and I resume my trudge to the center of the maze. He walks by my side as I move slowly. I catch him staring at my face. "That looks really bad." he says and points to my nose.

I lift my hand to my nostrils and it is quickly reddened with my blood. "Oh, shit." I say under my breath. I try to touch the rest of my nose, but I quickly pull away when my touch is greeted with a whole lot of pain. "Do you think it's broken?" I ask Sleepy.

He nods his head yes in response. *Shit again.*

A small gust of air that whips the hair on the left side of my head and a grunt signals Sleepy's encounter with a booby trap. I spin around to find no trace of him and immediately think he fell through another trap door.

Sleepy softly calls for me, "Um, Scar-face?" His voice comes from somewhere above me.

I lift my eyes and find Sleepy hanging upside-down just a couple feet above me. His hair falls loosely around his face and I have to hold back a laugh.

"Wren, can you...?"

I shift my gaze to the rope around his ankle and start to devise a plan to release him.

My attention shifts, though, when I hear footsteps nearby. I whirl around to see someone run by the entrance to Sleepy's and my corridor. I only see the person for a moment, but I could swear it was Swift. I shout his name and then wait for him to come back to me, but he never turns the corner.

"I don't think he heard you." Sleepy says above me. "The only way you could catch up to him is if you left now." He pauses. "But that wouldn't help me get out of here any faster so..."

He's right. I turn back to Sleepy and his predicament, "I am sorry, but..."

The hem of his light-blue shirt falls, revealing his stomach and covering part of his face. I can still see his dull grey eyes though, and they are begging for me to stay.

I look away from him and ignore the feelings of utter betrayal. "Thanks for saving me and everything," I take a few steps backward and toward the exit, "but I really need to go now." I spin around and run after Swift.

I move through this next hall quickly, but find another intersection at the end of it. I have no way of knowing which direction Swift went. *Damn it.* I decide to keep going straight and march through the identical corridors and walls that seem to be shrinking.

My arm brushes against the concrete to my right and I realize that the walls really are growing closer together and the corridor I'm in *is* shrinking. If I don't get out of here soon, I will be crushed. I forget Swift and just focus on not dying. I break into a sprint and keep my eyes looking straight ahead while the walls begin to press against me. The blood from my nose drips down and reaches my lips. I take a second to wipe my sleeve under my nose and trip briefly, but get right back up and keep moving forward, ignoring the dread and fear building up inside of me. I spot an opening ahead and put all of my remaining energy into getting there. The walls pin my arms to the side of my body and my legs together, making it almost impossible to move. But the end of the hallway is so close. Blood pounds in my ears and I inch forward as much as I can. *You're almost there, you can do it.* I pull my right arm free and reach my hand out. The tips of my fingers can feel the open air. The space shrinks even further, causing me to twist sideways so my hips won't get crushed. I release my other arm and wrap the fingers of both hands around the corners of the walls.

With one final effort, I pull myself out of the crack. I practically fall out of the space and stumble onto a ledge, narrowly missing the gaping hole of a giant pit. The center. I inch away from the small passageway I came through and a little ways along the ledge, taking in my surroundings and trying not to fall into the hole. The center is a perfect square, a pit in the middle of it. I move a little closer to the edge, trying to see the bottom of the hole, but all I see is darkness. On each of the four walls in the center are corridors. The one I just came through has almost completely closed.

I made it to the center, but now what? As soon as I think this, a body comes bounding through the opposite entrance. I am completely surprised when the person doesn't fall into the pit, but stops short.

The first thing he does is look up at me. My brown eyes meet his black ones and I feel a sudden chill throughout my body. He glares at me. I stare back. He is very tall and muscular, the perfect specimen of a Proxy. He moves his eyes from me to the hole.

"What now?" His voice is harsh and strong. "Jump?" The thought hadn't even occurred to me, but now it seems like the only answer. *Hawk didn't mention anything about jumping or a pit or anything. They just said that we have to reach the center, and I have.* I feel cheated.

"I don't know." I answer him, because I honestly have no idea.

Another body comes hurdling down the corridor behind my buddy. A ball of orange flies into the guy's back, sending both of them plummeting into the hole. I listen while they shout and fall. Just when I start to think they'll scream and fall forever, a loud thud comes from deep in the pit and then groans.

They landed somewhere. It looks like I have no other choice. I move away from the pit as much as possible, which is only like a foot or two, trying to get a running start. Leaping off the last stretch of floor, I start to descend right above the middle of the hole. As the darkness engulfs me, I place my arms across my chest and prepare for impact. It actually doesn't seem like I have fallen for too long when the tips of my toes reach the ground and I tuck and roll across a strange, hard surface. I stop in a crouch and then stand quickly, ready for anything.

"Nice entrance." Owl grins. He sits cross-legged in a corner of the odd place we're in, rubbing a bruised arm.

I am bending down to pat the dirt off my pants, when I notice the other guy behind me. He is pressing his hands against the walls of the structure we fell into, trying to find an exit.

"Where are we?" I ask and step toward him. I can barely see anything; my eyes haven't adjusted to the near darkness yet.

He turns around to face me when he speaks, "Somewhere underground. The perimeter of the chamber is a complete square." He talks to me as if I'm a soldier. Or maybe he's the soldier.

The air above us is filled with curses and insults as someone else comes flying down the shaft and down to the floor below. I step back just as the person lands, making dust rise and spread through the air. I cover my mouth and nose with my hands as the dust settles again. The woman landed on her stomach, but now rolls onto her side while swearing again. I reach a hand down to help her up.

The woman takes one look at my hand and practically sneers. I recognize her now, Sleepy's friend and the one in the group with me. I think she said her name is Nightingale. She ignores my attempt at being friendly and gets up slowly by herself.

"What's going on?" She asks when she is finally on her feet and nursing an injured elbow. She doesn't sound scared or worried, she sounds angry.

"Another test?" I theorize.

"Wren? Is that you?!" Someone yells from the edge of the pit above. I look up and can make out someone's form blocking out part of the square patch of light. I can tell by his voice that it is Swift.

Owl jumps up and rushes to my side. He stares up too, "Come on down, buddy." he shouts through cupped hands.

Another person appears over the edge and I dread the possibility that it's Blue-jay. For some reason that girl doesn't sit right with me. Owl goes back to his spot in the corner.

Swift's shouts distract me from my suspicious thoughts. And then he is right beside me, landing right on his feet. Swift only grimaces a little, which is quite surprising; he should be in a lot of pain. By now my eyes have adjusted for the most part.

"You should move." Swift warns and then grabs my hand and pulls me away from the landing zone. I move over next to Owl when Swift lets go of me.

Blue-jay, who was more that reluctant to jump down here, comes next, making sure to make a lot of fuss and noise.

"That girl should be coming down any second now." Swift says quietly to Blue-jay as he helps her get to her feet. Blue-jay agrees silently.

When she steps down on her left foot, Blue-jay stumbles and then leans on Swift for support. "I think it is sprained." she practically whispers in his ear.

"Maybe you just sit down then." Swift walks Blue-jay over to the nearest wall and then helps her sit gently.

Just as she does, another screaming and flailing person drops through the air and hits the ground hard, a sharp grunt escaping her mouth. She landed face down and after she doesn't move for a while, I begin to wonder whether she is conscious or not. The girl eventually does start to move and when she does, she says, "Thanks for leading me into another trap." and then crawls forward on her stomach.

I send a confused look towards Swift and he explains, "She was in our group. I noticed her following Blue-jay and I about halfway through the maze." Swift goes over to lend a hand.

She grabs his hand and says, "Agent Lark." When she speaks I notice her braced teeth. Lark gets up one leg at a time. I think she was the one that had the most painful landing. She looks pretty muscular for her size and age, with beautiful brown skin draped on her lean frame. She must be around Owl's age, and after dusting herself off and fixing her hair, she goes and introduces herself to him and then everyone else. Nightingale and that other guy barely look at her when she does, though, and don't respond.

I spot something out of the corner of my eye and lift my head to the entrance to the pit again just as two bodies descend through the hole. A man makes contact a few seconds before the other, landing even more smoothly and gracefully than Swift (if that's possible), and then helps his companion when she arrives. I recognize both of them. The female, of course, being Robin, and the male being another person from my original group.

"Robin!" Owl yelps and then rushes over to his sister. He is surprisingly happy that she's here. She, on the other hand, reacts just as I suspect she will.

"What are you doing here?" she hisses at him, trying not to make too much of a commotion, but they are the center of attention in the solitary chamber.

He backs away from her silently and returns to his spot next to me.

Two more. I count the people in the room. *Nine people so far, one spot left.* "The last one will be coming in next." I announce for everyone else to hear. I bet Nightingale is hoping it's going to be Sleepy. I kind of am too, even though it is highly improbable; he's probably back where I left him, still hanging upside down.

Swift walks over to the spot where most of the Proxies have been coming down and looks up. He stands there for a couple minutes and we all just wait quietly for the last Enhancement trainee. I hope we can go back to bed after this.

"See anything?" I ask Swift when I get too bored. I step towards him and Owl follows me.

125

"No…" Swift says, not taking his eyes off the entrance above. "Wait…" Excitement sparks in his eyes. "Someone is coming." Swift takes a few steps back, pushing Owl and I along with him.

Our last teammate arrives a few seconds later, landing on his side and then rolling a bit.

"Congratulations," Swift says and jogs over to the newcomer. "You are the tenth and last trainee accepted into the program."

The guy moans before rolling over so we can all see him properly. I notice the sweaty kid after a moment. It's Junior. *How the hell did he beat all of the others and get here in time?*

Junior gets onto his knees and then shakes the dirt out of his sandy hair. "Dirt." he says as if he is realizing something.

"Yeah…" Swift responds and lifts Junior off the ground and onto his feet.

"There is dirt here." Junior says as if we're all missing something obvious. "Smack dab in the middle of a maze made by computers in a building that has to be one of the cleanest in the country." I don't know what it means, but he is right. And I completely missed it.

As soon as he finishes his little speech, the ground below us begins to shake, the rocks and dirt bouncing against it and dust rising and filling the air once again. I stumble around for a second until I plant my feet and stick out my arms to keep my balance. Something covers the entrance to the hole and for a few scary seconds, we are cast into a pitch black and moving entity. Soon a dim glow emanates from the walls around us, shining a little light on our situation. Most of the others have adopted a stance like mine, trying not to fall over.

As fear builds up inside me, I know that I can't just wait around for something else to happen. "What the hell is going on?" I send a look at Swift, hoping he will have some answers. He isn't looking at me when I do, so I don't get an answer or any comfort from him.

I feel the ground actually start to move, tilting to my right, where more than half of the others are standing, and where Blue-jay is sitting and leaning against the wall. She begins to fall backward into the space between the square slab we're standing on and the wall. And that's when I realize that the walls are moving too; moving away and leaving us on a square island, trying not to fall off and into who knows what.

Blue-jay screams as she too realizes her situation and that catches Swift's attention. He dives and slides down the sloping slab, causing the whole thing to tip even more.

I grab Owl and pull him along with me, away from the center and more to the opposite side to the lower part. I lean back and try not to slip. Swift succeeds in catching Blue-jay's extended hand as she hangs halfway off the mass. The ground balances out a bit more, because of Owl and I, but not enough to make too much of a difference. If I don't do something, Swift and Blue-jay will fall off. The others are trying not to fall off too.

I shout across the expanse, "Help me balance this thing out! All of you over there come toward Owl and I." Nightingale, Lark and Junior start part walking, part climbing up the hunk of rock and toward the middle. Robin and her friend were already pretty close to the center, so I direct the other guy, who is near Owl and me, to move there too. The ground balances out nice and slowly until it rests with it leaning a little bit more on Blue-jay and Swift's end. Their combined weight is heavier than Owl's and mine.

Robin takes a step toward them, wanting to help, but I shout at her, "Do not move! You will throw the whole thing out of balance!" It feels good to shout at her after all she's done to Owl.

Swift manages to pull Blue-jay back onto the island and they both get to their feet slowly, holding onto each other to keep their balance. The ground shudders when Swift takes a step in our direction.

"Maybe you should stay there until we figure something out."

Swift smiles nervously is response and raises two thumbs at me.

"So what do we do now?" The guy that came down with Robin asks.

Nightingale moves from her place and shouts, "What the fuck are they trying to pull? Hawk said that all we had to do is reach the center and I'm here, so... Maybe we're supposed to jump again." She begins to walk towards the edge closest to her, on my left, and the rest of us have to deal with the consequences. I quickly move to the right side while the others stumble around in the center. Swift's and Blue-jay's side dips even further; Owl's rises.

"Don't you dare!" Robin hisses at her and steps forward to bring her back.

"Lark, get over here!" I shout in an attempt to even everything out.

Lark begins to make her way to me when Swift yells, "Robin get back, you are not helping! And you," he points at Nightingale, "are not going anywhere."

Robin goes back to the center, making Lark's journey futile. "Never mind, go help out Owl." I instruct her. "You too, Junior." Lark crosses over to Owl and so does Junior.

Swift takes over the leadership role and speaks, "I think this is another test. One to see how well we work together, and right now, I think we're failing." He almost falls when Nightingale walks back over to the center, causing my side to be the lowest one. I use all of my limbs when trying to reach the others. At least Nightingale is cooperating now.

When Swift regains his footing he continues, "The worst team player here, is the only one trying to do something." He means me and I am not sure if I should take is as a compliment or not. "So, let's take a moment to learn about our new friends and then finish up and go back to sleep." I think he convinced us all with the going back to sleep thing. He looks at everyone in turn and then introduces himself, "I am Agent Swift and I came here with this lovely lady—" he gestures to Blue-jay. I wrinkle my nose and then practically fall on my face because of my momentary lack of focus. My muscles ache from trying to stand still for so long.

His cue goes unnoticed until Swift nudges Blue-jay with his elbow. "Oh, yeah, I am Agent Blue-jay." she says and then tries to not catch anybody's eye. But how could we not? She's beautiful even down here, covered in sweat and dirt.

I notice Swift staring at me and I feel self-conscious for a moment, and then I realize that he wants me to support his idea and introduce myself next. "I'm Wren, I was the third person to come down."

"What happened to your face?" Nightingale asks, obviously trying to be disruptive.

I explain calmly, "I fell through a trapdoor and smashed my face against the floor. I think it's broken."

Owl takes over before Nightingale can get out another question meant to insult me. "I'm Owl, unfortunately the second one to fall into the hole," He pauses a moment to chuckle, "I literally ran into this guy and we came plummeting—"

Both Swift and the guy don't want Owl to go into details, the guy sending Owl a threatening look. "Yeah, I will take it from here," the man says in his harsh voice. "I was the first one to make it. Agent Koel." Koel has pale skin, straight black hair styled in the same way as Swift and dark, almost almond shaped eyes. It's pretty rare to see someone who looks like him. His pajama shirt is a tank-top, so I can make out a circular tattoo on his shoulder.

In the warm orange-y glow of the walls, I can finally see the people around me. The large group in the middle and the pairs on the sides. My teammates.

"Hey, you skipped me!" Lark exclaims in excitement. "I'm Lark." She flashes those braced teeth and twirls a tightly braided strand of her dark brown hair. "Figuring they're some of the smartest people here, I followed Swift and Blue-jay through the whole maze." Lark grins as if this is some big accomplishment.

Robin speaks, her bangs slightly askew, and then the guy she came with. His most noticeable feature is his golden blond hair. He smiles kindly as he says his name, "Jardah, I'm Osprey. It is a pleasure to meet you all." His pleasant voice wafts to every corner of the large and gloomy space.

Junior speaks up next; I can't see him in the midst of the giants Koel, Nightingale and Osprey, but he sounds nervous and out of breath, "Agent Goldcrest." I guess I'll have to start calling him by his Proxy name from now on.

Nightingale bursts into action, "How the fuck did *you* manage to get here?"

"It was quite simple actually," Goldcrest keeps his cool much like I did, "I just found three separate doors and answered the questions. I barely ran into any booby-traps." *Smart kid;* I praise him silently.

Nightingale is last and keeps her introduction short, then says, "So, what now, self-appointed leader?"

Swift rolls his eyes, but ignores her jab, "Balance this out completely."

"That isn't going to solve anything." Koel states.

"Do you have a better idea?" Swift challenges everyone.

Other than Nightingale's stupid suggestion of jumping off, there is no other solution. Swift recognizes the silence as him being right and continues with his plans, "I'm not the best at calculations, so... Wren, Goldcrest and Robin, if you could please help me out..."

Goldcrest steps out into the open to get a better look and stands next to me. Blue-jay and Swift are on one side, Lark and Owl are on the opposite one, while the rest of us are in the center. The slab is highly unstable, dipping on Swift's side and causing me to readjust my footing every couple second. "Okay, two in each side and then two in the center... Swift, how much do you weigh?" Goldcrest asks.

Swift thinks for a moment before answering, "Approximately one hundred and seventy-five pounds."

"And you, Agent Koel?"

"Over two hundred." Koel responds quickly.

"Hmm... So that will not work." Goldcrest concludes.

Robin joins in, "Maybe we should switch out Lark for Nightingale..."

Then I have the solution, "Osprey and I should switch out Lark and Owl."

Goldcrest's eyes brighten when he realizes that I am right, "Yes! That should work."

I grab Osprey's forearm. I don't usually like physical contact, but I need to keep an eye on him and this way we'll move faster together. He seems a little taken aback by the gesture. "Okay, we need to work in synchronization." I lock eyes with Owl and make sure he understands. He nods his head without a word. He and I take a step towards each other at the same time. Slowly, Osprey and I walk closer to the edge, passing Owl and Lark on our way. Owl takes a second to wink at me before continuing.

I stop Osprey about a foot from the edge and then turn around. The ground seems to be flat. I take a moment to grin.

While we four were switching places, Goldcrest was figuring the rest out. "Lark will go to that side," He points to my left, "with Nightingale, and Robin you should go over there with Owl." He, of course, gestures to the edge to my right. Koel and Goldcrest stay in the center.

At first I think that Owl and Robin working together won't end well, but neither of them say a word and the task is finished smoothly. I have to shift my weight while they move, but everything seems to be alright in the end.

When the four finish adjusting themselves, something clicks and the lights dim. The square hole above us opens again and another

131

shudder spreads through the ground. I start to worry that another test is about to start when, from the center of the island, a ladder grows. It rises and rises until it reaches the entrance of the hole. We can finally leave.

I step forward first and reach the ladder without any problems; the ground doesn't move or shift. I lick my lips and grab the third rung of the ladder. The taste of dried blood fills my mouth. I take my time climbing up.

When my head pops through the entrance, the bright lights make it nearly impossible to see, but my eyes soon adjust and pick up the now clear, and seemingly smaller, room and Hawk, who waits for me at the top. He holds out a hand for me to take and I do. Hawk pulls me up and out and I finally reach steady land, my legs feeling like jelly.

"Holy shit, what happened to you?" Hawk asks when he has had a good look at me.

I pause for a moment to think about that question. I was torn off from my friend, shot with a tranquilizing dart (and didn't even realize until now that I was bleeding from the puncture wound), fell through a trap door, broke my nose, practically betrayed a different friend, was almost crushed to death, fell about fifteen feet, and rolled around in dirt. I simply reply, "I had a rough night." and then step aside so the others can get up too. Although I don't exactly enjoy being tested in this way, I do see why it needed to be done. At least I passed and we actually work kind of well as a team.

I practically fall asleep standing while waiting for the other nine to climb out. All of the adrenaline is gone and I can feel every ache and injury in my body.

Swift touches my arm lightly and my eyes flutter open. He nods his head towards Hawk and I try to focus on what he is saying.

"This time I mean it when I say this—congratulations, you are the final ten." Goldcrest claps once and then realizes that maybe he shouldn't continue. Nightingale looks super pissed in general as well as Blue-jay, who leans against Osprey. "Tomorrow morning, in seven hours, we will officially begin. I will arrange lessons and team-building activities for throughout the week and then you will all attend the final Enhancer experiments." *Finally, we're really about to begin!* "You better head off to bed now, because the next few months will be very busy."

He doesn't have to tell me twice. I am the first one to start making my way out of the room. Some of the others linger and talk, but I am too tired and definitely don't feel like talking.

I notice Swift at my heel, "Exciting, huh?" he asks.

"Yeah, I guess so." I respond and then yawn.

"I've noticed that you don't express your feelings very often."

And...? "Emotions are distractions." I inaccurately quote my father; I don't have the energy to remember the correct phrase. "Goodnight, Swift." I get into the elevator and watch as Swift turns around and heads back to HABITAT.

I move like a zombie back to my dorm and somehow the key is still in my jacket pocket. It would have really sucked if I had lost it. I take a few moments to clean up, changing my clothes and washing off, and make sure my nose has stopped bleeding. Now that I have time to examine it, I don't think it's broken, but it will definitely be bruised for the next week or so.

I fall asleep almost immediately after getting into bed.

Chapter Thirteen

In the morning, when he sun has actually risen already, I hurry to get dressed and eat breakfast, and then head down to the basement. I find everyone waiting for me and then Hawk goes right into finishing the tour he started a few hours before. No one mentions my bruised nose or the other things that happened last night. I guess we're all a little relieved to have finally made it.

Hawk shows us some shooting ranges, more exercise rooms, the bathroom and a supply closet full of weapons. When he is done he says, "We won't do any training today, though. Let's head back to the classroom to just talk."

Talking? That's not what I want to do. I didn't go through all that crap to talk.

Going to the classroom we pass HABITAT, which calls to me silently. Half of me wants to train some more in it, but the other half wants to run as far away from it as possible.

Hawk walks into the room before us and then the rest of us run in, trying to find seats next to our friends. It reminds me of high school. I sit in the back corner. Swift is at the desk in front of me.

Blue-jay stares blankly near the entrance; there are only nine chairs. She runs her hand along the top of her head, smoothing down any run-away hair.

"Oh, Blue-jay, here have my spot." Robin jumps up when she notices. Swift and Osprey move too.

"No, it is okay." Blue-jay mumbles and doesn't take Robin's seat despite her injured ankle. Blue-jay backs up and leans against the wall.

Hawk types something into his T-Screen before stepping forward and taking control of the situation. I eye him suspiciously. "Sorry about that Blue-jay. The board wasn't sure if Agent Goldcrest would be able to join us today after last night's test, so we only had nine chairs set up. I'll be sure to get someone to set up another spot for you by tomorrow." Hawk consults the T-Screen again and then continues. "The order of today's lesson goes like this: We will spend some time getting to know each other better and then I will show you some of the new abilities I have because of the Enhancer." I grow excited about the Enhancer, but am not looking forward to 'getting to know each other'. "I'll read out some basic information about each of you and then after that; you should tell the group a little more about yourself." Before any of us can respond he begins, "I will begin with Agent Wren, who is not unfamiliar with the Enhancer. Your real name is Wren MacGregor." he starts. "Age eighteen, born November sixth. Height: five foot seven; and weight: one hundred and thirty-five pounds."

Why is he telling everything about me to these people? There are murmurs around the room as the others agree with my line of thought. I try to be as careful as I can while confronting Hawk, "Pardon me, but should you be—"

"Silence!" he shouts, and if I didn't already know Hawk, I would be really nervous right now. He turns to everyone, "You are going to work as a well-oiled machine. You need to know everything about each other so there won't be any surprises on the field. Secrets can get people killed. If I don't think you are working well with the others I can have you replaced." This shuts everyone up immediately. He gazes at me again, "Ex-Preacher. One of three children. Your father is Agent Hummingbird, developer of the Enhancement chip. Qualified for Security and Field, you have been a Proxy for one month."

Someone scoffs further down the aisle. I peer past Swift to see Nightingale smirking and talking to Koel, "I knew she had to have some reason to be here, there is no way they would have accepted her if her father hadn't have gotten her in." Then she looks at someone in the other corner, "Well I'm not too sure; *he* got in." She glares at Goldcrest. I pay her no attention. We both got in fair and square and she knows it.

Koel does not respond. He keeps a non-expressive face and looks straight ahead.

Hawk intervenes, "Okay, it looks like you want to be next, Agent Nightingale."

"No, it's ok—"

Hawk marches over to Nightingale and begins her evaluation, "Agent Nightingale, your real name is Dejah Smith. Ex-Preacher," A shot of anger appears on her face, but she quickly tries to hide her emotions. "Age: twenty-two, born on November thirtieth. Height: five foot ten, weight: one hundred and fifty pounds. You qualified for Security and Field and have been a Proxy for five years. You are an only child. Your parents are still Preachers." Nightingale scoffs again and tries to not look anyone in the eye as she reclines in her chair and twists her lip ring.

"Agent Swift." Hawk nods at Swift. Swift turns back to smile uncomfortably at me. Everything about him will be revealed to me soon enough, but not just to me, but to everyone. I furrow my brow in frustration as a strange pang of jealousy fills my gut.

"Also known as Sloane Ian Henderson. Twenty-one years old, born on March twenty-first, five foot nine, one hundred and seventy-six pounds. Qualified for Security, Liaison and Field."

Swift nods, like he is agreeing. Hawk doesn't mention his family. I want to ask Swift about his past, but I know this isn't a good time.

Hawk looks at the seat next to Swift. Owl bounces in his chair, grinning. Robin is on his other side. She sniffles quietly into her shirt sleeve.

"Agent Owl," Hawk reassures Owl with a smile, "Your name is… Dim… ri—"

"The 'M', 'H', 'I' and 'T' are silent. It is pronounced Di'ran." Robin explains.

Owl looks at her grudgingly. I chuckle softly. *How is his name spelled?*

"Okay... Di'ran Williams, you are fifteen years old, born on June second." Owl nods eagerly. "You are five foot three and weigh one hundred and thirty-one pounds. Ex-Preacher, orphan and brother to Agent Robin. You qualified for Security and Liaison." When Hawk finishes Owl wipes his brow dramatically. He gives Swift a low-five under his desk.

Hawk continues to Robin.

"Robin, your real name is Irene Williams. You are nineteen years old, born on April eleventh. Five foot five and weighs one hundred and forty-two pounds. Ex-Preacher, orphan, sister to Agent Owl." Hawk repeats their shared history. "You qualified for Liaison, Medical and Security." She looks solemnly at Hawk, silently asking if he is done.

Hawk turns away from us and talks to Blue-jay who stands because there aren't enough desks.

She doesn't look Hawk in the eyes and plays with the hem of her button-down white shirt. She yawns as Hawk starts her evaluation.

He moans happily, "Agent Blue-jay, real name is Wisteria Hera Conner. You are twenty four years of age, born on January first. Oh, happy birthday."

Today is the third. I wonder why she didn't say anything.

"You are five foot seven, one hundred and thirty-eight pounds. Your father is one of the founding members of NEST. You qualified for Security and Liaison."

Hawk finishes and goes to the back of the room, to the opposite corner from me. All of this movement is making my neck hurt.

"Agent Goldcrest. Your real name is Ronny Jones. You are sixteen years old." Goldcrest looks as if he might vomit. I have been introduced to two new names of his today. "Born on December thirteenth. You are five foot four and weigh one hundred and six pounds." He looks skinny, but I didn't know how thin he really is.

"Qualified for Security; you have only been an Agent one month."

"Agent Lark." Hawk side-steps to Lark in between Goldcrest and me.

"Your real name is Dot Alice Bradshaw. You are fifteen years old, born on May eighth. You are five foot two, one hundred and twenty-four pounds. Your family lives in the NEST civilian quarters, is that correct?"

"Yep." she giggles.

I sigh. *She is going to be a liability.*

"Very good. Agent Koel!"

"Sir yes, sir." Koel bursts into a standing position and salutes.

"Shichirou Timothy Crimson is your real name. You are twenty six, born on February twenty ninth. Six foot five; two hundred and three pounds. You are an orphan. You qualified for Security and Field."

"Am I excused, sir?" The way he speaks is like some sort of chant.

"Of course."

Even sitting, the guy is huge, his legs stretched out under the desk so he doesn't bump his knees.

Osprey smiles as he acknowledges that he is the only one left.

"Agent Osprey, real name: Hezro Leroy James. You are twenty years of age and were born on August twenty fifth. You are exactly six feet tall and weigh one hundred and seventy-nine pounds. You have five siblings who are not a part of NEST." *He could be an ex-Preacher.* "You qualified for Security, Liaison and Medical." Hawk returns to his place at the head of the classroom, "That is everyone, now onto more personal information." *Even more personal information? No thank you.* "So, Wren, how about you come up here and tell us a little bit more about yourself. I hope that sometime throughout the course all of you will share your backstories with us."

I slowly push my chair away from the desk, waiting for Hawk to change his mind. He doesn't.

I can feel everyone's eyes on my back as I walk to the front of the room. I tell myself to keep it short and not give away too much information.

"I'm Wren." I gaze at the back wall, not making eye contact with anyone. Well except for Swift occasionally. "I moved to NEST a few months ago and have been working in Security for the past month." *Tell them what they want to hear,* "And I am really looking forward to working with all of you." I try to look friendly with those last words. It doesn't seem to work. Swift gives me an encouraging smile.

Hawk sighs, obviously disappointed with my 'deep backstory.' "Come on, Wren dig deep. You need to trust these people. You will be working with them for as long as I can foresee, well unless..." He throws the whole replacement thing in my face, knowing that I will do anything to stay in this course.

Fine... I try to think of something that no one else knows except maybe my family. "Um, okay. Helena Bones was my birth name. I was a Preacher, along with my family, till I was ten years old. My father was very important so they could not just let us go. I spent five years on the run, changing my name so many times I cannot even remember all of them." Sabrina, Domino, Eris. It changed too often and I would never really be Helena Bones again. "Then I finally settled down in Tieced with the name Wren Paradox MacGregor."

"Paradox." Hawk ponders. "That is a very odd name. Did you choose it?"

"Yeah."

"For any particular reason?"

I chose the middle name 'Paradox' of course; thankfully I don't have parents that would give me a ridiculous name like that. I chose it because that is what I feel like. Technically my real name is Helena, but she doesn't exist anymore, and to the government and everyone else I am Wren, but she isn't real. So I am a fake person no longer existing or real. These names cancel out each other; I am a paradox. They leave me with nothing; I am nameless.

And besides, names don't really matter to Preachers; they see people as mistakes and failures either to be fixed or destroyed.

"No."

"Okay, Wren. Thank you for sharing."

"No problem." I mutter and stride away and sit in silence, crossing my arms over my chest.

"Would anyone else like to volunteer?" Hawk returns to the head of the room, "Nightingale?"

She shakes her head. *Of course I'm the only one who doesn't have an option. Well at least I got it over with.*

"That should be good for now, you all had a rough night." Hawk concludes, "This was just an introductory meeting, you can go back to your regular duties. I guess I will save the Enhancer for tomorrow." He waves his hand and dismisses us.

"That's it?" I ask Swift as we exit together.

"For now." Swift repeats what Hawk said. We continue down the hall and take the elevator with the rest of the crew. "Do you have a shift next?"

"Yeah." I say, disappointed. It's not like I don't like serving the refugees, but I had hoped to be free of those duties. I had hoped we would be busier and get through the training. At least I will be able to see that little girl again. I had recently learned that her name is Mara. It is nice to have a friend... who doesn't know anything about me.

Swift gets off of the elevator on the main level.

"See you later." He hugs me and then leaves.

My stomach twists into a knot. I must have eaten something bad. I put my hand on my stomach and look at it grumpily. *This is not the time, stomach.*

I walk back to my room after dropping Owl off at the cafeteria. I have noticed that he eats a lot.

I change my clothes into something more appropriate for guard duty and then attach the NEST symbol onto the sleeve of my shirt. I got it the day after becoming an Agent. It's a patch that I can easily put on any fabric, which is nice. The symbol is the same as any other Proxy's. It is hard to describe. It is kind of like a sideways curved 'Z' with a circle in the middle with zig-zagging lines coming from that dot. I never noticed them before I got my own.

I grab a weapon from the stock they keep on the main floor and head down to the living spaces.

"Agent Wren?" I hear that familiar child's voice. Mara. "I am bored."

I turn to her, "So am I."

"Can I ask you a question?"

"Okay." I wait for her to ask me.

"Do you know what the weather is outside?" She looks curiously at me expecting me to know the answer. I haven't checked the weather schedule in a while. I also haven't left the NEST building in a few months.

"Sorry, I don't."

She pouts a little. I can't do anything for her at the moment and anyway, it's not my job to entertain the civilians and refugees.

"Maybe you should find some other children to play with." I suggest.

"Okay." She says quietly and begins to walk away, looking back at me longingly, wanting me to stop her from leaving.

I shouldn't.

I can't.

I don't.

She sighs while rounding a corner and it kind of makes me feel bad.

These refugees were targets of the Preachers. For some reason, the Preachers wanted them out of the way. By murdering, kidnapping... any way possible; for reasons that vary from attacking Preachers to smoking. They don't understand that someone might possibly not think the same way they do. I certainly don't think like they do. And I'm proud of it.

These people are stuck down here for the remainder of... of this fight against the Preachers? Until some agreement has been made? Until Preachers don't have all of this power over the government...? I don't know the answer, I really don't. I wish I did.

Chapter Fourteen

As I walk into the classroom again, I notice that the furniture has been rearranged. Another chair has been added, for Blue-jay of course, so that there are two lines of four seats in the back and a line of two in the front. It messes up the whole dynamic of the room. Desks have also been added; I hope we won't have to write anything down. I have a T-Screen of my own, but I don't have the patience.

I decide to sit in the front, closest to the giant touchscreen board that Hawk will undoubtedly write all of the important information on.

"Hey, Wren." Swift calls to me, "What are you doing over there? Come sit with us."

I turn around and see him standing with Owl in the back.

"I think I will be able to concentrate better up front." I tell them.

"Come on, Wren." Owl begs and looks at me with those big green eyes of his. I decide to give the whole sitting-with-your-friends thing a chance and move to the back of the classroom.

"Jardah, Wren." Owl greets me. "Excited for the first—"

"I am just happy we are finally starting and cannot wait to be done with this." I interrupt him.

Swift stares blankly at me, meaning that I probably said something wrong. I need to stop acting so strange, but I can never read the situation well.

I should apologize, but I don't.

Right on time Hawk walks in, partially saving me from the embarrassment.

Blue-jay hurries to the seat to the right of Swift and the four of us make up the back row.

"So… How are you?" Swift asks, seeing if I am okay.

"Good, fine, great. You?" I splutter out. I close my eyes to calm myself down, wondering why I am acting like such a fool.

"Okay." I am not sure if he says that because of my response or if he is answering my question, but I don't care because when I open my eyes, he is smiling at me.

I clutch my chest as I almost hyperventilate.

"Are you okay?" Swift looks at me bewildered.

"Yeah." I croak out. "I think I'm coming down with something though; I'll see a doctor if this keeps up."

"Sorry to interrupt your conversations, but I think we should start our first lesson." Hawk says, perfectly impersonating a real teacher.

Swift does not respond to my mention of going to see a doctor, but looks right into my eyes and then pats me on the leg.

I turn away and smile at my desk. *Yep, I think I am going to be sick.*

"As you can see, we start at eight and have oral meetings until ten. Then there will be short break and after that we will start physical training until twelve." Hawk tells us our schedule. My grin disappears and is replaced by a frown. I had hoped we'd jump right in and finish as quickly as possible, not only meet for a few hours a day. "And I still have to demonstrate some of the Enhancer's powers for you guys." This lifts my spirits a little.

But Hawk gets back to the present lesson, "So what subject should we start with now? It should be something that has a connection with Preachers or the world today." I find it a little odd that he is letting us choose. "This course is a joint effort. We have to work as a team. I need your help and your input for all of us to learn new things." He puts on the friendliest face he can muster, but it still isn't very convincing.

Goldcrest slowly and cautiously raises his hand, "How about world history?"

"Good." Hawk says, "Now where to start?"

People start talking amongst themselves about what history subject we should learn until someone shouts, "World War Three!"

144

Everyone else stops talking at the mention of this and Hawk's face becomes dark. The worst thing that has happened in human history; leaving billions of people dead and North America alone in a cold world.

Lark was the one who shouted, but that doesn't really matter.

"A good place to start." Hawk approves. He stands and sets himself in the center of the head of the room. "World War Three started in two-thousand twenty four and only lasted a few years; but it was the worst war there ever was." He spins around quickly and writes the dates on the board. "Just like World War One there was a lot of tension beforehand and everyone was waiting for one thing to set it off and start the war. The match that lit the fuse was an unofficial American drone strike in a country called Iran. Something went horribly wrong when a missile hit a nuclear power plant setting off a chain reaction resulting in a huge nuclear explosion. Iran's ally, a country called North Korea, then blamed the UN, the international governing body back then, and all hell broke loose. Even though America caused the outbreak, the US tried to stay out of the war, recalling all of their embassies and troops from Europe, Asia and Africa and left them to kill each other in a global nuclear war. It's still unclear how we were protected from attacks from these other countries, when they obviously attempted. Some theories say that the government covered the whole country with a giant shield—" Owl and some others laugh at that. *People and their conspiracy theories.* "And that isn't altogether impossible considering we have a giant shield protecting us right now." They go quiet. "Others say that the US army had an 'air defense system' that shot rockets out of the sky before they were close enough to do any damage. Well whatever happened, North America sustained little damage."

"So what happened to everyone in other parts of the world?" Lark asks.

"Most of the major cities were bombed, in every country." Hawk pauses and looks down at his shoes, "And after that, the radioactive smoke rising from the resulting fires blocked sunlight from reaching most of Earth's surface." The dark years. Everyone suffered from that. Luckily we had protection, but outside North America, those people who had survived the nuclear holocaust were soon killed off by artic temperatures and lack of food. North America had its fair share of problems too; the many diseases that spread because of resulting close quarter living and hygienic problems and there was a lack of food here too. Many of the cities that exist today were built during the dark days. "When the smoke and ash finally cleared, it was discovered that most of the ozone layer was destroyed, leaving Earth vulnerable to the Sun's deadly UV radiation and other rays. Luckily, the government predicted this and prepared. That is why we have the force-fields surrounding the cities here. The force-fields contain high concentrations of the gas, ozone. And that is why we cannot leave the cities except by train."

"I guess there were no survivors, then?" Osprey asks.

"The government sent some men on an exploratory mission around the globe years ago to check. Only twenty of the one hundred and thirty man crew came back. They reported that outside North America was nothing but barren land; it was uninhabitable."

But how about now? If we could leave this stupid country, and the Preachers, behind without a fight that would be perfect. But I guess that's impossible. And a stupid thought...

Hawk begins to smirk slightly and I wonder what he's thinking about after that depressing speech. Then he says, "Now, for the demonstration..."

Owl whoops next to me and then the whole room erupts with noise of excitement.

I can tell that Hawk is gets a little annoyed and so do I. "Please control yourselves." He walks to the door and opens it and then walks out without saying another word.

Owl looks over at Swift, who just shrugs. I guess we're supposed to follow him. Slowly we all get out of our seats, exit the classroom and rush down the hallway to HABITAT. It takes a minute for all of us to fit through the doorway.

Hawk once again stands by the control panel and I'm anxious that it was just a trick to get us in here and we'll go through another test. I grab Swift's forearm so we won't get split up and prepare to run or whatever this test will require. I watch Hawk carefully as he flips a switch, causing a grey, thick wall to burst out of the floor. I didn't realize that I was holding my breath until now when I know that I shouldn't be concerned, and exhale deeply. I also let go of Swift without looking at him; I don't want to see his reaction to my silliness.

Hawk is now close to the new wall, "Please, gather around me." he instructs. He waits for the ten to surround him and then continues with his instruction. "The Enhancer is injected in your arm," Hawk lifts his right arm and points to a place on his forearm with his left. I remember exactly where it is, but it would be impossible to spot otherwise. "And gives you two different abilities beside the physical enhancements. One is called an energy blast and the other is a personal enhancement. Mine was based on my strengths, but yours will be based on your weaknesses." He pauses and then says, "Okay, get back now." Hawk moves directly in front of the erected wall while the rest of us move back only a few steps. We want to be close to the action.

Hawk gets into a fighting stance and then punches right through the wall, little pieces falling and dust flying into the air. He pulls his arm out of the wall, causing more of it to crumble and shakes the

147

dust off of himself. "So it turns out that my biggest strength, or asset, was literally my *strength*."

"That was amazing!" Owl tries not to shout.

Swift leans closer to me and whispers, "I've seen him carry a couch with one finger."

"Yeah, right." I push him away, teasing.

"Now the energy blasts!" Lark cries.

Hawk starts to walk back to the panel, "Fine, but this time you guys really do need to stand back, I am not always in control when it comes to the blasts." He types some things on a keyboard and the wall disappears, another appearing further down in the vast room. Hawk steps away and walks to the center of the ginormous room, still pretty far away from the new target.

Owl takes a step closer to it and Hawk, who is setting up for an energy blast, so I lift my arm against his chest and hold him back. I've seen what the Enhancer can do and that was just a couple minutes after injection.

Some of the others move to get a better look too and just when I'm about to yell at them, Swift does, "Hey, he said to stay away, so get back." And I am reminded that Swift was there when Hawk first used his powers too. It seems so long ago, and Swift seems like such a different person to me now.

A bright light comes from Hawk, bringing my attention back to him. The glow seems to move across his skin, first appearing around his right arm and then all over his body and then finally it all vanishes except for around both of his arms. I can barely see his arms the sparks are so strong. I shield my eyes and then look over at Owl, whose expression is one of joy and awe, the light bouncing off of his eyes.

Hawk shouts and I know what's happening now, I turn back to Hawk just in time to see him step forward and thrust his hands forward. The energy leaves his body and flies straight ahead of him and hits the barrier. It blasts a hole in the wall, but doesn't go all the way through. Hawk stumbles a little and then leans forward and places his hands on his knees.

"Wow." I hear Owl whisper.

Goldcrest is the first person to go over and help Hawk, "Incredible!" he exclaims and puts his hand on Hawk's back for support. I doubt Goldcrest could hold up Hawk if he collapses, so I grab Swift and rush over to Hawk too.

"Still having trouble I see." I mumble to Hawk so only he can hear. Now everyone is surrounding Hawk again.

He sort of glares at me and then stands up straight. "The Enhancer uses up a lot of your energy and I am still getting used to some of the side-effects of that."

"Will we have any problems?" asks Nightingale.

"If you eat properly and gets lots of sleep you should get over it pretty easily." He pauses and looks at all of us. "It also helps to be in good shape."

Goldcrest grabs Hawk's forearm full of curiosity, "How does the Enhancer work exactly?"

Hawk pulls away from Goldcrest, "The chip causes a huge amount of energy to be made in my body, which tries to get rid of it somehow. I can use this energy however I want, usually by throwing it, but sometimes it launches automatically from me in blasts." That's what happened the first time he used the Enhancer. "Are there any more questions?"

Robin raises her hand slightly and asks, "What did you mean when you said that our special power will be based on our weaknesses?"

"The new Enhancers made for all of you have been improved slightly from the original prototype that I have. Your most prominent weakness will be effected by the Enhancer and diminished, so you will be a well-rounded fighting machine." *That sounds reasonable.* "Therefore, one of the goals of this pre-Enhancer course is to find

149

out what your greatest flaw is. It will be very personal and could be emotional." *Unfortunately.*

I had already started thinking about my flaws when Dad told me about the adjustment, but still haven't figured out which is my biggest. I can be pretty stubborn and impatient, but those probably aren't things an Enhancer can fix. And they're not *that* bad anyway.

"While you think about that, we're going to have a group activity." Hawk steps out of the room for a moment and comes back with pistols.

He tosses one to each person. Goldcrest doesn't catch his and it clatters across the floor.

"Butterfingers." Nightingale smirks.

Goldcrest runs after it and then wipes his hands on his shirt before picking up the weapon.

"Swift and Koel; you are the team captains. Pick your teammates while I set up the lay-out of the room." Hawk grins mischievously and turns away to play with his toy.

"Do you want to go first?" Swift asks Koel. *He's too nice; he needs to take his shots while he can.*

Luckily Koel shakes his head and lets Swift choose first.

Please pick me, please pick me.

"Wren." Swift calls out.

Even though I was the most logical choice, because I am one of the best fighters and his friend, for some reason I'm relieved that he chooses me.

I don't need to move, because I'm already standing next to him.

Koel wants Osprey on his team next. He would have been my next choice.

"I really want Blue-jay on our side, but who do you think?" Swift quietly consults with me.

I roll my eyes. *What does he see in her? She has no personality at all.*

150

"How about Owl? He is our friend too." I would prefer someone who is a better fighter, but that would be Nightingale and we don't get along.

Swift nods and whispers, "Yeah, you're right." Then he says for everyone to hear, "Owl."

Owl jumps around and then joins us facing Koel from six feet away. This is on.

"Blue-jay." Koel announces while glaring right in to Swift's eyes.

"Crap." Swift mutters, "We should've picked her before." *Too bad.*

"Maybe Nightingale?" Swift asks Owl and me.

We both give him the same irritated look at the same time.

"Okay, okay, relax." Swift teases us and then tells Robin to come over to us, but that isn't a very good decision either. Owl has a hard time not exploding at Swift as Robin uncomfortably makes her way to our side.

Our opponents then choose Nightingale. It appears that they will have the strong team, while we'll be the loveable misfits. Will we make a miraculous comeback or fall flat on our faces?

Lark and Goldcrest are left; neither is a very good prospect. We can't go wrong with our choice. I find Lark annoying and I already know Goldcrest so I advise Swift to take the latter. He agrees.

Goldcrest stumbles over to us and I see a small smile appear on his face before disappearing in a pool of sweat and clammy hands. Owl and Robin greet him warmly and that leaves Lark to the others. Osprey is the only one who attempts to make her feel welcome.

Hawk returns from setting up the machine, "Everything is ready." He gathers Koel and Swift next to him, "The first team to have all of its members disqualified is the loser." *Basic stuff.* "The way to take someone out of the game is to shoot them with your gun. It will not do any real damage, it just shocks you. The worst it could do knock someone out, but at least you will know you are out of the game."

Swift doesn't look relieved at all. "There is one catch: each gun only has two good shots." That changes things a bit.

"What happens if you lose?" Swift asks, I don't think he thinks our chances are very good.

"All of the activities are here to test how well you work as a team and if you really fit in here with the group, so if you lose, that probably means you didn't work well with your teammates and that you don't truly belong here." *So this is another test after all.* Hawk raises his voice slightly, "Yes, if you have not already understood, you can still be replaced." His words leave a strange feeling hanging in the room. *So technically, this is a competition. And everyone will be trying their hardest.*

Hawk instructs us to move back to the opposite walls, "Are you all ready?" he asks. There are a few weak responses. "I am not going to make the room too hard to maneuver, but be careful. Good luck." *Stay safe, run and don't get too attached.* I finish his sentence mentally before he presses the button.

Barriers sprout out of the ground all around us, blocking our view of Koel and the others.

"You guys heard the plan, right?" Swift asks.

"I wouldn't exactly call that a plan; just the objective." I say, "I think we should be very careful with our ammunition."

"Who are the best shots here?" Swift asks the other members.

Goldcrest looks at Robin and Owl before saying, "I guess I'm okay." *Oh, boy.*

"Great." Swift tries to say as sincerely as possible, "So Wren, Goldcrest and I will be handling the weapons. We should get good positions and then—"

"And what about me?" Owl asks and stops before adding, "And Robin?" while handing over his gun.

"You guys will be the bait." Swift tells him. *What is he trying to do? If Robin and Owl work together, we are sure to fail.*

152

I almost come forward and tell him this, but decide to let Swift take the lead. I have to remind myself a couple times that Hawk made Swift the team leader.

"Great, I've always wanted to be bait." Owl grins.

Swift continues with his plan, "The three of us will go into the buildings and onto the rooftops, finding a spot with a good view of the area, where we will wait until we have a clear shot before firing."

"Yes, a clear shot." I emphasize 'clear shot' so Goldcrest knows not to fire without knowing for sure it's going to hit or I will hurt him myself.

"You two need to be good targets and make the other team come out of hiding to shoot at you. But you will have to either dive out of the way or we'll shoot them before they even put their finger on a trigger." Swift tries to put confidence behind his words.

"That sounds like a plan to me." Robin agrees to it.

Swift is doing a good job in his leadership role so far. "Sounds good to me too; they should already be on the move." I rush them, "You all in?"

"Yep." Owl puts his hand in the middle of our circle.

Swift places his on top of it and so do Goldcrest and Robin. I think the whole hand thing is cheesy and stupid, but incase Hawk is somehow watching us, I place my hand on the others' and wrap my fingers around them, trying to be as friendly and as much of a team player as I can. We *are* pretty close, at least compared to the other group. Then a thought comes to me — *why is Hawk pinning us against each other, making rivalries, when we are all supposed to get along and work together in the long-run?*

"Let's move. The minute we see a sign of the enemy, we split up into our respective roles." Swift breaks and I walk at his right side as we head straight ahead in the direction of our opponents.

I tuck one Taser in the back of my waistband and keep the other in my right hand.

Owl messes around with Robin and Goldcrest behind us, and I want to tell them to shut up, but I don't. Well I don't get the chance to. Believe me, if I could, I would.

First I hear the gun go off and then comes the high-pitched squeal of the flying projectile. A small, sparkling object flies overhead, missing us by a long shot, and hits the wall behind us. It sparks and then falls dully onto the floor.

"Damn it, Lark." I hear Koel's condescending voice say.

I pause and look around for them, not really paying attention to my surroundings, but searching for their hiding place.

A glint appears in the corner of my eye. I turn to see another electric pellet being shot at us.

"Get down!" I shout, pushing Goldcrest to the ground, as I dive behind some structure.

After a second, I climb onto my knees and blow my hair out of my face. Luckily, no one was hurt, except for maybe Goldcrest, who got bruised by the tumble. My team joins me behind the piece of cover, which is actually a bench. A concrete one.

Taking in the construction around us I notice the other benches and a fountain with a statue spraying water just a few feet away... And trees; they can't be real, though. A break in the close and crowded city; we're in a park. My mouth curls into a smile despite the danger I am in.

I love parks. I will have to come back here later with Swift.

"Did you see where it came from?" Swift pats me on the shoulder and I flinch.

"Um..." I try to remember. It all happened so fast and I wasn't even facing it at the time. "I think the shot came from that direction." I point across the street.

Swift follows the line from my finger past the top of the statue's funny cubic red hat and into an empty window.

"Are you sure?" Swift asks. "I was hoping they'd be on the ground."

"Not entirely. Maybe we can lure them out." I wink and say just loud enough for our side to hear, "We're going to split up now; Robin and Owl should try to get everyone else out of hiding and out into the open. Okay?" I ask to make sure they understand.

"Sure." Robin says.

Owl rubs his hands together while grinning devilishly and I know he's ready and excited to begin. I just hope we're not making a terrible mistake. Swift will probably get the blame if this goes wrong.

I say a silent prayer for success and motion Swift and Goldcrest forward.

The three of us take off from our hiding spot at the same time and then stop behind a short wall.

Swift asks, "Goldcrest do you want to take the other extra gun?"

My eyes get big and my expression wild as I stop and send Swift a message, 'What do you think you're doing?' behind Goldcrest's back.

Swift chokes back a laugh as Goldcrest tells him he can keep it.

Another gunshot blasts out from behind us. *We need to hurry.*

We run diagonally to where I think they're hiding while crouching.

I make a suggestion, "How about we take the three corners of the park that aren't already occupied?" Even though Swift is technically in charge, I can't not be in control somehow.

"Great idea." Swift approves. "You should take this one, Goldcrest." It's the closest one to us at the moment, the least amount of distance the better. "You will get to your position first, so you will have to cover us while we are on our way to our posts."

"No problem, I already have been."

What? I pause outside the entrance to where Goldcrest will be stationed. Looking back I see Goldcrest facing away from us holding out his gun shakily pointing in every direction. He *has* already been watching our backs. I was foolish to not be more careful. We've been walking in plain sight and I didn't even think to check if we were protected or not.

I take up his position and pat him on the back awkwardly, "Thanks."

He walks inside the empty and dark house and Swift and I wait until he has time to get to the top floors.

"You take that one, and I'll take this?" Swift suggests and for himself points to the building past Robin and Owl, the direction we just came from. It will take him the longest to get there. But my location is the closest to the enemy unit.

"I'll escort you, of course." He moves closer to me.

His decision is somewhat irrational. I can get there fine on my own and his going with me could put him in even more danger, but I'll risk it.

Swift starts toward the building. I make sure the coast is clear, signal to Goldcrest who is at the window on the third floor and then walk hastily after Swift.

Swift jogs in the tree line between the open park and the suffocating city. He tries to stay behind the trees as much as possible and stay out of the enemy's line of sight.

When I catch up with him I hear the whistle of a flying charged bullet. Before I have time to react, Swift is on top of me and we fall safely behind the trunk of a thick tree. Once I know we're safe, I quickly pull away from Swift. I push against the tree trunk while standing up. With my touch, the bark flickers blue for a second and then goes back to normal. This disappoints me, for some reason I had hoped they were real trees, even though impossible, especially in here.

I hear some shuffling and then two bangs ring throughout the area. Swift hops to his feet and then we begin to bob in and out of the branches. We stop to stoop next to a bush. Hopefully Robin and Owl have started running around and Goldcrest is picking them off, while Swift and I are making our way through the woods. We should move faster, get to our objective and then win this training activity. I can feel my heart beat in my chest.

"We're lucky." I whisper. Swift lightly bumps into me and leaves it at that. I feel my face slowly grow warm as I look away grinning, self-conscious. It must be red too.

I lift my free hand to my forehead, but quickly give up trying to figure out if I have a fever; I can never tell.

"Swift, do I have a fever?" I ask him and he quickly places the back of his hand on my cheek.

His cool skin on mine makes me shiver.

Swift laughs quietly at some inside joke, "You really must be sick, Wren." He takes his hand away and urges me onward, "You keep going; it's not that far. I'll head back."

"Okay." I sigh; a part of me doesn't want him to leave me. I try my best to suppress that part of me.

On my way to the doorway that leads to a black pit of a building, I look back at him once to make sure he is still squatting behind the bush.

I stop again in the entrance to see Swift running away swiftly, and then I plunge into the seeming darkness.

It's not as bad as I thought; my eyes get used to the lack of light quickly and I find the stairs in the back corner. After rushing up three flights of stairs, I'm tired and decide that this will be the perfect spot to make my little nest. I place myself at a window facing the enemy and take the extra gun out of my pants and set it on the window sill. Propped up on my knees I finally gaze outside. I have a perfect view of the battlefield and the enemy side. They are straight ahead.

Robin and Owl are doing an excellent job of keeping Koel and his team busy, while our snipers wait for an opening. I realize now how stupid of me it was to shame Swift's idea of giving his pistol to

Goldcrest. Swift and I have only reached our positions now and Goldcrest is probably out of ammunition while we haven't used any.

Owl stands in the fountain now, totally soaked and taunting Nightingale. That kid has guts. Nightingale stands in the doorway of their building and is one of the only ones not completely outside. I wait for her to step out in the open and when she does I aim, take a deep breath and pull the trigger while exhaling.

My charge hits her way before she has a chance to raise her weapon at Owl again. Her body tremors as she is electrocuted and then Nightingale falls flat on her butt. I laugh out loud.

I see something fly from Swift's area and then Osprey going down. We are winning.

Lark scoots lower behind her rock after my missile ricochets off of it. She cowers and doesn't even lift her head or try to help her team; she must have used up all of her bullets and Koel had sent her there in shame.

I pop up to reach the other gun when I notice Koel staring right at me from all the way across the park. My hand just grazes the steel as he rests his gun on his other forearm to stabilize it. I drop to the floor as fast as I can and only brush the last of the ammunition with my fingers. I hold on to the vain hope that I didn't knock it off the ledge and don't even pay attention to the bullet that misses me because I am listening so intently.

When the metallic clang of the gun hitting the pavement from four floors below reaches my ears, I shake my head in disappointment.

I lift my head just high enough to see out of the opening. Goldcrest appears flattened against a wall between my corner and his. I hope he is going to make a run for my gun. I dare to stick my neck out a little further to watch Goldcrest run in the other direction, to Robin who is jumping in the trees. Swift is the only one left to protect them.

I have to help; I think and make a dash for the stairs.

I make it to the last staircase easily, but halfway down the lights go out. Not just the lights in the surrounding park and buildings, but in the entire room. I can't see the ledge under me and go tumbling down to the main floor.

I moan at the bottom and lay there for a few seconds, but don't have time to assess my wounds because a blood curdling scream rings out, filling even the edges and corners of this gigantic room.

What happened? Who is that? I find the wall and follow it around to the exit. Everything looks exactly the same: a pitch black that no eye could get accustomed to.

"Robin? Where are you?" I hear Owl frantically calling his sister.

Someone is sobbing somewhere near me.

"Turn the lights back on!" Owl yells, a sincerity in his voice I have never heard from him before. "Stop messing around!"

The florescent lights gradually flicker back on.

Owl holds his crying sister on the floor. I have no idea how he could have even found her in this. Even though we all slowly gather around the siblings, everyone is completely still. No one even bothers to continue the training game, not even Koel.

"I-I'm sorry." Robin sobs, "It's just that they came in the night. In the dark-I didn't think—"

Owl quiets his sister and then raises his head, "If you haven't noticed Robin is afraid of the dark." He eyes us all, "Now if you could stop gawking at her..." He defends Robin sternly, but then his voice softens, "What she is talking about is the night my family left the Preachers. My mother was pregnant with me and Preachers came to abort me even though my mom was seven months along... My mother wanted to keep me so our family had to run- in the night... My father and brothers died letting us go free. Robin was only four years old." He holds her tenderly and I can sense that their feud will end soon if it hasn't already.

159

Robin calms down quickly and stands up again, still shaken, but alright.

Hawk jogs up behind us now, making me wonder what took him so long.

"I think we should stop the training for the day." *You think?* "That was... That was good. You can have the rest of the afternoon off." *Gee thanks, Hawk. Robin has a mental breakdown and you give us the rest of the day off.*

"We were winning..." I say to Swift after I catch up to him as he is exiting the room, "What was that all about?"

"I'm sure we'll hear all about it tomorrow, but until then I suggest you stay clear of Robin and Owl." Swift snaps at me, but soon changes his expression to a kinder one. I am surprised by his reaction. "I'm sorry about that. You have no tact, that's all. I don't want you to mess things up with either one of them before they've recovered. I can almost guarantee Hawk will have them elaborate on the subject during tomorrow's lessons."

I stay silent, because I know he's somewhat right.

"Anyway, you have guard duty now, right?" He asks, changing the subject.

"Yeah, but I am going to talk to my sister first." I understand from the expression on his face that he doesn't know what I am talking about. "About the symptoms I've been having. She's a nurse, so she should be able to help me."

"Okay, Wren. I might come find you later. I should have lots of free time because I don't really have a job anymore."

"What do you mean?" I ask him.

"I was a Field Agent and a Guide, in fact, I was supposed to retrieve another civilian next week, but because of the course I can't leave the building for extended periods of time." I don't respond.

"So is it okay if I stop by your station later?" Swift brings me out of unimportant worries.

"Uh, sure." I breathe, "Yeah; no problem." I pat his arm and begin to walk away, my head in the clouds, "I'm going to the communication center. See you."

I haven't exactly been there yet; I've only used the computers in The Viewing Deck up until now. I've heard that it is a room filled with mounted T-Screens and tech like that and meant for private Proxy work.

I ask Blue-jay, the residing Liaison, where it is. She responds with two words, 'Tenth floor'. Even after my attempts at being friendly and kind by saying 'thank you' she doesn't pay me much attention.

It turns out that I *have* been to the communications center before.

When I step onto the tenth floor, I recognize the hallway and then find the right room quickly; this is where I watched the introduction video.

The narrow room has a few Proxies working in it, most of them probably work with my father in the science department or whatever, but I shouldn't be disturbed.

I go to the back corner again and turn on the implanted T-Screen.

After waiting for the machine to turn on I type in my home number and security passcode. No one should be able to contact my house except my family or close colleagues.

I tap my fingers on the metal desk as I wait for my sister to answer. She should be home by now; she usually works the night shifts.

The screen in fuzzy so I sit straighter and fix my hair before the picture of my smiling sister appears.

"Jardah, Pip." I greet her. I do not mention the family. This is strictly a business meeting… Sort of. I *am* glad to see her.

"Jardah, Wren. So, how is my little sister doing?" she asks me.

"I'm okay, thanks for taking my call. I've been having a few problems that I would like your opinion on." I get right down to it.

"Oh, yeah? I would be glad to help." Piper smiles and it magnifies the dark circles under her eyes. She still has her scrubs on and they're all wrinkled. She must have slept in them when she got home and just woke up.

"I'm afraid that I'm coming down with something, but I'm not sure what kind of illness." I explain.

"Oh, I hope you feel better soon. Tell me the symptoms and I will give you my expert diagnosis." Piper pushes her messy hair out of her face after winking at me.

"So..." I dive in, "Fever, nausea, sweating a lot, blushing more than I'm used to..." I could go on, but for now that will suffice.

Piper giggles, looks away and calms down, but when she turns back to me she bursts into a fit of laughter again. Her tired demeanor is now replaced by a silly one.

I raise one eyebrow, annoyed, "What?" I ask. *Why is she laughing at me and not saying what the heck in wrong with me?*

"I cannot believe I am going to say this." Piper says in between giggles, "That sounds like symptoms of a crush."

"What?" My mouth falls open, "No, that's impossible..." I have never had a crush on anyone before. Well I guess I have, but nothing that hasn't passed after a day or two.

"Come on, Wren. You are a woman." *Ew, seriously, she has to bring 'girly emotions' up?* "I am sure there is someone you are working with now that you like... Is it a guy?" She pauses a moment, "A girl?"

My mind totally goes into abort mode and attempts to shut down, but I have just enough power to answer, "A guy." Then she goes on talking, I catch something about a bet she and Beck have. Finally she goes silent and I gain hope that she will drop the subject, but it's only to call to my mom who must be in the next room. "Wren is in love!" She yells in a sing-song tune.

"No. I'm not." I scoff at the insanity of the situation. "I have to go!"

"Wait, mom—"

I turn off the computer.

I spin around in panic, simultaneously leaning forward and putting my head in my hands and propping my elbows on my thighs. I can't believe I couldn't see it before.

Time seems to slow as I stand and then stumble through the room on my way to the door. My eyes can't focus on anything and my heart is racing. I bump into multiple workers, muttering my apologies, and almost knock over a desk filled with equipment.

I start going back to my dorm in a daze. I don't even notice the effects of the elevator; I don't think I could feel any sicker than this. I begin to wonder who I could possibly have a crush on.

Swift's voice trails out of the cafeteria. Right away my heart starts beating faster. He finishes talking with another Proxy and runs through the doors after me.

"So, do you have time for me now?" He grins. His expression changes when I almost walk into a wall. "Are you feeling alright?"

He's worried about me. That almost makes me feel better, but at the same time it doesn't.

My stomach gets all mushy inside.

I put the pieces together. I feel nauseated and hot whenever Swift is around and jealous if he talks to another girl. I have never seriously liked someone before so no wonder I couldn't figure it out. "You okay?" He looks at me nervously.

"Yeah, fine." I shouldn't let him see the panic on my face. "I have to go. I don't think I'll be working today, so don't bother checking on me."

I pretty much run to my dorm, leaving him staring, confused, at my quickly disappearing figure.

After fumbling with the keys for a few excruciating seconds, I slam my door behind me and then lean against it.

Nope, nope, nope, nope. I take deep breaths to calm myself.

How long has this been going on without me realizing it? I think back to the first day I met Swift. *He was quiet and self-preserved; now that I've gotten to know him, he is nice and funny and...* I yell at myself to stop thinking about him that way. But is this whole thing wrong? What could be the downside?

I get up and splash water on my face from the bathroom sink. I've never thought about having a relationship before, what is making me concentrate on it now? If Dad knew what was going on right now...

I need to stop asking myself questions and focus on what is really important—my Enhancement training.

I stop myself from thinking about such things with one quick sentence. *Who says I need a boyfriend in the first place?* I am doing just fine on my own.

Chapter Fifteen

Now that my fondness of Swift has been made clear in my mind, I start paying more attention to everything about him: Swift's long strides with his slightly bowed-legs as he walks into the almost full room; his round face and bright round eyes that seem to glow when he smiles as soon as he lays eyes on me. The way Swift is nice to everyone, not just me; but there is definitely something different about the way he approaches me. *Be quiet! Stop thinking about him.* It could be because he thinks I could explode at any moment—I'm actually thinking that that may happen—or maybe because he actually cares about me. I jump off the edge of the desk I was sitting on while talking to Robin and Owl. My body aches from my fall yesterday.

I have decided not to do anything at the moment concerning Swift and me. I will act the same and not let on anything to Swift. Our relationship will remain the same and I'll just wait till the stupid crush is over. I know it's not an answer, but it's all I've come up with for now. Hopefully this whole thing will blow over soon. I still can't believe it.

Swift greets Owl and Robin and then comes in for a hug. I'm close enough to smell him. I breathe in his scent of sweat and some sort of spice. I could never tell the difference between different spices.

The first hour passes without a hitch, Hawk comes in and we start today's lesson quickly. The ten of us seem to adjust quite fast to this new pace of life. Hawk tells us that because we learned the past yesterday, today we'll learn about the present world; the way things work now.

There are many subjects to choose from; Education, Government, Law Enforcement... a lot of big words that don't mean a lot when you get down to it, when you're alone in a corner being destroyed while no one even knows you exist.

He decides to go with the education system. But I already know all about that; I went through it.

Elementary school is from age five to eleven and then secondary school from ages twelve to sixteen. Elementary school is pretty basic, which is the exact meaning of the word. Every child learns the same thing, being put in the same box even though every student has their own needs and disadvantages. Well at least that was what it was like with the Preachers; having impossible things required of you when you are just a kid.

Secondary school is better. Was better. As soon as we settled down I was thrown into a society so different from what I had known. I was that girl in the back of the classroom who didn't have friends. Not because no one wanted to be my friend or because I didn't want one, but because I didn't need anyone. That was just a step in my life that would soon be over. Why should I get to know someone if one of us is just going to leave later? I was not particularly good or bad in any subject. I tried to stay hidden, even though I would get into fights every once in a while.

You get to choose most of your classes so there aren't any annoying kids whose only goal is to disturb the classroom. Age fifteen is when you really need to start thinking. That's the year you have to decide what you are going to do for the rest of your life. You choose your future occupation and go from there, taking special, more focused courses and sometimes even starting internships. Unfortunately for me there weren't any revenge-seeking instructors or training in martial arts or the sort.

I barely got by pretending I was interested in a teaching course. Like I would want to be a teacher or a professor… I have seen how messed up kids can be. I followed my homeroom teacher around for a couple weeks as part of my internship. I barely remember anything I saw except for the bad behavior from the kids.

"The question of the day is… 'What would you be doing right now if you hadn't have found NEST?" Hawk breaks into my thoughts as I almost drift off.

I blink a few times and shake my head to keep myself from falling asleep.

That is a good question.

"Who wants to go first?" Hawk asks and I don't expect there to be many takers.

But Owl raises his hand, "Dead." he states clearly for all to hear.

Wow, that's rough.

"I probably would be too." Robin adds.

I see Lark nod her head.

I would probably be living not very far from here waging war against the Preachers the best way I can. I smile; I can picture it now: me living in an empty warehouse with a police radio on full volume waiting for some sort of clue. If I heard anything suspicious I would quickly don a mask and hop on a motorcycle to follow the lead. That would be the life, a vigilante living on the edge of the law.

"Either still living with my family or on the streets." Osprey answers.

I think that's the answer most of us have; Nightingale, Koel and me. I'm not sure about Swift, but I see some kind of recognition in his eyes.

"I haven't heard answers all of you… Maybe I should ask another question: How many of you haven't left the NEST building in the past ten years?"

Blue-jay slowly raises her hand as do Lark, Owl and Robin.

"I think we should have a fieldtrip sometime soon then." Hawk understands that we should have some sort of connection with the world we are trying to protect. And I agree with him, but I doubt we'll actually ever leave this place if we're not on a mission.

167

Honestly, I hadn't thought this plan through. As soon as I heard about NEST I was excited and impressed. I thought I'd be joining a bigger family with the same goals as me and I couldn't believe I hadn't heard about them before. But I didn't think about how long it would take for everything to get up and running and the differences between our philosophies. I can't back out now though, I have to stick to this plan and get Enhanced. That is the only important thing at the moment; not Swift and not my family and I can't keep getting distracted by them.

But the thought of Swift itches in my mind. He has somehow found a home in my cold head. I try very hard to not grow roots wherever I go so I can leave at a moment's notice, but Swift has become something that I can't imagine living without. We spend practically every day together and when we don't it just feels wrong.

Some faces lighten in the room; excited to finally see the world, while others withdraw, not wanting to go back to the horrible place they ran away from.

I don't think we'll be leaving here anytime soon.

After a not very interesting class in the physical training room, Swift invites the other eight future Enhancements to join him and me in the cafeteria for dinner. It isn't a very special invitation, everyone eats there with friends, but I think Swift mainly offered because Hawk was still hovering over us. Hawk wants all of us to put our best effort into becoming friends.

So after freshening up in my dorm, I reluctantly go to the cafeteria where my new 'friends' are waiting for me.

Honestly, I'm just doing this for Swift. He's been distracting me all day. At least once a minute I would look at Swift and hate myself each time. *What would he think if he knew what was going on in your head?* I scold.

Swift stands up as I join the group and he walks with me as I retrieve my supper. A hot steaming plate of meat analogue, a somewhat special meal called "glarn", and gluten free pasta is plopped onto my plate. Then we sit.

Owl tells a joke and I laugh. I suddenly realize that that is strange; his jokes don't usually amuse me. I look at Swift to make sure he's laughing too. He is. Maybe that's why I am; to impress him or something. I still don't understand emotions and probably never will.

The Enhancements trainees have put two tables together so we can all sit and eat together. I guess we're all just putting on a show for the rest of the world; if we don't get along, we could be replaced and none of us want that to happen. I know that sooner or later we're going to have an argument. It has to happen; this little "family" cannot last forever.

Swift, of course, is seated next to me. So is Robin. I've been able to stand being around her now that she and Owl aren't fighting anymore. They haven't exactly made up yet, but at least they can stand to be around each other without bickering.

I haven't touched the food in front of me even though the pasta looks good today.

"Is something wrong?" I know Swift is looking at me, but I don't take my eyes off of my tray on the table. I don't think I could stand looking at him while it's obvious that he's worried about me. He is always worried about me.

I yawn, "Yes, there is, but I don't feel like talking about it." The truth is, I'm embarrassed.

Swift moves closer to me, inspecting my face.

I scoot back in my seat, "What are you doing?"

"You have dark rings under your eyes." He says bluntly.

"Oh, yeah." I recover. "I haven't been sleeping very well."

He scowls but doesn't continue the conversation.

169

Sleep deprivation and lack of appetite are not signs of crushing, are they? Why am I so helpless in the romance department? I hope he doesn't realize... But actually, a small part of me does want him to realize, because maybe he's thinking about me too. Usually, I am able to push away any unwanted and lingering thoughts, but not now. *I need help.*

Romance and all that garbage makes me want to hit my head against a wall. I have been over-thinking EVERYTHING. Why did he say this? Did he mean to touch me that way? What does that look mean? Why can't I just go back to the way I was? Oblivious, cold and keeping all romantic thoughts as far away from me as possible.

My eyes return to focus and I rest them on Nightingale as she asks, "Did you guys hear about that band's concert that was protested by Preachers?" I didn't think of her as one who pays attention to the news. The only way she could hear about it is through The Hearing or if she is actually a fan of the band.

"Which one?" I ask. The thought of my favorite band being targeted surfaces in my head, even though it seems quite silly. Most of the music these days doesn't even have any words in it, so that it can't be misinterpreted.

"The Chalk Outlines."

Of course it would have to be something I like. And apparently Nightingale likes them too.

"Crap." I exclaim. "How could the Preachers see anything bad in their music? It is just beeping noises for Pete's sake."

"Somehow it is unacceptable to Preachers." *Are Nightingale and I actually getting along?* "Which is total bullshit. If we weren't on lockdown, I would totally go to one of their concerts and be their bodyguard so I could beat the shit out of those Preachers. And meet the band members of course." She quickly adds the last sentence.

I would kill to be able to attend a concert (figure of speech), but most of them are held in bars. I don't usually go to bars.

I just sigh. What else can I do?

The rest of the meal goes along smoothly. Robin and I have a nice conversation about… well, about nothing in particular. Swift walks me back to my room when everyone else has dispersed.

As we navigate the hallways, I begin to wonder why Swift is walking with me. I begin to consider the possibility that maybe he likes me too, but he could just be being nice.

When we're outside my door, I begin to consider doing something utterly ridiculous, so I spit out "Goodnight." and enter my room before I make a fool out of myself.

As soon as the door closes, I peel off my day clothes and pull on my pajamas before finally turning off the lights and falling into bed.

Goodnight, Swift. Sweet dreams.

Chapter Sixteen

"There has been some very distressing news."

Hawk walks beside me on the way to the classroom. I'm not sure if I'm early or if he's late.

"Another congress member has been killed."

"Like Smith and Myers." I recall the news I heard after watching the recruitment video. I hadn't seen any more information on the incident.

"Yeah..." Apparently Hawk didn't think I would know about that.

"Why are you telling me?" *Well, only me; why not tell the whole group?* "Do you think it was Preachers?"

"Obviously."

"And what are they looking to accomplish by killing off these government officials?"

We're right outside the door now and that's where Hawk pauses, "*That* is our subject of the day." and then he turns the knob and swings the door open.

I could hear people talking while we were outside, but as soon as Hawk is seen, the room falls silent and everyone stumbles to a desk.

"Good morning, Swift." I whisper and fall into the seat next to him.

"Jardah." He greets me with a smile. "How did you sleep?"

I put a finger to my lips and shush him because I know that what Hawk has to say is important. He looks shocked that I would do something like that to him. I just smirk and turn my attention to Hawk.

"Government structure lesson, kids." To everyone else this will be a random discussion, but I know what brought this on. "Does anyone know the maximum amount of congress members during a single president's term?"

I doubt anyone will know, mostly from the fact that the only people who leave the NEST quarters have no interest in politics.

Hawk barely waits for us to even guess, "Twenty, only twenty." And then he goes into a long monologue of how the government is formed currently.

I try to summarize the important stuff and set it right in my mind.

Twenty congress members. If the president is impeached, resigns, or dies before the end of his term, then an election will be held and the candidates are only from those twenty members of congress.

By the end of the lesson, I am practically nodding off and Swift sweetly shakes me back into consciousness. *I should fall asleep more often...* That shouldn't really be a problem since I've been having trouble sleeping at night.

"Everyone up!" Hawk shouts randomly and I see Owl jump. Apparently I'm not the only one who was bored by Hawk's lecture.

Osprey looks around the room, unsure if we actually need to get up. We get our answer when Hawk suddenly marches out of the door. Shaking off the confusion and uncertainty, we follow Hawk from a few paces back all stuffed in a group. None of us wants to be first in line.

"We're just going to train, you idiots." That doesn't really make us want to move closer to him.

Hawk leads us to HABITAT. He waits by the door and watches each of us enter.

"Where are we going now, Hawk?" Owl asks as he passes Hawk.

"Nowhere." Hawk closes the door, "You will be running ten laps."

Hawk stares at us for a minute. His arms crossed across his chest, he waits. I'm the first one to start moving. Everyone else follows slowly. This is really the first time Hawk has acted so cold towards the team.

After most of us successfully run the laps, he orders us to do pushups and sit-ups. I take everything in quietly; in my opinion Hawk's just trying to do his best to lead the group. Usually I'm oblivious to what other people are feeling, but I can definitely sense that the rest of the trainees aren't happy with the way Hawk is treating us. *What did they expect when they joined? A summer camp?*

And then more laps.

By the end of today's lessons we're even more tired than we were in his class. And I still have to guard.

***

At dinnertime I decide to take a break from Swift; maybe now I'll be able to clear my head and set things straight.

As I retrieve my meal I notice Robin staring at me from across the room. It is obvious she has something to say to me and even though I'm not in the mood to get into an argument, I decide to walk over to her.

Robin watches me as I approach, getting more and more nervous with each step I take.

I sigh before asking, "Is there a problem we need to talk about?"

She looks away from me and at the table. "Well, yes. Would you like to sit down?" I set my tray down and prepare for a long speech about Owl and the program, and then Robin says, "What do you think about relationships?"

I almost laugh out loud when she says this. Partially because I am somewhat relieved that we won't be arguing about Owl and partially because I've been thinking about this subject for the past two days. But I decide to set my problems aside and focus on Robin.

Robin doesn't exactly let me answer her question, though. "Well, you see, I have been thinking about this Proxy…"

I swallow a spoonful of food before responding, "A Proxy?" I give her this look like 'really?', "Do you *really* think that is a good idea?"

She furrows her brow in worry and confusion, "What do you mean?"

I take a deep breath before going into a somewhat long speech about all the things that could go wrong, "Well, being in a relationship at all in this time isn't a very good decision. I mean it's dangerous out there, not just for Proxies." I take a swig of a berry flavored drink. "For Proxies it is especially dangerous—emotionally dangerous and physically dangerous. You could easily get hurt; the guy could literally die and you'd be stuck without him forever." The shocked look on Robin's face almost makes me stop, but I go on. "And you could be the one who gets him killed. He's not focused while out on the job, because he's thinking about you, and then wham, a Preacher shoots him." Robin's face begins to grow red. Her green eyes shimmer. "And since we're in the program, we need to be even more focused; we don't want anything to go wrong with the Enhancement or lose focus and get kicked out."

"Yeah," She swallows. "I guess you are right."

I nod my head, "Yep, I... guess I am." *Shit, I'm right.*

I head back to my room after dinner, only one thing on my mind—getting over Swift. Not because of all the things that could go wrong, but because I don't need that extra distraction and pressure, especially if I want to be Enhanced soon.

***

"The final testing and experiments, which I have already told you about, will take place tomorrow." Hawk paces in front of us at the head of the classroom. I think he's nervous. "Hummingbird and his team have already thoroughly tested the Enhancer and its safety, this

175

will just see what sort of effects the Enhancer has on my regular bodily functions and the Enhancer's limits." He pauses to look at me. "It will take place during our normal meeting hours, please arrive on time." *He must have heard about my psych evaluation.* "Now, onto our usual studies. Today I would like to take questions from all of you, I am sure you have some."

Robin and Blue-jay raise their hands, but apparently Nightingale thinks her question is more important than theirs so she speaks without even asking permission, "I have a problem with the whole 'don't leave the building rule'." The tone of her voice makes it seem like she's not really going to ask a question, but make an accusation. "Preachers aren't allowed to leave their compounds, and they believe it's for their safety, what's the difference between them and us— NEST?" I roll my eyes; Nightingale just made this session unnecessarily dramatic and hostile.

"*We* are actually protecting you." Hawk tries his best to remain calm and explain as best he can, "Most of the people living in this building were once targeted by Preachers. Preachers chose to attack them because of something they did or because they somehow 'threatened' the integrity of the Preacher ways. So, if they went out into the world again and Preachers found them, one: they would most likely either be killed or kidnapped, and two: Preachers would figure out that there is some sort of organization helping these people." Even though I don't really want to agree with him, because I don't support most of NEST's decisions and rules, this one *does* make sense.

Nightingale leans forward in her chair, "But if they're Proxies, they should be able to take care of themselves."

"That is correct." Hawk may be digging himself into a hole. "You may think that NEST's rules are stupid and it might be hard to believe, but all of them have good reasons behind them and are here to protect you."

"What about that no sharing information rule that Proxies have to follow?" Robin chimes in. "What if—and this is totally theoretical—I wanted to start a relationship with another Proxy? How am I supposed to have a healthy relationship without being able to know a single thing about said Proxy?" *Really, Robin? You're still on this? Haven't I scarred you enough?*

"No Proxy is allowed to give away personal information because that information could cause trouble. In the past we didn't have that rule and the refugees would have issues with the ex-Preachers. They didn't want them around and took out their anger and revenge against Preachers on them even though it wasn't necessarily their fault. There was a time that ex-Preachers were seen as lesser than others." That shuts the girls up, but I'm sure they're thinking of another rule to throw at Hawk. "Now please, one question at a time and in an orderly manner."

I'm not sure how I feel about what Hawk said. I do think that everyone should be seen as equals, but these ex-Preachers could have done something wrong and I sympathize with the refugees because I'd be angry with them too. But I'm an ex-Preacher as well.

I slowly raise my hand and make sure Hawk notices me before asking, "How long has NEST been around?" Hawk has been talking as if they have been formed for many years and yet I hadn't heard of them before a few months ago. Or heard of anything fighting against the Preachers at all.

"Around twenty years—" What the hell have they been doing up till now? "But it was small groups or rings that just defied the Preachers with our thoughts and words. It has only been twelve or so years since we broadened our operations and welcomed civilians to join us." My family ran away eight years ago. And my father knew about NEST, but kept that information from me for some reason.

"So you're saying we can leave?" Now we're back to the whole staying inside the building subject. Owl asks the question this time.

Hawk gets a little annoyed for a moment, "Please, wait your turn." But quickly turns back to his normal and somewhat distant self, "Proxies have always been permitted to leave the building during their free time." Hawk utters this with no emotion at all, and yet he makes the statement seem obvious.

Owl and his sister are taken aback.

'You are the only people standing in your way' seems to be filling everyone's minds.

"Except you all volunteered to train in the Enhancement program. And none of you can leave without permission until I or Albatross or someone else on the board gives the 'okay'. You must give up some of your liberties to gain others. Not everyone has this chance."

"And no one has put their lives on the line like this." Nightingale is back in the action. No one seems to be listening to Hawk's comments and it makes me want to get up and yell at everyone. "We might not even die in combat; the Enhancers could kill us before we even get a chance to fight."

Koel steps in to intercede, "I am happy to risk my life for such a great cause, sir," I don't think Koel could ever be happy, "But I would much rather go down in a storm of bullets."

"If you are patient enough you, should be able to do just that."

"So give us a taste of what we have to look forward to." Nightingale requests. The topic sure has changed. "Show me something from the Enhancer."

"Oh, yes, please!" Lark exclaims and soon everyone is in agreement with the two girls. Lark repeats after the room becomes quiet again, "Please." She pouts her lip. Lark probably thinks that it makes her look cuter or sweeter, but it just makes me want to smack her.

"No more questions, suggestions or comments." Hawk has officially become irritated. "I am not going to listen and be controlled by you. I gave you the demonstration and you will be there for the experimentation tomorrow. What more do you want?" Personally, I want to know everything that's going on with the Enhancer.

I feel something nudge against one of the legs of my chair and look down to find Swift's sneakered foot kicking it. I twist around in my chair to question him. He just stares at me and rolls his eyes. That's how I've felt about this whole thing.

Up until now I had kind of forgotten about Swift and can only take that as a good thing. Now that we have the thing tomorrow, I don't really have time to think about Swift or my problems with him. I keep reminding myself; I need to focus on Enhancement and training, not anything else.

But there is he is, right behind me and always around me. I can still somehow feel his foot touching my chair.

Chapter Seventeen

I have only been to the science floors of the building a few times, so I make sure to use my Guide wisely. This will be the first time I've seen my dad in a month, but he will not see me. I will be on the other side of a dark glass window.

Robin, Owl and Blue-jay are already in our selected room. The room we occupy is completely empty. Directly across from our window, in the opposite wall of the other room, is another dark, rectangular window. That must be where Albatross and the others are watching from.

Only after waiting in the room for a couple minutes do I realize that Goldcrest is here too, standing in the corner. The lighting in here is very dim, casting deep shadows that make the scene even more unnerving.

"A bit creepy." I mutter and nudge Swift who apparently also hadn't seen Goldcrest.

"Hey, Goldcrest. Come join us?" Swift asks him. I wasn't really suggesting that Swift should invite him.

"I will once we get started." Goldcrest has his hands behind his back.

"Sure thing." Swift agrees and then returns to looking through the one-sided glass to the empty laboratory next door.

A moment later doctors and scientists come in. I notice my father among them. They start fooling around with the machines in the lab, among them a huge chamber. I suspect that is where Hawk will be for most of the experiments; protection for him and for us.

Dad looks okay, or at least better than when I had dinner with him. Or maybe he is just more focused. My dad must have more time to relax now because they have almost finished manufacturing the new Enhancers.

Osprey pounces in, "Am I late?" he asks.

180

"No, you are just in time." Swift tells him, motioning toward Hawk who just entered the opposite room. "In fact, you are far from the last to arrive."

"Yeah, where is everyone?" I add.

"I suspect that Nightingale is taking the day off." Blue-jay draws out. "Despite the fact that she was one of the leaders of our little outburst a couple days ago."

"I bet she would do anything to get out of training for a day." I mutter.

"Now, I am sure she has a good reason for not being here yet." Robin forces a smile and then checks her watch, "Koel, Lark and Nightingale still have three minutes."

Even though we are shielded by tinted glass, Hawk still knows we are watching. He waves to us as my dad opens the door to the metal box.

Hawk's behavior confuses me sometimes. Most often he is our mature teacher and leader, but sometimes a smile, or something like that wave, shines through and it makes me wonder if he has always been so serious. Like most of us, he may have had to adapt and change his true personality.

I whisper so only Swift can hear me, "Hawk's family died, right?" I recall a memory from our first meeting.

I hope it is not some big secret that I just spilled to Swift.

"Yeah, but not many people know about it…"

That could very easily be a contributing factor.

"Sorry I'm late, guys." Lark's loud voice almost makes me jump. "I was helping my—"

"No one cares." Nightingale slips past her. Once again, I find myself being torn between agreeing with Nightingale and really hating her.

So Nightingale didn't skip.

Koel arrives a minute later, sneaking quietly in without bothering anyone.

"Looks like they're starting." Owl announces as Hawk climbs into the container.

Hawk sits in the metal contraption set up inside. I wonder what will happen if he cannot handle what they are going to put him through. The heavy door closes.

"Experiment number one." My dad's muffled voice tells his comrades.

All five workers gather around the machine as my dad stands beside it.

The whole thing is large enough to hold two people in it very uncomfortably. On the side near my father are buttons and levers, ready to deliver whatever horrors they have prepared for Hawk. Tubes and cables run from the top of the rectangular prison to other machines in the room and some lead out to the hallway. A small window in the front allows us to see Hawk's face. He has no need to act brave now and I can see his confidence wither away into fear.

"Hey, you think they are gonna do this to us?" Owl's breath fogs up the glass in front of him.

"No, I-I do not think so." Blue-jay exhales, but none of us are sure and none of us predicted this situation.

Goldcrest has moved closer now and his shaky breaths can be heard by all. "Sorry." He swallows.

T-screens ready, Dad pulls the closest lever and before anything even happens, the five other workers begin scribbling and typing.

The largest tube begins shaking and water pours down over Hawk's body, instantly drenching him. His jaw is clenched and his hands grasp the armrests. The water soon fills up the whole tank, but not a single drop leaks out.

"They are trying to drown him." Lark gasps. *That is pretty obvious.*

182

"Now, his time before Enhancement was one minute and forty two seconds." Dad reminds his colleagues.

"And apparently they did it before." I add.

"Hopefully, he should be able to hold his breath for a lot longer."

Hawk finally blacks out after eleven minutes and twenty seven seconds and we watched in anticipation the whole time. And then we watched some more when it took longer than planned to drain the tank.

Dad presses a button, releasing white powder onto Hawk, reviving him. Hawk gives us a 'thumbs up', but I doubt he means it. The tension seems to lift a little, but everyone is still nervous and so am I.

"Experiment number two."

I don't know why I am nervous and anxious; my dad created the Enhancer and should roughly know its limits, so Hawk shouldn't be in danger... but something about being stuck in a tank and experimented on over and over again makes me and the others scared. I guess we're worried that this will happen to us too. I don't want to be a test subject for the rest of my life.

Steam rises from the tank, but those on the outside are not affected. I can barely make out Hawk through the warm glow that Dad has caused to push Hawk to his limits.

"We will only be going to three hundred degrees today." That is slightly relieving.

The tank reaches the maximum temperature and then begins to cool down again. I watch as Hawk's heavy breathing and reddened face return to normal.

"So we will be able to walk through fire and stuff?" Owl asks rhetorically, "Sweet."

"Not really, basic candle fires are over nine hundred degrees." Goldcrest mutters. Owl shoots him a thanks-for-ruining-my-dream glare. "But you never know… they only put him past three hundred, he might be able to withstand much more."

"Nice save." Swift elbows Goldcrest in the ribs.

"His body dealt with that well. His vitals are fine." Hawk is panting, but seems okay. "On to experiment number three."

"What about a break?" Robin asks anxiously.

No one answers.

"Reaching minimal temperature now. Minus one hundred degrees." Now I can't see Hawk because the small window is covered in frost and frozen air. "He is okay. Bringing it back up again."

"This is getting ridiculous." Osprey mumbles. "They could accidently kill him."

"Someone has to do it." Nightingale of course.

"Why are you so quiet, Koel?" Swift asks out of seemingly nowhere.

Koel stands in the back, which makes sense because he is the tallest. He hovers over us, his broad shoulders tense. The strange light pouring in from the other room forms strange shadows on Koel, or I suppose on all of us, making his face even more foreign.

He stares blankly ahead, taking in everything that happens to Hawk. "My philosophies are being tried right now."

"Well I don't think anyone should be put through this." Osprey adds his point of view even though no one was asking for it.

Koel ignores Osprey, "It is for the betterment of the program and the organization…. but I really would not want to have to deal with that."

Like Swift, Koel believes in NEST. That they have a good reason behind every rule and everything they say. I know that there is definitely something wrong with the leaders of NEST; there has to be, right? There's always another angle.

"Experiment number four." Dad presses a button. "Saving the worst for last."

184

"At least this is the end." Robin relaxes a bit, but I wonder how this could be the worst.

"Carbon monoxide entering now."

I can't see the gas at all, but I know that that is one of the most dangerous parts about the poison. The silent killer.

"He is stable, as we thought."

"But it was a good idea to have the antidote on hand."

"It is over now, right?" Robin looks as if she might pass-out herself. "Do you think we would be allowed to talk to him?"

Swift answers her, "I'm not sure. They might want to keep an eye on him for the next few hours." It seems that he is our leader when Hawk is gone. He has the most connections and has our respect. Swift also knows how to talk to people, unlike me.

"So we have free time now?" Owl asks.

Swift isn't comfortable letting us go without permission, but says, "I guess."

Owl catches Robin's sleeve and pulls her out of the room. She is still affected by Hawk's pain and he must be going to try and cheer her up. Osprey goes after them. The friendly, happy group disappears.

It doesn't look like Swift is going to leave any time soon so I decide to stay with him and wait for everyone else to leave. Soon everyone leaves in their little groups and I am left alone with Swift.

Swift still stares through the dark glass, the florescent lights from the other side making his beautiful features distorted.

"It is amazing, right?" He suddenly acknowledges my presence.

Um, what? I was too busy staring at you.

"Hm?" I hum and turn my attention to the lab workers who run around turning machines off and on and check numbers.

"We will be able to survive underwater for longer and be exposed to high or low temperatures and toxins." I glance back to him once I

185

realize the engineers' actions have nothing to do with what he is saying. "Not to mention that we will have superpowers."

He looks intently at me now and I do not know how to respond.

"Yeah..." I breathe.

I study his whole face to see what reaction he wanted and notice the way his pupils are dilated. I wonder if his eyes are dilated because of me or because of his excitement about the Enhancers. Of course, I really hope it is because he is alone with me... in a dark room... talking about Enhancers... With me.

Stay focused. I remind myself.

The subject really does fascinate me, but I can't speak properly in front of Swift. His presence makes it hard for me to speak at all, and when I do, I either say something dumb or mean. He makes me feel stupid.

Finally his expression changes into one I can understand: disappointment.

Swift steps back and then moves toward the exit. I had not realized how close I was to him until he wasn't there anymore.

"Are you okay, Wren?" he asks very clearly while holding on to the door frame.

It takes me a few moments to answer while I think it over. *No not really, but I'm going to, I have to.* Of course I can't explain my feelings to Swift though, so I just say, "I guess so."

And then he nods his head.

I turn my eyes back to Hawk as he shakily steps out of the container and into the open room and bright lights. He rubs his temples tiredly. Just as I think that this whole ordeal is over, something catches my eye. One of the technician's lab coat flaps open for a second and I catch a glimpse of a pistol hanging on his hip.

I whip my head back to make sure Swift is still in the room. He pulls the door open and I ask quickly: "Lab workers aren't permitted to carry weapons, are they?" and then I impatiently wait for the answer that will either set me into motion or calm my nerves.

Swift's face scrunches up in confusion in the doorway, "No... Wr—"

The owner grabs his gun and reveals it to the rest of the room before I have a chance to decide whether I am going to fly through the door or the glass pane. My dad is in there.

Hawk is the first person other than me to see the weapon and does exactly what I would do if I was on the other side of this wall. He protects my dad. As the traitor pulls the trigger, Hawk throws himself over my father, getting right in the way of the projectile. I practically jump out of my skin to help them both. By the time the bullet has even hit its target Proxies begin rushing into the room and the assailant is pinned up against the left wall and has the gun knocked out of his hand. For once I am thankful for the Proxies.

I inch closer to the glass, keeping my eyes on the mound of Hawk and Dad. Hawk stands up straight and backs away from my father who seems to be perfectly fine, if not a little flustered. They *both* seem to be fine.

Swift practically falls back into the room as a female Proxy with long black hair bursts in, "You two cannot be here." she barks. "Leave immediately and keep this quiet." She grabs Swift above the elbow with one hand and me in the exact same place and then rushes us out of the room and down the hall to the elevator bank. Her rifle smacks the side of my leg the whole time. The Proxy practically throws us into the elevator when it arrives and says in a hushed tone, "Do not say anything until we have time to figure this out." The doors close between us and her half worried, half angry face. As we descend, Swift just gives me an incomprehensible face. I think it is something between shocked and worried and annoyed.

My father could be injured and dying, and so could Hawk... But they both seemed to be okay. How could they possibly be okay?

187

Chapter Eighteen

Breakfast is cereal. At the moment I am waiting for the dispenser to dump brown flakes into my dingy bowl. When it finally does, I pour water into the cereal, making an icky slosh. I barely slept last night. I usually do not sleep very well, but at least now I have a reason. Swift and I have not heard any news about Hawk or my dad. It was hard not to tell the rest of the group about the incident, but Swift convinced me to stay quiet. After we got off the elevator, we went back to my dorm and barely talked, both of our minds working overtime trying to understand what we watched. Swift left in the middle of the night without us finding an answer.

The dining-hall is surprisingly quiet today. No one I know is eating breakfast now. There is no reason for me to dawdle, so I shovel the food into my mouth quickly and set off for the bottom floor.

"It's about time you got here, slacker." Owl shouts at me as soon as I set foot in the classroom.

"Hey, at least I'm not a ginger." I sneer and jab at him.

We're both joking of course. And then it hits me—Owl and I are friends.

As I sit down and grip the sides of my desk, Swift gives me a grim expression. Everyone else seems to be fine and oblivious.

Hawk walks briskly into the room, "I am so sorry to interrupt your conversations." I stand up, surprised. "Because of my busy day yesterday, I didn't have time to plan anything for today, and I was wondering if someone who has not spoken yet is willing to tell the rest of the classroom about their past or family, or anything at all." For the first few moments I get lost in the normality of the situation and forget what happened yesterday, but I notice the dark rings under Hawk's eyes and that brings it back. He must have had a tough time getting to sleep last night, if he slept at all. I almost walk up to him and ask Hawk what happened and if everyone is okay, but Swift catches my attention and whispers for me to wait till class is over. I can't argue with him, so I sit back down.

I turn my attention back to the classroom and its students and try to remain in the moment. Osprey looks around. He rubs his hands on his thighs while getting to his feet.

The stage is his since no one else is stupid enough to take Hawk's bait.

As Osprey stands before us, I finally get a good look at him.

He is not fat or extremely muscular like Koel, or skinny; he just is. His nice, white smile, straight nose and wavy golden hair are a force on their one, but for some reason I am not attracted to him. He just does not seem like my kind of person.

"It seems to be my turn to speak. Which I do not really mind doing because I have forgiven…" He rubs the back of his neck. "Well, I should start from the beginning. Um, as you know my name is Hezro." He smiles. I have heard weirder names before.

"I lived with my family until three years ago when they kicked me out. Ah—" He makes a strange noise that sounds like he has been physically hurt; like he does not want his family to sound as bad as he makes them out to be. Maybe even as bad as they actually are. "Before you come up with any ideas in your head let me explain." He lifts his arms to stop us. "I am a Christian." Okay… I do not really have a problem with Christians, other than I heard theories that Preachers branched out from Christianity. But really any religion or ideology that wasn't supervised could have spiraled out of control and caused the Preachers. "So is my family. They are just… a little more extreme than I am…?" He doesn't know how to put his thoughts into words. "Most of the Christian community these days sits around waiting for the solution to magically appear. Some even block out the whole Preacher situation, not even admitting that there is a problem. My family is the latter." He pauses briefly before continuing. "I obviously do not agree with them, or I would not be here." He chuckles nervously. "When I confronted my family on this matter they were very upset. It scared me; made me think that they were more like Preachers than I had previously thought. I told them that I was leaving and that the Preachers need to be stopped. Arguments happened and then they made me leave. They disowned me and I have not heard from them in... well since I joined NEST. As I previously stated, I have forgiven those people a long time ago. If they showed up here tomorrow, I would greet them happily."

Wow, he is a better person than me. I can see Nightingale glaring at him; his approach is the exact opposite of hers.

To sum up he says, "I hope I will get closer to all of you and we can all be good friends." He specifically looks at me.

I artificially smile as best I can and he leaves me alone. Maybe all of my interactions with Osprey will be like that—fake.

Nightingale laughs hysterically. All heads turn in her direction.

"You think that's a sad story?"

"Are you volunteering to tell us yours?" Hawk asks. They stare at each other for a couple seconds before Nightingale looks away.

She swears under her breath, "Why not? But do I have to stand up?"

Hawk gives her this one and doesn't make her get up. Osprey hurries to his place before Nightingale can begin speaking.

"Well my life was pretty terrible, but whatever." Nightingale passes her hand over the desk gently. The only time I have ever seen her be somewhat soft. "I was raised by Preachers. Was kind of one myself, but I didn't really go along with all of their rules." She lifts her head and I can see the wildness in her eyes.

"I was a little rebel, getting in trouble a lot and the Preachers didn't retaliate that much until one day when I was fourteen..." She pauses for dramatic effect which makes me believe that this story might not be true. "One of my district's leaders cornered me after school. He told my parents that he was having talk with me about my behavior. That wasn't what he did though. He touched me." She doesn't hesitate while stating this, like it happened a long time ago to someone else. And as if it doesn't bother her at all. "I tried to stop him, but obviously I was not as strong as him or as strong as I am now. But that wasn't the worst of it. I made a horrible mistake. I told my parents. They never believed anything I said anyway, so how could they understand that I was telling the truth now, when I was accusing someone so important of something so… bad?" *It wasn't her fault, she shouldn't feel bad. It was right to tell her parents, but they should have responded correctly. Wait, what am I thinking? Preachers don't think the same way that we do.*

"My parents brought this issue to the attention of that specific Preacher. Things didn't end well. He admitted to my claims, but said that it was my idea, that I'm the one to blame, because I wanted it. I was punished. I begged for my parents to believe me. I screamed, I cried, I cursed at them. They did nothing and stood idly to the side."

No one dares say a word and the room feels cold. Goose-bumps have appeared on my skin. My story has nothing on this. I silently thank my parents for being so understanding.

Hawk almost whispers, "So what happened to you? What was your punishment?"

"At the weekly Preacher meeting I was whipped, in front of everyone. Flogged and crying and shouting and shrieking before my parents, my friends, my teachers, my spiritual leaders. No one did a damn thing." Nightingale smashes her fist on the desk, showing the first sign of emotion. "I was half thrown out and half ran away. Lived on the street for a while before finding my way here. Now I found the best chance to get back at those bastards—my parents, that worthless scum bag and the whole system." She abruptly finishes and puts her hands in her lap. Smiling sweetly at Hawk she asks, "Is that what you wanted to hear?"

She is insane.

Hawk blinks a few times before he can assess the situation, "Well, that was... interesting." I can see the regret of letting Nightingale into the program in the back of his mind. I honestly wouldn't be surprised if they let her go after this.

"Thank you both for opening up to us. I really feel that we are getting closer." Hawk says a little hesitantly. It must be the only thing he can come up with after being shocked. But that isn't what I want to do; I don't want to get closer to these people.

The rest of the lesson, Hawk splits us up into small groups to talk about our feelings and sparkles and sunshine.

At the end of the day Hawk tells us to prepare ourselves for the hard training session that will happen tomorrow. As soon as everyone else begins to leave, I silently tell Swift to stay behind. We need to talk to Hawk. Swift nods in agreement and watches as Hawk wipes the large T-screen of information. Blue-jay and a few others give us weird looks when we tell them we are staying, but they all eventually exit before Hawk is done.

"I guess you guys want to know what happened yesterday evening?" He knows we do so we don't respond. I sit with my arms crossed on the edge of a desk and Swift stands near the exit almost as if he suspects Hawk will try to make a break for it. "Agent Hummingbird, your father, is fine. Neither of us were injured from the attack." Hawk wants us to drop it now. I won't.

"How is that possible? You were in the direct line of fire." I dismount the desk to move closer to Hawk. He is not leaving without giving us an explanation first.

"Fine." Hawk surrenders, "Technically I was hit by the bullet, but it did not penetrate my skin..." His face breaks into a smile of amazement and surprise, "It left a dent, but bounced off." *Enhancements are impervious to bullets.*

"What?" Swift too half-grins and runs his hand through his hair. "Amazing." He says under his breath.

"And what happened to the attacker?"

"He was taken to an interrogation room for the night. I should be able to talk to him later today and figure out his objective." Most likely a Preacher trying to knock-off my dad. "That is all the information I have for now. You better get running, Wren; your shift starts in a few minutes. I will see you both tomorrow morning for our training session."

I follow Hawk out of the room and he closes the door behind us. "By the way, Hawk," *I really don't want to do this…* "Thanks for watching out for my dad." And then I run ahead of Swift and Hawk so I can get my Proxy clothes on for my Security shift. I can breathe better now. Dad is safe, as well as Hawk, and pretty soon I will be bulletproof.

Chapter Nineteen

I walk with a paintball gun in my hand. Hawk threw us right into HABITAT as soon as I stepped out of the elevator onto our floor. This time I'm not on the same team as Swift and it gives me a chance to see how I work without him.

I have Lark, Osprey, Blue-jay and Robin with me. We are always split into groups of five. There are no assigned leaders and we all have to work as a team. I only have one guy on my team, while the other has only one girl.

I wonder what Hawk is playing at. Whatever it is I'm going to make sure we win.

The goal is to disband the Preacher regiment in this newly formatted city while protecting the robot civilians. The robots are not anything special, just basic machines that Dad programmed to roam around aimlessly.

Swift, Nightingale, Owl, Koel and Goldcrest are the Preachers and everyone with me are the Proxies.

Two shots in the stomach and you are dead. Once shot to the head or chest means you're dead. You can still play if you get hit in the limbs but you have to act as if they actually have a bullet in them, so you can't use them.

My side can't shoot any civilians or we are out.

Easier said than done, I think as I wade through the sea of people while I try to look as innocent and robotic as I can.

My job at the moment is to search for any sign of the other team, Preachers.

Hawk made them wear hoodies and similar things to what Preachers wear. The important ones always have cloaks and masks while the footmen wear normal, but conservative clothing. I have never thought about it before, but how do they move so swiftly and silently in such uncomfortable and stiff clothes?

Blue-jay and Robin are waiting in windows for me to find a mark even though I told them that I am a better shot. Osprey is on the lookout like me and so is Lark. I think this is the worst plan that I have ever agreed to, but I am trying to not be bossy. Maybe Osprey, Lark and I should shepherd the Preachers into a certain area and let Blue-jay and Robin pick them off.

But first I have to spot one—the trail of dark cloth, rushed footsteps, or some voices.

Speaking of the devil, a blur runs past me, a gun at their side and not held up in defense. The blur actually does not move very fast so I can easily make out Lark's form as she gets paint splattered on her back and once in the head.

Damn it, she didn't run fast enough.

From the corner of my eye I notice a body gliding toward Lark's fallen and writhing self. I pull the nearest robot to my body as a shield and hide in an adjourning street before pushing it back to roam away. I'm not doing a very good job of keeping the citizens safe.

I look around the corner and gaze through the scope of the paintball gun at someone rummaging and grabbing Lark's unused weapon.

Preachers-1, Proxies-0

Should I take this guy out or let him lead me to the rest of their group? I can't make out who it is.

I decide to follow my friend who is dressed as a Preacher.

I wish Hawk would give us some sort of communicators so I can tell Blue-jay and Robin where I am going and where to meet me.

After sneaking around after this person for a while I begin to wonder if he knows I'm behind them. And I begin to notice his behavioral patterns; he doesn't walk like Swift and is too tall to be him as well.

Well maybe I just notice the differences between this person and Swift. But I still decide to not attack just yet.

195

Sometimes I hate this room, the HABITAT or whatever you want to call it, and sometimes I love it. Right now I hate it because it's so crowded and stuffy that I can barely move or breathe. For some reason the urge to shoot myself in the leg appears in the back of my head just so I can get out of here. I am not usually so claustrophobic and nervous.

Every once in a while I lose sight of my target amongst the bobbing heads but then spot him again a few feet away. I need to catch up without giving away my position.

He is too tall to be Owl or Goldcrest and he is definitely not my Swift. So those that remain are Koel and Nightingale. I did initially think that my prey is male, but I could picture Nightingale under that bulk of clothing.

Whoever it is, he begins to run. I am already falling behind so I leave all of my thoughts as I gather my gun and take off after him.

Hawk never told us what the Preachers of us were supposed to do; just regular Preacher activity I guess. That could mean anything from sitting in a stuffy room and talking about how bad things are in the world today to pulling out explosives and blowing up hospitals. I think my friends would go for the extreme and it is my job as a Proxy to protect the innocent civilians.

And that is what I focus on as I plow after this Preacher who keeps checking the watch on his wrist. *They are planning an attack...* An idea pops into my mind — *And this person is going to be late.*

There has to be some logic in the layout of this city. Some structure to show the center, the meeting point. Like the park in the previous city. And that is most likely where my adversaries would strike.

There is an opening up ahead. It could be exactly what I was talking about.

196

I have to get to my target before he can be seen clearly by anyone who could be in that clearing. I cross to the opposite side of the street so I'm walking at the same speed, paralleling the Preacher.

Then I wait for him to walk past the entrance of an alley and sprint at the silhouette, diving when I get close enough. *This going to hurt.*

I slam into the solid body and we skid across the cement. I can feel my exposed skin rip off as I keep sliding forward and it stays hanging on to the pavement. Just another thing added to my ever-growing list of injuries.

I get up quicker than my opponent, who must be in shock. I lift my rifle and shoot before Nightingale can react. I enjoy seeing the look of surprise that chances to anger on her stupid face. The pink paint splatters across the front of her coat. She throws her gun to the ground in anger. I am happy it is her, not only because I wanted to outsmart her, but because we are about the same size.

Smirking, I say, "You look great in pink, Nightingale." and then order her to strip off her costume. She knows what is up, but does it anyway because she is dead.

I make sure the coat is inside-out and the paint is not visible before fitting my arms through the sleeves and letting the hem drop to my knees. The fabric is not as heavy as it looked. The hood that lands on my head is soft, and when I tighten it to cover my face I can still see through it.

Where did Hawk get these? This is a legitimate Preacher cloak and it scares me. I never imagined myself wearing one and especially not in a game. Every training session is a game in my head. A game that I have to win. I need to prove that I deserve to be here.

I make sure Nightingale leaves in the opposite direction and does not tip-off her teammates before turning down the wider street.

Swift and the others have no reason to suspect that I'm not Nightingale so I don't think I'll have a problem until I get closer.

This clearing is not as impressive and pronounced as the previous courts. If I did not know my cohorts so well, I might have passed by here without noticing it too much. But this is the perfect place for them to attack. There are more 'people' on this street than any of the others and stores and restaurants line the sidewalks.

For the first time since entering, I notice the lack of vehicles. I suppose it's hard for HABITAT to create a large number of moving holograms.

Once again I have to walk some more while searching for the other team. My new clothes are definitely not as restricting as I thought they would be.

I spot some non-robotic movement up ahead and to the right. Two figures surround a bulky device. It looks like a bomb. *Where the hell did they get that?* I hold my weapon at my side, so they will not feel threatened. Only two of the remaining four are in sight. I should wait for the others before attacking.

As I get closer I notice Swift's walking pattern and height. He is standing behind one of his teammates as they mess with a bunch of wires.

I sigh. Swift looks strong and powerful, but I can block out everything about him for the most part. *Focus, Wren.*

Swift turns his head and his beautiful face is covered with a mask. "What are you doing here so early? Did you place the mines?"

I want to laugh nervously. I hadn't planned on speaking. *Should I try to impersonate Nightingale's voice or what? I must look like a fool standing here.*

I just nod.

Koel stops playing with the bomb and stands up. He is the only one that tall, so I quickly recognize him. "What does that mea—"

"We did it." The two shorter ones of the group, Owl and Goldcrest, save my butt in the last second.

"Then we should get started. It is a shame none of the Proxies will be here to see the end." Koel says. He really has gotten into the Preacher act.

"Yeah, it's going to be a blast." Owl contains himself from laughing.

If Nightingale was really here she would say something offensive. I shove Owl a little. Nightingale would do that, right?

My hand shoots out as Owl stumbles to catch his footing. I catch Owl by the wrist and he doesn't fall/

"What was that for, Night?" Swift takes off his mask and his confused and annoyed look sends shivers down my spine.

Owl pushes away from me and grasps his wrist. *Did I hurt him?*

"Are you okay?" Escapes from my mouth.

Oh, no.

I raise the rifle in my hands before they have time to suspect.

"Nightingale?" Swift walks towards me.

What do I do? All of their attention is fixed on me; I was not prepared for this.

"Put down your weapons!" Osprey shouts over the bustle of the city.

I take this opportunity to back away from the Preachers, still with my gun ready. When they look back to me, they are all in range.

I shoot a look around. Where is Osprey?

"Put your hands in the air and we will not shoot." Osprey's soft voice booms.

Swift, Koel, Owl and Goldcrest slowly raise their hands. I take off the hood just in case my team doesn't realize it's me.

I hear a rustle and then Osprey, Blue-jay and Robin come out of different buildings in unison. They saved my butt, and look good doing it. Their stances and the way they hold their guns are perfect.

They guide the Preachers away from the explosives and make them kneel.

We won. And I didn't even do anything to help.

But the Preachers surrendered way too quickly...

"Where did you get the bomb?" Blue-jay asks and prods Swift with the tip of her gun. First time in a while since she has been interested in something.

"We got them from Hawk." Swift answers.

Them. "Wait—"

Before I can react a loud boom rocks the square; a huge amount of heat and energy sweeps me off my feet.

I smack my head against a streetlight's pole and then land flat on my back.

"What the hell was that?" Blue-jay wipes off blood from her forehead and slowly gets up. She still holds her weapon high and covers Swift, Koel and the other two's flattened bodies.

I am impressed.

"That—" Owl coughs and sits up from his laying position, "Was us winning."

I still lay on my back; I don't feel like getting up.

The high, blank walls begin to appear again and we are left in the empty room. There is no sign of the explosion anywhere. Someone moans a couple feet away.

"You could have seriously injured one of us." Robin scorns and reaches a hand to Osprey who is laying on the floor like me.

"No, Hawk would not give us anything that could actually hurt us." Koel has confidence in his leader's decisions. "Look—no damage at all to the room."

I sigh. *Tell that to my whole aching body.*

Someone scuttles to me. "Wren? Are you okay?" Swift is by my side and has already knelt next to me.

I smile, "I'm fine; just taking a little break after you tried to kill me."

"I would never kill you." he teases.

"Are you sure about that?"

Swift helps me get up and I put most of my weight on him just because I can.

"Almost sure." he finally answers after pretending to be deep in thought as we all leave the surprisingly clean room.

When we get into the hallway, I let go of Swift and walk with the others.

This kind of quiet, friendly life will not last forever. We have already gotten in a few arguments. As soon as we all know each other well enough, we will be made to watch each other die. Thoughts like these make me want to scream in everyone's face to wake up and back off.

Hawk paces angrily when we walk in.

"That was the saddest thing I have ever seen." Apparently this exercise is more important that Hawk made it out to be.

Nightingale and Lark are sitting in their respective seats.

"And I thought that we were making such great progress." He pauses to collect his rushed thoughts and emotions, "Do you guys not realize how much is at stake? One more slip up like this and I can have you all kicked out and replaced. Not to mention that we are trying to win a war here." Hawk slowly calms down while the rest of us start to get worried. I didn't come all this way and spend two months here to not get Enhanced. "There is a meeting scheduled for tomorrow night. A get together to finally introduce you all to the NEST board that agreed to go through with the Enhancement program." News to my ears. "You will have tomorrow morning off to prepare. I expect you to be on your best behavior or they might just cancel the whole program." Hawk abruptly leaves his students and marches out of the room.

Robin looks just about in tears, "Can they really shut us down?"

"No." I am not trying to raise her spirits, I am just stating fact, "They have put too much time, effort and funds to give up on the idea now... But they could get a new team."

Swift goes to put his hand on Robin's shoulder while everyone else stands aimlessly around, "Wren is right." It feels nice to have someone agree with me, especially Swift. "I suggest we rest on our day off and be on our best behavior at the meeting." Swift is right. He is almost always right.

Chapter Twenty

My day off is enjoyable. I spend most of the time relaxing with Swift in the civilian lobby and the stores in that strip. The outside world is a real shock when you have been living in a secluded building for the past few months. The people and outfits seem to be bigger and crazier than ever, even if this area is still technically run by NEST. Robin joins us for a little while—Owl is actually hanging out with friends his own age—and she even convinces me to buy a dress for the gathering.

Robin is like one of those friends that you barely know anything about or have anything in common with, but you call them when you need help with something concerning the things they like. She is not all about clothes and shopping, but I would rather be with her than with Blue-jay, who was Swift's first suggestion. The dress I choose is not too flashy or big or costumey, like most of the other items in the store. The worker helping us is dressed in a large and heavy sweater, a short skirt and flashy tights. Her large hair barely fits under the small hat adorned with a lace veil. What I choose is just a simple and comfortable dress that falls to my knees. The very end is black and it gets gradually lighter to the top, which is white. Robin says something about the dress she is going to wear, but I don't catch it.

Swift compliments me many times as I try on the different outfits. His compliments don't affect me as much as they would have a couple days ago, which is good. Seeing Swift in this casual and more public setting is great. He seems much more relaxed and calm. His military cut has grown out and in everyday clothes he almost looks like a normal human being.

While we are checking out Robin says, "Owl should be done soon. We were planning to eat lunch together before getting ready." She does not invite either of us, which is okay with me. I would have declined anyway. "So I will see you both later."

Robin exits the shop just as I hand the cash to the clerk. My family started sending me money every month. I want to sever that tie, but I don't have any other form of income. Other than food and board, I don't really get anything for working as a Proxy.

Swift smiles and thanks the clerk and then grabs my bag before asking, "So what are your plans now?"

This has been the first day off in a while; it's weird not having my day planned out for me. "I was thinking about spending some time alone."

"Scar-face!" *Uh, oh.* Spaz's familiar cheerful voice breaks through the constant chatter yelling to me, "Wren."

I stop Swift and turn around. Spaz skips to me, a wide smile spread across her freckled face.

"Jardah!" Spaz squishes me with hidden strength. "It's great to see you." I try to hug back, but I'm not one for physical interaction.

I introduce her to Swift after she lets me go. I'm about to ask her about working in the hospital, because she wears a special white uniform, but I don't get the chance to.

"Oh, Wren. I didn't know that you have a boyfriend."

I look her straight in the face, with mine turning red, and say somewhat angrily, "We are not together."

"Really? You're not boyfriend and girlfriend?" It's not her fault, this is who Spaz is. Random and tactless.

Swift answers for me, "Nope, just friends. Right, Wren?" He nudges me.

"Yes." I say clearly.

"Alright." Spaz concludes, but she isn't convinced. "I'll see you around." She pats me on the shoulder and bursts from sight.

"We are just friends, right?" Swift repeats the question. I didn't want this to happen, I'm still in the process of getting over him.

I say, "That's the plan." before I can stop myself.

If I hadn't liked him this whole time, would I still have been friends with him in the first place? I have wondered why I was so easily attracted to him, why I didn't push him away, why I wanted to be friends with him. From the first moment I saw him I knew that that nervous, quiet boy would be important in my life.

I had no idea though how nice and supportive he really is and how close we would become. Or how much I would care for him now. But all of that doesn't matter right now.

"Good. I wouldn't want our relationship to be ruined." Swift says in a way that almost makes it sound like a threat.

I want to retort, insult him for making me feel bad, but I know that I can't. I can't hurt Swift. This causes an awkward atmosphere around us as we glide along the white, tiled floors. I want to run away, but I also want to stay as close as possible to Swift and not let on that I really am annoyed. The silence between us bears heavily on me.

As we get closer to the Proxy entrance he breaks the silence, "Enjoy your time alone." Swift hands me my bag. I lose sight of him in the busy shopping center.

After considering sitting in one of the small restaurants, I decide to drop my new things off in my dorm and then head downstairs to train for a bit. I need to get rid of this anger.

***

I take off my tank-top and collect the sweat hanging on my skin. I should be alone for a while; the only person I could think of training on their free day is Koel.

What time is it? I probably have an hour or two still to shower and get ready.

Deciding to check how much time I have left, I head to the elevator, but not before putting my shirt on again. *There is a clock in the Proxy lobby, right? Or I could just ask the current secretary.*

As soon as I step onto the main floor, I notice the giant clock straight ahead of me. *Holy crap, I have ten minutes. I don't have time to clean up and get dressed, so I might as well go up like this. The people might as well know what they are supporting.*

And just as I turn back to the elevator bank Hawk comes at me from the civilian section. "You have got to be kidding me." he tries not to shout.

"You look nice." I try to distract him and get on his good side simultaneously. Hawk wears a dark blue suit with a flashy tie. I guess he does look nice.

"You had better not be going to the dinner like that." He pulls me into the elevator going up. "Are you trying to embarrass me?"

"Of course not." The doors close. Hawk presses the button to the floor that holds my Proxy dorm. "I was training during my free time and lost track of time." I add at the end: "You should be proud of me."

"Wren, you are going to take the quickest shower you have ever taken and are going to throw on your nicest clothes." Hawk practically pushes me out of the elevator when the doors open on the right floor.

***

I am late, I am late, I am late, I am late; I repeat over and over again in my mind as I grab the piece of cloth from the edge of my bed and pull it over my head. The dress falls lightly around my body. I think that really was the fastest shower I've ever taken.

I flip my hair over my shoulder while putting on my nicest pair of shoes. I don't have time to do anything fancy with my hair, or even brush it. I also don't have time to notice the bruises on my face and arms and legs.

And then I run.

Past the cafeteria off of the courtyard, where I would be having dinner on a normal evening, and to the elevator shaft. Luckily I will only have to take one ride from here.

Why did I tell Swift that I could remember without him and for him to go by himself?

At least I'll be fashionably late.

I emerge onto the Viewing Deck and despite what I thought earlier, no one notices me. To be honest, it's a little disappointing. About twenty people, board members and trainees, surround the round table on the main level. I notice the many bottles and plates of expensive looking food. No one is working now; they must have cleared the place just for the meeting.

I sneak down the stairs as quietly as I possibly can and make my way to Swift who, luckily for me, stands at the edge of the group. He greets me with a wonderful smile, but stays quiet.

Of course I spend most of my time standing awkwardly half-way behind Swift. I know that he wants me to get out of my shell, but I have lived in it for so long that I don't want to. I search for each Enhancement with my eyes. Everyone seems to be wearing either a suit or a dress, even Nightingale. Blue-jay is perched next to an aging gentleman in a white tuxedo; they both hold glasses of champagne. Osprey has a small crowd of people surrounding him. Apparently he is quite amusing, because a second later the whole group bursts into laughter. I can hear Osprey's warm chuckle from all the way across the room. Robin stands idly by his side in a sparkling yellow dress.

Hawk clinks his glass to get everyone's attention even though the evening hasn't officially started yet.

Hawk lets Albatross speak, "Let us welcome our ten new Enhancements." Albatross waits a moment as everyone claps and then the attention goes back to Hawk.

"Thank you all for coming today to meet your Enhancements." *I am no one's Enhancement.* "Let me introduce them." Hawk motions to each of us in turn, announcing our names for everyone to hear. I nod my head slightly as he introduces me. I try to smile, but I don't think that's what it looked like. When Hawk is done he says, "There is no official schedule for the night, just mingle and have fun."

"Can we go now?" I whisper to Swift without moving my lips too much. My legs are cold because of the stupid dress; I wish I had not let Robin and Swift convince me into wearing one.

"I don't think so." He whispers back to me and smiles.

Swift relaxes and puts his hand on the small of my back, guiding me to a small group of well-dressed NEST members.

"I don't want to talk to anyone. I want to go home." Well, back to my room. I don't want to make a bigger fool of myself than I have already.

"Exactly." Swift winks at me, "Don't say anything. Just smile and nod your head."

Swift introduces me to the men here. He obviously knows some of them. I stand next to Swift and watch as he makes conversation with these people that he probably has nothing in common with. I wish I had such skills. They could be useful in a fight that is not in my favor; to negotiate my way out of trouble.

But I wasn't born with that skill and I keep my mouth shut and only answer with short answers if someone asks me a direct question.

Somehow I feel fake. And I guess it is sort of true. For now I keep all of my worries and anger inside for a few minutes and pretend to be someone else. Honestly, it is really painful. And I hope that I will never have to behave this way again.

Chapter Twenty One

"Keep the ball safe." are Hawk's last guiding words.

I think everyone is a little tired after staying up so late at that meeting last night. It was just light mingling and drinking sweet beverages, but I stayed up way past my bed time.

Koel takes the round black ball from Hawk, but stares at it, a little perplexed, "What does the ball symbolize in a real life situation?" He turns it over in his hands twice.

"Stop over-analyzing everything, Koel." Hawk scolds him, "It is just a ball."

It's pretty obvious that Koel isn't familiar with any games including a ball, well maybe any games at all.

But Koel asks another question, "Does the other team have a ball?" Koel has to be given precise orders. He can't make decisions on his own.

Hawk completely gives up and just walks away to the control panel. He spoke to the other group before us and we are still unsure of what we are supposed to do and if they have a ball too.

The ball somehow finds its way into my hand, fitting perfectly. Koel must not be able to deal with the pressure of the unknown. Luckily, Swift is with me once again.

"Are you ready?!" Hawk shouts from his safe position.

"As ready as we will ever be." I mutter because we still have no idea what the point of this exercise is.

Blue-jay has moved toward Swift now. I keep them in my sights. As soon as Hawk gives the signal that we have started, I ignore the rising walls around us and plow right through my team members—making Blue-jay step away from Swift—and then continue past them, almost ramming into rocks that keep appearing out of nowhere.

My teammates yell at me to come back, some even question my motives, but what really catches my attention is when everything goes silent and there is one single word shouted over the expanse, "Run!"

I don't know why I started running, other than to get Blue-jay away from Swift and wanting him to follow me, but I definitely was not expecting to be told to keep going. I can't keep going at full speed though, because the buildings and walls and barriers are forming too close together, so I slow down. After I walk a few steps I hear scampering behind me.

I know that it must be Swift or someone else from my team, but the way the area has been built around me makes me claustrophobic and paranoid. And the fact that I have some mysterious package that I have to keep safe does not help. *Who do I have to keep it safe from? The other team? They have Nightingale, Owl, Osprey, Goldcrest and Lark. I am not too worried.*

I take a break in a corner and wait for whatever is chasing me to catch up. I am a sprinter, not a long distance runner, so I'm already out of breath.

Just as I'm about to set the orb down beside me, Swift, followed by the rest of my team, bursts into view further down the alley that I had just come through.

They run frantically.

"Get up!" Swift instructs and without giving me anytime to respond, he grabs my arm and thrusts me forward, almost causing me to drop the ball.

The speed we're moving at and the narrow ways keep me constantly slamming into walls and I practically trip multiple times. If it wasn't for Swift's strong grip on my forearm I would have fallen and been trampled a long way back.

Blue-jay is right behind us followed by Koel and Robin. I have no idea how the other girls are keeping up. Or why we are running so fast and who we are running away from. Not even Nightingale could keep up with us for so long without being as driven as we are.

"Why." I take a breath. "Are." We turn around a corner. "We." The sphere nearly slips out of my sweaty palm. "Running?" *More like flying.*

We enter a wider opening.

"Swift, stop!" Robin practically screams. "It's gone!" And her voice seems strangely far away.

I snap my head back for a look, probably giving myself whiplash. The others have stopped dead in their tracks. I try to rip my arm away from Swift's grasp or at least to stop him. He still hangs onto me though and it's getting weird.

"Swift, you are hurting me." I say firmly and clearly while slowing my pace.

He freezes in place and turns to me. This whole time he had been looking away from me and I was unable see the fear in his eyes that I see now. My first instinct is to grab him and hug him as tightly as possible, but he is scaring me.

"Swift, what the hell is wrong?" I try not to yell at him and make the situation worse.

"Chasing us-terrifying-how did you know?" he stutters out an incomprehensible sentence. I have never seen Swift in this state; whatever is out there must be really dangerous.

"We should go back with the others." I say as kindly as possible.

He just stands and shakes a little. Realizing that it will be hard for me to get him to move, I slip the ball into his jacket pocket and tell him to sit down.

"Come on." I beckon to the other to join us over here.

I make everyone sit before checking out what the deal is, "What happened?"

Robin speaks first, still gasping for breath, "We were watching you take off and didn't understand why until I noticed a darkness starting to form to our right."

"It was not 'darkness'." Koel rolls his eyes, "It was definitely a Preacher. A ten foot tall Preacher."

"That is not what I saw." Blue-jay says solemnly.

"So you all saw different things?" I suggest.

Koel locks eyes with me, "Yeah, I guess so... Then it started coming toward me and I just knew that it was going to kill me." Coming from anyone else, I would think that this was an exaggeration.

Swift shivers, "Whatever it was, it was the most terrifying thing that I have ever encountered." Swift has recovered somewhat. At least enough to speak properly.

He wipes his forehead with the sleeve of his jacket, but loads more sweat linger on his neck and face. And he is really pale.

"Swift, you look like you've seen a ghost."

He takes a shaky breath. "I did." Swift puts his head between his legs and sits awkwardly like that for a few moments until he asks, "How did you see it before us?"

"Oh, um." I don't want to admit the real reason I ran and I don't really know why I ran anyway. "I can see through Hawk's tricks." *That doesn't clear anything up.*

No one speaks for a minute or so. I hope they don't question what I just said, because I have no excuse.

The silence is broken by Swift and I am very grateful for it. "We should have followed you as soon as you took off." Swift says and makes me feel good; falsely of course.

"But why did it come after us?" *And what the hell does it want? The ball? It can have it.*

"I am guessing the ball." Swift pats his pocket.

"That is stupid." Blue-jay points out and I agree with her. "What happens if we just give it to the thing?"

"Now, hang on." Koel interrupts, "Hawk told me to keep it safe."

Once again silence emerges as we debate the situation in our heads.

"Here, let me inspect it." Robin holds out her hand.

Swift reaches into his jacket, pulls it out and carefully places it in her hand.

I know what Robin expects to find—the reason 'it' wants the ball; for it to open and reveal something important or a button… anything.

"Nothing." Robin sighs.

We sit in a circle on the floor, which has transformed into a cobblestone, in a wide space surrounded by four buildings on each side. Arched doorways and gates open to our area. I suspect that we are in a sort of shared courtyard.

Robin rolls the ball into the center of the circle, "Black, made of ebonite. Nothing special."

Not even Swift asks her what ebonite is and how she knows about it. We don't have reason to question her. Why would anyone lie about rubber?

"Damn it." Swift curses under his breath. "What the hell are we doing here? Why is Hawk torturing us?" He is still shaking.

I don't like seeing Swift in pain. "Is anyone else cold?" I ask mostly to sympathize with Swift and to make him not so self-conscious about the fact that he is shivering.

I notice how his usually well-kept hair is now disarrayed when he nods his head yes.

"Apparently the monster went to haunt the other group." Blue-jay breaks the awkward quiet for the first time since I have known her. "I wonder what they are seeing."

We need to get somewhere safer; somewhere that will help everyone get back to their normal selves.

"Come on." I make one swift movement to stand up from sitting cross-legged. "We shouldn't just be sitting and waiting, Hawk sent us in here, with this, for a reason." I bend down and pluck up the ball with my thumb and index finger.

"Yeah, but we do not know what to do with it." Koel is the last person I thought would oppose. "All he said was to protect it."

Oh, I finally give him the orders he has been waiting for and he won't listen to me? "If we stay here, that thing will find us."

"Or we could run into it…" Blue-jay comments.

"Blue-jay, it is really nice that you are talking now and all, but could you stop being so negative?" I turn our treasure over in my hand. "And that is coming from me."

Of course, Blue-jay doesn't react as I had hoped. She doesn't move or get red in the face. If I had said that to Nightingale, she would have already been beating the crap out of me. Or at least trying to.

Still, Swift acts as if she did show signs of aggression, "Hey, hey now. You both need to calm down."

Calm down? "I'm always calm." I pause to think for a moment. "And you said that you like it when I'm more expressive."

"Yeah, but not when you're mean without cause… I agree with you though; we should keep moving forward. We just need to be careful."

"Fine." mumbles Koel. *Oh, so he listens to Swift?*

It takes a while for the three to stand. That run really wiped us all out.

"Okay." Swift clasps his hands together when we are finally ready to move out. "Wren and I will go first, she seemed to sense the monster quite well, and I think Koel should be at the back."

"Sure thing, boss."

The five of us stand in order and then move out.

Swift walks next to me and after a few minutes he asks, "So what did you see?"

214

It takes a moment for me to figure out what he is talking about. I hope he doesn't figure out I am lying, especially for such a silly lie. "Oh, you know... Like Koel, I saw a Preacher."

"You are pretty brave." he answers and I just shrug.

We walk in a line for what seems like hours, listening intently for any sign of life. Each of us is tired and annoyed; about to snap at any second. Even I feel the emotions bubbling up inside of me and threatening to explode. I don't like this feeling; I want to be my normal self again.

The buildings in here are not very tall, maybe three floors high. Every doorway is arched and it seems that we are either walking uphill or downhill, never on flat ground. It is especially cold and damp. Our shoes were not made for this kind of terrain.

"What the hell was he thinking?" Koel just sounds disappointed, not exactly angry.

"Wow." I exclaim in mock surprise, "Are you challenging your leader?"

"Shut up." he mutters.

And then we continue, sometimes making snide remarks or cursing.

The ball gets passed around between us while we walk. Currently I have it. The thought of smashing or destroying the ball enters my mind almost every second I hold it.

"We are going to find Hawk." Swift decides with anger in his voice. I don't think I've ever seen him angry before. "He has to be hiding here somewhere. I'm surprised we haven't stumbled upon him already."

"How is that any different than what we are doing now?" Robin complains. "I am sitting down, my feet are killing me." And she falls to her knees right there.

"Yeah..." Blue-jay too stops walking.

"Wait—" I lift a hand to silence them. "Get up, it's coming." I fake urgency.

They believe me without thinking and hop to their feet. It takes willpower to not start laughing right here and now. I can't tell if it's coming or not; I was just lucky earlier and now they go along with me. They were so frightened that they're willing to believe I have some magic detecting power. I just want us to keep moving and find Hawk so we can confront him. I don't mind lying to get what I want, especially when I am being taken advantage of.

I am the first to start moving again, but the girls follow me easily. My weary feet lift only a few inches above the ground and with each step they shuffle more and more. I try to push further and attempt to convince myself that this will somehow help me in the future. You never know, I might end up walking through an abandoned city for hours being chased by some crazy monster sometime again along my journey to get rid of the Preachers.

"Where is it now, Wren?" Blue-jay questions me after about ten minutes.

Stay cool, "It was—"

One shrill shriek erupts in the air further down this path and is then joined by many running footsteps.

The five in the other group collide with us, turn us around and push us forward. Once again, I am unwillingly being dragged around and hating myself.

"You guys found it?" I ask, anticipating the answer.

"Yep." Lark says through a hoarse throat.

My team is taken over by the wave of freshly frightened Proxies. Somehow, through this, we are united as one group and neither mention splitting up or abandoning the others. Even when there is a fork in the road, we all head in the same direction. Ten minds working as one out of pure fear. Everyone else is scared because of

216

what they've seen, I'm scared because something has the power to make usually reasonable people run around frantically.

"There!" shouts Osprey and points to an apartment building with a door facing us. He runs ahead and stops outside, ushering us in as we pass him. No one questions if we should listen to him, or if we should keep going. We all rush over the threshold and when Lark finally enters, Osprey closes the heavy metal door.

"Thank the gods we found this." Swift collapses against the right wall, completely winded. "That door should keep it out. Good eye, Osprey."

Pretty much all of us sit on the damp floor, or squat, trying to catch our breath. Only Osprey stands sentinel next to the doorway. He doesn't look scared, but as if he is trying to protect the rest of us. Maybe he hasn't seen the monster.

I sit in one of the corners, the cold stone on both sides of me. My pulse eventually slows down. No one speaks, mostly because we are exhausted, but also because we want to be able to hear if the monster is outside or trying to get in. Nothing attempts to get through the door. After long and excruciating minutes, we share a collective sigh of relief that the thing has left us alone for now.

"So what do we do now?" Owl asks. He lies on his back and stares at the domed ceiling.

"How about stay here to rest?" Lark suggests hopefully.

No one disagrees.

"Only for a little while and then we should find Hawk." Swift takes the reins, "He is the only one who can stop this and get us out of here." Swift is really set on finding Hawk.

We continue to rest, each person whispering to their friend. I stay in the corner to the left of the entrance and wait for someone to come to me, but no one does, not even Swift.

From my position though, I can hear Robin and Osprey's conversation. He hasn't moved from his place of guarding. Robin seems a little shaken up.

"What did you see?" Osprey asks, at first a little harsh, but then he returns to his normal self and puts his hand on her shoulder.

She is reluctant to tell him, but does anyway. "It was just this dark, dark force that was growing bigger and bigger, threatening to pull me in."

Everyone here knows that she is afraid of the dark. And everyone has seen something different. I speak clearly so everyone can hear me, "I think its form depends on the person who is looking at it. It becomes whatever the person fears the most." My words silence the chatting. All heads turn to me.

"That does make sense." Robin agrees, "My biggest fear is darkness and that is what I saw."

"Yeah," Osprey begins to object, "but I did not see anything at all."

Deep in thought, the room becomes still again. I am almost positive that all ten of us can feel the strange, dark pull in the air. Hawk probably put us in here to see how we deal with seeing our greatest fears. It makes sense for him to do so. I can see the logic in his actions, but I'm guessing some of the others won't.

"Like I said before, Hawk is the only one with answers." Swift stares blankly. He sits leaning against the wall opposite me. "We find him and we can leave."

We emerge from our hide-out after cooling down for at least twenty minutes.

"Hawk will have taken up refuge in one of the apartments. Look for a building that is different than the others." Swift instructs us.

Our heads turn in different directions, searching for a sign of our trainer.

Lark gives up first, "That will not help us much if we are on the grou—"

"Someone should get a better look by climbing a statue or something." Nightingale states. We wait for her to finish her sentence because we all know what she wants. "And when I say someone I mean me, obviously."

"Why not just look from one of the rooftops?" I say, trying to point out her stupidity.

Nightingale raises one pierced eyebrow, "Mostly because the buildings are completely hollow—no stairs or anything to climb."

She sets off to find a structure that she will be able to climb, but that is also tall enough. Nightingale heads uphill, which I guess is the best way. The rest of us follow her lead.

At the very top of the hill we find a statue not too different from the one in our first session in HABITAT. A man standing straight, a mop under his arm. He is the same dark grey of the stones and buildings, but with that red, cylinder hat. The whole thing is only about four feet taller than a human.

Nightingale approaches the statue, studying it as she moves closer. She only pauses a moment before attempting to climb, but her shoes slip on the smooth surface and slides back down. Of course, she tries again, clearly aware that we are all looking on. She grabs the statue's mop and hoists herself up onto the shoulder, almost slipping again.

Swift reaches his arms up, "Need some help?"

"No." she snaps and slaps his hands away, before he can try to touch her. He's too short to have succeeded anyway.

After regaining her balance, she shimmies up a little further, finally sitting on the head of the statue.

"What do you see?" Osprey shouts to Nightingale.

She grins, "Just a bunch of losers."

"Thanks a lot, Nightingale." Swift mutters and takes a few steps away from the group. *At least she kept it clean for now.*

"Okay, okay…" Nightingale pulls the attention back to her, "Um…" She squints her eyes and leans forward, "At the foot of this hill there is an opening. I don't think the land is clear… most likely a shorter house."

"So that is where we go." Swift concludes.

Before he has a chance to walk away I ask, "Wait, why?"

"Because Hawk would have his base of operations in a building that's different than the others." I give him a look. "I know Hawk better than you, okay?"

"Did you know that he could send a bunch of kids and young adults to face their worst fears in a never-ending maze?" questions Osprey.

"No…" Swift reluctantly confesses. "But that building is our best bet on finding him and giving him a piece of our minds."

"He's gonna get a lot more than a piece of my mind." says Nightingale from above. We ignore her.

"I don't get why all of you are so upset." I admit. "It makes perfect sense why Hawk would do this, it goes along with all of the other tests perfectly. What exactly did you expect when you joined?"

Swift steps toward me, "It may seem like the logical thing, but Wren it doesn't take away from the fact that it's not a humane thing to do. Something like this is emotionally scarring." I clench my jaw and roll my eyes in response. "I'm going that way, you can join me if you want."

The narrow streets are unwelcoming and the way they twist and bend makes it seem like they want us to get lost. For some reason there is not even one road that is straight, especially not one that will take us directly to the place Nightingale was talking about. So we follow her, stopping every minute or so she can find her bearings and then start again. We end up turning around a couple times, but it is not too bad. All of us decided to stick with Swift.

Suddenly, the ground evens out. I haven't been in this area yet.

Owl, who has been a little bummed out, returns to his normal self with this little bit of hope that we might be getting out. "Thank you for choosing Nightingale's travel services, we are looking forward to seeing you again soon."

"Great job." Osprey starts to pat Nightingale on the back, but thinks again and has to awkwardly put his arm down.

I don't have much time to take in my surroundings before we all see the house up ahead and, with one last push, one by one the other eight Enhancements sprint to this new complex. Swift stays behind with me while I jog. Of course, the two of us get to the house last.

No one dares to go in yet.

After a minute of silence and stillness, Lark whispers, "Should we knock or—"

"Hawk!!" Nightingale breaks down the door and then runs in.

"Well then..." Swift mutters and steps over the broken wood after her.

Swift and I enter the main room just in time to see Hawk sitting on a couch and then jump up as he notices the ten people breaking into his shelter.

Nightingale runs up to Hawk, pinning him against the far wall, "What the fuck?!"

Osprey quickly pulls her off of him, but he too is angry.

"It was not my idea." he says clearly, in his defense, still pressed against the wall. "Albatross... The board set this up."

The house we are in is a lot different than the other buildings in HABITAT. It looks familiar too... The length of the house makes up for the single floor. Hawk has been positioned in what I can tell is the living room because of the furniture. This has to be the only building that is furnished.

"They counted on your fear to keep you going."

Everyone is breathing heavily. Probably because we are extremely tired and trying to not be so angry with Hawk.

"And what the fuck is the deal with this?" Well everyone except Nightingale. She holds one of the balls violently above her head. I had almost forgotten about them. And I now notice the bulge in Swift's jacket pocket.

"Stop!" Hawk grabs it from her. "Who has the other one?" He searches us with his eyes.

I reach into Swift's pocket and try to hide it behind my back, but I am not fast enough.

"Wren, give that to me." Hawk beckons for it. "It is very important."

Swift wants me to be more expressive, huh? And I should try to be more of a team player, right? Just watch me. "Nope."

Hawk takes a step toward me and I rush past Swift on the way out. It only takes me a second to bound through the first room and then over the threshold. All of the other trainees wouldn't want to give it to Hawk, so I guess I shouldn't either. If I can do something to really annoy Hawk at the moment, then I'll do it, even if I am already freaking tired. Hawk tries to follow me, but is blocked by the others.

Outside, I try to put as much distance as possible between me and Hawk, but I don't get very far before running into the thing we have been trying to avoid this whole time. I see it on the opposite side of a long alleyway.

A figure stands before me, tall and lean. It wears a long black cloak that falls mid-calf. I quickly recognize the standard Preacher uniform. A hood casts a shadow on the person's face, so I cannot see who this Preacher is. I doubt it has a face anyway. *Why am I seeing this? I'm not afraid of Preachers.*

The form takes a step in my direction and I prepare for an attack. It stands still again after five paces.

222

"What do you want?!" I shout for some unknown reason. This image will not answer.

The hood falls to her shoulders revealing long brown hair, pale skin and brown eyes the color of fresh mud.

She whispers something to me. The distance between us is still too great for me to hear her properly, but I can read her lips... My lips.

"Come on." She smiles wryly. "We aren't that bad." A gloved hand reaches out to me, "They are not supposed to exist. Humans were created to be perfect... but look at us now." She sighs loudly and much more harmoniously than I ever could. Now she speaks normally, "We are only trying to return things to their former state." Her eyes become intense, "Their correct state!" She spits out the words and all of the kindness and pretenses fade away. What is left is a snake. A conniving, manipulative snake.

I find myself mumbling, "Go away, go away." *You are letting her get inside your head.* "You are not me." I say firmly, hoping she will hear me and go away. *Stop her.* And then I become rigid and powerful again, "I AM NOT YOU." Each word is shouted out.

Stop her! I take one final shaking breath and focus on the fact that she is a Preacher.

Her sweet laughter rings out, "We are the same."

"Shut up." This is my first feeble attempt to make her disappear. If she doesn't leave now, then I'll have to resort to violence.

Dark forms appear just out of sight, in the corners of my eyes.

She changes back to the smiling girl. "You want to murder and destroy us. You are exactly who you were raised to be." Her words are not reflected by her behavior and expression, which makes her even more frightening.

My stance changes as I prepare to fight. She mirrors my movements, still smiling. I put up my fists.

Those forms are whispering and muttering now. "You don't think she is actually gonna do it, do you?" "What is she seeing?" "You should shut it down." And finally the clunk of my shoes on the cobblestone as I shorten the distance between us. The Preacher version of me waits in anticipation.

"It was not programmed to—"

I swing my arm and I make contact with her face. It is weird to see myself from this point of view.

No pain or anger at all... just a slit in her bottom lip and an already growing bruise on my knuckles. *Man, her skin is harder than a normal human's.*

My other self spits blood at my shoes, but as the droplets fall they transform into metal bolts and bounce against the rough stone of the road. The noises they make echo off of the moist walls. She sneers, almost-black blood staining her teeth.

And then I punch her again, probably breaking her nose and after I knee her in the stomach she falls to the ground. I would have continued beating the crap out of her if Hawk had not shouted, "Grab her! She is going to break the machine. Stop her!"

I feel Swift's strong arms wrap around me from behind, restricting my movements almost completely. I try to break his grasp so I can hit that thing again.

Hawk goes up to the evil me and taps lightly on the top of her head. A metallic boom follows. Just before a medium sized machine flickers into view, the Preacher whispers, "Do you see what I'm talking about?"

I thrash one last time against Swift's restrictions and scream at what is now a simple robot, barely any better than an oven. It lays on its side with a few dents in it most likely made by me.

"What the hell, Hawk?!" I shout and try to attack him too. Now I know what everyone else was feeling and I hate it. I want it to go away.

Luckily, Swift is still holding me tight so I can't make any very stupid mistakes.

Hawk takes one look at the damaged machine and turns on me, pointing a finger at my chest, "You had better hope that nothing happened to the information."

My breaths come out in angry shakes. A retort has practically left my lips when Swift breathes into my ear, calming me. "Settle down."

He can sense that I'm upset and don't really have any experience with it. He's so close that I can feel the beat of his heart. A grin laces my lips when we break apart.

I notice some rolling eyes, but my friends beam to raise my spirits. I suppose having friends is nice sometimes. Swift probably would have done that for anyone else in this group.

Hawk doesn't say anything. He nudges the robot with his shoe.

I keep a very close eye on Hawk when he finally leads us to the main control panel. He ordered Koel to carry the robot back with us and in the one second before Koel complied, I saw doubt in his eyes. Even if this plan was not completely Hawk's fault, we are still going to have a tough time trusting him again.

"Set that down on the desk there. And sit down." Hawk says quietly. The group shuffles around, trying to find comfortable places. I bump into each desk I come across until I notice Swift sitting and then grab the chair next to him.

"I am sorry that you all had to go through that." No one makes eye-contact with him except for maybe Nightingale. And if she does, it is with glares. "The balls recorded what everyone saw. Everyone needed to see their fear and then the experiment would be over. Now that we have the information, you can leave."

"So how come you did not just throw us into a room one by one and study us that way?" Goldcrest is behind me but I'm the only one who can hear him, as no one wastes a moment getting out of the

225

plastic chairs and slamming them back into place. Whoever exits last slams the door behind them, leaving Hawk alone.

Chapter Twenty Two

It takes a couple days for each of us to recover. I know that a few of the others have had nightmares, but for some reason I haven't. Since the session I have been having trouble keeping my emotions in check at all. If something doesn't change soon I might have to do something drastic or search out help, which, in my book, is something drastic. The only thing I know for sure is that I am over any romantic feelings I had for Swift. Knowing this calms me a bit.

The classroom has been enveloped in a sort of numbness; none one of us have been very active and we strictly follow the curriculum. This is it; this is what I was talking about. The moment when we all slowly start hating each other and the group falls apart. That moment of unity we felt while being chased will not mean a thing anymore. Even though I was expecting this, I have to admit that I am a little disappointed.

On top of all that, Swift has started giving me the cold shoulder, but I have the feeling that it isn't because of the session. We only hang out together occasionally, and it is usually awkward and for some reason ends in bickering. About nothing really, or maybe about something that I don't understand.

***

A deep breath fills my lungs as I open my eyes and swing my legs over the side of my bed. After using the toilet, I hop into the shower for a quick rinse-off without getting my hair wet. And then, when I put on clean clothes, I feel so nice and smell nice... like I could take on a whole army of Preachers without breaking a sweat or taking a hit. I quickly put my hair in a ponytail and head out of the door. I do not meet anyone on the way to breakfast, but as soon as I walk into the dining-hall I see Swift and Blue-jay sitting at a round table.

The muffins look good, so I grab one before planting myself in a chair at their table. Their conversation stops as soon as I sit down. Blue-jay attempts to smile at me, but Swift, for once, does not greet me. We sit in awkward silence for what seems like an eternity.

"Wren," Swift catches me off guard as I'm looking down and picking at my muffin. "I wanted to discuss something you mentioned a week or so ago."

Okay... What the hell is he talking about? I say a lot of things.

"Maybe I should go..." Blue-jay says quietly and moves her chair out, but Swift grabs her arm and makes her stay. She sighs and blinks at me.

"You are aware that we aren't in a relationship, correct?"

I burst into genuine laughter, "Obviously." I try to say seriously.

"Great." His mood slightly changes for the better, so I drop it completely. Though there is something in his eyes that threatens to throw me off my game. I can't decide if it means that he is disappointed in my answer or unsure if I am telling the truth.

I devour the rest of the muffin quickly because I can't stand the quiet and tension between us. Now that I think about it, I haven't been eating a lot recently.

Swift finishes the same time as I do, but stays in his seat, pretending to be busy. After tossing the muffin wrapper in the trash without even looking, I go to my room one last time before class. I just want to splash water on my face and clear my head so I will be ready for whatever Hawk has planned for us.

As I take the elevator down to the basement, it stops on the main floor. The doors open to reveal Swift, who must have pressed the button and been waiting for the next elevator. As soon as he sees me he sort of flinches and then strides over to the secretary and speaks with him. I almost go after Swift, but the elevator doors close in front of me and I sink into the darkness.

What is up with him? I wonder. *Is it just me or is he acting weird?*

It doesn't matter anyway. After my breakdown in HABITAT and the past couple days of sulking, I just need to get back to how I used to be. After that, I won't care what Swift or anyone else does.

***

Instead of going to Swift and asking him why things are so weird between us, I go the reason I was so emotionless in the first place— my dad. So that evening I decide to visit him in his laboratory.

After making sure he's the only one left in the lab, I sneak in quietly. As I approach my father I watch as he puts things away for the night, his back to me.

"Hey, Dad." I say before I get too close; I don't want to startle him.

"Oh." He spins around to face me, "Hello, Wren." Dad walks back to his main desk and straightens the papers on it. "I was just about to leave for the night, is there a problem?"

I don't want to do this... He's gonna be so disappointed in me.
"Um, yeah." I take a deep breath before plunging in. "As you know, I am usually able to control my emotions because, well we both believe that they are distractions and keep us from behaving logically and correctly. The past couple weeks have been stressful and a couple unexpected things have caused me to have trouble controlling my emotions. I was wondering if you could help me in some way."

He sighs and sits on the stool next to his desk, but answers, "Of course, Wren. I am glad you came to me when you identified the problem. It is always best to keep your emotions in check, but are you sure you want my help?" I nod my head, grab another stool and sit next to my father. "Fine. I want you to close your eyes and imagine a switch."

229

"A switch?" I ask.

He explains, "As in a light switch or a lever."

Oh, okay. As I close my eyes I catch my father going back to his work. I continue anyway.

With my eyes closed, I picture a giant metal lever on a white wall. It is facing upwards.

"Can you see it?" asks my father. I nod my head yes. "Good. That switch represents your emotions and your feelings and your pain."

How does he know I'm in pain? I can barely recognize it myself.

A sign appears above the lever. Printed in red ink are the words 'Wren's emotions'. "Now picture yourself pulling it down, switching it off."

In my mind, I step closer to the lever and the wall. I see something other than those two things for the first time. Now my right hand reaches out and grab the black, rubbery grip and pulls on it. I don't try with my full force, thinking that it would be easy, but apparently I'm wrong because it doesn't move an inch.

"Did you do it?"

I ignore my father and try again, but this time harder. The lever moves slightly, but not enough to make a difference. I get frustrated and angry and almost give up on the whole thing until I realize that that's the reason I'm doing this in the first place. I don't want that frustration and anger.

So I roll up my sleeves and grab the damn lever with both hands, pulling as hard as I possibly can. As the lever slowly falls, the anger disappears as well as all of the other things I've been feeling the past few weeks—the fear and anxiety from the session in HABITAT, the worry that I might get kicked out of the Enhancement program, my feelings towards the other trainees and then most of my feelings for Swift, leaving only the important ones there.

I let go and open my eyes after making sure the lever won't budge for a long time.

***

The next day I feel a lot better and hope to get back into Swift's good graces, maybe pretending that nothing happened yesterday at all. He isn't in the dining-hall when I eat my small breakfast, so I rush through eating and down to the classroom in hopes to find him there with Robin and Owl. No one is in the room except Koel. That's how early I am.

Even when there's only a minute before class starts Swift still hasn't appeared. I have been able to relax and talk with a couple of the others until now, but I am starting to get worried. *Maybe he is sick.*

Just as I am about to stand up, Hawk enters with Swift on his tail. They seem to have been deep in conversation.

"Let's get right down to business." Hawk says and Swift and the others who are still standing grab a seat.

I offer Swift the place next to me, but he just shakes his head solemnly and sits somewhere else. I dimiss his behavior and focus solely on the lesson.

Hawk tells us all about the production of modern food and the effect of the Nuclear Winter and Summer had on natural produce. He mentions the different sources such as 3D printing and lab-grown meat. Most of the discussion bores me and I get lost in the bright photos and sketches on the T-screen board.

Afterward, I help Hawk teach some of the younger Enhancements useful fighting techniques based on their small size.

***

Swift sits alone now. I have been joining him for a few meals here and there since our 'conversation', but we have not really 'clicked' like we used to. I think that now would be a good time to bond again.

"Jardah." I greet Swift who practically glares at me. "What's wrong?" I set my tray full of extremely runny meat and sauce on the table in front of me.

"Why do you want to know?" he grumbles in a voice close to a growl.

I am surprised. I know I'm a little new to the whole 'friends' game, but we are supposed to worry about each other, right? "Because I care about you." I say more violently than I meant to.

The way Swift doesn't meet my gaze really irritates and concerns me.

Swift picks a point above my head, still not looking directly at me and abruptly says, "Do you have something to tell me?"

My throat closes as it dawns on me that he knows that I like him—liked him—and he is waiting for me to admit it. Is his behavior an act to get me to confess or is he really mad at me?

Without thinking it through I say, "No, everything is normal now."

Swift jumps to his feet and slams his fists on the table, "Wren, we have been going back and forth for a while now. Just spit it out!" For once he towers over me. I thought that Swift was angry that time in HABITAT, but this is even worse. It scares me and I almost can't say these next words.

I lower my voice so people will not hear. "Fine, Swift, since you are acting like a child I will explain it to you. I liked you... romantically."

Just before I'm about to say that that doesn't really matter *at all*, he looks sternly straight into my eyes. A crease appears between his eyebrows. "Wren... I don't feel that way about you. I—"

"Yeah, I know, I am okay with that. In all honesty, I don't have those feelings for you anymore."

This causes his anger to leave, but he is still very emotional. "Oh, well I—" He looks confused and slightly worried.

I notice the sweat growing on his brow and the apologetic look that begins to grow on his face. "What did you do?"

"Listen, Wren," Swift lowers his voice and sits back down at the table. "I-I didn't know…"

His words and his expression worries me immensely. "What did you do?" I ask again, with more force behind my question.

"I may have told Hawk and Albatross that you have a crush on me and that I think it could cause trouble in the team."

A fire sparks before I can calm myself or think straight, "You did what?!"

"I didn't know, Wren." He pleads with me with his eyes.

My nostrils flare as my eyes move back in forth between Swift and the table. "You have so little faith in me… no one could ever get over you, huh?" I say somewhat quietly. "Do you know what this could have done? Why didn't you just come and talk to me?!" Now it's me who jumps up and smashes my hands against the table between us.

"You're right." Swift says softly and looks away from me.

I can't look at him right now. He could have ruined my chances of ever getting Enhanced because of this nonsense. "Whatever. I need to get out of here." I back away from the table, holding my hands to my head. I am just shocked that something like this could happen. "And do not think of talking to me after this." I turn around and violently make my way out of the cafeteria and into the courtyard.

Outside, I close my mouth that has been hanging open for the past minute and try to act casual. But I can't do much with a thousand thoughts running through my head at the moment. About how one of my only friends practically betrayed me, about how I should probably talk to Hawk as soon as possible and clear things up with him, about how my dad will eventually hear about this and probably disown me, about how I won't be able to look Swift—or anyone else from the team—in the eyes again.

I want to vomit, I want to burst into tears. I feel like slamming my head into the wall, or falling, right here, to the ground and crawling into a little ball of sadness.

Compared to what I'm feeling now, everything that I've been through in the past few months seems like nothing. Now it seems all of these emotions will make my heart and head burst. In my mind, the lever breaks, the bar snapping off and then sparks erupting from the base. And nothing can stop the oncoming storm of grief and anger and pity that I feel towards myself and Swift. I don't know what will happen after this.

I could get a message any minute now saying that I've been replaced. It might not be that good of a reason to kick me out, but Hawk and the others aren't willing to take any chances when it comes to making the perfect team.

I shake my head of all of my bad thoughts. I can't give up just yet, I have a purpose in life; I have a goal. This isn't the end yet.

Standing on my feet, I raise my head high. I hadn't even realized I had sat down in the middle of the courtyard.

I need to talk to Hawk. — I decide with conviction and then run off in a sprint, not caring who sees me or who I pump into because none of that matters to me at the moment.

***

"Hawk, I need to talk to you." Hawk stands five feet away from me, busy talking to one of the Viewing Deck Liaisons.

He looks at me for a moment and then turns back to what he was doing, "Just a second, Wren."

Hawk finishes up his conversation with the worker and focuses on me, taking me to the side. "What are you doing up? It is almost midnight."

"Swift told me about his meeting with you and the others... You need to know that my relationship with Swift is purely platonic and is not going to interfere with the program."

Hawk keeps his eyes locked on mine. "I did find it a little unbelievable when he told me..."

I ask the most important question now, "Is what Swift said going to have any effect on my position on the team?"

Hawk thinks before answering. "If I have anything to say about it, it won't, but that is because I know you personally and knew what Swift didn't make sense. I do not know what the other will think, but I will let you know if they make a decision."

That isn't quite the definite answer I was looking for, but it will have to suffice for now. "Okay, thank you." I salute quickly, turn around and hurry back to the elevator.

On my way back to my room I focus on the next task at hand— falling asleep. I know that my brain will be active all night trying to think of ways to convince Hawk and the others that I am worthy of staying, but, unfortunately, I will also be thinking about Swift and what he did.

I turn to my hallway. Two people talk ahead of me and it takes a second for my vision and mind to clear and recognize the young woman.

Blue-jay walks quickly away from him and towards me, but he grabs her arm.

I hide behind a corner so they can't see me. I stick my head around just enough so I can see who she is talking to. An older man with whiting blonde hair and Blue-jay's crooked nose. He must be her father.

"Wisteria, do not walk away from me."

"Fine, Dad. What do you want?" She pulls her arm away from him and glares right into his grey eyes. His whole being screams power and authority, just like Blue-jay, but she also has a certain frailty.

"I heard that you were not fully participating in the Enhancement training. You know how much this means to you." He towers over her, but she stands her ground.

"You mean 'how much this means to you', right?" She spits back.

This is the first time I have ever seen her so emotional, so expressive. She can be scary if she wants to be.

"We agreed that you—"

"No, father, you volunteered me and I did not object because I was too scared, because I was doing it for you. I never wanted to be in the program. You are lucky it is too late to back out, and unlucky because I am finally strong enough to take on my powers. You just wanted to look good with Albatross, and the other leaders. The only one to have a child in the program, 'you are so proud'."

That's where I saw him. He was one of the NEST leaders at the meet-and-greet.

"I am sorry; I did not know how you felt about this—"

"Because I was taught to accept what was given to me and do as I was told." Blue-jay starts walking again back in the direction of my hiding place.

Her father looks astonished at her outburst, "I am worried about you."

Blue-jay spins on her heels quickly, her hair flipping over her shoulder. "You should be." she hisses and stomps right passed me.

I'm not sure if she saw me, but she didn't act like she did. I sigh in relief and then rub my eyes. I break away from the support of the wall and slowly walk to my apartment.

Blue-jay's father stands where she left him with an expression I cannot interpret. I glare at him as I scoot past.

The shock that Blue-jay caused me and my anger towards her father distract me from my real emotions.

I now feel anger towards someone I thought I never could. I slam my door behind me and I am surprised it doesn't break.

I begin to cry. A deep, bitter cry that makes me shake every time a breath escapes. I haven't cried in years, not since we escaped and were on the run and I was in so much pain. That's when I first learned to control myself, and now there isn't a lot left to hold onto. Not even some stupid imaginary lever that my dad made up to make me feel better.

No crying, no crying, no crying. — I furiously tell myself over and over again.

Showers always help me feel better. — I think as I pull my sweater over my head. I kick my sneakers off and then slide my pants down my pale legs.

A small sink and mirror are next to the toilet and the shower-dryer is opposite to that. It is hard to not hit anything while I violently undress. The tiny bathroom isn't much, but I am very thankful I don't have to share one with the other Proxies.

I take a moment to look in the mirror and see all of the bruises on my body. My nose is still bruised as well as my fists, every muscle in my body hurts. I can still feel the impact of the explosion and the pain in the back of my skull.

I don't need to wait for the water to warm up. There are only two temperatures—hell and Nuclear Winter.

I turn away from my tortured body and jump into the shower without thinking and close the curtain behind me. The burning water doesn't bother me; I have more important things to worry about than that.

The liquid flows over my aching, bare body and the water and tears mix together gathering in a pool around my feet. Soon I cannot tell the difference between the two and can't tell if I'm even crying anymore. The thing is though, I know I am.

I feel the pain and ache in my very bones; they guide me to the floor. Gravity finally has a hold of me and I don't dare try to break its grasp and stand again. Every emotion and injury and pain comes together in this moment, when I'm not sure what will happen to me tomorrow.

I sit there for who knows long, hunched over and naked.

I haven't given up yet. I'll never give up.

Chapter Twenty Three

Can't move. Don't move. Please let today be canceled. Not just the lessons, but the whole freaking day. After talking with Hawk, I came back to my room and tried to sleep. It took me a while to actually fall asleep, but I slept for a couple hours. Now I lay in bed and wondering what happens now. *How do I move forward? Ignore Swift, forget what he did, get revenge?* I don't know if I can stay friends with him.

I get out of bed and dress slowly, hoping that I will receive a message that today's lessons have been canceled. No such luck. After leaving my dorm I notice a greasy smell come wafting from the cafeteria, but I won't be able to swallow anything. I can barely swallow my own saliva.

I sneak through the hallways and down to the bottom floor and, of course, arrive early. Surprisingly, by the time Hawk starts talking, Swift still hasn't arrived. I say a quiet, 'thank you' that I don't have to see him, and then try to focus on Hawk. Emphasis on try.

I don't realize that I'm daydreaming until the door creaks open a few minutes later and Swift creeps in.

He doesn't sit right away, "Sorry, Hawk." Swift salutes like Koel would.

"Just don't let it happen again." is all Hawk says and lets Swift sit before continuing. "What are the Preachers' goals? What is the point of their killing, what do they achieve at the end of the day? How many people are they actually going to kill before they think they are done with the job? Swift has arrived just in time." Hawk smiles without showing his teeth. "I want you to split into small groups to discuss these questions. There is no right answer, because we really do not know. But it is good to try to understand the reasons behind your enemies' actions."

I make eye contact with Swift. For one second I think he'll come over to me and we'll forget what happened. But I'm not sure I really want that, so I glare at him till he backs off. Swift turns away and weaves through the standing people to get to Blue-jay. She stands next to Nightingale. Blue-jay's hair frames her face perfectly.

"How's it going?" I read Swift's lips as he places his hand on her back.

I expect Robin and Owl to peer over my shoulder and join me, but I see them laughing with Osprey. I am used to being alone.

Owl and Swift are the only people I would actually spend my time on, speaking with anyone else would be pointless.

I gather myself and leave the room without a word. Hawk's eyes burn into my back, but he doesn't stop me for some reason.

I'm alone and have free time. It's the opportune chance to have a little adventure in the room that I have been wanting to explore. This time my feet listen to the calls of HABITAT and step into the empty, huge rectangle that can change into anything I want.

I flip open the control panel and turn a knob at random and then press a few buttons. I really hope that a giant robot won't appear out of nowhere and attack me.

Instead, a few small buildings, like huts, flicker into existence. Trees and many types of plants grow out of the floor that becomes dirt.

It's perfect; one of those things that you didn't know you want until it is right before your eyes. Or even worse, already gone. But I have this place to myself for the time being. Even the door to the outside world, the one I am so willing to run away from, has disappeared.

I stay in this universe for a good amount of time just wandering and thinking. I even think about the things Hawk brought up so not to be a bother later.

The Preachers have given up on trying to convert the sinners and have decided that there is no hope for the human race. They won't stop until every unholy person is gone; they believe that is what they

240

are supposed to do. I'm sure they wouldn't mind sacrificing innocent lives or even themselves to help their crusade.

I reach for a tall and bare tree trunk. Until now I have tried to avoid coming into contact with anything so as not to mess up the beauty, and so I don't see the shimmers every item gives off when touched. I want to keep the illusion up and running for as long as I can. Light flashes and then vanishes under my fingertips.

Despite my long shower last night, there is dirt under my fingernails.

The small houses are rectangular and have pointed tops. They look so peaceful...

How can anything be peaceful when there's so much anger and sadness inside? I need to disturb them! I decide and then run towards a ring of four houses.

It doesn't take much to get me angry and soon my blood pressure rises and I have the confidence for destruction. I know that this is all some creation by the program, but smashing through the wooden doors and breaking off tree branches makes me feel better.

But a few minutes after, while I cool down, I regret ruining my dream landscape.

A gap appears in the horizon. Owl's red head pop through it and the images around me disperse. "Sorry, but we have to continue with the lesson..." He really does look sorry. And full of pity. *Does he know what happened?*

Owl runs ahead, leaving me alone. I slowly walk over to the control panel and return HABITAT to its normal state.

Everyone stares at me when I return to the room. Well everyone except for Swift; he looks down at his desk.

I march to the opposite side of the room to my empty chair.

Robin is nearest to me and she touches my arm lightly.

I pull it away and turn on her, "What do you want?" I whisper violently.

241

"So-sorry." She mumbles and gulps. "I was trying to help-you have…" Robin leaves the thought all together and goes back to listening to Hawk.

Focusing on a point straight ahead, I try to cool down.

I am all sweaty and my hair is a total mess from my earlier activities. That must be what Robin was referring to and one of the reasons I grabbed so much attention.

"Wren." Hawk stands between me and my focusing point. "Did you hear what I asked?"

I groan, "No."

"Will someone help Wren by repeating the question and answering it?" This isn't helping my mood.

I don't move, but can tell that someone has raised their hand by Hawk's reaction.

"You just repeated the main question before we split into groups." Swift is trying to kill me. It is he who 'explains' this to me. "The Preacher's goals and motives. What my group thinks is that the Preachers are trying to purify society of people who do conform to their view of an ideal human being."

"People from a certain background, ethnicity, whose ancestors are from a certain place." Blue-jay finishes Swift's thought. "Or religion."

"Very much like the twentieth century's Nazis." Hawk concludes. "I agree."

Osprey represents his, Robin's and Owl's group, "Our group thinks that Preachers are trying to take control of as many people as possible so that the Preachers can brainwash them."

"In my opinion they have given up on the idea that they can change the world." I throw out their idea completely. "They realize that their actions of trying to save others are futile—that's why they barely ever have meetings open to non-Preachers—and they are focusing on eradicating the people they were once trying to save." I like making the room go silent, "They have changed their philosophies."

Koel's watch beeps twice; signaling to us that today's lessons are over.

I prepare to get out quickly to avoid Swift anyone else who might want to talk.

"It would be wise to continue talking about Preachers tomorrow, so start trying to remember any important information on how they work from your experience."

I am already walking through the doorframe. That will be my goal from now on: Get to Enhancement training exactly on time, leave as soon as possible and avoid everyone during my free hours.

***

In my mind, there's an inner war about who is stupider—me or Swift? I'm an idiot for falling for him in the first place and he's an idiot for not checking with me before possibly ruining my life. And I could have talked to him about my predicament in the first place, but I knew that I would be over him before long anyway. I sit behind a round table in the cafeteria at the moment, thinking about all of my problems. The whole situation with Swift gives me so much anxiety, plus I behaved quite poorly earlier today. I am afraid to confront Hawk about the situation because he could have decided to lay me off.

He should have just kept his mouth shut, that way I would still have a friend and a guide. Now I have neither.

I stare blankly at the wall, not focused on anything and only thinking about my failures. I may take a few bites out of the feithid that I got from the lunch-line a few minutes ago, but I don't really pay attention. I have always liked the different kinds of feithid, but now I do not find any joy in watching the few surviving insects try to scurry away before falling under my blade.

The cafeteria is pretty crowded now; I am slightly surprised that no one has asked to sit at my table. It could be because of my bad mood and sour expressions that people are avoiding me. A hovering roar of sounds and voices fill the dining hall. All of the voices seem to be mocking me somehow. Whispering about me, laughing at me, spreading rumors. These things have never bothered me before, but for some reason I can't ignore them now.

From my right an annoying man bumps into the table and chuckles, "Hey, can you—"

I had already been unconsciously clutching onto the knife on my tray and in one swift movement I stand up, push the guy against the nearest wall with my left hand and shove the knife an inch away from his throat with my right. My chair flies back and hits the front of the food stand. "What did you say about me?" I ask through clenched teeth. I grip the front of his shirt.

The Proxy holds his hands up in surrender, "I could never beat you in a fight." I don't focus on him, my eyes move from one place to the other fast. The knife, the throat, the face, the shirt, the contact, the wall, the Proxies behind me.

"Whoa, man. Leave him alone." Someone places their hand on my shoulder. I almost thrash at the hand, but instead I just shrug it off.

"Wren, are you okay?" Sleepy's grey eyes pull me in for a second. In that moment I realize what I am doing and where I am and snap back into the present. I let go of Sleepy's shirt and drop the knife before going back to the table and knocking my tray of food off the table.

Proxies try to stop me as I make my way to the exit. They grab at my clothes or my arms and the whole time I hear Sleepy's muffled voice shouting at me, but he isn't angry.

***

The bed is not the only thing that groans as I roll out of bed. My muscles ache and so does my brain.

I can't let another incident like last night's happen again. I need to let Hawk and Albatross know that I am fine and that there is no reason for them to kick me out. I can't get into any more embarrassing situations, especially when I am around Swift.

I can barely lift my legs to slip them into pants and even debate whether or not I should put on real clothes.

My long brown hair does not want to cooperate, so after I simply run my fingers through it, I give up.

None of the food for breakfast looks good and I end up just grabbing a handful of breakfast flakes and picking at them at a table in the corner facing the door. From here, I will be able to see everyone who walks in. I finish my breakfast quickly and then make my way to class, trying to behave as good as possible in case someone is watching. Just as I had planned, by the time I have arrived they have already begun.

"Did you do what I asked you to?" Hawk asks right as I walk past him on my way to my desk.

I am not sure if he was specifically asking me, but I tell him that I did anyway. I mean... I kind of did.

"What do you have to tell us?"

This time I am definitely not sure who he is talking to because I had my back to him.

No one speaks up so as soon as I am situated in my chair I begin, "Um, like I mentioned yesterday the Preachers don't really... go out and recruit. Which is pretty good for us; that way it is harder for them to get followers I guess. I heard from my dad that they used to spread their ideology more, but stopped around ten years ago." *The exact time Preachers did certain things has never been clarified.*

245

When they formed, when they gave up, when they started killing...
No one knows. Maybe they have been around for a hundred years
and only now have been publicly known.

Blue-jay throws in some stuff she overheard her father saying and soon Robin and Owl are relaying news from the refugees and Koel is telling us things about his homeless friends.

Hawk writes down each point on the board and we fill up every inch of it quickly.

"This is what happens when you work together." Hawk points out. "Each one of you, each one of your thoughts, your experiences, they are pieces of a puzzle and together, we get a look at the whole picture. A picture and a solution."

Working as a team and getting something done has really raised my spirits.

Now I know that Preachers raid the Circumference—the edges of the major cities—once a month. These are always the slums, where the poor population lives and there is usually a high crime rate.

I am also informed that not just political figures have been going missing, but also famous club owners, big designers and the like.

And that Nightingale is still upset that The Chalk Outlines are in danger.

Preachers are taking action against humanity and everyone knows it. People may try to ignore it, but they could also be the next to be targeted. But still, no one is retaliating; the Preachers must have a strong hold in the government and in other fields.

"I am really proud of the work you have done today, team. Take a break for a few minutes and then meet me in the smaller training room." We barely do anything in there except for martial arts training.

"The one that does not turn into a giant maze and try to kill us?" Owl asks, his hand under his chin.

"Yes, that other one."

These past couple days and the exercises Hawk has come up with have dispersed the tension between us and him, but not with each other. "Sure thing, boss."

In the break people move their chairs around to form small groups. All of them excluding me.

I close my eyes. *Cool. Everything is cool.* I have to remind myself to breathe.

I use the break to pee and then wash my face, water splashing out of the small basin.

There is a knock on the door as I dry my face with the bottom of my shirt, "Occupied." I shout.

"It is me." Hawk. "Are you okay?"

I am not going to open the door, "Yeah, I'm fine." I can barely say that without becoming angry.

"I heard about what happened in the cafeteria." He pauses for a moment in hopes that I will reply. His words just make me worry about my position on the team. "You will be glad to hear that you have not been kicked out. Yet. Watch your behavior the next few days, or you will have something to worry about."

"Okay, thanks." is all I manage to say without my voice breaking. Staring at the door, I wait for him to leave.

He sighs, disappointed in me. "Training time."

I wait until he walk away before exhaling all the stress that has built up the past few days. I can still feel the anger and emotion just inches away, so I will have to watch myself.

After taking a few moments to breathe, I creep through the clean hallway, making my way to the sound of some force hitting a punching bag. Ducking through the doorway, I try to not make eye-contact with anyone.

The way the team has fallen apart is apparent as I look in from the outside. Cliques have formed: Osprey, Robin, Owl and Lark; and then two pairs: Swift and Blue-jay, and Koel and Nightingale. It is obvious that Koel doesn't enjoy Nightingale's company that much though. I don't understand why they hang out. Goldcrest is the only one not in a group.

Koel and Nightingale are sparring on the mat. I haven't been in a good fight since Proxy training. I almost run up and challenge one of them when I hear a muffled cry.

Everyone stops what they are doing and crowd around Owl who sits awkwardly on his butt. He grips his right wrist and winces. Owl tries to not make such a commotion and to muffle his moans, but I can tell he is in pain. A red rubber ball, slightly larger than a human head rolls slowly away from the scene.

"Are you okay, buddy?" Osprey holds his right hand out to help Owl up, then quickly realized his mistake, retracts it and jerks out his left arm.

"Yeah." Owl grabs Osprey's hand with his weaker, but not injured hand. Robin helps him get to his feet properly, "Well no."

"The thing is…" I can tell that Owl is going to drop a secret on us. "I have problems with my wrists and other joints… some kind of weird disease that's pretty rare for someone as young as me. I have trouble lifting heavy weights and flexibility. It's one of the main reasons Preachers wanted me dead… "

"Do not worry about it, Owl." Osprey tries to make him feel better. "I am sure the Enhancer can help with your injuries and until then we will try to make everything easier on you." *Should Owl really be treated any differently just because he has a disadvantage? I know that I wouldn't want that.*

"Thanks." Owl tries to smile despite the pain.

Osprey and Robin take him to a bench on the side and then return to training.

Before I have time to walk to my own punching bag I hear Nightingale call, "Hey, Goldcrest, how 'bout you come up here and fight me?"

"Yeah, I was not planning on getting beaten up today." he responds and then adds, "Plus I have to look good for my date later..."

"You have a date tonight?!" Robin exclaims and makes several of us jump. Everyone stops working. "Why didn't you tell us?" She genuinely looks hurt.

Goldcrest answers candidly, "Well, none of you are really my friends... Expect for Osprey, maybe."

Robin's eyes grow bigger and she rushes up to him, "I am so sorry if we ever made you feel unwanted." she says sincerely. Then she smiles and asks, "Now who's the lucky girl?"

Goldcrest blushes and grins, "Well actually, it is a guy."

Lark turns to him, confused. "Wait, what?" she asks.

I want to laugh at her and smack her at the same time. I can't believe how much of a closed-off life she's had. Sexual preference barely has any importance in the outside world. Well except to the Preachers.

"It means that he is homosexual." Koel mutters in explanation. "Gay."

Osprey sighs and shakes his head. That really irks me. He doesn't think anyone saw, but I did. *He thinks he is so much better than the rest of us because of his religion, doesn't he?*

"Well you see, Osprey? Goldcrest is gay." I send a gesture in Goldcrest's direction while moving away from Osprey. "Do you have anything to say about that?"

Osprey is calm and does not respond in an emotional way like I had hoped. I am just picking fights now. "I don't know what you are trying to insinuate, Wren. As you already know, I am not a Preacher." He takes a step closer to me, "I am not going to try to convince

249

Goldcrest to change his ways or act like a child. It is obvious that he has made his decision.

"What I am going to do is be Goldcrest's friend, help him as best I can and just be there for him. If then after that he decides to ask why I am being so nice to him, why I am so happy all of the time, I will explain my beliefs to him and maybe change his mind about the way he sees the world." Osprey says louder for everyone to hear, "The way all of you see the world. I do not have a problem with Goldcrest even if I do not agree with him completely."

Whatever emotions I had related to this subject have left me.

"Christians are supposed to spread love, not hatred." Osprey smiles an infectious smile. "Are we good?"

Despite my better judgment, I relax slightly and nod. I guess Osprey is just a nice guy.

He wraps his arms around me and almost lifts me off the ground.

I will never admit it out loud, but I have missed hugs and human affection. His blonde hair smells like... Chocolate. Which is odd because it's hard to come by.

When he puts be down I straighten my shirt and pretend like it didn't happen.

Swift stares at me from a little ways off; he hasn't dared come close to me, though.

I jump when Osprey puts his hand on my shoulder, "You seem a little stressed. Has something happened?" He looks at me with his big blue eyes.

I hesitate for a moment. "Yeah, but I don't really want to talk about it."

Osprey's voice surrounds me in warmth. "I am sorry if you are not feeling well." He sighs. "Maybe we should go sit over there with Owl and rest. We don't have to speak."

"Yeah, okay. Thanks." I give him a small smile.

I walk over to the bench with Osprey and sit there for the remainder of the lesson. He doesn't ask me anymore questions, in fact he does not say anything for the whole twenty minutes we are together. His presence is enough to calm me down again and to stop thinking bad thoughts for the time being. He is like a buffer.

My mind silent, I watch the others take turns fighting on the mat. No one really gets hurt and the fights are not very intense, but it serves as a good distraction.

"Hey, get up." Osprey pats me on the back and I realize that I zoned out.

The eight others have grouped around Osprey, Owl and I in a semi-circle while Hawk stands in front of us. Osprey helps me get to my feet.

"Despite the sudden outbursts and an injury, today was a good day for our team. Tomorrow we will be visited again by the leaders of NEST that you met a couple weeks ago. They want to get to know you a little better so I will be presenting the information I have collected on all of you from the past weeks, including the fears you saw. This is just one more step closer to Enhancement. I am not allowed to give you too much information, but I think we are really close." He half smiles. "You are dismissed. Be on your best behavior tomorrow."

I prepare myself to leave quickly when Hawk catches my eye. I reluctantly go to him. "You, especially, need to be on your best behavior tomorrow. Do you think you can handle that?"

I almost tell him what I really think—that maybe I won't be able to handle it because the stress and my problems have messed with my brain and emotions. But I put on a brave face and say, "Yeah, no problem." with as much confidence and sincerity I can muster.

I can *handle this.*

Chapter Twenty Four

I stumble out of bed in the morning, throw some clothes on that I am not sure even match, and wander into the cafeteria craving pastries. No such luck for me.

I end up leaving a few minutes later without eating anything and hazily going to the elevator bank. I am so tired. Last night I couldn't fall asleep for thinking about Swift and Hawk and Enhancement. I have the small feeling that I'm forgetting something, but choose to ignore it.

On the bottom floor, a dozen or so people talk in groups in the hallway. I walk right past them without giving them too much attention. But as soon as I step past the door to the training room, Hawk pulls me in and starts ordering me around.

"What is wrong with your hair? What are you wearing? Are you trying to give me a heart attack?" are some of the things I hear. I slide my hand over the top of my head in a feeble attempt to tame my hair and then straighten my shirt.

Hawk continues to run around like a maniac, poking each one of us and putting us in proper places.

I'm not exactly sure what is going on. Hawk stupidly places me between Swift and Osprey. Hawk probably thinks that I'll behave better next to those two. But in reality, I can't even look at Swift without, one: hating myself, and two: wanting to punch him in the throat. I either stare at my feet or try to pay more attention to Osprey.

Swift touches my arm lightly, "Wren, I think we should talk."

I pull my arm free of his grasp quickly, "I don't want to talk to you." I say under my breath, trying not to shout.

Hawk walks past me and I grab his attention, "What is going on, sir?" I ask as politely as possible.

He turns off the tablet he was holding, "I told you yesterday. The people who overlook the Enhancement program are coming in in just a few minutes to see our progress." *Crap he did tell us, and I forgot.* Hawk speaks louder now, so that all of the future Enhancements can hear, "This is not a physical test, but a mental one of sorts. They want to know your advantages and disadvantages; your weaknesses and strengths. Just like we have talked about before. Apparently they were not very impressed from the dinner.

"I will address each person individually, but you are not allowed to respond unless you want to make a bad impression on your bosses." *He doesn't want us to embarrass him.* He does have the right to worry—most of us are insane.

The door creaks open behind Hawk, signaling that we have begun. The Enhancement program leaders file in and stand around us in different areas of the room.

Albatross hobbles in the lead, heavily relying on his cane. This is the first time I notice the handle on his cane, it is the head of some sort of bird made of silver.

Most of our spectators are older, already graying and have just enough wrinkles to make a difference. There are a few women among them, but most of them are men. I recognize a few of them from that evening when Swift and I still liked each other. I notice Swift shift his weight from one foot to the other.

I shake my head and try to stay in the moment. *Who will Hawk target first?* I wonder.

I expect Hawk to dive in right away, like he is known for, but instead he welcomes the leaders and thanks them for blah, blah, blah.

My feet start to hurt from standing still for too long.

"Now that you have had a good look at everyone," By this time almost all of the birds of prey have circled us at least once. "I think it would be wise to start the evaluations."

I have gone through way too many evaluations in my short time as a member of NEST. I guess that the purpose of this evaluation is to show everyone their limits and where they need to improve.

It will be uncomfortable to have my flaws broadcasted for complete strangers to hear. SO far only the leaders of the program know who we are, but I wonder if we are ever going to be shown to the whole NEST community.

"Agent Osprey." Hawk indicates that Osprey will be the first to be embarrassed.

"Jardah." Osprey greets our 'bosses'. "I—"

"Osprey is too soft." Hawk interrupts him, "And that causes him to not always follow instructions. He does not do this out of malice, but because he does not always agree with what he is told to do. Osprey is not willing to physically harm any person, not just his fellow teammates. And that is a huge liability in the field. I suspect that his Enhancement power will have something to do with that lack of ambition to fight." Osprey still smiles, despite what is being said about him. "The interesting thing is, during the fear session, nothing appeared before Osprey."

That actually *is* interesting. I notice some pens moving across paper, or typing on T-Screens. They are taking notes.

"Agent Lark." Hawk moves on to his next victim. "She is inexperienced in almost everything. She is not serious, but silly." It is kind of nice to hear the things I have been thinking out loud without me getting in trouble for saying them. "Lark is also not physically fit; she is the slowest runner in the whole group, which I do not think we can really do anything about. Her greatest fear, or at least what appeared before her in the session, was fire."

I study Lark now to see her reaction. I notice that her bottom lip quivers and she is trying very hard to hold herself together. I can almost imagine what is going on her head; she is imaging fire like Hawk mentioned. Licking the walls, heating her skin, causing sweat to drip down the side of her face.

"Agent Blue-jay." A man moves behind me. "She is willing to do anything and does not have any personal opinion on any matter."

"That a good thing, correct?" The same man asks. I can't see him from my position.

"I guess so, but we do not want our Proxies to be robots, Agent Ostrich. We want them to have voices and not be afraid to tell us what they need. She also has not left this building in some time, and that is a bad decision at best." Hawk pauses a moment to get back on track, "What she saw in that room, her fear, was her father." A few shocked looks appear on the onlookers' faces and Hawk leaves it at that, letting them draw their own conclusions.

I take a quick look over my shoulder and easily recognize Blue-jay's father as the man that spoke. He could never admit that he may have been wrong in the way he raised her. He probably thinks that fear only comes from respect.

Blue-jay tries to hide her face in her hands.

"Agent Koel. He is altogether a good Proxy, but that does not mean he can work properly in this format. Koel has trouble working in a team and he is too serious. He needs to loosen up a bit." *So Lark is not serious enough, but Koel is too serious. There is a very narrow gap we have to fit in.* "Understandably, the robot took form as a monstrous Preacher in the eyes of Koel." A strong guy like Koel wouldn't want his weaknesses and fears told to strangers, or anyone in fact.

"Agent Wren." *Oh great, my turn to hear what other people think is wrong with me. They will probably be right, but not understand the reasons behind my actions. There is always a reason.* "Like Koel here, she has trouble working with others. She does not make friends very easily and shuts people out almost immediately." *Unless I know they are going to stick around.* "Wren also has a hard time reading people, knowing what to say or what not to say during specific moments, and that usually ends up with someone having their feelings hurt." *Okay, that is true and I don't have an excuse for it... How 'bout genetics?* "Oddly, the thing

Wren saw was herself, and she was the only one who tried to fight her fear instead of run away from it."

The spectators nod their heads and write more things down. I don't know if that means they like me or hate me. I am thankful that Hawk doesn't mention my 'relationships' with anyone from the group.

Hawk tries to draw the attention back to him. "Agent Nightingale. Like Wren, Nightingale says whatever comes into her mind, but in a different way than Wren. Nightingale knows exactly what she is doing, while Wren is simply tactless." *It's funny and slightly annoying how she is always being associated with me.* "She does not think before she acts, which gets her into a lot of tough situations especially in combat. Nightingale is also very rebellious and stubborn." I am surprised Hawk didn't include that in my assessment too. It frightens me somewhat that Nightingale and I are so similar. "Nightingale's fear took the form of the man that sexually assaulted her as a young teenager. Nightingale's reaction to the image was not exactly fear, more anger than anything else." Nightingale wants to say something to Hawk and to the leaders, but she knows to keep her mouth shut.

She would probably say that it is no one's business knowing her deepest, darkest fears. Nightingale still stands strong though, as if to explain that she actually isn't afraid of that guy anymore.

"Agent Owl is a pretty good team member. Other than his knack for wrong-timed jokes and problems with strength—which are totally unsolvable at the moment—he behaves properly." Owl cracks a smile, looking at only the good parts of Hawk's assessment. "Owl fears something that he has not seen, but something he has been told about his whole life—Preachers."

"Agent Swift." *Hawk's pride and joy.* Swift tenses beside me. "Swift bruises easily." *That is a weird thing to say.* "Both in the mental-emotional way—he gets offended easily—and also in the physical way—it takes him longer than it normally would to recover from any injury no matter how small. Swift likes to play it tough even though he has a soft side." *Huh? I would have never thought those things about Swift. He always seems so strong and protective.* "I do not exactly understand what appeared before Swift in the fear session. It was a simple boy." *A boy?* Swift clenches his jaw and tries to not show any emotion.

"Agent Robin is a great addition to the team. She is bright, energetic and always willing to help. Despite her obvious fear of the dark, she has no major problems." The ginger family is looking pretty good right now.

Well that just leaves Goldcrest, he already has self-esteem issues so I wonder why Hawk would leave him for last.

"And now for our last Enhancement, Goldcrest. Hmm…" Hawk picks at his chin, "Where do I begin?" *Great.* "Goldcrest has many problems. He has health issues, being sick and frail most of his childhood." *He is pretty much still a child.* "He is weak in many areas, physical and mental. But Goldcrest is a good person; he speaks the truth and is a good friend if people let him be, he is also very smart."

That's it. That is all the members of our screwed up family. Well honestly, these people will never be my real family. Not even my real family is my real family. I've never felt like I click with them and can be myself around them. I've always been trying to keep my distance from my family so they won't get hurt if something happens… I guess you don't exactly get a real family in this line of business.

"Well thank you for holding this meeting, Hawk." Blue-jay's father steps forward to speak for the group of leaders. "We are happy to inform you," he does not look happy, "That this program is being advanced. Enhancement will take place in a week's time and until then special sessions will take place including placement. Each of you will pair up with a partner from the team. Good luck, stay safe, think fast, run, and do not get too attached." I wonder if that is his motto. He kind of ruins it for me, but the saying is branded in my mind.

Hawk breaks away from the rest of us and begins speaking to some of the 'important' people.

These people will decide my fate. They will choose my partner for… well, until the end of this war… if whoever they pick survives that long.

I don't like standing around and doing nothing, so I burst out of my position and walk away from everyone.

Someone shouts to me as I leave the room, but I am not really in the mood for talking.

The hallways are gloriously empty, so it takes no time for me to travel back to my dorm.

I pause for a second when I reach the Courtyard. The Proxies still eating breakfast and chatting make too much noise for my fragile ears. The pace of my feet and steps slows and I watch as many agents trickle out of the cafeteria. Many of them are laughing. It seems odd to me that the Proxies in here could be laughing while people are dying out in the real world. But I suppose people die all the time anyway.

I nap for a few hours and when I wake up, not knowing what time it is, I grab a snack from the cafeteria. That is my day: sleep and eat, sleep and eat. When I notice the setting sun out of one of the windows, I decide that I can officially go to bed for the night.

***

"This next week before Enhancement we are going to focus on the weaknesses we discussed yesterday." *Great. I thought we were done with that.* "We can either go over them in small groups or all together."

I prefer small groups, but Lark exclaims, "All together." with a stupid grin on her face.

"Very well." Hawk agrees, "It would be better to advance with everyone, as a team."

My 'problem' is not letting people in, so to advance I will probably have to discuss some personal matter. This arrangement annoys me, but I wouldn't mind watching Lark run around like an idiot.

"Wren, get up here." Hawk instructs me. I guess my issue is the easiest to attend to. "Tell us something that no one else knows about you."

I want to growl at him to leave me alone, but I shuffle to the front of the classroom and lift my head high. I don't need to tell them anything too important and personal.

What is the silliest thing I have done recently? Hmm... "Sometimes I talk to my stuffed dolls." is the only thing that comes to mind. *That has to help them get an idea of me, right?*

"Wren MacGregor." Hawk scolds me like he is my father and I am a child.

My whole life I have been running away from everyone. Even my family, because I knew that I would leave them one day and I didn't want to hurt them... or get hurt.

Even in the NEST training I was meant to stay away from everyone, not get attached, not to ask personal questions and I was more than happy about that. I got attached to Swift and I got burned. Now they expect me to pour my soul out to these people, to trust them with my life, to be friends with them. Even when they are most likely going to die.

I know what Hawk wants me to say, and I can't risk failing this test, so I go back to when I really was a child.

"I had friends when I was a Preacher, people I trusted and would give my life for. And I was just a child.

"One day my father walks into my bedroom and tells me to pack. We had been talking about leaving recently, but I never thought it was true." I gulp slowly and take a break. I tell my burning eyes warning me about the oncoming tears that I don't want to cry. Usually if I let some emotion leak, a whole wave of emotions will break through, and I can't handle them right now, not ever. "My family lived on a block where only Preachers lived. My dad warned me not to say goodbye to anyone, not to tell anyone that we were leaving. I had seen others leave and had heard terrible stories of what happened to them after they did, after they left the Preacher lifestyle. The others didn't really have trouble going, no one reacted as badly as they did to my family's departure.

"I snuck over to the neighbors' house after my father left. My best friend lived there. She and I sat in their living-room and I whispered to her about our departure. I expected to receive tear-filled goodbyes and hugs from her at least—" I stop, I don't know why. Maybe for dramatic effect, maybe because my throat is closing in on itself. "She nearly dropped the glass she was holding as she stood up. She spat on me and called me a traitor. I ran out of the front door and slammed it closed as she called for her parents. Because of me, we had to flee that night with barely any of our belongings."

"It wasn't your fau—" I put my hand up to stop Robin from continuing. I know that, but my actions caused us to walk around for a weeks without any clothes or food.

Swift stands up and then leaves. *What the hell?* I practically run after him just so I can ask what his problem is.

I hold back my tears until I sit back down in my spot. There, I let a single tear roll down the side of my face and then stop the rest.

Osprey pats my right shoulder.

"That was... more than I was expecting." *At least I surprised Hawk.* "Osprey would you willing to go next?"

"I would be happy to." is what he says, but I can tell that he doesn't mean it. I think that he is just trying to get the attention away from me.

I can now put my focus on Osprey's weakness, if it even counts as one. *Osprey has trouble harming people... so will he have to hurt someone? Fight them, kick them, punch them?* I find the idea to be ridiculous.

Osprey pats my head when he gets out of his chair and then does and stands a little ways away from Hawk. I realize that Hawk actually will have Osprey hit him.

"It may be a small achievement, but Osprey, I want you to punch me," Hawk turns and flexes his arm. "Right here." He points.

Osprey ruffles his wavy hair. "Hawk, I don't really want to... It's against my belief system. I—" *Then why did he join the program? That's kind of silly... What did he think we'd be doing?*

"No, it is okay." Hawk encourages Osprey. "I want you to hit me. It would be a sin to not hit me."

Despite the fact that Osprey does not fall for Hawk's stupid attempt, he prepares to attack. "Are you sure?"

Hawk rolls his eyes in response and pats the same area on his upper-arm.

I slide forward in my seat and then notice that everyone else wants to get closer to the action too.

Will Osprey go all out and punch Hawk really hard or close his eyes and throw one?

Both Osprey and Hawk are ready, as well as their ogling fans.

In the last second, right before Osprey moves, Hawk pulls away.

"I could see that you were really prepared to harm me." Hawk motions that it is okay for Osprey to return to his place. "But I do want to ask you why you do not feel the need or want to physically harm?"

"Because I do not think violence is the answer. Violence only brings on more violence which causes more violence. It is a cycle that never ends unless we make it end. Someone needs to be the bump in the road that throws the whole system."

Unfortunately Lark doesn't have to run around the room while I laugh at her. I could use a good laugh, but Hawk thinks that she can't be helped, except by the Enhancer. Maybe he knows more about her than he is letting on.

Like Hawk said, some weaknesses can't be dealt with and solved. Some of our weaknesses are actually what make us special and unique; and worth something. Without us and our so called weaknesses, the team would be missing a potentially great asset that we can't see at the moment because circumstances have not evolved to reveal the need for these certain attributes. Humans cannot foresee the future, something that seems small and insignificant now might be really useful later.

To help with Blue-jay's and Koel's problems, instead of having normal activities we're all heading out to a restaurant so even our strictest members can have some fun. Some of our members will be seeing the great outdoors for the first time in a long time or for the first time ever. Whoop dee doo dah. We collect Swift from the hallway—who knows what the jerk was up to—and head up to the lobby. The group stays on Huntington Street, which I learn is the name of the street the NEST headquarters are on, checking out some of the shops and stands. Hawk manages to get a few drinks into Koel and he relaxes a tiny bit. It's crazy to see the difference between life inside NEST and life outside, even if we are only feet away. The way people dress and the way they behave is already so much different depending on whether you live near the center of the city or in the

Circumference. People in the Inner Ring can laugh and not worry about tomorrow and for just a moment we are like the people here wearing bright colors and only thinking about the next drink we're going to order.

Chapter Twenty Five

"So continuing the fun exercises from yesterday," *Oh, I can't wait for this,* "Each of you will pair up with someone you would most likely not talk to." *So at least Swift is off of the table.*

"Will these be our official partners?"

"No, but it could affect the decision." Hawk pauses a moment before throwing us into the activity, "Swift and Goldcrest, Osprey and Blue-jay, Wren and Lark, Nightingale and Owl, and last but not least, Robin and Koel. Go talk for a couple minutes or play a game or have a brawling match or something." *Yay. I am so good at improvisation.* I wish he would have told us to go be sarcastic together, I would succeed in that.

"I guess I should introduce myself properly, since we've never actually spoken." Lark comes right up to me and holds out her hand for me to shake. "Agent Lark, also known as Dot, it's nice to meet you." I wearily take her hand.

"Wren." And then after a second, "Just Wren."

She waits for me to continue speaking or do something. With her hands fiddling behind her back, her smile slowly fades as time goes on and I don't say anything at all. There are a few couples still in the room, but I think Nightingale left with Owl to torture him in the training room.

Reluctantly, I start the conversation, "So… what do you want to do…?" Lark perks up in response to my words. She seems to be only a few inches shorter than I, but she stands on the balls of her feet so in reality she is probably half a head shorter.

"Well, um, do think Hawk would mind if we left the Enhancement floor?" Her warm brown eyes bounce around, not focusing on one thing for more than a few seconds. Her words come out fast and somewhat childish, "He did tell us to do anything and I was thinking that maybe we could go see my family, they live only two floors above us."

"How old are you?" The words come out of my mouth before I can stop them.

"Well I would have to be at least fifteen to be a Proxy. And I would have to be a Proxy to be in this program."

"So fifteen."

"Yeah."

I know how she got through the maze, but how did she pass all the other stages of testing? She has to be super smart or something.

I take a glance at Hawk who has taken a seat in the front row. He already looks like he's ready to take a nap. "I think Hawk would prefer us to stay down here." I am not looking forward to meeting a whole family of Larks.

"That's fine with me."

I sit on the nearest chair and she grabs another one and makes it face me before sitting herself.

Her mouth turns back to a firm line after a minute or two of silence and then it opens, "Yesterday was pretty fun."

"Yep." I send a grim smile in her direction.

"How often do you see the city?" Interest has returned to her eyes.

"Well when I was living in Tieced, before joining NEST, I would leave the house at least once a day. But I didn't pay much attention to my surroundings." After a moment, "Was yesterday the first time you've ever been outside?"

"Do I look like I've never been outside?" I have no idea what that means or how to respond. "Not my first time, but it's been a while."

"It was great to see everyone relax. Especially you, Wren, you have been a little—" *Yeah, I know my problems with Swift have caused me to act a little weird...*

265

"Yeah, yeah, I know." She doesn't have to continue. I could try to justify my actions, but that would mean explaining what happened and I don't really want to tell anyone what happened, especially Lark.

I decide to change the subject, "Do you have any hobbies?" I practically wince while attempting small talk.

"Not really." She ponders my question while chewing on her bottom lip, "I don't have a lot of spare time with this course and my job and helping my mom with my siblings. You know how it is."

I nod my head even though I don't know how it is to take care of younger family members.

Lark begins to ask me a different question, "Do you—"

"Hawk! We need your help!" shouts come from down the hall. I suspect they're from the training room.

I recognize one of the voices to be Swift's. My first instinct is to rush to his aide, but I quickly remember what he did and instantly feel angry again. I know we'll have to make up sometime, but I don't really want to.

I grip the sides of my chair to keep myself from jumping up. *Hawk can take care of it. Let Hawk deal with whatever Swift did.*

"Wren, Lark, come with me." Hawk calls us to join him in checking on the others. Everyone else must already be in the training room. *Fine.* I actually don't mind seeing Swift screw something up for once.

Lark hops up and I follow her after Hawk. We walk at a normal pace to the training room. As I get closer I can hear mutters and then one loud, "Hawk, come faster!"

"Not in HABITAT." Hawk tells us and we begin jogging the short distance and arrive at the smaller training room a few moments later.

The mats are out and I notice a punching bag still swinging on its chains, but no one touches it now. Goldcrest hangs in Swift's arms, his body looking even smaller now, compared to Swift's.

266

"What the hell happened?" Hawk wastes no time in trying to help and takes Goldcrest from Swift, who looks like he might start crying.

"I was trying to show him some good fighting techniques and he just got really sweaty and said he was tired. Then all of a sudden he passed out." Swift runs his fingers through his dark hair multiple times, rubbing the back of his neck in between. His lower eyelids quickly become red and for a second I am worried that he really is going to cry.

"Robin?" Hawk turns to her as if she will have all of the answers.

She too, doesn't look like a happy camper, "Fatigue?"

This is the moment I take a look at Goldcrest. I couldn't before when Swift was holding him with that look in his eyes. It made mine burn. I guess I never really actually looked at Goldcrest, he has always been in the corner of my eye or just a shadow.

Goldcrest is like a baby in Hawk's arms, resting his sweat-lined face on Hawk's pecks. His sandy hair sticks to his forehead while his eyes flutter open every once in a while revealing icy-blue eyes. The bright color shocks me every time they appear; I'm surprised I haven't noticed their beauty before. His limp arm, hangs over the side of Hawk's grasp. He was doing so well.

"I should get him to the clinic." Hawk turns abruptly, almost whacking me with Goldcrest's lifeless legs. I back out of the way as he marches toward the exit and the elevator. "Robin, walk with me." he calls over his shoulder.

Robin snatches up her sweatshirt from the floor and runs after Hawk and Goldcrest.

We wait and stare at the empty doorway for a minute. *Will Goldcrest be okay or will we lose a team member even before being Enhanced?*

"You think he is going to be alright?" Swift whines.

267

"How should we know? You're the one who messed up." I turn around to face him, simultaneously crossing my arms across my chest.

"I told you, it was an accident." he tries to convince me and the others in the room.

"Was telling Hawk an accident?" I try my hardest not to shout.

"What?" he can barely manage to get out.

"Either way," I let our relationship go. "It still happened and now Goldcrest is in the hospital. Whatever you did may have caused us to lose a teammate. Nice one." I stomp out of the room before Swift can retort or anyone can comment. If Robin was here, she would tell me I'm being mean. She's like the mom of the group. I never liked my mom that much anyway.

***

I go up and check on Goldcrest a few hours later. Not because I'm trying to be nice or anything, but because I have nothing else to do except guard and I can't be alone for more than five minutes or so without stressing out too much. I know that my position in the Enhancement program is safe at the moment, but the way Swift treated me was the real problem. It's obvious that he doesn't trust me enough.

Osprey is in the room with me for most of the time so at least it isn't too awkward. I just hover over Goldcrest's body or sit on the chair in the corner, thinking. Usually thinking is a bad thing for me, but this is a different kind of thinking. I imagine myself in Goldcrest's spot. Who would I want at my bedside? Definitely not some angry teenager who doesn't like me. Maybe I just give off that vibe.

Other Enhancements float in every once in a while. Every time a new one appears, I ask about Swift. Not that I actually care about him, but I need to know if he's coming to visit in case I need to evacuate. I don't pay attention when the doctors announce what is wrong with Goldcrest. Does that make me a bad friend? Hell yes. Either way he's going to be fine in a few days and almost definitely be healed with Enhancement.

After staying with Goldcrest for another hour, I hear that Swift will be up soon to apologize and see how he's doing. Nothing should have kept Swift from coming and visiting the poor kid he put in the hospital. I leave as soon as I can after hearing.

I pop into my dorm to put on guarding clothes and then rush to pick up my weapon from the weapons cache. When I arrive at the desk the resident clerk seems pretty grumpy.

"Been a while since you have come around." He notes as he goes into the back and looks through the shelves of supplies. I guess I have seen him here a few times.

"Well yeah, I've been pretty busy." I answer. "Enhancement training and such." This is my excuse even though we have had plenty of time off.

"Oh, you are one of those crazy kids, huh?" He drops a rifle on the desk in front of me. A Tirian-AK. "Do you really think it is going to work?"

"I have faith in my-in the Proxies in charge of the program." I don't usually like going around flaunting the fact that my father is a genius.

"How long do you think it is till the Preachers have the same technology and come busting in here?"

I adjust the rifle's strap over my shoulder. "Huh?"

"They are working on these Enhancers too."

"How do you know so much about the Enhancers?" I narrow my eyes and step closer, leaning against the desk.

He steps back, "Word travels fast around here..." and then he goes back to arranging the weapons.

At least now I know that I can still scare people.

269

Chapter Twenty Six

"Emergency Enhancement meeting!" A knuckle knocks urgently on my dorm's door. It sounds like Osprey's voice, but I can't quite identify it through the door.

I quickly throw the blanket off of me, toss the T-Screen I was using aside and hop off of the couch and rush to answer whoever's calling.

I was using the T-Screen to check up on the news. Another congress member has gone missing in the past week. That makes seven over all. Whatever the Preachers are up to, it's happening faster and sooner than we are ready for.

I unlock the door somewhat hesitantly; I forgot that I was in my pajamas already. It's only five o'clock in the evening.

To my surprise, Osprey is not waiting outside, but my father. He smiles brightly and opens his arms wide for a hug. I accept his hug without too much complaining.

"Should I change or—?" I point at my outfit, but he just waves my comments away.

"We need to hurry, the others will be waiting." He starts off toward the elevator bank and I try to cover up as much as possible.

"What's the big rush, Dad?" We walk past the cafeteria and I hide my face nonchalantly.

"I suppose you have been keeping up with the Hearing?"

"Actually I was just—"

"Another disappearance means that either Preachers are killing off their competition or making their members go into hiding. Either way, a storm is coming and we are not prepared." He stabs at the down button when we reach the silvery elevators. His brown eyes flick around in his skull behind his glasses. He is definitely nervous. "The Enhancement is being moved up and so are all of our other plans." I sneak into the elevator beside him while other Proxies file in behind us.

Dad is the only one here who seems to be worried or scared. So maybe he's overreacting like he sometimes does when he's overworked, or maybe no one else has been told so as not to cause mass panic.

"Other plans?" I whisper to my dad after we exit and then wait for the next elevator to take us past the civilian quarters.

"I will be heading home tomorrow for a few days before returning to start the next batch of Enhancers."

This time we have the pod to ourselves.

"More?"

"You did not think that we would stop with you ten, did you? Come on, Wren, think logically. Like I taught you."

"I just thought that I would be..."

"Special. I know. You always wanted that and you should know that you have always been special to me." He smiles and touches my cheek before exiting. I hadn't noticed that the doors had opened. Dad is acting weird...

Pausing for a minute, I take a deep breath. *Of course, he will be making more. How else are we going to win this war?* Then I run to catch up to my dad, which only takes a few seconds, and continue marching at his heel. "But for now you will receive your partner for the rest of the war." *Great way to put it, Dad. I'm going to be stuck with someone until the Preachers are stopped or one of us dies.* I just wanted to fight Preachers alone and now I am stuck with ten other people; not to mention the NEST leaders breathing down my neck.

My father walks ahead of me into HABITAT, "Dad, you really screwed me over—" But he's already gone, busy corresponding with Hawk.

Almost everyone is here, but I notice that a couple of trainees are missing. The large room seems so empty now without the buildings and landscape. The tall white walls, my teammates roaming around. I wish they would put some chairs in here or something; we always end up standing around while 'adults' talk about us.

The last two people trickle in and we, without speaking, make a semi-circle and wait for Hawk and my father to announce our fate. I positioned myself as far as I can be from Swift, but now I just glare at him with his stupid face and bright eyes and the way that he can still smile. When Hawk finally joins us, he is smiling too.

I make the effort to purposefully scowl, but I don't have to try too hard. Anger and sadness seem always just beyond the surface, hiding underneath my skin. But I don't let it show until I need it.

Dad joins the group and stands next to Hawk.

"Agent Hummingbird and I have gathered you here to bring you great news. My associates and I have finally put you into pairs and decided who your partners are going to be. I know the timing may be a little inconvenient, sorry for interrupting your activities. Especially you Goldcrest." He must have been brought down from the hospital.

There is a rumbling of comments. Some happy, some nervous. I, for one, think that it couldn't have come at a worse time for me personally and even though Hawk tries to make it seem otherwise, I know that this is only happening now because they are scared Preachers are going to do something.

Hawk casually stands in front of us, "Are you all ready?" Multiple people nod their heads while Owl squats slightly so he can drum on his thighs. His sense of rhythm isn't very good.

Hawk draws in our full attention; I can feel the energy in the air. "The first pair is…" He pauses for dramatic effect. You could hear a pin drop. "Robin and Osprey."

Everyone must have been holding their breath, because now there is a collective sigh. That match seems like it will work pretty well, their personalities aren't very different. Plus they're already friends.

"Yay!" Robin exclaims and gives Osprey a hug. They were already standing next to each other. Owl, who is on Robin's other side, congratulates them.

Hawk prepares to speak again. *Please not me, please not with Swift.* "Nightingale…" Nightingale cracks her knuckles. "You have been paired with Goldcrest."

"No fucking way!" She breaks out of formation and jabs her finger at Goldcrest angrily, "I'm not going to work with this weakling! How the hell did I get put with him? We are NOTHING alike."

"That is exactly the point." Hawk says. He isn't disturbed at all from Nightingale's outburst, unlike my father who has taken a step back in case she starts swinging.

Poor Goldcrest stands there dumbfounded and takes the insults in silence. He looks like he might faint again. Osprey places a hand on Goldcrest's shoulder for support.

"Now stand down and calm yourself." Hawk instructs a little stricter. "The next match is Blue-jay and Owl."

Swift's face drops. *He wanted to be with Blue-jay.*

So that just leaves Koel, Swift, Lark and I. I can already see it coming. How could this not happen? Just my luck.

"Wren, it is your turn and you will be with…" 'Not Swift', I almost scream out. I don't know if I'll be able to take it. *No, no, no, no. It's going to be Swift.*

"Swift." Hawk smirks slightly, making me wonder what he is thinking. My dad steps forward again, as if he wants to congratulate us. He must not know. I'm a little thankful for that.

Swift sighs in pain. I give Hawk a death stare and before anyone realizes it, march up to Swift. My fist lashes out and makes contact with his annoying face. He falls to his knees and doesn't even attempt to retaliate. With everyone shocked and looking at me, I run.

I burst out of the room, anger coursing through my veins.

273

I charge into the first elevator, crushing the up button with my fist. Blood pumps in my ears.

I look down at my hand; it has turned red and is swelling already. I know that Hawk and my dad are going to be disappointed in me, that my fellow teammates are going to be utterly confused and that Swift could be furious. But who the hell cares about them? I need to get out of here. I can't be here anymore. I can't be around Swift or any place that reminds me of him, which is everywhere in this freaking building. Maybe I should take this as a final sign to leave for good.

Bump. I run into a solid force: a body.

"Watch where you're going." I grumble and attempt to walk past the person.

"Wren?" an annoyingly familiar voice says. He grabs my arm.

"Oh, hey, Sleepy." I say sheepishly.

I had gotten out of the elevator and accidentally ended up in the Proxy lobby without realizing it.

Sleepy looks… better somehow. Maybe it's the lack of dark rings under his eyes or maybe it is the fact that I need someone around who doesn't know very much about me.

"Wow, it is great seeing you." he begins and then picks up on my angry vibes, "Are you okay? Hey, a few friends and I are going out later. It looks like you could use a night out." *It's great seeing me? The girl who left him hanging upside down and randomly attacked him…?*

"Where are you going?" I ask, slightly intrigued by his offer. I need to get away from here.

"Just a club in town." He shrugs like it's no big deal. "Club Scarlet."

I've never been to a club, never even drank alcohol.

"So, do you want to join us?"

"Uh, sure." I agree on a whim. *I'll go with Sleepy tonight, see how things are tomorrow and then make my decision on whether*

274

or not I'm staying in this damned building and damned organization. I need to take a moment before making a rash decision.

He smiles widely like he didn't think that I would say yes. I don't even know why he'd still want to hang out with me.

"Okay, I'll stop by your dorm before I leave," He thinks for a few seconds, "In about two hours? One hundred and forty five, right?"

"That sounds fine." I answer and start to walk away, "Wait, how do you know—" I twist around, but he's already turning the corner.

***

"You ready, Wren?" Sleepy asks outside my door.

I look at myself in the mirror one last time. I had looked through my almost empty closet for something appropriate to wear. I ended up borrowing a shirt and nice pants from Robin. Thankfully she didn't ask any questions. During my search I found that stupid dress that I bought with Swift and... Well I burnt it.

"Yep." I open the door and lock it behind me.

Sleepy whistles. He gets up from where he was leaning against the wall.

"You look nice." he says and we begin to make our way to the exit of the headquarters.

"Thanks." I say quietly. My cheeks warm. "I actually haven't really been out of this building since I moved in a few months ago."

"Then it's been way too long."

We walk past the secretary into the civilian lobby. I stop in the middle of the shopping center. *What would Swift do, would he go out to a club?* I ask myself hesitantly. *No he wouldn't* — I think confidently — *so I will.*

"Are you okay?" Sleepy asks me while touching my arm.

I quickly move away quickly.

"Yeah, we should go." I say a little too eagerly and walk through the large entryway to the Phoenix Center.

We hop on a bus and ride it through the center of the city. I gaze up at the large Center Building. Every major city in UCNA has one—a tall building right in the middle of it that holds the political and government workers and the police headquarters. At the top of the building is the control room that supervises the security of the entire city—the light-train, the force-field surrounding the city, and the water and sewer system. If somebody got up there who shouldn't be, we would be screwed. The sun sets just as we zip past the building, the lights on its sides finally lighting up.

"So, Nightjar, you go partying a lot?" I ask Sleepy. Most of the Proxies are very strict and don't seem to leave.

"Oh, yeah, almost every weekend." he says like it's obvious. "This is our stop. And by the way, out here my name is York." He winks at me. I doubt I'll be able to keep track of so many names.

Sleepy and I jump out of the slowly moving bus and walk down an alleyway. We're near the Circumference. The stench out here is awful.

A small group of people stand outside a metal door, they are huddled together smoking and goofing off.

When we get closer Sleepy raises his hand in greeting.

"It's about time you got here!" A man breaks out of the group and pats Sleepy on the back. He has long black hair and many tattoos.

"And who is this beautiful woman?" he asks Sleepy and then extends his hand to me, "Jardah, my name is Apollo."

I reluctantly shake it.

"Everyone, this is uh—" Sleepy stops. He doesn't know that Wren is my real name too.

"Wren." I finish.

I shake the rest's hands. Someone else is standing in the shadows, out of the club's light. "Fancy seeing you here." Nightingale's voice says and she steps into view. "Shall we go in?" she asks and they all mumble in agreement. I should have known she would be here; she *is* part of Sleepy's crew.

We step slowly to the entrance in unison. Almost at the door, Nightingale bumps into me. "To them I'm just Dejah." she whispers, creepily close. Nightingale seems at home with these people. In this place. She blends in with the surroundings. Her spiky purple hair seems tame compared to the other bar-goers. I have a feeling that I will be the odd-looking one tonight.

Loud music blasts through the open door, if this is even called music. As I walk into the club, I am bombarded with too many attractions that distract my senses. Most of the club is dark except for the middle, where red strobe lights illuminate the dance-floor. A bar is to the left, lining the wall, and dark red couches and chairs border the elevated dance-floor. Windows line the top of the tall walls. A slight burning smell emanates from somewhere across the room, but the club mostly smells sickly sweet.

All of my senses are working overtime. This place reminds me of the battle scenarios in Proxy training. I almost say so to Sleepy, but he speaks first.

"Do you want to dance?" he asks.

I laugh at his question, "No."

"Okay…" he replies, a little disappointed.

We stroll slowly over to the bar and sit down on the high stools.

Nightingale is on my right and Sleepy is on my left, like my bodyguards. I have a feeling that in a place like this I might need bodyguards.

Nightingale takes off her jacket, revealing a crop top that perfectly shows off her tattoos. The chains inked on her collarbones seem to glow in this light as well as the noose behind her left ear. The back of her top consists of only loose threads and I can make out dark wings on her shoulders and back.

The music explodes in the background, but my spirits are not lifted. I put my head on the table. It reeks of alcohol.

Sleepy puts his hand on my back, "What's wrong?"

"Yeah, you've been upset for a while now." Nightingale adds. I didn't know she was paying attention.

"It's nothing." I sigh and sit up straight again.

"Come on, you can tell us. I can't make you feel better if I don't know the problem."

Nightingale whispers beside me, "And I'm going to find out eventually."

I stick my tongue out at her.

"Fine." I begin to tell my tale of briefly being interested in Swift, him risking my job and then me telling him not to talk to me. And how, of course, I would be lucky enough to be paired with him. Sleepy orders us drinks during my monologue, I tell him non-alcoholic for me.

Purple liquid in a thin, tall cup is handed to Nightingale who starts stirring the contents nonchalantly. Little bubbles reach the surface and keep my attention until a blue beverage is given to me. I take a small sip to make sure it really is non-alcoholic. Sleepy's green cup is filled with clear liquid right before our eyes. For the first time, I notice a pattern tattooed onto the inside of his wrist. The whole club is mesmerizing.

"What I just don't understand is Swift's reasoning for talking to Hawk and Albatross before me." I pause to take a sip of the delicious drink. "Plus, what was Hawk thinking when he paired me and Swift together? I can't stand being ten feet away from Swift and it's clear he doesn't trust or respect me. If Hawk thinks this will help Swift and I reunite then he is sorely mistaken."

278

Nightingale moves closer me and says, "You know what will make you feel better?"

I nod my head no, and worry about her answer.

She gets that crazy look in her eyes right before saying, "Meaningless sex."

I spit out my drink. I'm a virgin.

Nightingale seems surprised, "Don't tell me…"

I nod my head sheepishly.

"I never drank alcohol either."

The whole time I've been telling my story, Sleepy has been quiet, but now he speaks up, "Well that is about to change."

He calls over the waiter, a red foamy liquid—the house specialty—is set in front of me, and then all hell breaks loose.

Well to me it seems like the worst thing that could happen.

***

A faint buzzing fills my ears, and some snoring. I don't dare to open my eyes because it feels like my head is going to explode. A gentle breeze blows in from an open window somewhere. It dances across my skin and I can sense that I am shirtless.

I quickly open my eyes. I still have my bra on, but my shirt is nowhere in sight.

The sunlight burns my eyes. I hold my head in my hands and will myself to get up and look around.

What happened and where am I? I take a peek at my surroundings. I'm on one of the couches below the dance-floor; other people are sprawled around the room. A red-eyed bartender wipes off the bar. And then some of last night comes back to me.

After Sleepy got me the drink, Apollo and his other friends came up and asked us to dance with them. I remember dancing with Apollo, but not much else…

279

Apollo is on the couch with me, but not right next to me, which is slightly comforting.

It has to be morning by now, the Proxies must be worried. I should get back, but where is my damn shirt?

I hear some moans and see a body move to my right. Another person stands up and begins to throw up on his friends.

I slowly stand up and stumble around the room, searching for my clothes with squinted eyes. I pick up what I think is mine on the other side of the club and start for the door. When I finally get there, it creaks open, but hesitate when I remember Sleepy.

I look back over my shoulder at the crowded club, but decide that it would be better to leave. Hawk will be furious.

I close the door quietly and pick my way through the alleyway. It takes me awhile to walk down this short alley, avoiding garbage trying to keep my eyes open despite the burning sun.

I hear voices and heavy footsteps ahead and press myself against the wall. *Why am I so afraid and paranoid? People should be out already, it is probably just the regular bustle of the city. I need to get rid of the fog in my mind.*

I breathe in and out and then round the corner, right into a group of marching cloaked figures. It takes me a moment to realize what is before me but when I do, I don't waste time in my retreat and turn on my heel. Rushing back into the alley, I almost trip over my feet. When I see the group turn too, I rip the club door open and jump inside.

Preachers, and they have guns. Leaning against the door I wonder what they're doing here. *They seem like a pretty elite team too.*

I can hear them outside, they're getting closer. This is no mistake, they are coming to the bar.

Frantically, I search for a place to hide and find a janitor's closet. I throw myself in it and slam the door shut just as cylinders roll across the dirty tiles and start spraying gas.

The white smoke billows up from the crack between the floor and the door. I try to cover my mouth and nose with my shirt.

How did I get in this situation? I am going to kill Sleepy and Nightingale when I get out of here. Wait, where is Nightingale? I didn't see her earlier.

Despite my shirt, my head begins to spin and it takes everything for me not to fall over. I stumble around, though, and have to balance against the back wall.

Pop! One round is shot off and then what seems like a million rounds are fired after it.

I scream into the cloth in frustration and fear and panic.

The gas is too strong and I am too weak—I collapse onto the dirty floor. I don't think I'm unconscious, but I'm too tired to get up and my brain feels like there is a heavy weight pressed down on it. So I lie on the floor and wait for the noise to stop, or for someone to burst into my hiding spot.

Thankfully no one does, and the noise eventually disappears. And then I am left in silence until my head clears.

The Preachers can't still be here, they had to have left — I think to convince myself to get up. I should find Sleepy and Nightingale and then get back to HQ.

Still on the floor, I slowly and gently pull the shirt over my head and put my arms through the sleeves.

I reach up and turn the handle, then crawl out.

"Sleepy?" I whisper, "Um, Nightjar? York? Where are you?"

I continue to crawl to the exit, but my mind hurts.

I squeeze my eyes shut and move forward. "York?" I say a little louder.

My hand lands in something wet and sticky, I lift it to my nose. Blood.

My eyes burst open and I come face to face with Sleepy. He lies on his side, among the littered bodies on the trashed floor. They are all dead.

I gasp and scurry backward. His grey eyes look blankly up at me, blood drips down the side of his face.

No. I take in a heavy breath, trying not to scream. *I have got to get out of here.*

I shakily get on my feet and run as fast as a hung-over person can.

***

Club Scarlet isn't too far from the NEST building by foot, it didn't make much sense to take the bus last night.

I try to ignore all of the early risers who are probably going to work, but my easily distracted brain focuses on people randomly.

It's like every person in this city is trying to be the opposite of what they really are. Naturally tan or dark-skinned humans wear pale and boring colors of clothing and makeup, powdering their skin until it looks like they are ill. Light-skinned and pale people artificially tan their skin into weird shades. Orange, red, sometimes even green. Hopefully it's just accidental.

Big hair-styles and costume-like designs are everyday appearances. Or at least in the Inner Ring.

It could be the alcohol, but they seem more strangely dressed than usual.

The months of staying in NEST headquarters have gotten me used to plain clothing and plain makeup, which is the opposite of the world outside. The world that I am trying to save. It's clear to me that I can't stay in hiding forever, away from the people I need to keep my eyes on and connect with.

I trip through the glass doors and into the lobby. Then I save myself from falling at the last second. *Whoa, that was close* — I laugh and stick my hands out to keep my balance. The curved, tinted-glass ceiling spins above me.

The civilian lobby secretary looks at me revoltingly, "Excuse me, what are you doing here?" That reminds me of what happened just a few minutes ago. *I have to warn them.*

"There has been an attack!" This is my first time trying to really talk since I woke up. My words come out in slurs.

"You are not authorized to be here."

She doesn't recognize me. And I don't have any identification on me.

I get closer to her in case anyone else is near and could overhear, "I am Agent Wren." I whisper.

She waves her hand in front of her face, dispersing the nasty fumes coming out of my mouth. "You. Are. Drunk. You cannot be here." she says slowly like I am an idiot.

"No, you don't understand. I was almost killed at this club—"

"Of course." She presses a button under her desk.

"Wait—"

Three Security Proxies march out of a side room.

Oh, crap. I rip past her and run through the first floor shops that are just starting to open. If I can get to the Proxy front desk, I could explain.

It doesn't take too long for the Proxies to catch up to me. Especially after I practically run in to a wall. Reminder to self: don't do any running while intoxicated. Never mind, just don't get intoxicated at all.

"Get on your knees." orders a guard. I have trouble just doing that, and after trying to slowly drop down, I fall on my face.

"Come on. We need to take you to a holding cell."

"But I'm a Proxy." I mumble against the floor.

They grab me near my armpits and guide me to the hole they came from.

They pull me down the squeaky clean white hallway. This must be where they take intruders.

There is someone walking up ahead. As I get closer I recognize the person.

"Wren?" Swift asks, confused, at a distance.

I try to ignore him, but he intervenes.

"Sorry, there must be some sort of mistake." Swift says politely to the Proxies.

"I don't need your help." I hiss.

"Oh, really?" he laughs. "This is Agent Wren." he tells them and then explains after they still don't release me, "Part of the Enhancement program."

"Oh." They exclaim and let go of me, "Sorry, we did not know." They must not want to get in trouble.

"It's okay. It's a common mistake." Swift says.

He can be so infuriating.

Swift reaches toward me to take me in the opposite direction. I brush past his hand and walk away.

Swift follows me, "Wren, what happened?"

Tears appear in my eyes and I run, again, through the Proxy lobby and up the back stairs, not having the patience to wait in the elevator. After fumbling with my keys for a couple infuriating seconds, I slam the door to my dorm behind me.

Swift gets there a few seconds after, "Wren!" He pounds on the door, but I don't answer him.

He continues pounding and waits outside for a few minutes. "Come on, Wren! Come out already!"

"I already told you that I don't need your help! I can take care of myself!" I yell back to him on the other side of the door.

I glare at the stupid barrier between us. A salty drop rolls down my cheek and to the corner of my mouth.

"You are so stubborn!" He hits my door one last time.

"Yeah, well I'm not the only one!" I yell with venom, remembering his last words.

"I thought it was the best thing to do at the time. Apparently some people don't agree with me." His voice is calmer. He asks hesitantly, "Wren, what happened last night?"

"Oh, you don't remember? After you sabotaged my Enhancement career a week ago, we became partners!" I do not want to think about what happened afterward.

"That's not what I meant to do." he mutters and then adds, "You know what I'm talking about. Are you okay?"

I take a shaky breath. *Sleepy is dead and so is everyone else in the bar. Some of them may have done some bad things, but that doesn't mean that they had to be killed. They still had time to change, but the Preachers took away that time.*

I'm not even allowed out of the building in the first place... I shouldn't have been there.

"You'll find everything out in the incident report. I will be sure to send you a copy."

"Okay." he says, giving up. "So you're not leaving?"

"What?" I say and then remember my resolution—go out and then decide. But Swift couldn't know about that. "I guess I'll stay for the time being."

"Good. I just hope you are okay." *He has to, he's my partner now.* Swift stays silent after that and I don't know if he has left or is still standing outside my door.

Hawk and Dad will expect me to reveal all of my secrets and stories to Swift. How long do I have before I will have to tell him everything?

Chapter Twenty Seven

I take my time getting ready the next morning, dreading the idea of walking back into class. After the trouble with Swift and then the scene with the secretary, I really am surprised I wasn't kicked out or something.

Apparently, they canceled yesterday's session when I didn't show up, but no one went looking for me. Dad left early yesterday morning to go back to Tieced. Maybe instead of going partying I should have waited till the next day and gone home with him. Well it's too late now.

I make sure there aren't many Proxies in the cafeteria before walking in. Luckily the cooks have some left-over bread and jam. They scowl at me as they hand it over like it isn't their job.

I eat the stale food in silence and try to not think about what happened yesterday.

After taking a nap yesterday, I filled out the most excruciating form ever. It tortured me and made me remember everything that happened earlier that day. I eat my breakfast slowly, staring blankly at the wall and trying not to think. Of course it doesn't work.

It's funny how twisted the Preachers thoughts are; killing people is not seen as forbidden, but all the things the people they killed did were forbidden. So forbidden that they were killed for it. The Preachers can no longer convince non-Preachers of their ways and help them join their cult, so they decide to kill them or scare them into submission. Sure the people they murdered yesterday weren't the most innocent or spotless people, but they didn't deserve to die.

I realize that I'm late, and notice the glares I'm getting from the workers here, but it takes all of my energy to push myself away from the table and stand up straight.

The lobby is filled with buzz about the attack and I see a few stray dirty looks aimed at me. I pull the hood of my sweater over my head in shame and ride to the bottom floor, trying not to think too much about what happened.

The lights down here make my eyes hurt — is the only thing that comes to mind as I walk through the open door to the classroom. As soon as I enter someone flies at me, pinning me against the wall. "What happened to them? Where the hell are my friends?" Nightingale breathes into my ear and then yells for everyone to hear, "Where the fuck is Nightjar, Wren?" and punches me in the gut.

Swift pulls her off of me before she can do anymore damage.

I wipe my mouth and straighten my shirt before answering. I know I shouldn't be such a smart-ass, but I can't help it. "I think the real question is: Where did you go? Hmm?"

Fire lights in her eyes and she tries to grab at me. Luckily Hawk is there to restrain her.

"Wren, just tell her what happened." Swift says calmly, but it makes me that much angrier.

I don't want to remember, you ass.

"Wren." Hawk pushes.

Fine. "Sleepy i- Nightjar is dead. They all are." I say quietly, drawing people in, "And you weren't there to stop it!" I shout at Nightingale.

"And you were, but didn't do anything." she snarls and rips away from Hawk.

She's right, I didn't stop them. I could have warned some of them, but instead I found a hiding place and cowered in the corner. I was just looking for someone to blame before and now I see the truth. It may not be entirely my fault, but some of it is. That is why I don't stop her from punching the side of my face and then in the stomach again.

287

I would have let her continue, but Koel, Hawk and Osprey peel her away. Swift stands from a distance now and doesn't even look at me.

"Get back to work." Hawk instructs and the rest of the trainees split into their pairs.

I see Swift coming, "I have been waiting for you." he says and then catches me up, "We're supposed to be working with our partners now. The first assignment is to find out why your partner joined the Enhancement program. We can go anywhere we want, but have to be back in an hour."

Personally, I don't want to go anywhere with Swift. "It probably won't take that long." I inform him.

We exit.

"Where should we go?" Swift asks, but I can tell that he doesn't really care about my opinion.

"How about my place?" Wrong answer. He turns and stares at me sternly so I change my answer, "The Viewing Deck?"

"Fine."

This new silence between us is not the usual silence we had. It is hollow and empty, like a vacuum leaving it very hard for me to breathe.

"Why do you think they put us together?" I ask quietly, hoping he won't have another outburst.

"Probably because they saw how well we worked together before."

"Well, things have changed."

"But why are you so angry with me?"

How could he still not understand? "You and I were supposed to be friends. Friends are supposed to talk about potentially dream wrecking problems."

"Yeah, but—"

I stop walking to make sure he's paying attention. "Yeah, but you could have talked to me. Yeah, but you could have trusted that I have the situation under control. Yeah, but you could have respected me enough to warn me that you were going to the leaders about this. Stuff like this might not mean that much to you, but we're dealing with something I've been working towards my whole life. We're talking about my birthright."

Swift looks at the floor and nods his head slightly, "Do you ever think we could be alright again?"

"I think so."

We have made it to the Viewing Deck. People work as usual, ignoring us and ignoring how I feel.

Swift and I stay on the platform overlooking everyone and lean against the railing. The huge screen is being used. Photographs from Club Scarlet being displayed for everyone to see. I try to avert my gaze.

"So... Do you want to start? I want to know why you're here. You had a nice life, you could have stayed with your family and be safe and never have to worry about the Preachers."

Oh, hell no. I keep my mouth shut, and it must be apparent that I won't talk to him.

"Okay, then I will." *Mind-reading wizard.* "As a kid, my parents were very anti-Preachers. They never told me why, but it was always a given. We lived in the Circumference and my parents were very poor and couldn't find work. When I was a young teenager I led a group of homeless and runaway kids my age. We would sabotage any Preacher activity we came across, or did odd jobs for people and had a fun time doing it." He smiles, obviously remembering the times he had with his friends.

"One day, I overheard a rumor that a Preacher rally would be taking place in this old factory also on the edge of town. The gang and I went there with our loaded guns and weapons." I am surprised they were so organized. I would have joined them if I had lived in the same city. "We were prepared and fairly well trained, but there were way too many Preachers. And it wasn't just some ordinary rally, something was off. We were spotted almost right away and by then it was too late. I was the only one that escaped that I know of. Though someone else might have, or they could have been captured."

His eyes become all misty. *He must have survivor's guilt.*

"It was my fault. That's why I joined NEST, why I'm in this program. In memory of my fallen brothers and to make sure it doesn't happen again." He takes a shaky breath. His hands are wrapped around the railing and his knuckles are white from holding on so tight.

The Preachers spread hatred and sadness, they destroy everything they come in contact with.

"This is why I couldn't stay with my family. I couldn't leave it up to fate or other people to solve the problem. Preachers have caused so much pain and have taken so many loved ones away. I need to stop them, or help in some way, and I know that I can do that here." I don't tell him that I want my revenge for all of those years on the run. "That has always been my goal, I only came to NEST because I felt that it would be easier to take down the Preachers with NEST's resources and forces."

I am a little annoyed that Swift actually got me to talk about the reason I'm here, so I try to change the subject, "We should head back. The others might be done by now."

He nods his head despite knowing that I just don't want to be alone with him.

This talk has made me feel closer to him, almost like the gap he made between us when he did what he did is being closed, but I don't know if I will ever feel like I can trust him again. I hope I can, because we need that trust if we're supposed to be partners.

He walks away. I take a second to clear my head before following.

Swift punches in our floor on the pad and then crosses his arms against his chest. "Things are always going to be this way, huh?" he asks after the doors close.

If he keeps bothering me about it, he could set us back even further. "I can't tell you right now. Just give me some space to figure it out."

The elevator's doors open and we emerge onto our floor.

Hawk is surprised we're back so early and gives Swift something to do.

"This is not going to be a problem, is it?" Hawk looks right into my eyes after Swift walks away.

"I am trying, Hawk." I have to try for all of us.

"Get your shit together or I will have to suspend the whole program. We do not have any time to spare."

"Yes, sir." I say instead of making a big fuss.

"Go... drink some water or something..." Hawk instructs me.

"Fine." I wave my hand over my shoulder while walking away.

I leave the room quickly, and try to clear my mind of anything while searching our floor for a water fountain or something. But I can't find one.

There has to be one around here somewhere — I think and decide to explore. I push an unfamiliar door open slowly.

The room is dark, but I can see Lark's bright pink tank-top from here. She sits on a desk against a wall. Across the room from Lark, I can make out Koel's huge form sitting on a backwards chair.

Koel moves abruptly and I close the door quickly, but stay leaning against it so I can hear what they're saying.

"I am just from the streets. I saw the things Preachers do first hand. My other homeless friends kept disappearing and most people would ignore it." I hear a scrape against the floor. "I could not ignore that fact when I knew that I could be next."

Lark for once doesn't speak at all.

"I tried everything I could to keep away from anywhere I thought had to do with the Preachers. But one day, when I came back to the place I was staying for the night, I saw the people I was staying with being round up. Cloaked figures with guns came and pushed them against a wall in the alley outside our building. I was too afraid to do anything so I hid behind a corner and watched."

That sounds exactly like what happened to me hours ago.

"Luckily, before anyone was killed, a few people came out of the shadows. They attacked the Preachers and saved my companions. They were NEST agents. They took us to this facility and I have been training ever since."

"Have you left since then? I mean before last week." Lark asks. I can hear the curiosity in her voice. She has tasted the life outside, had a glimpse of it, and now she wants more. She wants to know what it's like outside, but also knows that most people don't like talking about it because of the darkness out there and the bad memories. There has to be good somewhere, though.

"A few times. But nothing has changed. In some places the crime is even worse." Koel tells her without giving up too much information. "When we left the building a few days ago… it was just really hard for me."

"And what happened to the Preachers that attacked you?" Lark asks another unexpected question.

"Um, I do not know." I can tell Koel hasn't really thought about it and doesn't care what happened to those murderers. "I guess the Proxies killed them." *Good, they deserved it.* I wish I could get my hands on Sleepy's murderers.

"Oh, okay..." Lark trails off.

She hasn't been out there. She hasn't known death. If she had seen what Koel and I have seen, then she would be happy the world is rid of them.

If I was just a little bit crazier I would barge in and tell her all of the scary Preacher stories from my childhood, but I leave the new partners to get to know each other.

Out of everyone I think that is the most difficult pair.

"We should probably head back to our class." Koel looks at his watch and then stands. Lark jumps off the table and I leap away from the door and down the hallway before they know I was there.

Swift has returned from Hawk's errand and sits alone toward the front of the room. I bump into his desk as I walk passed. Luckily he doesn't notice it as most of the other Enhancements come back.

I notice Goldcrest walk in slowly. I had forgotten about him and his condition. I'm surprised that he has survived even one day with Nightingale.

He sits in the chair behind me so I turn to him, "How are you doing?"

He looks at me with surprise in those blue eyes. Not sure how to respond, he plays with his hands on the table. "Eh, I will be alright. I am just waiting for Enhancement right now." He looks a little healthier.

"And how are you managing with Nightingale?"

"Not to be insensitive, but it is better now after the attack." He sees the growing anger in my eyes, "I mean, she is dealing with a loss so instead of just being mean and angry all of the time now she is also sad. I can deal with sad. Nightingale is just really in pain."

Nodding, I take note of Goldcrest's perceptiveness and sit right-way in my seat.

The rest of the group has returned and Hawk takes the lead again. "I trust you all had a fruitful experience." He pauses, maybe waiting for a response. No one gives him one. "I wish we could have more meetings like this, and I will try to put as many as I can in the schedule, but for now we are going to try and get you guys Enhanced

293

and trained with your new powers as soon as possible. Because of the new attack on Club Scarlet—which is in our city—we have to speed up our procedures, which were already sped up because of the cabinet members' deaths." Hawk sighs. He really does look more tired than ever before. "In summary, I wish I had time to properly train you, but I am afraid we will not be given that pleasure… The board has given us three days. We have to use them wisely."

In one way it's a shock that we will be Enhanced so soon, but in another way it isn't. I mean… it's the most logical move. But I'm not sure if any of us are ready for this, or as ready as we say we are. Then there's the possibility that you could never truly prepare for this.

Hawk seems to still be pretty normal. So far we haven't seen any random breakouts of his powers, so that is a good thing. Hopefully after we are all Enhanced too, we'll get to see the Enhancement side of Hawk. All we know is the teacher and instructor, but with his powers, Hawk is a hero. We will need him so much more now.

***

The remaining days until Enhancement, Hawk has us do bonding activities with our partners. It seems like the other pairs are really growing closer, but that Swift and I are further apart than ever before. He and I keep getting into arguments about the littlest things, usually with deeper meaning, but everyone else thinks that we are crazy because they don't understand. After every fight Swift runs back to Blue-jay, probably to tell her secrets about me or something. Every physical training activity, like facing off against another pair in HABITAT, Swift and I lose. We stumble over each other's feet and argue the whole time, no one wonder we get our asses handed to us. We might be the worst pair of the whole group, even worse than Nightingale and Goldcrest, and Koel and Lark who are also having a tough time. Poor Goldcrest has to listen and do everything

Nightingale tells him to do. At least Lark stands up for herself most of the time. With every day Swift and I seem to be getting closer and closer to failure, not Enhancement.

The group barely has any breaks, even in the evening. If it isn't fighting, running simulations or time with our partners, then we are preparing for Enhancement in other ways; like having our measurements taken again for special Enhancement clothes—tank-top, pants, jacket, and boots that are supposed to keep us safe as we get used to our new powers.

Tomorrow we will be Enhanced, finally. I have waited patiently for this moment and it is here, almost in my grasp. Everything has to go smoothly for just a few more hours.

Chapter Twenty Eight

Today is the day. For once I smile as I get out of bed.

More like tonight is the night. — I think as I get out of bed and switch on the light. I don't know why they chose to Enhance us in the middle of the night, but I think it might have something to do with secrecy. No one is out of their dorms at night except for the Security Proxies on duty.

The hour makes me want to be sneaky and quiet, so I make the least amount of noise as possible while tying the laces on my boots and wrapping a sweatshirt around my shoulders. We will be given our new uniforms after Enhancement. As I leave my room I hear another door clicking shut down the hall.

Robin raises her head and smiles when she sees me. I am glad that she is also wearing her pajamas. I wait for her to reach me and when she does she throws her arm over my shoulder and I decide to let her. That's how we walk to the elevator. In some ways Robin reminds me of my sister, Piper. I'm sure she's happy I'm here with her in this dark hallway.

When Robin and I make it to the elevator shaft, I make out Koel's dark form waiting in the shadows. He has already pressed the up button, so all we have to do is wait in silence behind him.

Robin puts her lips right next to my ear, "He seems excited."

I try to get some sort of vibe from him, but he seems to be the same old Koel to me.

It takes my eyes a minute to adjust to the light in the elevator and by the time we emerge onto the laboratory floor—the only lighted floor in the building—I can see just fine.

An eager assistant pops his head through a doorway as we step into the hallway. He rushes out, fixing his glasses, and types stuff into his T-screen as he half leads us, half circles us to the right room and laboratory.

The four of us enter a large, rectangular room. A long table runs through the center, split into different sections by dividers. A computer is fixed in each section as well as a chair similar to the one in my dad's basement lab, the one Hawk sat in when he was Enhanced.

Swift, Blue-jay and Osprey have already arrived and are being prepped by a team. I spot my dad instructing two young scientists in a corner. I had been hoping that Piper would be here, since she helped my father develop the original Enhancer, but I cannot find her anywhere. I spot Albatross sitting comfortably on a chair in the left corner, his hair disarrayed.

"The party has arrived; we can start now." Owl stands, while holding his hands up, in the doorway, ready to receive our praise.

Nightingale forces her way passed him a second later and Goldcrest follows close behind.

My dad looks up from his work, "Great. Every Enhancement should grab a stall; you will each have two lab technicians to administer the Enhancer chip."

For once, no one looks sad or depressed. It feels good to know that our hard work will finally bring forth fruit.

I want to talk to my dad before the procedure, but he looks busy and stressed and I am already being rushed into a cubicle. I smile nervously at the lab technician as she helps me into the chair. Another one comes out of nowhere, rolls up the sleeve of my sweatshirt and wipes the length of my left forearm with a disinfectant. Then the magnificent injector is placed on the section of table in front of me.

My dad pops into my cubicle for a moment, "Ready?" he asks.

I look over the dividers at the rest of my team. Swift is beside me and Owl is across from me. Almost everyone looks nervous except for Nightingale. She looks determined. I decide to choose that path too, so I grit my teeth and say, "Yep." with as much confidence as I can muster.

My dad pats my shoulder and for a moment my bravery falters as he says, "There is no turning back after this." with a hint of sadness in his eyes.

"I know." I breathe out.

"Okay. Good luck." He leaves me to check on the other Enhancements. I can't believe that that nickname will soon be true. I am going to be Enhanced in a minute.

The female scientist grabs the injector. "There is a needle at the very tip of this device. After it punctures your skin, the chip will be shot through the needle and into your flesh, embedding in your tissue." *Thanks for explaining that to me, I feel so much better now.* I think I might throw up. "We have Proxy doctors and nurses standing by if anything goes wrong."

A silenced scream comes from three cubicles, it makes me jump. Someone must have just been Enhanced.

"Get it over with." I gulp and lean back against the headrest, sticking out my left arm.

The lady moves to my left side and brings the device close to my skin. I close my eyes before contact and breathe nervously through my nose. My whole life is going to change.

The cold needle pierces my warm skin and I know that the chip will now be shooting into my flesh.

I wince; it definitely hurts more than a regular needle. My eyes open to see the woman pull away, the device in her hands.

My first instinct is to rub the injection area, but I know that that will just aggravate the wound. Instead, I stare at the bleeding speck on my forearm. I can't see the Enhancer, but I know it's in there and somehow I can feel it. I don't know how, but I do.

"Are you okay?" she asks when I stay seated for too long.

298

"Yeah." I hold my arms at my side so not to be tempted to touch the penetration area.

"Oh, yeah, do not touch that yet." she warns me. "Wait here a second until I activate the Enhancer." She taps a small button on the side of the injector. A small square shaped area beneath the wounds lights up and then pulsates five or six times before disappearing. I take a deep breath. "Do not try to use your powers yet either. You are free to check on the other Enhancements now." It *will* be a great way to keep myself distracted. I jump out of the chair. "Maybe you should see how your partner is doing."

My first thought was actually to stay away from Swift, but I guess she's right. I won't mind seeing him in pain.

I quickly enter the cubicle to my right, where Swift is. He still hasn't been Enhanced. I try to stay out of the workers' way, but it always seems like I am in the wrong place. Finally, the doctor brings out the injector. As soon as Swift sees it, his jaw locks and as the needle grows close, he looks away. Sadly though, no pain is shown on his face. I am slightly disappointed.

I pop my head over the middle barrier just as Owl is injected. He smiles right until the needle goes in, then he cries in pain.

Everyone else seems to take it pretty well; groans can be heard from a few people though.

When all ten of us have been Enhanced, Dad stands at the head of the table with Albatross and looks at us proudly.

"This is a very important day." he announces with relief and joy. "You should be very proud at making it this far. Now, let us get right down to business. Rules. First of all, you will be watched and studied every waking hour. You are not allowed to use the Enhancer's powers unsupervised until I say so. Because of the changes I made to this batch, we will have to keep a very close eye on the side-effects and abilities these Enhancer's have. I expect to have varying results." *Fun; I love being constantly watched.*

"Now, before you run off to the training room, I think you should head back to your apartments and get the rest you need. The Enhancers will really drain you if not used properly." I was hoping we could get right to the butt-kicking like Hawk did, but I guess he's right. "Security and Medical Proxies will be standing right outside your door for protection. If anything, even in the slightest, happens please tell the Proxies." He locks eyes with each Enhancement in turn. When his brown eyes meet mine, his lips curl a little in a small smile. "Good night."

I cover my forearm with my jacket sleeve again and intend to leave as soon as possible. But something catches my attention. *Where is Hawk?* I grab my dad's elbow before he can hurry past me to continue with his research.

"Hey." I try to greet him before getting down to business. "Where is Hawk? Why isn't he here with his students?"

My dad scans the room, but not with intentions to help me, he is making sure everything is flowing smoothly. "I do not know, but it is rather peculiar."

Dad looks too distracted to answer my questions properly, so I let it go. "Congratulations." I remember that these are his inventions that are actually working properly, "And thank you."

He nods his head absent mindedly and walks off to talk with one of his colleagues.

Swift sees me about to leave and says, "Sweet dreams." He makes me want to hit him.

I just roll my eyes and march out of the room.

I try to make a beeline to my dorm, but almost as soon as I exit the room, Albatross is at my side. "Is everything alright with you and Swift?" he asks with that old man voice that you can't be cross at. But he isn't really that old.

"Not really." I admit. "And I'm afraid you really made a terrible decision of putting us together."

He just nods his head as if he knows what I mean.

I choose to change the subject and get some information, "Why wasn't Hawk here?"

He ponders the question for a moment before answering. "I do not know…" And then he adds mostly to himself, "He should have been back by now."

Before I exit the elevator on my floor I say good bye and goodnight to Albatross. He seems more sullen than usual. I watch as the doors shut between us and he begins to descend again.

I notice two Proxies tailing me after landing on my floor. I don't pay them any attention and let them think I don't see them. But it would be pretty hard for me to not hear or see them, because we're the only ones awake at this time of night. I close my door quietly before flipping on my lights, but turn them off a few seconds later after throwing my jacket on the couch and kicking off my shoes.

Usually I sleep on my side, but tonight I lay in bed on my back. My right hand grips my left forearm, both on my stomach. I hear one of the Proxies' feet shuffle outside in the hallway. At least I can feel safe now, but tomorrow will hold new wonders and new powers. Am I ready for this?

Chapter Twenty Nine

I can barely sleep the rest of the night and morning, but in the brief moments of slumber, nightmares flicker on the back of my eyelids. Apparently they are back, but who knows for how long. Hopefully they will fade again.

At breakfast I shovel three servings onto my plate without even realizing it. I join a table with a few other Enhancements and soon we have the whole room's attention as we scoop everything we can find into our mouths.

"I did not think it would be this bad." Robin mumbles while taking a break.

"Huh?" I say in between bites.

"We are eating so much because of the Enhancers." *Oh, right.* "It might just be like this in the beginning, or at least I hope so."

"At least we won't be getting fat because of it." Nightingale has eaten the most out of all of us.

"Hey, where is Goldcrest? Why isn't your partner here?" I set my silverware down for a minute.

"I won't mention the absence of your partner…" Nightingale gives me a stink-eye, "Anyway, you didn't hear? Goldcrest was sent to the infirmary again last night." *But he was doing better… And the Enhancer should have cured him.* "But he will be joining us for the first lesson, at least."

We have finally been Enhanced and now we get to use our super-cool powers. Of course, we will really have to learn how to use them properly before setting out and fighting Preachers.

The small group of us head down to the basement slowly, trying not to exert too much energy. We head straight to the training room with all of the mats. I have a feeling we'll need a little precaution while beginning our training. One wrong move and someone's head could get blown off.

Hawk, Swift and my father are already waiting in the training room.

"It is nice of you to show up." I mutter to Hawk as I brush by him. He just responds with a raised eyebrow.

"Nightingale, I think it would be best for you to go retrieve your partner now. I am sending a Medical Proxy with you." Dad twirls Nightingale around and nudges her back through the door before she can answer him, but I see a snarky comment behind her closed lips.

The rest of the team has to wait impatiently for Nightingale to return with Goldcrest. I can't help but feel a little irked that I have to wait more even though I am already Enhanced. If I didn't know for certain that I wouldn't be able to hone my new skills by myself, I would have left this morning.

When Nightingale, Goldcrest and the Proxy do finally show up, I let out a sigh and say, "Thanks for coming." The look on Goldcrest's sickly face and the silence from the rest of the group tells me that I have said something wrong. *Whatever.*

Goldcrest lets go of the Proxy's support and slowly makes his way to where the other Enhancements have sat on the floor. I sit across the room from everyone else, my back leaning against the wall. Swift joins me while Dad and Hawk talk quietly. Hawk seems to be nervous about something, but I can't tell what.

A few lab technicians wait on my father's every wish, which I'm sure he's happy about, and more Security and Medical Proxies wait outside. Apparently they expect something bad to happen. "Don't they have anything better to do?" I ask Swift after a Proxy ogles me for too long.

"No, it's their job for now. They had to sign up for this."

"Yeah, Nightjar would have been down here with us, if he hadn't died." Nightingale says from across the room, obviously overhearing our conversation.

"He was murdered." Swift reminds her.

303

"He volunteered so he could see us more often." *She means Nightingale and I. He could have been standing just outside the door, peeking in every few minutes to make faces at me. Well at least he isn't here to distract us.*

"Sorry for the delay." I snap my head back to look at my father who stands above Swift and I. He addresses the ten new Enhancements. "Now, how about we start the official Enhancement training?" Everyone else smiles and agrees; I am just glad he saved me from getting murdered again by Nightingale. "I think we should start with basic activities."

We all get to our feet. "I want you all to get used to your body again. Overnight the Enhancer may have caused slight changes, making muscles stronger than they were before, making your reflexes quicker, making your mind sharper. Hawk?" He motions for Hawk to step forward. Up until now he has mostly been lurking in the corner, a grim expression on his face.

Hawk steps in front of us, bows his head slightly to my father and then turns to us. "First, I am going to show you all techniques from the martial art, Tai Chi, in hopes that it will help you discover your new found abilities and keep you... balanced. I used this when I first started out to calm myself down." *Calm himself down? What exactly does that mean? Did Hawk have more trouble with the Enhancer than he told us?* "And to direct my energy." I know about the directing energy part. It's weird to think that now I can do everything I dreamed about. To be honest the energy and powers frighten me a little. "The excess energy can be released from anywhere in your body if you are trained well enough. The easiest spot is from your hands with punches, then from your feet with kicks and then from your chest."

The next hour or so consists of Hawk demonstrating different positions and movements. I find the session hard and discover that I am not graceful. At all. I don't possess the patience that is required to deliver each form, like Blue-jay or Osprey.

Dad is right, though, I do feel different. I find it easier to maneuver my own body in a way I never felt before. Even my eyes seem to have been Enhanced as things appear to be so much clearer and brighter and beautiful. But I don't have time to look at beautiful things right now.

Right after I stumble for the hundredth time, my father steps in again, placing a hand on Hawks shoulder. "Thank you, Hawk. I think that should be enough for today." Hawk nods again to my dad, but he seems to be in a better mood. Maybe this stuff actually works.

A Proxy enters the room, carrying a box of protein bars and without a word all ten Enhancements surround him, taking as many bars as we can carry. Even Hawk reaches over me to grab a few.

After we have stuffed our faces full and all that remains are the crumbs on our shirts, Dad looks at us for a moment and exclaims, "That reminds me!" then leaves without saying anything else. Luckily we don't have to wait in suspense for too long, because he comes back a minute later with a stack of clothes in his hands. "Your new uniforms and training outfits." He reads something on each set before handing us our uniforms. My name is written on a piece of paper nestled on top of my new shirt.

"Put them on." My father urges.

Most of us take turns changing in the bathroom, but a couple decide to strip right in the training room.

The training outfits are plain sweats—a light grey tank-top and light grey pants. The pants are lightweight and comfortable, while the shirt fits into every nook and cranny in an annoyingly stiff way. The uniforms consist of a dark jacket and dark pants; they too are made out of the uncomfortable fabric. "You will get used to it." Dad says when he notices I am wiggling in discomfort in my new clothes. "It is made out of synthetic textiles, aramid fibers and olefin fibers, making

305

it flame-retardant and hydrophobic, as well as sensors that will adapt the shirt to your specifications." *Whatever that means...* "And look at the jacket sleeve." He points to the jacket in my arms. I fumble around with the cloth for a few seconds before I find what he was talking about. A design is sewn into the top of the right sleeve. "Enhancement patch. I designed it myself." *He is dorking out about his own creations.* I grin.

I fix my ponytail as he steps back to address the whole group, "Everyone in their training outfits?" He beams at us for a moment, proud of his inventions, and then speaks again. "Good. Let us head to HABITAT for some actual training with your Enhancer powers." *Finally. It has been hours since actually being Enhanced, Hawk got to fire up his powers only seconds after activation.*

The ten of us rush to the large room, Dad and Hawk trailing behind, talking.

When we burst into the room, the remains from our last exercise are still standing.

"The more room, the better." My dad says and collapses the structures.

Targets appear on the far wall. The others in my team move further into the room.

"This is awesome, Wren!" Owl nearly shouts in my ear. "I feel stronger already. Your dad is so cool."

I get caught in the excitement too and smile with him. Swift stays with me close to Dad and Hawk near the entrance.

"They are acting like children." Hawk comments while checking out the rest of the team, who are running around. He should be happy for us, not grumpy. He is acting like me.

"Ease up a little, Hawk." I tie my sneakers tight. "We are children." Just then Koel falls flat on his butt after Lark jumps out and surprises him. It makes the ground around him shake. "Very large children, but still children." I laugh. Swift walks over to help Koel up.

"Yeah, Hawk, let us have a little fun!" Swift shouts back to us.

He ignores Swift, "Be careful!" Hawk shouts and rushes over to Nightingale who looks like she's about to use her powers. "Only fire at the targets and only if you're sure no one is near and could get hurt." He shifts Nightingale until she is facing a target instead of Owl. "I will let you try stuff out by yourselves for now, but if you want to continue training like this, everyone will have to be on their best behavior. I will give a few pointers while you all work." He reluctantly steps away from Nightingale and takes up a position near the door and the control panel. We take that as the final authorization to basically do whatever we want. As I walk away, he shouts out, "If you start to feel tired, you should take a rest and maybe eat a snack."

It might be a little dangerous to let a bunch of kids with superpowers run around even though they don't exactly know how to use said superpowers, but I'm too eager to use my the Enhancer to complain. Besides, if anything happens Hawk, Dad, and a bunch of other Proxies are right here. I'm surprised my dad is letting us do our own thing. He either has a lot of confidence in us, or his invention. I'm betting on his invention.

I might as well enjoy a little freedom now, because I will be spied on and watched twenty four-seven for the next couple weeks…

To get the Enhancer to work, I will need to concentrate. I breathe deeply and forget about everyone else in the room; in the world. All that matters right now is my new-found powers and what I will be able to do with them. Strike down Preachers with pure willpower, save innocent lives and finally give the Preachers what they deserve for causing so much pain and destruction. For trying to kill me and my family and for killing Sleepy.

I remember the position Hawk was standing in the first time he used the Enhancer, it's similar to one he showed us before.

I walk to the middle of the room and stand with my knees slightly bent and face the nearest target. Focusing on the pull in my gut that I have been feeling for a few minutes now, I will the Enhancer to start up.

Come on, Enhancer, work.

"There may be a weird feeling at the beginning, maybe even a little pain." Hawk's voice drifts past. He must be right behind me, but he seems to be miles away.

My soul feels like it is drifting away, like that moment right as you're falling asleep, or when you wake up from a dream. An in-two-places-at-once kind of feeling. The sick feeling moves from my gut to my left arm, more specifically—the Enhancer. I look down and see the tiny square begin to glow.

My heart rate gets faster and my breathing does too. Something inside me begins to change and I can't stop it. For once in my life I am worried about one of my dad's creations. A fire seems to grow in my very bone and flesh, starting out in my left arm and then quickly spreading to my enter body.

"Dad…" I open my eyes wide and turn to him; begging with my eyes from him to instruct me. I am freaking out. *My blood is on fire.* "Dad!" *This was a bad idea. I wasn't ready for this.*

"Just go with it! Everyone get back." he says and doesn't look worried.

The other Enhancements back away slowly, stopping their activities, but don't do anything to help.

Swift barely looks at me, but I see the worry on his face.

It feels like my hands are in flames. I actually make sure they are not. My skin is a little red from the heat, like I am blushing. My shirt flashes red for half a second, making me wonder if I imagined it.

Hawk steps forward in case I need help, but I motion for him to leave me alone. I can do this by myself. *Just go with it, Wren. Ready, set, go.* I exhale while thrusting my burning hands forward. All of the heat seems to leave my body now, sending a cold shiver over my skin. Red light flows out from my hands and chars the wall above the target's head.

My head spins and I fall to my knees.

Hawk runs to me and puts his hand on my shoulder. "Are you okay, Wren?"

"Yeah, I think so." I slowly stand up, still dizzy. "That wasn't fire, but it sure looked like it."

"I think that was energy just like mine, but red."

I stumble over to my dad to see what he has to say.

"I think you should take a rest."

That's fine with me. A second ago I was excited and felt like I could run a whole marathon without breaking a sweat, but now I sit on the floor, leaning against the entrance wall. The rest of the group goes back to what they were doing a little hesitantly. Honestly, I don't want to feel that sensation again anytime soon, but no pain, no gain.

Dad looks down at me, "The Enhancer causes the energy we make through cellular respiration to multiply. That great amount of energy has to go somewhere."

"Heat." I mumble.

"Yes, but not hot enough for combustion. At least I hope not."

That really makes me feel better.

"You burned a lot of energy with just that flare. Your diet will include a lot more food." *Yeah, I noticed.*

I watch Swift as he figures out the Enhancer. After performing some of the stances Hawk showed us earlier with no success, he tries to do what I did, but fumbles around. He is frustrated.

Haha, I am better than him at something.

Osprey gets a few good sparks and so does Nightingale. Their flares are different colors than mine. Owl's lights up next as a bright orange being flies past and almost hits my dad. Good thing he has fast reflexes. I duck.

"Yes!" Owl whoops and throws his arms in the air, "I mean, sorry."

He doesn't look very apologetic as he runs to Swift who gives him the nicest high five he can while still feeling down.

Then the whole room turns dark in the shadow of something huge.

I search the room for the source and lower my head. Koel drops his hands. That black shape came from him.

The black wave is sinister, but beautiful to watch as it rises, blocking out the lights, and then quickly descends in Swift's and Owl's direction.

"Run!" Hawk yells to them.

It moves too fast and there is nothing they can do. Owl flattens himself against the floor and Swift lifts his hands to protect his face. I block my eyes just as it hits them, the impact being way larger and brighter than it should be.

When the black glow disperses I expect to see a disaster; Swift and Owl's mangled bodies, like the ones I saw in the club. But Swift and Owl remain in the same place, a blue dome surrounding them like a shield.

"Holy crap." I mutter under my breath.

Swifts lowers his hands and their protection disappears. I want to run up to him and give him a huge hug. But I know that I can't do that. At least he is safe.

I get to my feet. No one else dares to move.

"Now you see the power of the Enhancer." my dad breaks the awed silence. "From what I have witnessed, every one of you has a different color to the energy you produce. Wren: red, Osprey: green,

310

Nightingale: purple, Owl: orange and Koel: black. This change may be caused by the difference in each of your personalities, but that is just a theory for now." He gazes at Swift who is looking for an explanation for him still being alive. "It also seems that Swift is the first one to reveal his new strength and his old weakness. Everyone's unique power will be revealed as time goes on, ranging from a few minutes," he waves his hand at Swift, "to a week." Hopefully that won't be me.

"I think that you should practice a little more and then take a break."

After two accidents, the team realizes that we should calm down a bit and focus more on shooting at the targets like Hawk said. I line up between Swift and Robin and then get ready for more pain. I assume that if I get rid of the energy quickly it won't be so painful.

I spend time hurling the produced energy from my left and right hands. Using the left hand is pretty much painless, but with my right hand, the one I write with and undoubtedly use more often, I sense the energy climbing up my left arm, across my chest and into my right arm. It hurts. Then I try using my feet, like Hawk said. Performing a spinning hook kick, I turn around hundred and eighty degrees and then bring up my right leg in a sweeping hook motion. In the last second I remember that I am also trying to produce energy, so only a little red emerges from the ball of my right foot and I land unbalanced.

By the time I notice Swift watching me, I'm getting pretty good punching and kicking and am little tired. "What?" I ask him and decide to take a break.

"You're just really good at it. Already." He is envious.

"Yeah, but you produced that shield thing." I say to make him feel better.

"And so far it hasn't come back."

311

"Fine." I say and putting our problems aside, decide to help him. He's my partner after all. "You are feeling a little nauseous, right?" I leave my target and stand next to him.

"Yeah, but what does that—" I place one hand on his stomach and the other on his lower back, trying to position him, but Swift jumps.

"We're all feeling nauseous; I think it has something to do with the Enhancer."

"Okay, but—" Swift slaps my hand away from his body.

"Stop arguing with me and listen." I say clearly. He rolls his eyes, but does what he is told and keeps his mouth shut. "Close your eyes."

He doesn't trust me, but does so anyway. "Just don't touch me again."

"Oh, so now you don't like to be touched?" I say loud enough so the people closest to us can hear. Nightingale snickers. One of my many skills is making people uncomfortable. Sometimes without even meaning to. "Focus on that sensation. On the place it is coming from."

His eyeballs move behind his eyelids and he sways slightly. I should be holding onto him.

Swift's gray shirt flashes a dark blue and then returns to its normal color. Something is happening, it has to be working. I move away quietly, not wanting to disrupt his concentration.

Blue light bursts from his chest, hitting far away from the target, but it doesn't matter; Swift used his powers. That was fast. His entire face turns into one big smile and he shouts with joy.

"Great job, Swift!" Owl exclaims and smacks him on the back. "Welcome to the big leagues." Owl winks at him and sends a quick blast from his hand to the wall. It chars the area above the target's shoulder. "Hey, at least I can do that." Owl's joy cannot be deterred today, not by anything.

"So how did it feel?" I ask Swift. *Like you were on fire? I hope so.*

"Cool..." *Huh?* "It spread in a cold way, not like how you described it at all. Like my veins were filled with ice water."

We continue practicing like this for hours, only taking breaks to eat, drink and use the toilet. But no one takes long breaks and no one complains or mentions the time. It's only after Dad comes in looking more tired than us, does anyone mention calling it a day. But still, we soldier on.

"It is getting late guys." Hawk stands up and rubs the back of his neck. Most of the time he has just been watching us, sometimes giving tips. Once or twice he joined the line-up to practice too. He has impeccable power and accuracy. Hawk's energy is plain white, and it is apparent that whatever changes Dad made to the Enhancer have caused the energy blasts to be personalized. Everyone has a different color, mine is red, Swift's is dark blue, Owl's is an orange that matches his hair, Koel's is black, Nightingale's is purple, Robin's is yellow, Osprey has gotten out a few good green sparks, and Blue-jay, Lark and Goldcrest... well, we don't exactly know because they have not been able to produce anything, not even their power based on their weaknesses. No one except Swift has been able to use his special power and hasn't been unable to produce it again.

My dad tries to comfort the three by saying that it they will figure the blasts out eventually. I guess that isn't really comforting though. Multiple times Swift has left my side to help Blue-jay even though I'm the one who originally helped him. Her partner, Owl, of course has tried his best to guide her, but he isn't exactly the teaching type, no matter how kind and supportive he is. Most of the pairs have been working pretty well despite their differences.

"Fine, Hawk." Owl stops instructing Blue-jay, "We get it; you're tired and want to go to bed." He is joking, of course.

"Yes I do. And you guys need to get some real food into you." We all stop training now. "Class dismissed. Head up to the cafeteria and then straight to bed. That is an order."

"Fine." I mutter and pick up my new jacket. I put it on to cover my sweat-drenched training tank top.

The ten of us march up to the Proxy living quarters, filing into the almost empty cafeteria. It is way past dinner time, so we scoop up all of the left-overs. Without any planning at all, we sit next to our partners.

Because all we have are the remains of the previous meal, Osprey and Robin decide to divide the food evenly among the ten of us. Of course there is a tiny bit left over that no one can decide who gets it.

I hadn't realized how hungry and tired I was.

Hawk comes in a few minutes after we start digging in. He joins us at a table, but leaves a few moments later to get food. Somehow he convinces the kitchen staff to cook him up something; he probably mentions a thing or two about the Enhancer. A group of Proxies who volunteered to guard us watch from a table near the entrance.

"I was thinking, Wren," Robin passes me the toppings, "That I could use the light from the energy blasts as something like a flashlight. It could help with my fear of the dark."

I think about what she says for a minute before answering. "Sounds like a great idea, but we aren't exactly allowed to use the Enhancer without supervision yet."

"Oh, so you're following the rules now?" She laughs and jabs me in the ribs with her index finger. "I got permission from Agent Hummingbird, but keep it on the down low around the others." She winks and goes back to eating.

Apparently Dad trusts her more than some of the other people here. "Okay, just be careful. Those blasts can be pretty powerful."

I notice Hawk looking at me from the corner of my eye. I can tell that he was paying attention to our conversation, but has kept quiet. Hawk has been acting strange lately and he didn't show up to the Enhancement last night. I decide to have a talk with him before I head to bed.

"When did you unleash your super-strength, Hawk?" Swift asks. Up until now Swift has been quiet. I know this whole Enhancer thing has gotten him worked up. He is used to being good at everything and everyone liking him. Now he will try anything to fix the one thing he can't get right.

The rest of the table grows quiet with his question.

Hawk is caught off guard, "Oh, um." he mumbles and sets his silverware down. "It was actually an accident, which I suspect will be the same for most of you." I study Swift's face. He stares at Hawk, trying to gain as much information and wisdom as he can from him. "I was helping Agent Hummingbird and Albatross construct HABITAT, when a piece of machinery fell and threatened to crush Agent Hummingbird. I ran over quickly and caught the part. Any normal human would have been killed; luckily I had the Enhancer to save me from my stupid split second decision." Hawk has saved my father's life at least twice already. "You see, the Enhancer I was given chose one of my greatest strengths and amplified it, causing my special power. With this new Enhancer, the one you ten have, it will select one of your greatest weaknesses and get rid of them by giving you a special power, one that cancels out the weakness or the exact opposite of your weakness."

"Dad gave an example of speed." I add to the conversation to hopefully explain better the way the Enhancer works. "Like if someone's greatest weakness is speed, their special power would probably be super-speed."

315

"That is one way the Enhancer's solves your weaknesses..." Hawk says and I know he is going to add something more. "Let us say that someone's weakness is getting hurt too easily emotionally, then the Enhancer might give them some sort of shield to protect them." Swift turns away from Hawk now.

Everyone else returns to their food and conversations, but Swift, Hawk and I remain silent.

I notice Hawk eating his food quickly, so I follow suit and shove spoonful after spoonful into my mouth so it will seem like we finished at the same time. I want to talk to him in private.

I jump up with him when he clears his place and walk out of the room with him too. I stay two steps behind him and for a second I think that he may not notice me.

"You are not going to say goodbye, goodnight, something?" Hawk asks when the cafeteria doors slam shut.

"Huh?" I wanted to be the first one to speak. He turns around.

He puts his hands in his pockets. "To your friends..."

"My what? Oh, friends. Nah." I didn't come to him to get socializing lessons. "Why were you acting so weird today?"

He seems taken aback by my straightforwardness. "I am just worried about you guys. Do not tell anyone, but despite Albatross and your father's faith in you guys, I do not think you were ready to be Enhanced."

"I concur." I pause. "But we have to move fast, it's getting more dangerous out there with every new day."

"I know..." I can tell that there is something more that he isn't telling me. I wait for him to complete his thought. "I went out between class and Enhancement yesterday. It was just supposed to be a simple job, but I needed to do something. They have kept me cooped up here teaching you guys because they do not want the Preachers to know about the Enhancers." *I bet 'they' are Albatross, Blue-jay's father and his associates.* "The mission almost went to

316

hell, and I barely got out without revealing my powers. And I missed the Enhancing." He doesn't tell me any details about the mission, for all I know it could have been to go get coffee for Blue-jay's dad. "It shook me up and reminded me of the dangers that are out there." It doesn't really explain his behavior today. Something else must have happened that he isn't telling me.

I tell him "It's a scary world out there." but then let the subject go. It is obvious he will not tell me what else happened.

"You have got that right." Hawk agrees. "Anyway, get some sleep, Wren. You look like crap." He chuckles and that makes the lines around his eyes and mouth be even more prominent. It is almost as if he has aged ten years in the past two days.

"You're one to talk, old man." I grin and begin to walk away, back to dorm number one hundred and forty five. "Oh, and thanks for saving my dad's life."

Chapter Thirty

I am back home in Tieced. I don't know why I'm here or how I got here. It's a normal day, I hear noises come from downstairs—my dad undoubtedly making another one of his crazy inventions—and my brother, sister, and mother are off at work. For some reason though, I just sit on the couch watching the time fly by. No training, no research, just staring off into space. Time must fast-forward because what seems like a second later the rest of my family is home doing their own things and the sun is just about to set, casting long shadows across the wood floor. And I am still sitting. My ears ring, but hear nothing.

Someone pats me on the shoulder roughly, and slowly I am able to focus again. Beck's face is inches from mine, "Dinner's ready. Mom called us five minutes ago." He looks as if he's worried about me; worried because I didn't hear my mother's call.

"Oh, okay." I get off the couch and straighten my shirt, "Sorry."

The front door flies off its hinges, into the house. Next thing I know, cans dispersing billowing smoke, like the ones from the club, are rolled across the floors. The floors of my house. A wave of anxiety washes over me as I realize what this means—Preachers. This time there is no way I will not run and hide, so I prepare for a fight.

Dad, Mom, Beck and Piper run into the living room from the kitchen. "Cover your nose and mouth!" I shout, but nothing comes out. I lift the collar of my shirt over my nose and continue to tell them to cover up, but they can't hear me and just stand still, in shock. Almost immediately after their bodies fall to the floor, heavy steps land on my front porch. I have to think fast.

If they were still awake we could have put up a good fight, but I can't take a whole army of Preachers on my own. But I also can't leave my family to be killed. Well my dad would most likely be taken alive, but the rest of them would be gone.

In a feeble attempt to stick it to the man, I remain in my position, ready to throw myself at the first person through the door. *Wait! The Enhancer!* Just as the first person comes through the entryway, I thrust my arms out in front of me, expecting a wave of red energy to overwhelm them and send them flying backward. Nothing happens when I try the Enhancer and I just end up looking stupid in front of an army of Preachers.

They waste no time in filling the room, restraining me (despite my kicks and punches and hidden knife), and rounding up my unconscious family members.

"What do you want from us?" I shout and for once my voice actually works, but it just sounds weak. Of course I know the answer to my question, but I have to try to stall and save my family.

No one answers me for a minute or two and then the sea of black parts and someone walks towards me. It must be their leader.

The Preacher stops a couple feet from me. I try to sound threatening when I ask, "And who are you supposed to be?" but inside I know I am probably going to die. I have no weapons and no backup.

The Preacher rips their mask off and grins before me, "I think we have met before…"

I spit on the Preacher version of me and try to break loose of my bonds, hoping that just maybe I can see her blood again. But this time I can't get away from the Preachers holding onto my arms and she steps closer to me. I kick at her legs, but she keeps coming and finally, when she is inches from me she reaches into her cloak, bringing out a beautiful knife with a nine-inch blade. In normal circumstances I would stop and admire the blade, but now I know that I should be afraid.

Her face being so close to mine, it's like a mirror. Shifting her gaze to the knife she asks, "What do you think I should do with this?" Her breath crawls into my nose and throat. I swallow, but stay quiet. She turns on her heel quickly and starts walking away.

I stick my head out; it's about the only thing I can move, "How about you shove it up your ass?"

She throws herself at me, the knife clutched in her claw-like hand. With one move she brings the knife to my head, lodging it in my right eye. A burning sensation rips through my head. I try to keep my jaw locked, but cries escape my mouth.

The Preachers let me fall and writhe in pain. She just fucking stabbed me in the eye. I scream and howl on the wooden floor. *My* floor that is now covered in a fresh coat of *my* blood. I can see the tip of the handle with my left eye when it isn't closed or rolled back into my head.

Lying on my back, I rip out the knife, not knowing if it will help or make the situation worse.

Lying on my side, I clutch the side of my face, my head in a quickly growing pool of blood. *Just leave me here to die* — I beg. From my position, I can see my father, my mother, my sister and my brother through the Preachers' legs and feet. And I can see their bodies as bullets rip through their skulls and I scream and cry, still in pain and still gripping my bloodied face.

"Wren? Wren!?"

The floor is gone; it is now replaced with my queen-sized mattress. I shiver and cover the right side of my face with my hands. Swift stands above me. "Wren, you're okay." is all he says to me and sends a small smile in my direction. For some reason this pulls me out of the dream right away.

I sit up straight in my bed. The blanket, top-sheet and pillows have been thrown around the room in my terror. That nightmare was something different. Usually I can tell when I'm dreaming, but that felt so real.

I sit still for a minute to calm my heart and steady my breathing.

The main light is on, but I know that it is still night time. Swift has to be here for a reason. "What's wrong?" There is no way he could have known I was having a nightmare. And if he did, he probably wouldn't come here to wake me up.

He sighs, rubbing his neck. "Something is wrong with Koel. He's up in the hospital. I don't know the exact details, but I'm pretty sure it has something to do with the Enhancer."

It was just a nightmare, it isn't important — I remind myself and try to set my emotions aside. "Let's go then." I swing my legs over the edge of the bed, grab my boots and Enhancement jacket and head out the door. The two Proxies standing guard follow Swift and me. They must have let him into my room.

We remain quiet the entire trip upstairs to the main hospital floor. Swift doesn't mention my nightmare or ask me what happened or even check to see if I really am okay. I am somewhat grateful for that. I hope he has finally understood that I want there to be distance between us.

In the middle of the level is the circular main desk. "An Enhancement was brought here a few minutes ago...?" Swift asks the nurse behind the desk.

"Yes, he was—"

Koel's head pops out of a doorway to our right, "He's in here, but watch what you say, he's pretty grumpy." He disappears back into the room so Swift and I give each other a look and then follow him. *That guy looked just like Koel... Maybe he has a brother?*

They must have given Koel the largest room in the entire hospital section, because it miraculously holds all ten Enhancements, at least three lab technicians, Agent Hummingbird, Hawk, Albatross and patrolling Proxies, still with enough room to shove some more people into it.

There is a nice hospital bed, with mechanical devices set up next to it, but no one occupies the bed. Koel stands at the window that overlooks the city and he is also sitting in a chair next to Robin. *How is this possible?* Two Koels occupy the room as well. Both looking identical and both looking very much real and alive.

The one in the chair speaks first, "This has to be some sort of joke…" Koel sounds like he is begging.

"Jokes?" The second Koel turns around to face the first Koel, his face bright. "I love jokes."

"Shut up." Sitting Koel groans. *This has to be the real Koel, while the other is what? A clone? A copy?* I close my gaping mouth.

Silence. No answers. I can't take it. "What happened? How did it happen?" I motion to the two Koels.

"Yeah, one of us was bad enough." Window Koel jests.

Sitting Koel leans further back in his chair, "Well as you can see," the double steps forward, waves and then sits on the armrest of the other Koel's chair. "Something weird is going on."

I look to my father for an explanation. Dad hides the smirk that appears on his face.

Lark moves closer to Koel's double, looking him over. "He is a perfect copy." she says in surprise.

"Tell us everything." Father instructs.

"There is not much to tell." Koel mutters, "I woke up and he was sitting on the edge of my bed. Scared the shit out of me."

This whole time the second Koel has been making faces behind the real one's back. There *are* differences between them; personality is the most obvious.

"Come on, it can't be too bad." Number two says and slaps Koel on the back.

Pop! Koel vibrates before turning, annoyed, on himself.

A shape starts pulling away from Koel and another version of him appears to his left, pushing Robin's chair away.

"Oh, hell no." the original Koel says. "Not another one."

This one has longer and shaggier hair than the real Koel. He has bags under his eyes, "I'm not too thrilled about it either." he says in monotone.

"How many more are there?" Koel asks, frustrated.

"I am not sure, but I think they appear when you are not focused. This first one appeared when you were sleeping and were in a state of unconsciousness. Then the second came when you were surprised."

"I think we should keep hitting you, until new ones stop popping out." grins the first duplicate.

"It sounds like you're giving birth." Owl laughs and studies the joking version of Koel, "I like this one better than you-know-who." he whispers to Blue-jay.

"Since this is your special power, it would be best to try everything to reach its full potential." I think my dad is enjoying this whole situation.

It is the first time Koel has shown any real emotion.

"Fine, go ahead." Koel surrenders, stands and leaves himself open to be attacked.

The second twin unleashes a hard punch to the back of Koel's shoulder and **Pop!** Koel stumbles back and through the doorway.

"That gave me no pleasure." mumbles the long-haired Koel.

"Did it work?" Dad calls.

"Yeah." says a voice that is somehow different.

Two Koels walk in, both rubbing their shoulders.

"Which—?" Lark asks. It's hard to remember that she and Koel are depending on each other. Especially now that Koel has these different partners. She will have to remember who is who and get to know each and every one of them. I have never been more grateful that I wasn't paired with Koel.

Someone moans from outside the room, "I am the real one." Another Koel stumbles in behind them.

"Well it should be me." grunts one of the new ones.

It's too hard to keep track of all of them. I count them in my head—one, two, three, four, and then the real Koel.

"Maybe we should come up with a way to tell them apart. Give them names?" Lark suggests.

My father steps forward to inspect them, "Maybe once we get to know them. It is obvious that they behave differently."

"My turn!" shouts one.

Before the real Koel can react, he gets kicked in the groin by himself.

Pop! A new one morphs into creation. All six of them react to the pain, shooting their hands down to protect their manhood.

"The more the merrier." someone says and greets the newest Koel.

This is ridiculous.

"Why am I here? I want to go back to bed, what is going on?" whines the newbie. He is shorter and has messed up hair.

"Shut up, loser." says the same one who kicked Koel.

Another puts himself in between the shorter one and this aggressive bully, "Why can't we all just get along?"

I feel like laughing out loud because of this ridiculous situation, but I keep a straight face because this could potentially be a serious problem.

The original Koel stands closest to the exit, watching everything play out.

This is probably the only time I will be able to hurt Koel without repercussions, "Surprise attack!" I yell and tackle Koel.

Pop! He slams into the wall and suddenly I am holding onto two identical bodies.

I back up before Koel does anything to me and smile apologetically.

A Koel puts his arm over my shoulders, "I like this one." He has dark eyes and is somehow buffer than the real Koel. Apparently there are some physical differences too.

"Slow down there, animal." Swift nudges him away from me.

Robin and Osprey mutter things under their breath to each other and Nightingale is about to go in for another strike.

"Stop hitting me!" Koel yells and the room goes quiet. "Isn't there some other way to get them out? And how am I supposed to fit them all inside of me again?"

"Don't you have any control over us?" The seventh Koel asks. He's right and Koel knows it too.

Koel shuts his eyes. The six other versions of him freeze and then salute at the same time. Koel lifts one eyelid and smiles after he sees what he has done. "I can hear what you guys are thinking too."

"Really? What am I thinking about?" challenges Animal.

"Violence." Koel announces. "And girls."

Animal's reaction is the funniest thing I have ever seen. He flips out and thinks that it is the coolest thing in the world. "We should be able to communicate then."

A different Koel steps forward and agrees, "A telepathic link, I would assume."

"Now you should try to get them back together and then release them all at once." Hawk instructs, finally taking initiative. He knows more about working with Enhancers than anyone. "Relax."

Koel slows his breathing and sits on the floor leaning against the wall. His six personalities stand around him. Koel crosses his legs.

He closes his eyes really hard and one by one those other Koels get pulled into the real one.

A strange silence fills the room after they disappear.

If I was one of the volunteer Proxies, I would be freaking out right now. Even though I have seen some weird and incredible things already, it is taking a lot of willpower for me not freak out.

Koel opens his eyes slowly, hoping the others are gone. He hops to his feet when he realizes that he did it.

"Good job. Now show us the others again." Hawk says in a hushed voice.

Koel shoots out his arms and the loudest popping noise yet rings out. Owl and I put our hands over our ears.

One by one seven more Koel copies are projected from Koel and take form. I notice that there is one more than before.

Each copy goes to the Enhancement that is most similar to them in personality. It is like a gravity field pulls them without them even noticing. The 'animal' is next to Nightingale; they both cross their arms over their chests at the same time. That joking first one moves towards Owl and they greet each other like they're old friends. The friendly duplicate stands in between Robin and Osprey. That whiny kid flops over to Goldcrest and an extremely depressed Koel sits beside Blue-jay, who I haven't noticed was in the room until now.

Two of them stay next to the original Koel, the brand new one among them.

"That should be all of them." Dad says. "Koel, this is a very big responsibility, you could be in eight places at once. You must have constant control over them when they are separate from you. If you ever feel like you aren't focused or if you're tired, angry, whatever, you should retract them as soon as possible. I think your duplicates will help you learn how to work as a team." My dad takes them all in. These are his creations. He has made seven new human beings, if that is even what they are. "We should give them names. It is vital that you remember that these duplicates are not really you; they are merely different parts of your personality."

Koel closes his eyes again, reading and feeling his new companions with his mind. He knows their thoughts, opinions and emotions in seconds. He knows them better than anyone else can and ever will—well, because they are him. He raises his arm.

Koel points to Owl's companion, "J—short for Joker." Koel turns to the copy sitting next to Blue-jay, "Dark, because you are really pessimistic."

"I am not pessimistic, I am realistic." sighs the resting Koel like this is obvious, and then flips his long black hair out of his face.

"You," declares Koel, "Are Light, the opposite of that one."

Robin and Osprey smile with their friend. *Joy and happiness to the world* — I roll my eyes.

"As was stated before, Animal." Nightingale's friend smirks when he hears this.

Koel turns to the copy to his left, "Nerd." Then wrinkles his nose as he speaks to the duplicate paired with Goldcrest, "Annoying-worthless-baby and I am not sure about the last one... Awesomest?" Koel puts his arm around the version of him that is closest. *What?*

"Most awesome." corrects Nerd.

Annoying-worthless-baby, the one with Goldcrest, pouts his lip and is on the verge of tears. *Seriously?* At least we now know that Koel has feelings.

"We will just have to see how this plays out." my dad concludes, obviously not too happy about the results of Koel's name-giving experience. "You all need some sleep."

Lark puts her hand on A. W. B.'s shoulder, "It's going to be alright. I won't let Koel be mean to you." She turns and sticks her tongue out at the real Koel, "And I will find you a real name." I'm guessing it will be Sunshine-sparkle.

"I think it will be safe for you to return to your dorm." Hawk tells Koel. "I don't think any of you will be getting a lot of sleep, I know I didn't." He chuckles briefly. "Get back to bed while you can."

I leave with the rest of the large group. It gets smaller in the middle of the hallway, when Koel retracts his duplicates so he can fit into the elevator.

It gets smaller still as the group stops at the different the Proxy floors and splits up more as the hallways on my floor go on. Each person drifts off to their own dorm, leaving Robin and I alone for a short while until I reach my door. Robin says goodnight to me while I rifle through my pockets for the key.

"Goodnight." I respond, open the door and push it closed.

I curl into bed after taking off the jacket. Pulling the blankets, sheets and pillows up with me on the bed, I surround myself with them. I tell myself that I need my sleep after minutes of just staring at the wall. And then I let myself admit that I am too scared to close my eyes again, scared to see images that I can't control. But I have to sleep; I have to be ready for tomorrow. But I am scared of the Enhancer too. I am scared to feel the burn again and I am afraid that I might lose control of my powers like Koel did. Who knows what my 'special power' is going to be, I might not be able to contain it.

Chapter Thirty One

Over the next week, the ten of us work our butts off. Not only do we have to perfect our aim and the strength of the raging energy blasts, but we also have to worry about a random power possibly appearing out of nowhere and what it means if it doesn't show up soon.

My dad was right of course, I don't get much sleep after the night that Koel's duplicates appeared.

Koel has been pretty good at training with them. Controlling eight minds at once must be really hard, but he makes it seem easy. But of course there are some malfunctions—Koel will sometimes wake up to multiple versions of himself standing around and staring at him. I even heard him scream in the bathroom; apparently J had popped up while he was peeing. His partner, Lark, isn't having as much success. She has a hard time producing her pink energy and even if she does succeed, they are weak flickers. Lark has been successful in finding A.W.B., Koel's duplicate, a new name, though. It came to her after exclaiming, "Leave him alone, he's just a kid!" when Animal was picking on him. Thus, was born the name, 'Kid'. It isn't that great, but it is better than Annoying-worthless-baby.

Swift has had no luck in recreating his shield and I haven't had any luck with my special power either. At least he knows what his is; at least he knows what he is looking for. I, on the other hand, could have it right under my nose and not realize it. I still have one of the best sparks but am being quickly overrun by Swift. While I have been good from the beginning, I haven't progressed at all. Swift on the other hand, seems to be getting better every day.

Throughout the week, the special powers of the other Enhancements begin to reveal themselves, along with each other's strength of character. I must admit, it has been a tough seven days physically and emotionally. I think the Enhancer might be doing things to my head. I am having nightmares again. And they are so much more powerful this time and so real in my mind.

For once, Goldcrest is ahead of Nightingale because he has discovered his power before she has. Well I guess she kind of helped him… in a way. During one of her rampages, she stabbed his hand with a butter knife. This was during breakfast, so we were all quite taken aback and ready to rush Goldcrest to the hospital, but as soon as he removed the knife, the wound mended itself and the skin closed. He was healed. Which is great, but now whenever he and Nightingale have to fight on the mat, she shows no mercy. I'm sure he has suffered a broken rib or two, but has come back completely fine and completely healed.

Owl has gotten better with his energy blasts, which are pretty easy for him to produce, but he doesn't know what to do with them once he has got them. He and Blue-jay haven't discovered their unique powers yet, or at least not that we know of.

Osprey can produce energy, but doesn't like using it because all it can really do is cause destruction or bodily harm, so he really has no use for it. Robin has been mastering those energy flashes, to be used as a sort of light instead of a weapon, and Osprey is willingly helping her perfect the maneuver.

Exactly a week after Enhancement, Robin has figured out her powers. I was told that during the night, she woke up, completely convinced it was morning, and since she had plans to meet up with Osprey before breakfast the next day, she walked right to his dorm. I don't know how she didn't realize that no one else was up. After knocking on Osprey's door for a couple minutes, he finally answered and opened the door, greeting Robin in only his boxers. The situation isn't that bad, but Osprey was so embarrassed when she relayed the story later that it made it so much more amusing. Robin smiled the entire time she was telling us. So she has night vision now. So much for being afraid of the dark.

The sleepless nights plus the mental and physical strain have me on edge as well as all of the other Enhancements. Even Hawk has been working harder than I have ever seen him, but we are running on fumes now. Thankfully Albatross has taken control of the situation and given us tomorrow off.

What I really want to do on our day off is sleep, but I know I can't allow myself that indulgence, or at least not for too long. I made plans with Swift to help him with his force-field tomorrow and in return he said he would help me figure out what my power is. I suppose you could say that we have somewhat made-up, but we'll see tomorrow.

Of course this won't really be a day off, I severely doubt any of the Enhancements will really be resting, but working on their powers in other ways, outside of the classroom.

***

Swift sits cross-legged on my bed making weird movements with his hands. He pays me no attention, keeping his eyes on his work.

I just sit on the desk and stare at him, but not how I used to. Now there is caution and distrust. Now there is animosity, or at least from my side there is. The situation isn't as bad as it was, say, two weeks ago, but there are still boundaries that can't be crossed, on both sides. I'm afraid that our relationship will never be the same again.

I stare at him now because I am bored, and because I am waiting for something to happen. He has been trying for several minutes to get his powers to work. We have taken a break from helping each other and are working by ourselves now. I have no idea how I'm supposed to trigger my power, so I do nothing.

I turn my attention to the couch for a moment. *Man, I'm bored.*

From the corner of my eye something flashes above Swift. I turn my head quickly to see what it is, but nothing is there.

"What?" Swift asks and gazes up. He is slightly alarmed by the look on my face.

"Nothing, I thought I saw something above your head… But it wasn't blue."

"Okay… Maybe you're just tired." Swift says and goes back to trying to produce the shield. *I actually got a full night's rest; I don't think that is it.*

Words rush out of my mouth, "Are you okay? You seem upset."

"I'm worried about the stupid shield, of course, and stressed out from the program and exhausted from working so hard…" He catches his breath and calms down, "Why do you ask?"

Why did *I ask?* "I don't know. It just sort of popped into my head that you weren't feeling one-hundred percent okay." And obviously he isn't. Which is to be expected.

I decide to do something about it, "I will help you develop your force-field, don't worry." I hop off the edge of the desk and go to my closet.

"How…?" Swift asks and watches me walk past him. "Wren, what are you doing?"

"Helping my partner." I tell him and come back out with two pairs of shoes.

Without thinking and without warning him I chuck one shoe at his head. It bounces off of his forehead and flops to the ground.

Swift stares at me blankly, "Thanks for that, Wren. What exactly were you trying to do?"

"I was hoping the shield would pop out to protect you. Let me try again."

Swift sighs, "Don't you think I've already tried something like that?"

"Yeah, but not with me." I grin confidently.

He rolls his eyes, but I know he concedes because he stands up. He'll be ready this time.

I run around the room, hoping to surprise him. Finally, I jump on my bed before throwing my weapon at Swift.

It doesn't touch him, but stops abruptly in the air in front of him and falls to his feet.

"I don't know how or why, but something definitely happened." His face brightens instantly, "Throw another one!"

Swift's eyes follow me as I streak past him and into the entrance of the bathroom. I lob the projectile as hard as I can as Swift shoots out his hands with force.

A blue wall appears in front of him and the shoe bounces off of it, flying in my direction. I dive over the couch to get out of the way.

"Yes!" Swift cheers. "I can't believe your stupid idea worked."

I pop my head over the top of the couch. The wall is gone now. His expression glows radiantly.

Happiness burns into my retinas, first appearing over Swift's head and then everywhere I look the word flashes in red.

"Shit!" I exclaim in pain and cover my eyes with my hands, while falling to my knees.

"Wren?" I look up at him. Swift's expression and body language have completely changed.

The happiness is replaced by *fear*. The change makes it even worse. I cry out again.

He quickly realizes that something is wrong with me and jumps over the couch, landing beside me. "What's wrong?" Swifts holds on to my arms and keeps me steady.

Burning, burning, but no fire. I can't take the pain. "Burning, but no fire." I repeat out loud. "It has to be connected to my Enhancer powers." I try to hide my agony, but I can't contain it. Everywhere I look emotions brand themselves onto my eyes. My eyes begin to water. "Help me." I say through gritted teeth.

"Oh, um…" He looks around the room, and must think about calling for help. Swift doesn't know how to help me. He puts his warm, hard hands on the sides of my face. A tear rolls down my cheek. "Uh-close your eyes." he instructs with uncertainty. "If it's your eyes that are bothering you then close them." Swift urges me. He is right, so I listen to him. With my eyes shut the words slowly fade and the pain recedes.

I let Swift guide me the couple of feet to my couch.

"What happened?" Now Swift sounds more excited than worried. He sits next to me, still holding onto me.

"Emotions." Even I can hear the wonder and confusion in my voice, "I could see what you were feeling."

"Yeah, Wren. Most people can." Swift tells me.

"Well not me. I have always had a problem with… reading… people." I say the last words slowly as I realize that that was my worst weakness, "And now I won't have that problem." *Unless this torture continues every time my eyes are open. Imagine what would happen if I was in a room filled with people.* "The emotion is clearly written out for me above the person's head. At first you were happy, because you triggered your power again and then you were scared because of my reaction."

Swift removes his hands from me, "Are you okay now?"

"I think so." I answer. I am still too scared to open my eyes.

"Check if it's still there."

I slowly lift my eyelids and see Swift's anticipating face with concern still in it.

Nothing but Swift. I smile. "It's gone."

"Great." he says and pulls me into a hug.

My instincts are to shout 'Get off', but I just pull away quickly. *What the hell is going through his head?* For a second **sad** glows above his head and I recoil, shutting my eyes, ready for the burning, but this time I don't feel anything.

334

"You okay?" Swift asks.

A look again, this time everything goes back to normal.

I nod, "I should be." I reassure Swift and then mutter under my breath, "With time."

I wonder why Swift was sad. He doesn't seem like a person who regrets his actions, but I could be wrong. I will find out soon enough with my power. I wonder what secrets I'll unveil with this new phenomenon.

We sit in silence on the couch for a few moments. I hate this distance between us, but also want to be as far away as possible from him.

"You should probably rest." he says and nods to the bed. "I'll practice some more."

"Fine." I walk slowly over to my bed. Almost as soon as I pull the covers over my shoulders I fall asleep.

***

"Wren! Swift!" Robin's voice comes plowing through my closed door. I worry at first, but soon recognize the happiness in her tone.

Rejuvenated from my nap, I hop up and open the door for her. She stands in the hallway with Osprey at her side. They both smile as per usual. "The whole team is going to grab some food from the mall." Then she notices my bed head and Swift on the couch, "Oh, I hope we didn't interrupt anything." She giggles and turns to Osprey.

"I have a feeling you will not be interrupting anything, ever." I say to stop her thoughts of anything going on between Swift and I. I won't let anything happen.

"Okay…" Robin isn't convinced. "Well get ready quickly and we can go together."

Swift appears behind me quickly, "I don't think that is a very good idea. Maybe Wren should spend some time alone." I can feel his breath on the back of my neck.

I turn on him, "Excuse me—"

"There will be lots of people," he says quietly, "With lots of feelings." *Oh, shit. That's true.*

"Right." I say to Swift and then speak to Robin and Osprey, "Swift is right, I should stay home for now. Maybe you could bring me something back?" I try to sound as nice as possible.

"Sure." Osprey says and then beckons for Swift to leave with them.

I watch Robin, Osprey and Swift walk away with a pang of jealousy or some other emotion in my stomach. Just think, a month ago I would have tried anything to stay away from them, but now I want to be with everyone. Maybe I am growing too attached, and maybe Swift realized that too and it's another reason he told me not to go with everyone, beside my special power problems. But I need someone to talk to.

I find my father in the Viewing Deck and seeing the bags under his eyes and his disordered clothes, realize that he too needs a break. So I invite him to lunch and he accepts my offer.

My father and I have never had much to talk about. Neither of us like to talk much anyway. But I'm the only family he has here, so after we get our food from the cafeteria I try my best to have a real conversation with him.

We talk about his visit back home and how the family is doing. He was only there for a few days, but he got to catch up a little with each of our family members. Piper is busier than ever at the hospital, more attacks from Preachers bringing more injured to her. But Beck's situation is the exact opposite; no one comes to the museum he works at so it might be closing altogether. Mother has been going to local homeless shelters to help out and get information, which is dangerous on any day, but especially if a Preacher uprising is starting.

We talk about the Enhancers. Of course. One of the only things we have in common really, except our logical thinking. He claims that everything is running smoothly and that the new batch is easier to control than Hawk's was. I ask him when he will officially start making the next bunch of Enhancers. He tells me he is uncertain.

Apparently Lark's power manifested last night. I would undoubtedly have learned this while out with the team. She and Koel came to my father early this morning after she woke up in HABITAT, unsure of how she got there. At first he thought that she melted through the floor since she lives directly above HABITAT, but later Dad concluded that she has the power of teleportation. She dreamt of being in that room and appeared there. Thinking is all it will take for her to appear in a different room, or possible a different city.

I let him know about my Enhancer power at the end of our meal. He gives me its name—empathy. He isn't very surprised.

"Try it out right now." Dad says and after seeing my doubting face he adds, "There are not many people here and I can help if something goes wrong." He convinces me, but I don't exactly know how to activate this empathy. So I look around the cafeteria at the relatively small crowd. I try to imagine what the other Proxies are thinking, what is going on in their lives and how they are feeling. And before I know it, words show above most of their heads. The empathy doesn't hurt as much this time; maybe I have gotten used to it. Now it feels like a bright light being shined in my eyes.

"So what do you see?" Dad asks. "What is that girl feeling?" He nods to a teenage Proxy a table away.

I see nothing above her head, but I go with my instinct. "She is calm. Content." My power is not that impressive when you think about it.

337

"And him." He subtly points to a tattooed Proxy leaning against the wall across the room. Dad and I do this for a while. He asks me about a person, I read them and then answer.

"It is not that hard." Dad says.

"I guess not." I must admit that I was quite concerned before.

"Now turn it off." *Turn it off? How do I—* I shut my eyes and count to five. If it worked with Swift than it should work now. When I open my eyes, the emotions are still there, written above my dad's head, the cook's, that tattooed Proxy's, above almost everyone's.

"I can't turn it off."

Chapter Thirty Two

"I would like to introduce our newest Enhancement—Wren!" Owl announces my arrival at the training room. "Her powers appeared yesterday." I told him and Robin earlier during breakfast. So far the empathy has not turned off since lunch yesterday and I have the feeling that it will always be there.

Nightingale stops attacking a punching bag, "Congrats." she says while smirking. I am very suspicious of that. "So I'm sure you wouldn't mind a round with me on the mat?" Of course that's what she was getting at.

I am about to agree to fight her, but Hawk comes striding in and starts ordering us around. "Not today, girls. I want Robin and Koel on the mat first."

"What? Me?" Robin mouths in shock. 'Scared' glows above her forehead. "But I don't have my—"

"I do not care." Hawk interrupts her rudely. "Both of you, up there now."

Owl pushes Robin to the slightly elevated mat, she hops on it nervously. Koel gets up more confidently. He has seven more versions of him at his disposal, I would feel pretty certain of myself if were him, too.

"Everyone will fight today. It ends when one of you surrenders—bringing much humiliation—or if you are unable to continue to fight. Use your energy, Enhancer power, whatever." The rest of the team surrounds the fighting area. "Ready?" Hawk asks and Robin and Koel get into fighting stances. "Go." he commands them.

Koel takes a step forward, and Robin takes one back. Koel punches the air, black energy emerging from his fist aimed at Robin. But she is fast and dodges it while kicking two yellow balls in his direction. Koel is a big target, so even though he dodges the one, the second one hits him square in the chest.

"S-sorry." she exclaims.

Without speaking, Koel releases his duplicates, all seven lining up next to him. Koel is in complete control of them. As they prepare for a combined strike, I prepare for the worst. Robin is rightfully scared.

"Robin! The flares..." Osprey hints.

"Oh, yeah!" she says quickly and a second later her hands are in the air, releasing some sort of bright energy. The energy flies in a ring at the Koels, popping and flashing brighter, blinding them completely. I can't believe she figured it out.

Screaming in pain and covering their eyes, the seven retract to the one real Koel.

Robin steps toward Koel, her fist glowing, ready to deliver the final blow. But Koel lifts his hands in front of him, "You win, I surrender." He backs off the mat. "I can't fucking see." he mutters. *Anger*.

"He will be fine in a minute." Robin steps off the mat with Osprey's help.

When Koel's eyesight returns to him, Hawk states the next pair. Owl and me.

I jump onto the mat with ease and Owl follows.

"Come on, Owl!" J, Koel's duplicate shouts. The others are out again too, but are mostly ignoring the fight and doing their own thing.

Animal likes violence and fights, though, so he is up close to the mat. "No! Go Wren!" he shouts not really for me, but at J. They continue to shout at each other a few more times before launching at each other and wrestling on the ground. Koel just rolls his eyes and walks away.

"Okay..." Hawk brings the attention back to the real fight. "Get started."

Even though Owl is my friend and weaker than me, I decide to take this fight seriously. I have a feeling Hawk wants our fight to trigger his powers, so I might as well go all out. "I have my special power now and I'm not scared to hurt a kid." I smirk.

"Oh, yeah, I'm really scared that you are going to beat me with your emotion sensing powers." Owl jokes. He isn't worried.

"Okay…" I crack my knuckles, red energy flowing between them and then I shoot them out at Owl. Eight different small sparks, like glowing knives, fly at him. He runs fast enough to dodge most of them, and when I think he's about to get hit by the last two, he waves his right arm in front of his face, letting out a wave of orange energy. My sparks hit his wave, causing a small explosion, but both of us are left uninjured. J whoops for Owl. Then we spend several minutes throwing energy, dodging and throwing again. No one gets hit, but Owl gets grazed a few times. As time goes on I notice that Owl is only using his energy blasts as defense, and isn't actively attacking me. So I decide to take things up a notch.

Stepping forward, I bring my hands together in front of me. The clap releases a large surge of energy that Owl won't be able to run away from.

Up until now Owl has been pretty calm, but now *fear* appears above his head in red. Animal cheers me on just as Owl rolls under my soaring energy. I hadn't realized how close he was to me until now, when he rolls right through my legs. I'm about to turn around, when he places his foot on my lower back, and pushes. I land flat on my face. That stops Animal's roaring.

At the sight of me, J bursts into laughter and so does Owl. I roll over onto my side and while Owl stands and helps me get up, J doubles over, howling.

"S-S-Sorry." Owl says between giggles, tears forming in his eyes, "We shouldn't be making fun of you." He wipes away a tear.

Watching Owl try to be serious and considerate instead of laughing, makes me crack a smile. When I finally get to my feet I begin to laugh too.

"I am calling off the fight!" Hawk shouts, which makes us laugh even more. Neither of us were intending to finish, not in our condition. Hawk throws us off and Owl and I leave, laughing hysterically.

"Nice moves." I tell him as I alight.

"Not so bad yourself." He chuckles.

I go over and stand with Swift and Owl goes to help J, who has now collapsed on the floor in his fit. Swift smirks, but other than that, everyone else seems to not have found the situation that amusing. I try to calm down.

"Next up, Swift and Lark."

"These pairings are really unfair, Hawk." Lark whines, but goes to the platform anyway.

"And who has been winning so far?"

Swift leaves my side and climbs up. The two prepare for battle and then Hawk starts them off. They both take the match quite seriously. Swift's energy blasts are clean and swift, sliding off his fists with each mid-air punch. Lark knows her limits, and keeps the offense to the minimum, mostly teleporting out of the way of Swift's attacks. She seems to be in control of her power. The pink energy surges through her body only a second before she disappears and reappears a foot away a moment later.

"Strike!" Koel shouts to her through cupped hands.

Swift stands in the middle of the platform now, his eyes on Lark's movements. She teleports from the top right corner to the bottom left and then to the top left and then to the bottom right. *What is she up to?* — I wonder.

With a flash of pink, Lark is gone and then at Swift's back. Her fist alive with energy, she punches him in the back. The pink energy lingers on his skin for a moment and then seems to be absorbed by his body. His back bends at the point of impact. Swift roars. He turns around quickly, prepared to topple her, but she has already teleported away.

Lark continues to circle Swift and then jump right next to him, delivering an energized punch or kick. Chest, right knee, jaw, side, back again, stomach. And Swift can't do anything in return because she keeps teleporting out of the way. But he has to do something.

Hawk subtly calls Goldcrest over to him and whispers, "Be on stand-by." Hawk thinks Swift might need to be healed.

"Swift, for God's sake use your force-field!" I yell at him. If he doesn't do something fast he will be seriously injured and I know that he won't want to surrender. His power usually emerges when he needs to be defended; where is it now? I can tell that he is in a lot of pain.

Swift tries, I can tell that he really tries, but nothing happens. No blue force surrounds him and absorbs Lark's attacks, and his energy blasts are futile. Lark circles again now, Swift stands alert.

"Finish it!" Koel tells her.

Lark appears at Swift's side and knocks his feet out from under him. Swift's head hits the mat with a lot of force. Knees bent, Lark leans over Swift, a fist in his face. "Surrender." she orders. And he does.

As soon as he says so, I jump onto the stage and help him up. I grab his arm and put it over my shoulders. His shirt is drenched in sweat, but somehow it has survived the bombardment. I carry most of his weight down and over to Goldcrest.

A few other Enhancements crowd around. "Swift, I think you're the first person alive to actually be hit by an energy blast. How does it feel?" Owl asks just as Goldcrest places his hands on Swift's arm.

"Not very good." Swift winces. The veins on Goldcrest's hands turn a sickly grey and then the area of contact on Swift's arm does too. It spreads all over Swift's body and then finally fades. This is the first time I have witnessed Goldcrest heal anyone. It is quite strange.

Goldcrest lets go of Swift, "You good?"

"Yeah." Swift says and nods, "Thanks."

Goldcrest pats Swift's shoulder and then walks off.

While Swift has been being healed, Koel and his support team have been congratulating Lark on her work. Yes, it is a great achievement and all, but Swift was seriously injured. We're lucky we have Goldcrest.

Robin runs to get Swift a chair from the classroom and then she sets it up beside the fighting square. I help him over to it while Hawk announces the next showdown.

Next up is Nightingale and Blue-jay. A very aggressive fighter against a more passive one. I am sure Nightingale is going to win.

"You can beat her, Blue-jay." Swift shouts as Blue-jay walks up to the mat.

She responds with a nod and a grim face. She knows her chances are slim; she doesn't have any of her Enhancer powers. The mat shivers when Nightingale jumps on.

"Get ready." Blue-jay and Nightingale prepare themselves. Feet apart, knees bent, fists up. "And go."

"Oh sweet, a cat fight!" Animal roars and the rest of the duplicates rush to the mat.

Blue-jay stays in her place when Nightingale takes a step forward and lets loose two small, purple energy blasts. Blue-jay waits until the very last second to move out of the way, causing much terror in the eyes of the other bystanders. I have never seen Blue-jay in a real fight before. She is lean and tall, like Nightingale, but she is also very graceful and lithe. She is pretty fast too, but still gets bombarded by Nightingale's pure power and aggression. At what seems like the end of the battle, Nightingale releases one large wave of energy that Blue-jay couldn't possibly dodge. But for some reason Blue-jay rushes Nightingale at high speed, pulling up right before the wave overruns her. She bends her head back and falls to her knees, Blue-jay's blonde hair flowing beautifully behind her. Her momentum causes her to slide across the distance between her and Nightingale. Animal and J whistle. She learned a thing or two from Owl's fight with me.

Blue-jay stands inches from Nightingale now. Blue-jay pulls back her arm and for a second we all think that she has won. But of course Nightingale isn't going down so easily. She brings the excitement of Blue-jay's impressive maneuver to a complete stop by grabbing Blue-jay's fist just when Blue-jay's fist is inches away from Nightingale's face.

"Nice try." Nightingale sneers and twists Blue-jay's hand to the left, getting a wail out of her, but still Nightingale doesn't let go.

Nightingale threatens to twist further, but Blue-jay lets loose a mighty snarl, white light burning through their clasped hands. Blue-jay's energy. Nightingale releases quickly and jumps back.

Blue-jay then thrusts her arms forward while taking a step, causing an enormous torrent of energy to come raining down on Nightingale. She gets hit square in the chest, and is thrown back over the edge of the mat and onto the cold tile floor. Nightingale is fine, or at least that's what she says through clenched teeth. She got beat by Blue-jay.

Happiness glows above Blue-jay, and she has every right to be happy and excited.

Before Blue-jay has time to even fully realize what she has done, Animal and J rush onto the mat and lift her onto their shoulders, "You destroyed the witch!" J hollers. I'm sure that isn't going to make Nightingale any happier about losing.

Nightingale gets up slowly, brushes off her clothes and retreats to a corner. Goldcrest joins her a minute later.

Blue-jay eventually gets away from the duplicates and rejoins the rest of the group.

"That was very good work, Blue-jay." Hawk commends her, "Congratulations on gaining your energy blasts too. The final pair is, of course, Goldcrest and Osprey." The two most well-mannered

345

Enhancements in our team. "I want to see some real action, Osprey." Hawk instructs him.

"Come on, Osprey!" Robin and Owl cheer.

Owl then hops onto the mat with Goldcrest and Osprey, makes them huddle around him and says, "Now I want this to be a nice, clean fight. No funny business or you're both off the team."

Hawk rolls his eyes, "Get off, Owl!"

With this rate of the underdogs finishing on top, Goldcrest should pull ahead.

His grey energy against Osprey's green is a sight to see. They both have different fighting styles than the others. While most people used short, fast blasts, Goldcrest and Osprey have long, fluid attacks. Osprey actually does his best to hit Goldcrest, but when he does Goldcrest simply heals. So even though Goldcrest doesn't usually land a hit and Osprey does, Osprey seems to be on the losing side. Then with one fair sweep, Goldcrest releases a mighty blow that erupts from his chest and then hits Osprey's chest. Osprey goes flying off the mat, flipping end over end. He sets down near the right wall and Goldcrest is the first to run to him.

"I did not mean to hurt him." Goldcrest says when I arrive with Swift and Hawk. He really is sorry. Osprey's eyes are closed and he is completely still. Goldcrest knocked him out cold.

"Do not worry about it." Hawk ruffles Goldcrest's hair. *Don't worry about it? Osprey is unconscious.*

"Goldcrest, you heal him." Swift points from Goldcrest to Osprey. Then he turns to Hawk, "Just because we have a healer doesn't mean you can make us beat the crap out of each other." But Hawk ignores Swift and walks away.

I have to keep Swift from marching after him and giving him a piece of his mind. I don't think we can still get kicked out, but we don't need any problems within the group, especially with our leader and mentor.

***

Beep, beep, beep, beep.

I lay in my bed with a pillow over my head. For some reason I keep hearing beeping… really loud beeping. I am not alarmed, I'm tired. Soon the beeps turn into one loud wail. The urge to get up and check out the problem evades me so I continue to kick around in my comforter. *This could be in my head; this could be another side-effect from the Enhancer* — I succeed in convincing myself further to stay in bed.

Next, knocks join the siren. I wait for the knocks to go away but they continue. Fast and urgent.

"Who is it?!" I shout and rip the pillow away.

"Wren, get dressed quickly and get out here." It's Swift. Focusing, I read *fear* through the wall and it moves back and forth. Swift is pacing now.

I throw the covers off finally realizing that something really must be wrong. Some security system alarms are blaring. I am stupid for ignoring it.

After throwing on my Proxy uniform (which is the first thing I find and seems safest), I leave my room.

"How couldn't you hear that?" Swift grabs my forearm and I rip it away from his grasp.

"What's going on?!" I choose to not tell him that I was ignoring the cries.

Swift is taking me to the street level.

"Security says that the building is under attack." We emerge into the Proxy lobby. The breath catches in my throat. The first thing that pops into my head are Enhanced Preachers.

I swallow slowly and try to remain calm. "So what's the protocol?" I ask.

There are a lot of Proxies in here, some of them running around, coming in and out of doors; some standing and talking with fast words and others just sitting on the floor. It isn't organized at all.

"Usually the refugees go to the very bottom floors." That means our training rooms are filled with families. I hope no one bumps the control panel in HABITAT. "Security Proxies grab their weapons and secure all of the exits, while Liaisons and the people who work the computers try to pinpoint the attack."

Now that I understand what is happening the gravity of the situation finally hits me. The Preachers might be finally making their move and we aren't prepared. The Enhancements aren't ready.

But where are the explosions? The screams of pain instead of the normal crying caused by fear? And what about the damage?

"We aren't really under attack." I say out loud mostly so that I will believe it.

Swift grins and turns to me, "You're right, this is just a drill. Hawk and the leaders thought up a new plan in case the building is really attacked, which could happen any day now…"

"Good thinking." This place relies on the hope that Preachers don't know who or where we are. If they did send in forces we would be taken out quickly; if it came down to it, this building is impossible to defend. The only way we could try is if hundreds of Proxies would flood the streets but then our cover would be completely blown. "So what's the new protocol?"

"Hawk will be able to explain it better than me, I haven't even heard the whole plan yet." Swift tells me. *Could he make a force-field big enough to surround the whole building? Probably not, and definitely not at the moment.* "He and a few others were in the Viewing Deck before I came to wake you up."

"So let's go."

348

We wade through the sea of people to the next elevator. It is weird to see all of these Proxies who usually represent power and protection being so helpless. Hopefully they won't lose their heads.

The siren's scream is blocked in the elevator and soon it's like Swift and I are just taking a casual trip up to the Viewing Deck to talk to Albatross or Hawk like we used to do when I was working Security. Especially because I am wearing this uniform. I do not mention this though.

Swift is calm now; I finally have time to check up on him again. I didn't bother focusing my powers in the lobby; I would probably get a giant wave of emotions and pass out.

I fear that the electricity might go off and the elevator will stop working, but Swift and I arrive safely on the top floor.

"It is about time you got here!" Hawk rises from his hunched-over-the-table position.

"Someone couldn't hear the alarm." Swift replies and quickly descends the stairs to the main area.

I glare at him for throwing me under the bus, even if he is somewhat joking.

"So, the new plans..." I try to get the attention away from me. Swift and I join all of the other Enhancements at the round table.

I sit between Swift and Osprey. Osprey smiles at me in greeting.

"Right. Because of the Preacher's increase of activity, the board decided to go over old protocols and renew any of them that needed to be renewed. I decided that it would be best to go over these plans with all of the Enhancements, so when an attack really happens, we will all be on the same page." The others are surprisingly quiet. They must be tired.

"Each Proxy group has a different job," Hawk continues, "Liaisons contact the local police and care for the refugees; making sure they get in the basement quickly and that they are calm. Medical Proxies will take up shop in the first floor below ground, so it will not be too hard for injured soldiers to get to them, but they will have some sort of protection. Most of the upper levels will be cleared out in case of aerial attacks, which would be quite rare because of the force-fields and the limited air space, but we still need to be cautious. Security, of course, stays close to the building and guards it while Field Proxies find their way out of the building to fight on a battlefield. All eleven Enhancements would go out with the Field Proxies and rage war against the Preachers." Hawk pauses a moment to make sure we're all still awake and following along.

Then he finishes, "There are a few underground tunnels leading from the NEST building to surrounding buildings and streets. They have not been used in years, so they are currently being cleared out. The Field Proxies will use them to get further away from the building and strike from behind the enemy forces. And even if we do not need them for that purpose, I am sure that the refugees could escape through them if they ever need to."

Goldcrest's head falls forward and he makes a weird noise as he is thrust back into consciousness. His eyes roll back into his head before focusing on Hawk again.

Hawk looks slightly annoyed, "If everything is clear you can all go back to bed now..."

"Yes, yes, everything's clear..." Nightingale mumbles, "Everyone else to their separate areas and jobs while we go out and kick Preacher butt, I think we got it."

"Fine." Hawk concludes, "You are dismissed."

I hop out of my seat and try to leave as quickly as possible. I take one last scan of the room before walking up the stairs.

Owl hasn't made it through. His red hair hides his face from me, but I am almost sure it is covered in slobber. His head rests on the table.

Robin shakes his shoulders and it takes a while for him to wake up. While watching Robin and Owl I realize that, I too, am exhausted. I rub my eyes.

Lark is just as energetic as usual despite the late hour. She runs around Koel saying things that I can't hear.

I climb the few stair to the elevators and then press the button.

From the lobby, I can see the sun just start to rise behind the buildings. The other Proxies and refugees must have all gone back to their rooms and apartments while we were up there. Hawk's debriefing didn't seem to take that long though...

"Goodnight." Osprey tells me.

I jump because I hadn't noticed that he was in the elevator with me.

"Yeah." I mumble back.

Chapter Thirty Three

I can only read the most basic emotions and can sense others. From what I've gathered by watching random people, those basic emotions are happiness, anger, sadness, and fear.

I like sitting in the busy civilian lobby and reading everyone who passes by me. It is great practice. Sometimes if I see someone who is having a particularly bad day I get the urge to talk to them—to try and make them feel better. But that is stupid. Helping people may be my job, but not individually. I am working on a higher scale. Or at least I will be eventually.

I have been able to ignore the Empathy when I don't actually need it. The words are still there, but they look out of focus or I can see through them.

Sometimes Swift joins me for these sessions and sits silently beside me, sometimes asking me questions about certain people in whispers. He has to practice too, but his power is corporeal and can be seen so he has to do so privately. NEST is trying to keep the whole Enhancement thing on the down low, so it would be unwise to go around broadcasting our powers. But we are going to be out in the real world, using our powers, sometime soon and I am sure everyone will know about it.

It has been two weeks since Enhancement and soon the ten of us will be released and more people recruited for the Enhancement program. I kind of feel sorry for Hawk because he has to stay behind and train everyone, but I guess that's the way it has to be.

I haven't left this building since the incident. I am not sure why; I'm not one to be scared.

Okay, I was terrified when the club was attacked, but I was under the influence. If I hadn't been drinking I would have fought instead of hide, but I did drink and I paid the price, even if it was a little extreme.

I'm not exactly sure what we'll be doing once the program ends other than fighting Preachers. I sincerely hope I won't be expected to stay at NEST headquarters, but as long as I'm doing something, I will be happy.

***

"Why are you always happy?" I ask Robin who is sitting to my right at a table in the cafeteria. We are eating breakfast together.

She spoons cereal into her mouth, "Huh?"

I tap my finger against my temple and she gets what I'm hinting at. "Um, I guess because I want to be happy and I try to be." *It can't be that easy.* "I try to do things that make me happy and surround myself with people that make me happy. If someone does not, then I leave them behind. I do not need their negativity." Robin tucks a loose strand of orange hair behind her ear.

I put down my bowl. "So having friends makes you happy?"

"Yes." Robin laughs like this is obvious.

"So I guess if you hang out with me that means I make you happy." *That is odd.*

"Most of the time. At first you didn't." Robin laughs again while standing up. Her bowl is empty now. "Now come on or we're going to be late."

I pick up my unfinished breakfast and follow Robin to the trashcan and then out of the cafeteria. She whistles as we descend to our floor. Robin, Osprey and Owl are some of the happiest people I have ever seen. They must be doing something different, because everywhere else I look, my Empathy shows me anything but happiness. When we emerge into the basement, I can hear Hawk's voice bellowing throughout the entire floor. *What is he going on about now?*

I quicken my steps and Robin follows suit.

"Sit down." Hawk orders and points to the chairs as soon as we enter.

Robin and I rush to free chairs as quickly as possible. Thanks to the Enhancer I know when someone is super pissed and try to avoid conflict with them. I tuck my legs under the desk quickly. Swift is at my left and Blue-jay is on my right.

"Now, what I was doing before you girls got here,"—annoyance drips from every word—"was trying to figure Blue-jay out a little more. What makes her tick, who she is." He stops pacing around the room and plants himself in front of Blue-jay's desk. "So what is your deal, Blue-jay?" Hawk places his hands on her desk and leans forward so his face is quite close to hers. "You have been taught all of your life that you should not have emotions or at least not let anyone know about them. Your father and mother do not want you to have your own opinions. So what do you feel now, huh?" He is angry. I don't know what at—Blue-jay or her parents or NEST or maybe something else entirely.

"I am pretty annoyed that you are asking me." Blue-jay crosses her arms across her chest to form a barrier.

"No!" Hawk hits the desk with his fists and spins around in fury. Blue-jay flinches and looks at the ground. "What are you feeling?!"

"Anger." she says in an almost inaudible voice.

"And who or what are you angry at and why?" Hawk seems to be calming down.

Blue-jay's voice rises, "My father because he never lets me do what I want. I never wanted to be in this damned program and risk my life." She looks Hawk straight in the eyes. Admitting that in front of all of us is pretty gutsy.

"And who else?" he pushes her further.

"Swift." Her eyes look to him even though her head doesn't move. "I wanted to be partners with him." *And he wanted to be partners with her. She should be mad at me instead.* "And at myself because I let my dad push me around and make me join this. And now I can't even get this stupid device to work!" She throws her hands up, knocking the desk over. Hawk jumps back before it crushes his foot.

"Great." he breathes. Hawk is happy that Blue-jay is showing some emotion now.

"Great?" Fire sparks in her eyes and burns brightly. It won't be put out easily. "You get me all riled up for a stupid exercise and expect me to be okay with it?" She sidesteps the desk to get closer to Hawk. "Well I'm NOT!" she yells and pushes another desk out of the way.

"Hey, Blue-jay everything is going to be alright." Swift stands from his desk and attempts to touch her arm, but she pulls it away.

"No! I could die!" Her body begins to pulse with white energy and for a moment her emotion changes from *anger* to *fear*, but the rage soon returns. I grip the sides of my desk.

"Blue-jay, please calm down." Hawk goes near her, "I never meant to—"

"You knew exactly what you were doing!" The energy swells and leaves Blue-jay to form a large silhouette beside her. A great beast takes shape next to me; I am so close I can see scales covering its sides and hide. Its claws dig at the ground and it keeps growing. *Shit, Blue-jay's power.*

I pull the chair from under my body and slowly back away from the giant. The rest of the class jumps to their feet and backs away from the thing. The monster being caused by Blue-jay's anger already reaches the one wall, while its horned head grazes the ceiling.

"Um, Blue-jay?" calls Goldcrest, who is almost crushed by the beast's spiked tail.

"Everyone just shut up!" she shouts. Even though this thing just appeared, she seems to be fully aware and in control of it.

"You really need to relax now or you are going to crush us all and make the room cave in." Swift warns her.

"Maybe I want that to happen." she utters and the tail of the beast swings, knocking a line of desks into the wall. Lark has to teleport out of the way. The animal snorts and then begins to move through the small classroom, destroying anything in its way. Blue-jay and Hawk stare each other down, but the rest of us squish in a cluster at the wall furthest from the monster.

"Hey, Swift, a shield would be good right about now." I say and then have to jump to avoid a giant paw. Everyone else disperses too.

Swift joins me, "Yeah, I don't think I can." He looks at me apologetically. He hasn't been able to work the force-field since that time in my dorm. I glare at him.

Fear is the popular emotion in the room right now as Blue-jay's creature rampages. The nine Enhancements do our best to dodge and run away. Blue-jay yells insults at Hawk, and he just takes it. Lark teleports all over the room, never staying anywhere more than five seconds. She should just get out of here. Robin and Osprey try to use the flares against the beast, but it doesn't have any effect and Osprey gets hit by a paw because they got too close to its face. Nightingale even tried to jump on its back and bring it down, but of course, she failed. Koel thinks it's better to stay singular right now and I agree with him.

"Hawk, you better do something quick or you are going to lose one of your Enhancements sooner than you thought!" I shout and roll out of the way of the swinging tail.

"You are right." Hawk tells Blue-jay and the beast freezes in place. "It was not right of me or anyone else to mess with your emotions to test you. I am sorry."

Blue-jay's monster flickers and shrinks until all that remains is a small animal. It floats over to Blue-jay and sticks his head underneath her hand so she can pet it, but her hand dangles limp. Her head hangs low, her hair hiding her face. The adrenaline from the anger is gone. *That was easy.*

"I am sorry too." she says. The new creature has a small body and head, whiskers, big ears, a small tail and antlers. It floats up until it is right in front of Blue-jay, stares at her. Its whiskers are so long that they tickle her face. Blue-jay can't help but smile and pet its head.

The rest of the room sighs with relief.

Hawk takes Blue-jay aside to speak with her further and leaves us to deal with the aftermath of her little breakdown.

"Oh, dear gods, we're alive." Owl says, surprised.

"Barely." Koel says, "And what the hell was that thing?"

"Obviously her Enhancer power. It changes with her emotions." The eight of them stare at me, "I could see that when her anger disappeared, so did the beast. I would think that you guys could too." They shake their heads no.

Blue-jay comes back into the room. Her head still hangs low, but not as much as before. She is sorry for almost killing us at least. No one says anything for minutes, even when Hawk enters after her.

I look at Swift for the first time since things settled down. For some reason **anger** appears above his head. "You say your apologies and make up and I'm going to talk with Hawk." Swift instruct the team and then passes Blue-jay as she approaches everyone else.

Swift pulls Hawk away from the crowd and towards the exit. "What the hell happened to you?" I hear him try to whisper.

Since I have no interest in 'making up' with these people, I decide to follow the two, curious. They stop halfway down the hallway, so I stay just inside the classroom doorway

Hawk pulls away from Swift's grasp, "Life happened." In this light Hawk looks like an annoyed teenager. They continue speak in hushed tones.

"You are putting our lives in danger, pushing us to the max. Why?"

357

"You think it is going to be easy out there? In a week all of them are going to be out on the streets fighting for their lives and the Preachers will not give them second chances. Real life is not like it is in a classroom, there is no 'trying again', no second chances to get it right and succeed. I thought you understood that. Your partner sure gets it."

I glance over at the rest of my team; Blue-jay sits in a circle with the rest of them. Things seem to be alright; they goof around now. And then I look at Swift. He stays silent for now.

"We are all getting too close together. I thought you realized that when you found out Wren had feelings for you." *Getting too close? He's the one who wanted that. He forced us to get along and be friends.* I begin to grow angry like Swift.

"Don't talk about—"

"Do not pretend that you cared about her." Hawk begins to walk back to the classroom.

"I do care about her." Swift pauses, "But not in that way." *Good.* "Just a few weeks ago you were apologizing for pitting us against our greatest fears, but now you are doing this?" Swift tries to shift the subject back to Hawk's behavior. He follows Hawk.

Hawk stops and glances down at his shoe for a second. I can tell that Swift has hit a nerve. "Albatross was right about that stuff." As they grow closer, I move further away from the doorway, so it won't seem like I was listening.

"Shut up, Hawk." Apparently Hawk has crossed some sort of line; Swift wouldn't say stuff like that to Hawk otherwise. "Whatever happened, you need to realize that most of us are children. No forget that, we are human beings and you need to respect us."

They both walk in. "I am respecting all of you by not bullshitting you." Hawk says this loud enough for the whole room to hear and then approaches to the others, "And tomorrow you are going to be

358

challenged even more." Swift isn't wrong, something has changed a little. But Hawk is right too, we need to be prepared.

Chapter Thirty Four

"An exciting new activity waits for you guys tomorrow, so I think it would be best if you got your sleep." Hawk walks up behind Swift and I while we eat our dinner. He sits down at our table for a moment.

Swift mumbles to me, "I sincerely hope he doesn't have any more of his deadly games planned."

I smile nervously at Hawk. For the most part I agree with him and not Swift.

"Then I am sorry to disappoint you..." Hawk escapes his seat quickly, knowing that Swift won't take kindly to his words. Swift glares at him as he leaves the room.

I put my food aside for a moment, "Come on, Swift." I think he needs to take things easy. "Albatross and the others put Hawk in charge, my dad practically chose him to be the first Enhancement. Shouldn't we trust him and his plans? You're the one who loves your precious NEST so much."

Swift rolls his eyes. "Nobody, not even Albatross, can be right one hundred percent of the time." He pauses and then adds, "Not even you or your father."

***

"Even though this is the first real training activity with Enhancer powers, I do not want you to go easy on each other." According to Swift, Hawk wants us to kill each other. "So the people who have not released all of their powers yet will be the only ones who receive extra weapons. More powerful stunners than the first training session." Hawk hands out rifles to Nightingale, Osprey, Owl, and Swift. "And as you already know, the purpose of this 'activity' is to help your fellow Enhancements' special power to develop and emerge, so one point will be given to the pair that somehow gets a new power to surface."

"What are the points for?" Koel asks.

"You will find out once the session is over." Hawk says, and to me that only sounds like a good lie to make people listen to you.

Most likely, most of us will be playing it safe, but a couple—like Nightingale and I—will go all out like Hawk wants. It's a good thing we have such a good medic.

"Teams!" Hawk brings the attention back to him. "You will not be working with just your partner. Two pairs will join for this challenge."

There is a collective groan.

"And I will choose."

Another groan.

"So, Koel and Lark will be on a team with Osprey and Robin." There aren't an even amount of pairs. "Swift and Wren, you are with Goldcrest and Nightingale."

As usual Blue-jay is left out. And Owl, of course.

"Blue-jay and Owl will work with me." Hawk grins, "That is right—you will have to fight me too."

Plot twist.

"I do not want you to be happy with your teammates; I want each of you to be out of your comfort zones. If anyone gets seriously injured, I would suggest sending up a flare and the game will pause while Goldcrest makes his way to you and then heals you. Albatross and others are watching our little game, so try your best to impress them and make me look good. Good luck." Hawk dismisses us and everyone walks slowly away. I look around awkwardly, wondering just exactly where we're supposed to go.

"Oh, and by the way." Hawk pulls us back, "I set the room on the most complex level architecturally. I am not sure what that includes, but be careful." Hawk turns his back on us again and stays away from

Blue-jay and Owl. "Each team will start separately. On my command, the computer will change the room. I have a safety word to stop it if anything happens." *Dammit, Hawk, stop telling us things last minute!* "Now for the voice-activated password to start HABITAT…" Hawk pauses to make sure everyone is ready.

Swift and I stand prepared. I have one hand on the wall and prepare to run. Swift has his gun slung over his back. Nightingale and Goldcrest stand at the opposite wall. Goldcrest is nervous while Nightingale is determined.

"Freya." Hawk says clearly and the lights dim.

Four walls grow around Swift and I and concrete appears above us almost knocking into my head. I feel us rise with the building and have to keep my balance. This time we start in a building with multiple floors. The room we occupy is completely dark and windowless.

Swift finds the staircase and I go down ahead of him. "I don't feel comfortable doing this." he says quietly.

I hold onto the wall and the railing. The first floor is lighter and we can see the empty doorway from the stairs. I stop short near the last step and turn around to face him, "Swift, we are almost done. Just go along for the rest of our time under Hawk's command." He nods silently in response. I just hope he'll listen to me. "We should find Nightingale and Goldcrest and set up a base and plan—who to target and how to trigger their powers into manifestation."

"Okay, but we need to be careful. Make sure you are focusing your Empathy; we might be able to tell if anyone is coming." *Good thinking.*

I stay alert as we exit the tall building and scour the streets for our partners in crime. A few times I see someone else's emotions through a wall or even a complete building and I use the knowledge of their whereabouts to easily sneak past them and throughout the whole city.

I know what I am looking for—Nightingale is usually fuming and Goldcrest is frightened.

I am sure we go in circles a few times. The streets curve in odd angles and turn randomly as well as dead end, it's a nightmare. Most of the buildings are a lot taller than the one Swift and I started in, reminding me of the Inner Ring of most cities.

After about twenty minutes of searching, Swift and I hear fighting. Battle cries as well as cries of pain erupt from about two blocks down. I recognize one of the voices to be Nightingale's.

"Come on." I urge Swift to walk faster and, as we get closer to the scene, we see a lot of destruction.

Nightingale is in the middle of the wide street swinging her gun widely and shooting at a large piece of rubble that must have fallen from one of the close buildings. Goldcrest hides behind a corner.

"Hawk!" she calls out, "Is that all you have?" Nightingale challenges Hawk; he must be behind that hunk of concrete. Goldcrest comes out from his hiding spot and joins her barrage.

"Fine!" I hear Hawk bellow and the chunk begins to move. Slowly at first, but then it is launched into the air and comes tumbling down on Nightingale. She jumps out of the way, but the rock still manages to partially roll over her leg.

"Cover me!" I yell to Swift, running faster. He stays behind and starts shooting at Hawk as I sprint over to Nightingale, who tries to crawl away from the scene. Taking her gun, I help her stand up straight and then we begin hobbling back to Swift. "Goldcrest come on!" I shout, thinking that he was hiding again. But a second after I call for him, a white blob of energy that soars toward my head is knocked out of the air by a grey one. Goldcrest had joined Swift in covering Nightingale and I.

I send Hawk a nice, red present before yelling, "We are getting out of here."

After that, Goldcrest rushes to Nightingale's other side and pulls her arm over his shoulder. Swift continues to protect us with his fire, until we all reach a spot that we think is safe.

We enter the bottom floor of a large, circular building and I practically throw Nightingale on the ground. I am dripping in sweat and exhausted already. "You're a lot heavier than you look." I say between deep breaths.

Nightingale scoots to a wall and leans against it. "Gods, it hurts." she says and looks down at her leg. Most of the foot and calf of her right leg has had the skin scraped off of it and looks slightly mangled. Blood covers her pant leg. I wouldn't be surprised if we accidently left a trail of blood to our safe house.

Goldcrest gets to healing her even though he looks like he might vomit. Then we rest before starting to strategize.

My mind races — *Technically Owl and Osprey are the only ones we could target because Swift and Nightingale are on my team. Owl's weakness is Robin.*

The four of us devise a plan to get both Owl and Osprey.

Somehow we have to get Owl to believe that his sister is in danger; he will try to help her no matter what, hopefully triggering his powers. We'll convince Owl with Robin's flare—like Hawk said, if anyone is seriously injured send up a flare. Nightingale says that she and Goldcrest will take care of that, which I am a little worried about, but agree to let them do it anyway. We decide that Swift and I should go after Osprey after they get Robin to release a flare. Nightingale thinks that a bullet will help Osprey, and I don't have a better plan so I agree. I wonder if the 'friendships' between Enhancements will still be intact after this.

364

Chapter Thirty Five

"Get out of my way!" Owl screams at Koel—the only thing he thinks stands between him and his sister. Where has the funny, joyful little boy gone?

Nightingale succeeded in forcing Robin to release a flare. It shot right up into the space between the top of the buildings and the ceiling; everyone could see it. Then they retreated somewhere to wait for Owl to respond. We tried to lure Owl out and it seems as if the whole team has showed up in a chain reaction. Well at least Osprey is present; now it is up to Swift and me.

Owl strikes in a blink of an eye, lifting Koel without even touching him. Then Blue-jay's monster slams into him while he is still in the air.

"The plan worked, Owl has some sort of controlling power." I tell Swift. The only reason Owl attacked Koel is because Koel was in his way. Blue-jay is just doing all she can to help her partner. It's a good thing we've kept our distance.

Owl stares at his hands for a second, fear filling his expression, but he doesn't waste time on his new power. His sister is in trouble, or at least that is what he is made to believe. I kind of feel bad about doing this to the others.

I study Swift while he waits for the cue to shoot. He is worried too, but I wouldn't know it without my powers. I can feel remorse in every movement of his. We are on one of the top floors of a tall building, overlooking everything. Swift rests his gun on the window sill and peers through the scope.

"Wren, get ready." he warns and I focus on the task ahead—shooting Osprey.

Osprey and Robin come into view, running around the corner that blocked us before.

"Three... two..."

Robin flings her head in our direction. *Damn it, she saw us.*

"Duck!" I yell.

A yellow ball of light comes flying through the open window. I cover my eyes and wait for it to explode.

It does, but the light ignites the room and then disperses. Just a flash-bomb. But Swift is temporarily blinded. **Pop! Pop!** The room is filled with more noises as Lark and Koel teleport in, and then Koel releases his friends.

I dive next to Swift. *So apparently Lark can teleport with other people; that will come in handy in a real fight.*

"Swift, trust me on this one. Open your shield now!"

"I don—"

The pink and black start to bombard us just as the blue shield encircles us.

"Shit." mutters Koel. I am forced to read his lips, because no sound penetrates Swift's barrier. Then he yells louder, "You are going to have to come out sometime!" He isn't playing games. After taking that hit from Owl—a child—getting someone to unleash their powers isn't his plan. And he is the only one who has fully mastered his so far.

Swift is scared, and I would be too if I didn't have a plan. Luckily I do.

While he is still blinded, I help Swift get on his feet. Facing our foes, I smile politely and wave. I grip Swift's jacket, "Bye." then sit on the ledge and push off.

"Wren!" Swift yells as we fall the many floors to the street.

I laugh when I see Koel's and Lark's faces as they rush to the window to see if we made it.

Swift's shield absorbs the impact and we bounce around on the ground in the bubble a few times. *Now to find our teammates... And where did Robin and Osprey go?*

"Get up." I say to Swift. He can manage on his own now, his eyesight is recovering.

I scan the area for any Enhancements, but they must have scattered.

All of the other groups must be re-forming. We need to find Nightingale and Goldcrest again before anyone else finds them.

I think fast — *Enhancements yet to unlock their powers are Nightingale and Osprey. We can either get Nightingale to use her power and get the points or wait for some dangerous situation to come up because of the other teams. Swift and I don't have any points yet.*

"We need to find the others." I say before Swift can.

We pick a random direction and start running. This thing is huge. It seems to go on forever; maybe it keeps making more and more buildings as we move forward. A labyrinth that I would hate to be in alone.

Swift makes us stop, "There is no way we're going to find them in this maze; we got lucky before."

He is right, even though I would never admit it.

"We could send up a flare." I almost whisper. It could either save us or cause our demise.

"Only as a last resort." Swift decides, "Have you tried scanning with your Empathy for emotions again?"

I forgot. "No." I admit. He understands my powers better than I do and vice-versa. And suddenly I understand one of the reasons those scientists and important Proxies put us together. *Shit, why do things like this have to happen? Why can't I hate someone without them turning out to be right?*

"Wren?" Swift pokes me and I realize that I have been making a grumpy face.

"Oh, yeah…" I have to blink a few times before I can focus again.

Nothing is in this area. "Nope, let's keep moving."

I walk down a side-street. *Who thought up this city? My dad? I doubt he has a big enough imagination and architectural knowledge for all of this.*

Something flickers up ahead.

"Did you see that?" I ask Swift. If he didn't, then my powers might be picking up something.

"No." he says in a hushed voice. He understands.

We slowly and carefully advance. Two structures are on our left and right, someone is in the building directly in front of us. But this is a dead end and there is no door on this wall.

"Looks like we are going to blast our way through." Swift says and gets into striking position.

"Wait." I need to make sure this is really Goldcrest and Nightingale, not another team or we could be walking right into a trap. I try to find the area that the flickers came from. With my power it is almost like I have x-ray vision, except only with humans. Maybe with animals too, but there aren't a lot of them running wild.

Anger paces on the second floor, *fear* stays motionless a little further away.

"Anger and fear. Second story." I inform Swift. "Who else could it be?"

"Animal and Kid." he contradicts, but not seriously.

I roll my eyes, "I'll hit and you'll protect." He doesn't like that idea. "It will be good practice." I support my plan.

"Fine." He makes a face at me that he thinks I don't see.

"Right after the blast hits the wall, you have to put up the shield, okay?"

"Fine." he repeats.

"Three…" I rub my hands together. "Two…" The palms begin to warm up. "One." I hold my arms bent in front on my body, so I won't feel the recoil as hard. It's like holding a gun.

The energy goes out from me and strikes the wall with amazing strength. Dust covers the immediate area so I can't tell if Swift is doing his job or not. But if we aren't being hit with rubble and debris then I guess he is. When the air clears I can see the blue shield. But Swift is really straining. He loosens up just a little bit and the shield is gone.

I pat Swift on the shoulder, "Good job."

The hole I made is completely square. Probably because of HABITAT's holographic system.

I can hear scuffling upstairs and can sense that whoever is up there is ready for to attack.

I know it's hard for Swift, but he just has to deal with it. "Power up, now!"

Swift does right as Nightingale comes down the stairs.

Her gun in swung limply over her shoulder and she greets us, "Jardah, nice of you to drop in."

Goldcrest hops down after her. Swift lowers his force-field and studies them quizzically.

"How did you know it was us?" Swift asks.

Nightingale smiles. I could never trust that smile. "I saw you guys coming for a few minutes now." She taps her temple with her index finger.

"Your pow—"

"Yep, I got it almost at the beginning of the game, when I couldn't decide which way to go. I follow a path around two minutes into the future and then am transported back to the present. It helps me make good decisions."

"Why didn't you tell us earlier?" Swift asks, annoyed by her secrecy. We could have used her power.

"So that no one will know." *Obviously.* "So the other teams will think that I'm still powerless and they will try to 'help' me show it." she tries to explain to us her line of thought. "So they will come to

369

us. I am the bait and we will set a trap. Really people, use your brains!"

She had time to think about her plan. Maybe it will work. Maybe that is what he power is all about, to help her plan ahead and make wiser moves.

"Yeah, but Osprey is the only one left. Who says he'll be in the team that gets to us first? I really don't want to fight Hawk." Swift tells her the flaw in her idea.

"I will see if it is anyone other than Osprey and readjust my plan accordingly." Nightingale seems to have everything ready, and according to my senses, she is calm. "And if anything goes wrong Goldcrest can help us."

Swift gives me a look like 'we might as well go along with it'. I agree, but we still don't have any points. We need to be the ones who get Osprey.

"Can Swift and I talk about this in private?" I ask Nightingale.

She is confused, "I do not see why you would need to because we are all on the same team, but whatever." She waves us away.

I grab Swift's arm and pull him into the corner.

"I know that sound can't travel into the barrier, but can it go out?" I whisper.

"I think so. Why?"

Damn it. If he surrounds them with his bubble then they'll get suspicious.

"Never mind." I brush it off, "Not to be rude or anything, but we need to get that point." I gaze over my shoulder. They are talking to each other. "And that means going behind their backs. We can't risk them getting the last point."

He sighs and realizes that I'm speaking the truth, "Yeah. So what are we going to do? It's not like we can surprise her. She can see the damn future!"

"Be quiet." I hit him lightly on the shoulder. "That really does limit our options. Don't think too much about it. When you see an opening to get them out of the way then take it."

He nods, but he is worried. I wouldn't want Nightingale against us either.

"Okay." I conclude.

We break apart and go back to where Nightingale and Goldcrest are.

I smile, and after realizing that she'll be suspicious because of it, change my expression. "Sounds good to us."

Nightingale studies my face. I try to stare back.

"Good." she finally says.

"Should we wait around or send a signal…?"

"Oh, no. Robin is going to be here in about—" she stops and counts under her breath, "Thirty seconds."

"What the hell?" I shout at her and spin around, watching and waiting.

This is the most stressful training exercise I have ever been through.

"Five, four, three…" 'Two, one.' she mouths.

Nightingale and Goldcrest step back when we hear a large explosion and debris start to fall in from the destroyed roof.

The blue energy envelops Swift and I as Hawk jumps through the hole.

The chunks of ceiling bounce off of the dome and go in different directions. Hawk dodges one and then Goldcrest gets hit in the head by another.

He starts to bleed but the wound is easily healed.

Swift and I back away toward the exit, leaving Nightingale and Goldcrest to fight for themselves. Nightingale moves two seconds before every one of Hawk's attacks and he gets frustrated quickly. Nightingale doesn't use her gun or her energy blasts for some reason.

371

She gives Goldcrest signals when to fire upon Hawk and when Hawk fires at Goldcrest, he just heals a few moments later.

Nightingale suddenly flashes a smile and I know that all hell is going to break loose. She must have found an opening.

She tells Goldcrest to stop and then moves so fast she had to have thought out every single step. She zigzags around the room before she gets behind Hawk. When he spins around she ducks and goes the other way. He turns again, running right into the butt of Nightingale's gun with his head as she thrusts it down.

He twirls and then hits the floor really hard.

Swift gets rid of the force-field and we run to Hawk.

"Is he okay?" I ask.

Goldcrest checks his vitals. "Yeah, he should wake up soon."

"Then we should get going." Nightingale rushes through the hole I made. "Thanks for the help by the way."

"It was a little surprising, that's all. And where is Robin like you said?" We follow her in and out of the alleys and streets.

"I don't know much about my powers yet, she must have changed her mind." Nightingale says lightly. "But I have a feeling they'll show up soon enough."

Roar! A white glowing beast breaks into our sight right ahead of us.

We stop short and turn to the left.

"Run! Before Owl catches up!" I shout, bringing up the rear. I don't want to cross paths with Owl. That kid can do some serious damage.

I can hear the beast's growls and heavy paws hitting the ground. *Blue-jay has to be pretty angry to keep this up. Where is she anyway?*

I quickly turn around to get a good look at the monster that displays all of Blue-jay's angry and bad vibes.

The amount of emotion coming from it makes my head hurt.

Its head is huge with long curved horns. Scales line the heavy-set body and legs. Blue-jay sits on the creature's back and gazes down upon us unchanged. She looks beautiful, even royal as her white-blonde hair swishes with each step. She terrifies me.

My quick look wasn't as fast as I thought and I run into Swift before getting a chance to turn and see where I am going again.

"Why did you—?"

Swift points somewhere in the distance above the buildings. His mouth is wide open in surprise. "That pair is way too powerful."

An orange dot slowly glides towards us. We are now between a flying Owl and super-powered Blue-jay. Stuck between a rock and a hard place. *Shit.*

"What the hell are we going to do?" I shout to the others.

"Well if we keep standing here we are going to be smashed. Goldcrest will be the only one who survives." Nightingale says.

Holy-We're going to die.

Swift steps up, "Not on my watch." That line sounds really cheesy, but fits Swift perfectly.

"Do you really think your force-field will be able to hold all four of us?" I try to speak fast because Blue-jay is—

"Ten seconds to impact." Nightingale chimes in.

"Probably not, so I'm going to try something else." Surprisingly, Swift is calm.

Nightingale grins, but does not say a word. She can probably see what is going to happen, and according to that smile at least she will live through it.

"Go for it."

Swift nods his head and turns away from us to face Blue-jay's magnificent beast. "You guys will have to handle Owl."

"Okay." Nightingale and I say at the same time and then lock eyes in a glare.

I stand back to back with Swift. I can see Owl a lot clearer now. He stands at the top of the structure closest to us. His ginger hair moves without there being any wind.

I feel something change about Swift, but I can't check it out because Owl jumps off of the building and heads straight for us.

I feel like running away or just disappearing. I don't want to hurt this boy—my friend.

He isn't scared or nervous. I wonder how he will behave after this session is over.

"Hit him now!" Nightingale shouts.

I lift my hands, which start to warm up and then send two energy-blasts his way. It still hurts when I use my energy blasts. The pain just keeps my adrenaline pumping.

They hit, but Owl keeps plowing through.

"Another!" Nightingale yells at Goldcrest.

His grey energy makes Owl stumble, if that is possible while levitating.

Owl drops a few feet to the ground and stares at Nightingale.

We stand twenty feet apart. Owl is angry and shows it by scowling at us.

I count off everyone in my mind. *Hawk was taken care of, but could recover and be here any minute. Swift is off fighting Blue-jay. Owl, Nightingale, Goldcrest and I are here; and Lark, Koel, Osprey and Robin should be heading our way soon. Osprey is the target, how will I draw him out?*

Goldcrest and I aren't fully committed to this fight, neither wants to hurt Owl, but he can surely do more damage to us than we can to him.

"Get your act together." Nightingale says. She is only one of us who actually wants to fight him.

Owl figures she is the leader.

"Ready, g—"

Owl raises his hand and waves it to his left.

Nightingale is thrown into the wall to our right. *Owl did that.* Nightingale's body lands limply on the floor, she doesn't move.

"I had hoped that would trigger her power." Owl is confused and stands regularly.

"She already knew her power." Goldcrest mutters and starts making his way to her.

He doesn't pay attention to Owl at all, like he doesn't think we're still enemies in this game.

Goldcrest's body becomes rigid and stops short.

"Come on, Goldcrest, you know I can't let you help her. She'll be fine." Owl is completely focused on Goldcrest.

"How are you doing that?" I ask. I know it sounds stupid, but I need to distract Owl.

Swift and Blue-jay are nowhere to be seen, they must have taken their battle elsewhere.

"Seriously, Wren? My power. I can control objects with my mind." His green eyes flicker to my face.

Goldcrest can move again and slowly inches towards Nightingale.

"What is that power called?" Another stupid question. Goldcrest has reached her now and puts his hand on her.

"Telekinesis." Owl announces. "And don't think I don't notice you. When I focus, I can feel every movement around me." He turns back to Goldcrest.

Owl raises him off the floor and suspends Goldcrest in the air.

Goldcrest mumbles a curse, making it appear as if he didn't have enough time to heal her. But her eyes flutter and she props herself up on her elbows.

Nightingale puts her finger to her lips telling me not to say anything. I roll my eyes, I'm not stupid.

But how can we take down a boy who can move things with his mind and can feel everything?

I'll talk to him. "Who do you think will win?"

He doesn't know what I am referring to.

"Blue-jay or Swift? Blue-jay's holographic monster is pretty impressive, but she won't be able to stay mad for too long and Swift has gotten very handy with that field of his." I bluff.

Nightingale takes hold of her gun and swings it into position just as Owl's full attention is on me.

"Blue-jay—"

I can hear the crack of the trigger right before the bang.

"Stop that!" Owl shouts and his face turns the same color as his hair.

The bullet hovers in mid-air. Owl eyes flicker to the right and the projectile follows them.

"Why—"

Pop! Lark appears between Owl and I. She gives him one nice Enhancer-powered blow to the stomach and he goes flying into the wall above Nightingale.

Nightingale scoots out of the way of his falling body.

Now that is how you fight a telekinetic.

Lark vanishes.

"Remember, we are aiming for Nightingale." Koel says. His voice bounces off the walls and I turn and twist to find the source. Robin, Osprey, Lark and Koel stand on a roof two buildings to my right. They all mumble in agreement and get ready to attack. Koel and Robin put their hands on Lark's shoulders.

"Stay away." Koel instructs Osprey. He knows that Osprey is a liability at this point.

Robin gives Osprey a faint smile before they disappear.

Osprey turns and runs along the rooftops and before I even see where the three resurface, I take my shot and run as well. I track Osprey in the same direction Swift had gone a few minutes before. I wonder where he's going.

Chapter Thirty Six

I sort of feel bad about leaving Nightingale and Goldcrest, but this was the plan and I *have* to fight Osprey. Hopefully they'll be able to distract the others so Koel or Lark won't follow me.

I keep an eye on Osprey who is still running and jumping from rooftop to rooftop. I try to stay at a safe distance so he won't see me until he lands on ground level.

I hear noises up ahead. Fighting. Growls and another sound like something is being hit by a battering-ram. It could only be Swift and Blue-jay.

Osprey stops short, almost skidding off the edge of a roof, and then freezes in his tracks. He is tired; his face is red and his breathing is heavy.

I move forward in the shadows. The sounds are really close now, like if I turn this next corner—the corner of the building Osprey is resting on—I will see Swift and Blue-jay.

I don't know what I expected, really. I lean against the wall and peek around the corner. Blue-jay and Swift are close to each other; both are exhausted, but Swift is winning.

He uses his powers in a way I have never seen before. The force-field is pulled close to his body, fitting every curve perfectly. It's like personally made armor. I wonder how strong it is, how strong his punches are now. I don't know how or when he learned how to do this.

Blue-jay stands back and lets her illusion do all of the work. Well, that isn't exactly true, she is controlling it. Does the pain inflicted on it hurt her as well?

The beast flickers after one more punch and she winces. She must feel it. The hologram shrinks until it is the same height as Swift. Swift knees it in the stomach. Blue-jay doubles over and slowly makes her way to the floor. I don't know if she has passed out, but she is definitely out of this fight.

377

Swift is relieved and wipes his forehead. He lowers the shield and heaves. Swift sits and then lies with his back on the ground. His chest rises and lowers quickly. *Poor guy, he didn't even want to do this in the first place. I'll let him rest; let Swift and Osprey rest.*

These people aren't really my enemies. This is just a training activity; they're supposed to be my friends.

Swift's head slumps and he rests the right side of his face against the cool ground. He closes his eyes for half a minute before I try to get his attention.

I let my hands spark for a brief moment. From this angle, Osprey won't be able to see it, but Swift does and he jolts.

I put my finger to my lips. I don't want Osprey to know he knows. He lies still as I point above me. He follows my finger and catches a glimpse of Osprey before looking away again.

I point up again, trying to get through to Swift that I am going to climb up. He closes his eyes and nods.

The building is about five floors high. I go around the back searching for a way in and find an empty rectangle—an entrance with no door.

There are a few windows facing Swift, so he'll be able to signal me if Osprey moves.

I run up the stairs as fast as possible without making too much noise.

On the last floor I check out the window. Swift is still in the same position.

Swift suddenly jumps to his feet and starts bolting away; Osprey must have seen him and is trying to escape.

I take the next flight of stairs three steps at a time. I burst onto the roof and see Osprey two buildings away. I run after him, of course. Swift is still on the ground, running at the same speed as Osprey.

I come to the edge of the first rooftop. The jump scares me a little bit, but the gap isn't too large and I have enough momentum. I land on the other building with ease and grin a little. It wasn't too bad; it was actually kind of fun.

Osprey is still way ahead of me. I need to speed up if I want to catch up.

I sprint to the next ledge and almost don't have enough time to leap. I tiger-roll into a standing position when I hit solid ground and try keep going.

Osprey hears my landing and turns to look at me. It slows him down a little, but he keeps running.

I am catching up — I think while leaping across the next open space. Only one rooftop's length behind him.

Osprey stops running up ahead. *What is he doing?*

I notice his roadblock. The distance between the next couple buildings is much greater than before. He won't make it.

He can either get captured by me, here, or risk it all and jump. I can sense his fear.

He steps back, turns his head to look at me, shrugs and then goes for it. The fear disappears and is replaced by... Trust? Faith? I can't tell. He runs a few paces and then jumps as far as he can. It isn't good enough.

My legs have turned to jelly and I can't continue moving, it makes me stumble.

I watch Osprey fall for a brief second before a green light appears on the bottom of his feet and he receives a push that is just enough to get him to the other side. *Holy crap.*

He stops when he lands and smiles. "Thank you, God." I can hear him say before he continues.

How the heck am I supposed to get across? I have never tried anything like that with my powers.

I peer over the edge. It's about the same height as when I fell with Swift, but I had his force-field then. The distance between this building and the next is way too far, but I have to try.

379

I back up, take a deep breath — *I can't believe I am doing all of this for a stupid point in a stupid training activity* — and let loose all of my anxiety. My eyes pop open right before my foot hits the last bit of concrete. I can tell that I didn't push off hard enough.

I fly shortly in the air, get about halfway to the other side until I start to fall. The fear and anxiety settle within me when my feet and shins land on a hard surface. I put my hands out to get up and stare in wonder at the blue, flat bridge that is under my feet, holding me up.

Through the blue I can see Swift with his arms raised high above him. Sweat gleams on his face, but he smiles.

'Get going.' he mouths to me.

I give him a thumbs up and dash across his force-field.

He has learned so much in just this lesson while I can barely understand what I am picking up about other people. My power is not that useful anyway... In all honesty, my power sucks.

My anger at the Enhancer makes my drive stronger and makes me able to run again. I quickly cross Swift's bridge to the connecting rooftop and soon catch up to Osprey.

Osprey leaps over another gap one last time before I am on top of him. I jump right after he does, and as soon as he lands, I am already flying towards him and I punch him in the back of the neck.

"Ow, Wren." he mutters. *What the hell did he expect me to do to him?*

He rubs the spot and turns to face me.

"I really don't want to fight." Osprey explains before putting up his hands in fists.

"Preachers will though." I tell him. "And the whole point is to release your power, Hawk just thinks that you need something to push you along."

"Fine."

I kick him in the gut and he stumbles back. Hitting him endlessly isn't going to be fun. It'll be tough hitting a nice guy like Osprey. The way he slowly gets back into a fighting stance makes my heart ache.

I throw a punch and he blocks it. I try to knee him in the groin, but that doesn't work either. He is very good a protecting himself, at least. Only about a third of my strikes actually land, but he doesn't try to fight back, so he is bruised and battered before long.

"You have to at least try, Osprey." I say through clenched teeth. I am getting frustrated now.

I try to punch him in the jaw, but he blocks it with his arm and sees an opening. I'm not usually happy to get punched in the chest, but this time I am okay with it. Even the short loss of breath isn't too bad.

But after that he doesn't do much but defend himself again.

Tired of his crap, I grab his arm, turn quickly and then flip him over my back.

I keep a hold on his hand and place my foot in the nook between his arm and shoulder.

"Now you're going to stop me, by *HURTING* me. There is no way you can talk me out of this, or I will dislocate your shoulder." Hawk is right. There's no point in sugarcoating our training or making it any easier. When we're out in the field it's kill or be killed.

"Wren, I—"

"I said no talking!" I shout at him.

"Well you didn't actually—"

I glare at him and it makes him shut up.

"I will count to ten." I inform him, "One, two…" I twist his wrist harder. "Three… Four… Five, six, seven, eight, nine, ten." I rush the last five numbers and twist and pull.

"Wren!" he shouts as the loud popping sound erupts.

I let go of him and he rolls over on the floor in pain.

"What the heck, Wren?" he heaves.

I need that goddamn point.

"Get up!" I shout.

Osprey is seriously worried about me now, I can tell from the look in his eyes and the word above his head. He is probably thinking that I've gone insane. Maybe I should show him just how crazy I can be.

He gets up on his good arm with lots of moaning.

I roll my eyes and kick him in the nook of his elbow. He falls on his back again.

I get on my knees next to him and put my face very close to his ear. I put on my best crazy voice and whisper, "Now I am going to choke you until something happens."

Osprey doesn't respond so I prepare to put my hands around his neck.

I situate my body into a comfortable position while Osprey lays and looks straight up, not paying me any attention at all.

Fine — I huff.

I wrap my skinny fingers around his neck. My hands are small compared to him.

Come on, do something! I cry in my head. I tighten my grip until his face becomes red.

Swift appears at my side.

"Whatcha doing, Wren?" he asks, very much concerned.

"Proving a point." I mutter through a tense jaw.

"Well you have an audience." he informs me.

I lift my head a moment to see Robin with a look of horror on her face while Koel holds her back and Lark stands beside them silently.

"Osprey, do something!" Robin begs him.

Osprey's face is purple now.

He slowly lifts his arm as his face turns blue. I pay no attention to it until it gets too close to my forehead and he lets his last breath out. His finger barely touches my skin before it drops.

"Go to sleep." My brain, soul and body tell me. And I do.

"Good night." Osprey wheezes, he peers at me through one open eye.

My eyelids fall over my eyes that flash all over the place, searching for an answer. My body tries urgently to stay awake.

"Go to sleep." A voice says somewhere off in the distance. *Okay... I really am tired anyway...*

***

"Wren? Wren?" Swift calls to me.

"Is she going to be okay?" Owl is anxious.

"What did you do to her, Osprey?" Swift yells again.

"She was strangling him!" Robin comes to Osprey's defense.

Maybe I should open my eyes and grace them with my presence now.

When my vision clears I notice almost all of the team standing over me, but no one is actually paying attention or looking at me. They fight amongst themselves and don't even notice the could-have-been-dead girl.

"Hey, guys." I croak. My throat is super dry. "Swift." I hold out my hand and he helps me stand up.

The battlefield has returned to normal. The structures have collapsed and I can see the ends of the room.

"How are you feeling?" he asks. Now that I'm awake, he doesn't sound so concerned.

"Actually, I feel fine. Great in fact." I haven't been this well rested since forever.

"Really?" Osprey asks. He doesn't want to be responsible for any of my injuries.

"Yeah, I think that I was just sleeping. You didn't hurt me at all. How long was I out?"

Osprey smiles. "Thank, God." he mumbles.

"Around ten minutes." Swift tells me quietly.

"Great job, Osprey. With your new power you won't actually have to hurt anyone." Hawk slaps him on the back.

"Yeah, I guess that is true." Osprey is really relieved.

"So what's the situation with the points?" Nightingale asks. She doesn't care about my condition or Osprey's power, she just wants to know who the best Enhancement is.

"Koel and Lark helped unleash Owl's telekinesis, so you two have one point." Koel nods. "Wren used some unusual methods to trigger Osprey's." Hawk pauses to think, "I am not sure what to do about you, Nightingale, though."

"Her powers came to her without any help but her own." Goldcrest says. "We should get the point." he insists.

Goldcrest has been more outgoing since being Enhanced and you can see how big of a difference the Enhancer caused physically. He looks healthier—his skin isn't sickly, he doesn't sweat as much and he is gaining weight.

"Fine." Hawk agrees. When someone like Goldcrest, who is usually quiet, actually speaks up, it's probably because he's telling the truth. "I saw some great progress from Swift and good teamwork with his partner."

Ding!

We all freeze and hear this floor's elevator doors open down the hall. I didn't think we were expecting visitors.

A shorter man wearing glasses and a Proxy uniform runs through the door and almost bumps into us. He backs up and is obviously surprised to see eleven Enhancements standing right in front of him.

He clears his throat and runs his hair through his disheveled hair. "Oh-um, sorry." I can tell that he works in the Viewing Deck; he has that sort of air about him—a Proxy, but not in combat and he looks smart, but that could just be the glasses.

Hawk gives him a get-on-with-it glare.

"Oh, yes. Albatross needs all of you,"—he waves his hand in a circular motion surrounding us—"Right now, upstairs. There has been some distressing news."

"Then what are we waiting for?" Hawk says, "Albatross was watching us from the Viewing Deck, let's go." That is our signal to head to the elevator.

I decide to take the stairs because there isn't enough room for everyone in the single pod and I don't feel like waiting for another. I glance over my shoulder to see the metal doors block my view of Swift. We barely walk anywhere with each other nowadays.

Owl floats up the stairwell past me. I bet Lark just teleported. *Lucky them.*

I take the steps two at a time, but still get to the lobby last. Why did I have to get stuck with the lame powers?

I'm winded from the session and the climb, so I head to the elevator bank. Just as I arrive, the doors begin to close. I run the final few feet and shove Goldcrest further into the cabin so I won't be crushed by the metal doors. The floor isn't visible, only feet and the bodies around me keep me upright.

When the doors open again, I pour out onto the platform overlooking the busy Proxy workers.

The windows have dimmed. The table in the middle has been cleared, most likely so we can sit there and hear whatever important news or information has been discovered. The staff is noticeably thinned out, or maybe that's just because of the special situation.

Hawk is the first person who steps down and approaches Albatross and Ostrich, Blue-jay's father, who stand at the head of the table.

Never have I seen Albatross so worried. Ostrich looks unchanged with the same cold expressions.

The rest of us trickle down slowly after our mentor. No one speaks, not even Lark.

"What happened?" Hawk asks and as soon as he does Albatross makes the large screen-window behind him show a video.

It's like he was waiting for Hawk to say something. "We received this footage fifteen minutes ago from the president's estate." *The President? What does he want with us and how does he know who we are?*

"Okay, show us." Hawk doesn't seem too concerned about communications with the president.

Albatross presses play and I quickly pull out a chair and place my rear in it.

"Is-is this thing working?" The president's face is way too close to the camera. All I can make out is his forehead. He turns to speak to someone else, "Gemma, is it working?" His secretary I assume.

"Yes." a bored woman says like she has to deal with this on a daily basis. Poor Gemma. "Move back a little."

The shot shakes and makes me feel sick, but when it stabilizes I can clearly see my country's leader. Well that is what people say he is.

I haven't seen a photograph or video of President Napier since I came to NEST. His hair has definitely gotten lighter and more wrinkles have grown on his face. It makes me wonder what has made such a change in these past months.

Napier twists in his chair, looking over his shoulders. He is worried someone might be listening in. "I hope this is reaching you, Ostrich, if you are still the head of NEST." Ostrich's nose sticks up a little higher. *Since when is he the head of NEST?* "I am scared." Napier continues, "The Preachers have been getting more violent and vocal publicly. They are not afraid to be noticed anymore. I am worried they will not see any use in me soon." *They're using him?*

He moves closer to the camera and says in a hushed voice, "They might try to kill me."

Albatross pauses the video and the screen shows the leader of the country mid-word making a really stupid face. "Apparently the

Preachers have been using President Walter Napier and many other leaders as puppets. Recently he has been trying to restrain the Preachers power, but with no success. He has a past connection with Ostrich and NEST, so he sometimes contacts us with important information." Albatross moves away from blocking our view of Walter.

"I am holding a press meeting later this evening and I think that is when Preachers plan to strike." he continues. "I will be out in the open for anyone to attack. I am hoping you will receive this message and send reinforcements to help protect me. Thank you."

That's it. The windows go blank.

"Not only should we help him because he is a human-being being threatened by the Preachers, but he also is our eyes on the inside and the president."

"What are we going to do?" Swift stands and brings his fist down on the top of the table.

Hawk speaks, "I think I should go." Hawk is still seated and doesn't raise his eyes to us. He speaks as if he is going to his death sentence.

"And we will be right behind you." I offer.

"I could teleport you there right now." Lark contributes.

"No, no." Hawk shakes his head. *Why isn't Albatross telling him off?* "It would be best if I go alone. I mean, come on—" Hawk finally looks at us—his students. "You guys are not prepared for this at all. Any one of you could be injured… or worse."

This doesn't make sense. Why is he speaking like this?

"I concur." Albatross' words hang in the air.

All heads turn to him; no one can comprehend this.

Even Ostrich looks bewildered, but recovers. "Well… I guess it has been decided. Hawk will go immediately to the meeting in Tieced and protect the president."

387

"Nobody agreed to anything!" Nightingale's stands. Not even she can consent to letting Hawk go on his own.

Every single one of us begins to give reasons to why he can't go alone, but Hawk brings us to a halt. "Stop it!" he yells. I feel so helpless. "It is final." *Not it isn't.* "I need to get ready."

Hawk pushes his chair away from the table and we have to sit in silence as we watch our leader face a great challenge alone. He has to protect the president of the United Countries of North America from being assassinated by the most dangerous terrorist organization in the world. "Thank you for trying to help. It has been an honor working with each and every one of you." *Why is he acting like he isn't going to come back? I don't understand this.*

Hawk shakes hands with all of the Enhancements, even giving Robin and a couple others hugs.

When he approaches me to say goodbye I grab his hand tightly and slap him on the back, "You're coming back, aren't you?" I say for just him to hear. He ruffles my hair like I'm five years old but doesn't answer. I want to smack his hand away and ask him what's really going on.

He lets go of me and looks into my eyes, "If I have anything to say about it, I will be."

He climbs the stairs to the platform and when he reaches the top, he waves.

I turn to Swift hoping he has some answers. I plead with him with my eyes.

"I don't know, Wren." His mouth forms a grim line. "But something's up."

Chapter Thirty Seven

President Napier stands at the podium, ready to make his speech, while Hawk and more government officials stand behind him, their hands behind their backs and staring straight ahead.

I wish we could be there. *We are ready; we shouldn't waste our training by waiting around while we could be helping people.*

Hawk left only an hour after we all heard and raced to Tieced. The ten Enhancements and many other important NEST figures watch the President's speech from the Viewing Deck's huge screen. Something big is going to happen and we can all feel it.

The president starts his speech, "Citizens of the United Countries of North America, welcome. I am standing here today, making this speech, because I have betrayed you and everything that this country supposedly to stand for." Many gasps come from the audience and I turn to Swift. He is just as bewildered as I am. *He's going public about the Preachers.*

"I am supposed to stand for a united people—the united survivors after the terrible war in two thousand twenty-four, but instead I represent an evil organization that has been using me for many years. I have turned a blind eye while innocent people have been killed and families have been ripped apart.

But I say: No more. No more hiding, no more being afraid of death and no more lies. The organization I am talking about is the Preachers! They use religion as an excuse to murder people and for personal gain!"

A scream erupts as two men climb onto the stage wielding crowbars. The president was right—Preachers are here. The people in the crowd begin to panic, most of them trying to get away from the danger. For some reason Hawk is the only one of the guards that steps forward to intercept the men. He quickly takes them out even without using his powers. We wouldn't want the Preachers to know yet.

389

The president continues and this time he speaks even louder and faster so he can be heard over the roaring of the crowd. "I am truly sorry that I have done this to you; that I have let people die because of my fear.

I have kept so many truths and secrets from you all." He pauses, trying to think about his next sentence. Almost everyone has stopped in their tracks and gone quiet again.

One of his bodyguards pulls out a gun and steps forward. I move closer to the screen. *Be careful, Hawk.* Hawk kicks the gun out of the guard's hands and then punches him in the gut. The guard doubles-over and falls to the floor.

Three more people come on stage and try to get to the president, but Hawk stands between them. The first man crouches and attempts to wrap his arms around Hawk's waist. Hawk waits till he is close enough and knees the guy in the groin. The guy jumps a little into the air and Hawks grabs him before he lands, throwing him off the platform into the crowd.

The second guy comes at Hawk, anger in his eyes. Hawk steps out of the way just in time and trips him. The second guy lands on the floor and the air escapes him.

While Hawk is still focused on the second guy, the last one holds up a gun behind him. He aims for Hawks head. There is no way he could miss.

"Hawk watch out! Behind you!" I yell at the screen.

Hawk turns around just in time and rolls out of the way and off the back of the stage. I quickly lose sight of him in the wild crowd.

"Where did he go?!" I yell at Swift and Albatross. This all happened so fast. The others stand around, feeling just as helpless as I am. The cameras stay focused on the third and last guy, who is making his way to President Napier. *Damn you, cameramen! Where is Hawk? What happened?*

The third man grabs the president's shoulder and pushes him down onto his knees in front of the podium.

"Do you have any last words?" he asks with an evil smirk. His voice is familiar, strange. He places his gun to the back of the president's head.

"Do not give up, there is still hope. We are not alone. There are still people alive—"

The trigger is pulled. The bullet enters the back of the president's skull, exiting through his forehead which is now blown to bits. Blood trickles down his apologetic face, and he falls forward. Screams fill the air.

We have failed.

Printed in the USA
CPSIA information can be obtained
at www.ICGtesting.com
LVHW040325260724
786575LV00005B/28

9 781329 341234